WORDS OF BLOOD

DEACIS'S HOLY ARSE, but I'm bored out of my wits. All my bitching about suicide missions and getting my face blown off aside, I'd much rather be out there with the Colonel doing whatever insane thing it is he's doing, than stuck in here slowly getting older, with my brain dribbling out of my ears. Another month here and I'm going to be smashing my grey matter out on the walls of that cell, screaming and damning Schaeffer's name to the Abyssal Chaos and back. I have to get out of this fragging tower. – *from* **Liberty** *by Gav Thorpe*

WITH A ROAR of primal ferocity that spoke of millennia of hate, the Night Lords Chaos Space Marines finally revealed themselves. Battering through the wreckage came five ornately carved Rhino armoured personnel carriers, coruscating azure flames writhing within their flanks. Uriel was speechless.

They resembled Rhinos in name only. Bloody spikes festooned every surface and leering gargoyles thrashed across the undulating armour, gibbering eldritch incantations that made Uriel's skin crawl. – *from* **Chains of Command** *by Graham McNeill*

IN THE NIGHTMARE world of the 41st millennium, humanity is locked in a desperate struggle for survival against a relentless tide of aliens. Read tales of heroism and valour in this action-packed selection of savage science fiction stories ripped from the pages of *Inferno!* magazine.

More Warhammer 40,000 from the Black Library

WARHAMMER 40,000 STORIES

WORDS OF BLOOD

**Edited by
Marc Gascoigne
& Christian Dunn**

A BLACK LIBRARY PUBLICATION

First published in Great Britain in 2002 by
Games Workshop Publishing
Willow Road, Lenton,
Nottingham, NG7 2WS, UK

10 9 8 7 6 5 4 3 2 1

Cover illustration by Clint Langley

A CIP record for this book
is available from the British Library

ISBN 1 84154 230 X

Set in ITC Giovanni

Printed and bound in Great Britain by
Cox & Wyman Ltd, Cardiff Rd, Reading, Berkshire RG1 8EX, UK

See the Black Library on the Internet at
www.blacklibrary.co.uk

Find out more about Games Workshop
and the world of Warhammer 40.000 at
www.games-workshop.com

CONTENTS

WORDS OF BLOOD

Ben Counter

DAY HAD NEARLY broken on Empyrion IX. Commander Athellenas glanced above him at the stars fading against the light of the planet's sun. He could still just see the silver dagger hanging in orbit, the renegade ship that was waiting to drop down onto the lone spaceport and rescue the heathen horde that was stranded here.

He had thirty Marines. Thirty Marines to halt an army which never gave up, never felt pain, existed only to draw blood from the holy Imperium of man.

But Athellenas knew he must succeed. This temple on the outskirts of the planet's lone abandoned city dated back from the Great Crusade, when the people of the Imperium spontaneously elevated the Emperor to Godhood before His worship was taken over by the bureaucrats of the Ecclesiarchy – and it was by the faith that had built this temple that he swore no heretic would leave this planet alive.

Sergeant Valerian scrambled over the ruined outer wall of the temple, keeping low to avoid detection. 'Commander, they are sighted. They have left their ship.'

'Damage?'

'They came down shallow. Most of them survived.'

'Numbers?'

Valerian paused, a frown passing over his old, gnarled features. 'It is better that you see for yourself, commander.'

The Devastator sergeant handed Athellenas the scope from the squad's lascannon. Athellenas made his way to the temple perimeter, from where the great smoking hulk of the crashed renegade craft could be seen, scarred and pitted, against the grey pre-dawn sky.

He looked through the scope and saw the enemy for the first time. He counted them automatically – one batch stripping the dead, another, cavalry, dragging stubborn horses from the ship's hold, a third group, the largest, surrounding the leader. They were cultists, and far gone – most of them shirtless and wearing the jackets of their uniforms tied around their waists; barefoot, their skins scarred and painted with blood, armed with whatever they had salvaged. Lasguns, knives, shards of twisted metal, a couple of heavy weapons on carriages pulled by the riders' horses. Every cultist had that same wide-eyed look, the look of rage mixed with desperation and unacknowledged fear, the emotions of treachery waiting to boil over at any second. Athellenas added up their numbers. Six thousand, give or take.

And the leader. If proof was needed that this was the work of the Blood God, he was it. Tall, not massively muscular but wiry and powerful, almost glowing with pent-up energy. Dressed only in bloodstained cloth wrapped around his waist, black straggly hair, a violent, unshaven face, his skin covered in scars and branded with heathen symbols. One arm was gone, replaced with a pair of hydraulic industrial shears so big the tips reached the ground. The blades were pitted and worn, but even in the weak light the savagely sharp edge shone silver. He was talking animatedly to the heretics who surrounded him, his eyes flashing, his words so charged and evil that even though he was out of earshot, Athellenas could feel their power.

'Valerian?'

'Commander?'

'Take note. We have found the Gathalamor 24th.'

'The Manskinner? But he's–'

'He's a lot more than a rumour, Valerian. He's real, and he's here. He has the four thousand from Gathalamor and more. Probably the Guryan mutineers, and some cavalry.' Athellenas handed back the scope. 'Prepare a defensive position. The Manskinner will know we are here. He will attack with the sun.'

As Valerian gave instruction to the dug-in Devastators, and the tactical and assault squads checked their weapons again for the fight that was to come, Athellenas ran over the rumours and official denials. That the famously pious planet of Gathalamor should supply the renegades for the Manskinner's army was too much for the Ecclesiarchy to admit. They had insisted the Manskinner was a rumour dreamed up by their enemies in the Administratum.

Athellenas's loyalty lay with Terra, not the Ecclesiarchy. But he, for one, would be happy to do them a favour and quell this rumour for good. And what rumours...

They said the Manskinner was nothing more than a criminal. He was being transported from a hive world – some said Necromunda, others Lastrati – when he broke out somehow. A bulkhead used to seal the brig had taken his arm off during the attempt, but the massive shock and blood loss had not killed him; he survived and fought on, and the last entries in the log of the drifting, burnt-out prison ship recorded how the plasma reactor was being tampered with and was about to go critical. The charred bodies of all those on board were recovered, save one.

It was on Gathalamor that the Manskinner turned up next and earned his name. Those officers in the regiment he infiltrated who opposed him were butchered in the night and their flayed skins run up the barrack's flag poles. Within three days of his arrival, it was said, several thousand of the planet's most trusted Guardsmen had disappeared, taking a troop transport ship from orbit as they did so, leaving a blood-soaked altar of skulls in the centre of their parade ground as if to mock those who stayed behind.

These were the tales that seemed to have substance. Others were just anecdotes and stories, about how the Manskinner could turn men to Chaos with his words alone, about the strange omens that accompanied him and the abnormalities in the Astronomican which had confounded the spacecraft attempting to persue his army.

Athellenas had been a commander for a long time, and a Space Marine for longer. He had learned that when cautious men believe nothing they have not seen, a true leader can sift the truth from lies.

And there was a truth here, of the sheer monstrosity of the Manskinner, a force that corrupted the staunchest of men with horrifying ease. From foes such as him the Imperium had the most to fear – for it was built on the souls of its subjects, those same souls that the Manskinner was making his own.

'BROTHERS! SONS OF blood! This day, we face the final enemy. Some amongst you may believe the Blood God has seen fit to test us once more before we can truly worship him with the sacrifice of a million Macharian lives.'

The words of blood cut right into their minds, driving them to further heights of bloodlust. The Manskinner had never felt more grateful for the gift of the words – no army, no Marine, could stand before men who knew nothing but the joy of carnage.

'But the truth, sons of blood, is that such have we pleased him that he has given us yet more skulls to take! And what skulls! The Marines, the scum of Humanity, the Imperium's blind machines, are here, to die in His name and prove His power to the weak!'

The Manskinner raised his remaining arm high and the crowd around him cheered madly, screaming their insane joy at the battle to come. Many had died in the crash, and still more were wounded or weak – their very bloodlust would kill them. But still, they were many. They would charge across the planet's lone city and take the spaceport, and their brothers in orbit would carry them the rest of their journey to Macharia, and on that world of thirty billion souls, his army would die in an orgy of carnage in the name of the Blood God. It was impossible to imagine the numbers that would die, the mindless hordes of the weak put to the sword before the last cultist died.

And then, such would be the pleasure of the Blood God, that he, the Manskinner, would become his chosen, an immortal champion murdering the very stars in His name.

'Brothers!' he called again over the din. 'Tend to your arms! the Imperial filth will die at the rising of the sun!'

The cultists scattered to prepare themselves: to load guns and sharpen blades, scar themselves and contemplate the glorious acts of murder to come. Recoba, once a corporal, now commanding the four thousand Gathalamor rebels, bellowed orders and cracked heads. Kireeah, who had joined the Manskinner with over two thousand men from the Planetary Defence Force on Guryan, was rather more subtle, making sure his men could see his finger on the trigger of his duelling laspistol at all times.

'Diess!' yelled the Manskinner. The rider galloped up on his jet-black horse. The beast's nostrils were flecked with foaming blood and its eyes bulged, but even this animal was infected by the power of the words of blood. Diess himself, young and breathlessly eager, sat bolt upright, cavalry sword raised in salute, still wearing his tattered officer's uniform.

'Sir! My Lord Manskinner!'

'Diess, to you goes the honour of first blood. You and your men will be the first to hit the Marines' position. Hit hard. If you can take some alive, do so. They will provide sport for the rest. If not, let nothing survive.'

Even Diess smiled at this. 'Thank you, my lord! This is a glorious day for Colcha!'

'Everyone on Colcha wants you dead, Diess. This is a glorious day for the Blood God.'

'Sir, yes sir!' Diess galloped off, infused with that strange joy that only the Blood God could give a man in the moments before battle.

The Manskinner could taste his victory on the air. The dry ground of Empyrion IX would run red before the day was out.

The first rays of the sun broke around the hulk of the cultists' spacecraft. Diess's horsemen, three hundred strong, spurred their mounts into motion as one and thundered across the plain towards the broken obsidian shell of the temple. Many of the foot troops followed them, waving their salvaged weapons and screaming with bloodlust, hoping that when they reached the temple there would be some Marines left alive for them.

Even as the first lasgun shots cut through the air, the Man-skinner could feel the Blood God smiling down upon him from His throne of skulls in the warp.

Blood, keened a familiar voice in his head.

Blood for the Blood God.

'FIRE!' YELLED VALERIAN, his old, battered face creased with rage and indignation. The Devastator squad's weapons sprouted sudden blossoms of flame and the first wave of heretic cavalry fell, some men shot off the backs of their mounts, some with their horses cut in half, all falling to the ground in clouds of dust.

But the horsemen kept on coming, their horses' hides smeared black with engine oil, beast and rider branded and scarred, the eyes both black with blood-madness. Those who had weapons which could shoot returned fire and a score of lasgun shots impacted against the black stone of the temple. Some hit the armour of the dug-in tactical and assault squads. None penetrated.

Athellenas flexed his hand encased in his power glove, feeling its power field leap into life around it. He raised his uncased hand, and brought it down in a swift chopping motion – at the signal, the tactical squad's bolters spat a rain of explosive steel.

Another wave of cavalry went down but they were closer now – and their leader, an officer in a ragged, stained parody of a uniform, still lived, holding his sabre high, leading his troops into the fray.

Shots kept coming and the assault squad Sergeant Kytellias took a hit on the arm.

'Status, Kytellias?'

'Not serious,' replied the sergeant. 'Lost a couple of fingers. Ready for your order.'

'Hold, Kytellias. Hold.'

Another volley from the devastator and tactical squads cut down a swathe more horsemen, but the enemy were within laspistol range now. Athellenas's auto-sense warning icons flashed against his retina as one shot rang off his shoulder pad. He aimed his bolt pistol and took revenge for the firer's presumption, the shot taking a cultist in the neck and sending him somersaulting backwards off his horse.

They were close. Their horses were foaming. The officer raised his sword, ready to bring it down on the first Marine in his path.

'Charge!' yelled Athellenas. Before the word was out of his throat, Kytellias and his men had rocketed out of their dugouts, jump packs roaring. They came down on the heads of the nearest riders and each one cut down his opposite man. Kytellias himself sought his next target without breaking stride. Ignoring the cultists whose blades and clubs were turned aside by his armour, the sergeant ran at full pelt towards the officer.

He wants revenge, thought Athellenas. Revenge for his fingers. In any other army it would be considered ill-discipline – but for the Black Templars, for all Space Marines, everything they did was revenge.

Athellenas led the second charge himself, charging into the now-confused horsemen with the tactical squad. Plunging into the swirling dust and screams of the dying, he ducked the first blade and struck back with his power fist, a great pendulous blow that lifted rider and horse and threw them seven metres in a shower of blue sparks from the power field.

'Again!' yelled the officer. 'Again! Hit them again!' But his horsemen were too scattered and confused to regroup and counter-charge. Those who still had mounts were trying to wrestle their horses back under control through the hail of bolt pistol shells and the screeching walls of chainsword blades that lanced out of the dust and cut down a cultist with every stroke.

Athellenas's auto-senses picked out Kytellias, duelling with the officer. The officer was good, using his height advantage on his horse to keep Kytellias's power sword at bay. An aristocrat, thought Athellenas, raised in the saddle just as Athellenas and his Marines had been raised on the battlefield. He met Kytellias's every thrust, turning the blade so its power field didn't shatter his own.

Then Kytellias stopped toying with him and brought the power sword down so fast the officer didn't have time to cry out as its point came down on his shoulder and carved him open. The officer dropped his sword, convulsed as his blood flooded out onto the dry earth, then toppled to the ground. His horse bolted and took many of the surviving animals with it. Those who were without mounts still fought, but they were so consumed with madness and confusion that the Assault and Tactical Marines picked them off at will with the chainsword tooth or the bolter shell.

'Sergeant Kytellias, report,' said Athellenas over his communicator.

'Seventy per cent enemy casualties, sir, no losses. Injuries nominal.'

Athellenas hurried forward through the clouds of dust and gunsmoke. He looked in the direction of the cultist spacecraft, auto-senses magnifying the image and picking out the sounds of the approaching horde.

The rest of the cultists were following. The Manskinner was acting true to form: the cavalry had been sent to draw out a counter-charge and break up the Marines' position, so the main body of cultists would hit a compromised Marine line.

'Valerian?'

'Sir.'

'Take your squad and fall back to the city's outskirts. Prepare another defensive position. Kytellias and I will join you there.'

Silence. Then...

'Sir, we cannot fall back. We cannot surrender this position.'

There was a quality in Valerian's voice that every commander came to know. The sound of rebellion.

'Valerian, you will fall back immediately. The enemy is too great. We cannot face them here.' Athellenas could see the

Manskinner, claw swinging as he ran, the mass of cultists swarming around him.

'Sir, I cannot retreat in the face of the enemy. The Inititate Doctoris states as much–'

'Questions of doctrine will be dealt with on Terra. For now you will follow orders.'

Again, silence.

'Yes, sir.' But this time, rebellion was clear in Valerian's voice.

Athellenas signalled to the tactical and assault squads, and they moved as one back through the temple towards the outskirts of the city, leaving behind them a field of two hundred dead and an enemy who would not give up.

THE MANSKINNER KICKED over the worn marble icon of the Imperial eagle and watched it shatter on the ground. All around him his men were taking out their rage on the fabric of the temple, firing shots into the carved walls, defiling the altars with their own blood.

'Where are they?' yelled Recoba. 'Where are the dogs? Cowardly dogs! Too afraid to face Khorne's wrath!' An untrained eye would see Recoba as a burned-out corporal running to fat, now turned to madness with the worship of the Blood God. But the truth was that he was strong – that bulk was muscle, not fat, and he held the minds of his men in bonds of iron that the Blood God's worship had only forged tighter.

He spoke for all his men, and the Manskinner knew all his men were angry.

They had run. These Marines, these defenders of humanity, who should have died a hundred times over rather than yield one inch of ground to the Blood God's followers: they had retreated. They had fallen back in the face of heretics. They had surrendered this place, a symbol of their Emperor's false godhood, a place that was as holy as could be.

This was wrong. This was not the way of the Imperium. They were supposed to underestimate the Blood God's power in their arrogance, and die beneath the blades of His army as it swept them aside.

And his men, they all felt the same. They had been robbed of their battle, the ultimate deceit. The bloodlust was building up in them unchecked, a destroying hunger that only violence would satisfy.

'Brothers!' The Manskinner felt the words of blood hot in his mind. He had to use them wisely now, and mould the minds of his men just as he wished. 'The enemy has shown its true face! Not merely weak, but cowardly! Deceitful! With their trickery they defy all that the Blood God has shown you! But we will not fall prey to their lies. We will wait here, in this, the very place they hold as a symbol of their weakling Emperor, and gather our strength before we strike and brand our victory against the spirit of the Imperium!'

Recoba strode forward, out of the gathered crowd. 'We cannot wait! By the Blood God's throne, the enemy are in flight! We must pursue them and run them down, not cower like children!'

The Manskinner fixed Recoba with a glare. The man was as dangerous as he was useful. He, amongst all the cultists, must be brought to heel. The Manskinner raised his claw so the steel tips hovered in front of Recoba's face.

'Recoba, my brother, you know nothing of the ways of the enemy. The Blood God has shown me the truth about the feeble ways of Man. The Marines wish to draw us out in pursuit so they can destroy one part of our force at a time, until finally there are none left to take to Macharia and begin the slaughter. They will use the commands of the Blood God against us, knowing we will become blind with bloodlust. Even now, when you wish to pursue, Kireeah's forces and half of your men have yet to arrive here. You would take on the Marines with a third, with a quarter, of your forces, only to let them run once more when the rest come to avenge them?'

The Manskinner turned once more to the rest of the cultists, who listened to his every word as if they were those of the Blood God himself. 'But we will not let them, my brothers! We will all strike as one, so they will not break the back of this army before we reach the spaceport! Blood for the Blood God!'

But even now, the Manskinner could see a cohort of Gath-alamor men gathering around Recoba, the old corporal's face twisted further with hate. He would break off, and lead them right into the Marines' trap.

Well, let him die, thought the Manskinner. Maybe his men would inflict some suffering on the Marines before the rest of the horde could reach them. It was for the good. To stop Recoba would be to fight him and his men, and he could not afford to have his army fall apart now. Let the Marines think their plan is working, that they will eliminate the Blood God's army piece by piece.

It will be all the more joyous when the enemy's skulls litter the ground of Empyrion IX and our army is on its way to begin the holy slaughter.

Let him die.

THE MIDDAY SUN CAST few shadows through the outskirts of the deserted town. Empyrion IX's only settlement had been abandoned, along with the rest of the planet, when it was realised that its mineral deposits were far scarcer than the Adeptus Mechanicus Geologis had thought. And so it had stayed, for hundreds of years, until today, when the fates had chosen it for the conflict that would decide the fate of a billion lives.

Athellanas had chosen to set up the second Space Marine line in a string of decrepit residential blocks, ugly grey blank plascrete. His squad were in the upper floors of one block, with the Devastators in the neighbouring building. Below them, the broad streets, designed to take mining machines and trucks of ore, were empty, scattered with fallen masonry and fragments of broken glass. Everything was quiet. Even the air was still. It was only Athellenas's enhanced auto-senses that registered the scent of blood.

'They haven't actually... said anything, sir.' Kytellias, speaking to his commander face-to-face, was choosing his words carefully, for this was an area a Marine would normally never encounter. The area of rebellion. It was a dark, unfamiliar taste in the air. 'But I can tell. The way they move, their voices. They... they're not happy, sir. Not happy with you.'

Commander Athellenas looked at his assault sergeant. Like all the Black Templars, he had been tested without his knowledge back on Terra for the risk of disobedience – and Kytellias had been designated the most likely to rebel in Athellenas's whole command. Kytellias's capacity for initiative and self-reliance, that made him an ideal assault sergeant, at the same time made him headstrong and potentially dangerous. Yet he was the Marine Athellenas could most trust here.

This was not a question of a Marine being required to sell his life for the fraction of a victory. This danger was not born of cowardice or malice. Valerian, and perhaps others, were being ordered to abandon their whole system of values, to change the way they saw right and wrong. Retreat in the face of the enemy – in the face of Chaos – was a fundamental evil to a Marine.

He was asking his men to do wrong. What commander, what Space Marine, had that right?

'You have done well to tell me this, Kytellias,' he said. 'What of your squad?'

'They are sound. But no more.'

'And your hand?'

Kytellias looked down at his wounded hand. His blood had crystallised quickly around the plasteel, where the lasgun blast had sheared off three fingers. 'I still have my trigger finger, sir. No operational concerns.'

'Good. The next wave will be poorly led but larger. We will use the streets. You will use your squad to draw the enemy in, funnel them into the street below. My squad and Valerian's will open fire on them from above. Understood?'

'Understood, sir.'

Kytellias's jump pack flared and he leapt through the wide, glassless window, across to the roof of the opposite building to enact the equipment rituals with his squad.

'Valerian?'

'Sir?' Valerian's voice was clear with suppressed anger over the communicator.

'Have your squad move into position. The second wave is here.'

'Nothing on the auspex, sir.'

'They're close. They will be hard to break at first but soon their formation will disperse. When Kytellias withdraws, you will open fire. Kytellias will chase down enemy stragglers.'

'And then, sir? The next wave?'

'You have your orders, sergeant.'

Athellenas and his squad gathered on the fourth floor, bolters checked, ready to turn the street below into a river of fire.

The horizon shifted, turned dark, and began to spread through the outskirts towards them.

The second wave.

'FOR EVERY GREEN and sainted isle, of Gathalamor's blue sea, for the sake of every man that's lost, we'll die or we'll be free!'

Recoba's spirit rose with pride. His men, his personal command within the Gathalamor army, had sided with him to a man – fully a third of the cultists in number. As they marched in time, as they had been drilled, it was like they were back on fair Gathalamor, before they had lost so many brothers and friends to the idiocy of the Guard's commanders, before they had first encountered that madman with the voice of a god who took them at their lowest hour and changed them into his own private army.

They didn't need the Imperium. But they didn't need the Manskinner either. He was just another fool who would throw away the lives of Recoba's men. Well, if they must die, they would die face-to-face with the enemy, the Marines.

Space Marines. When the Guard threw billions of men to be chewed up by whichever foe their wrath fell upon, it was the Marines who survived, who delivered the killing blow to an enemy the Guardsmen's deaths had laid open.

They would know what it was like to feel that utter despair. Recoba would see to that.

At the front of the marching formation some of the men were falling out of step, breaking into a run to get to grips with the Marines who lurked in the residential blocks around them. As they headed down the town's main road, lasguns ready, still singing, the men were breaking off, kicking down doors, hunting for the enemy.

His men. Recoba was proud. They were still his men, even after all the Imperium and the Manskinner had put them through.

The smell came first, the burning, metallic reek of fuel. Then the white noise as they descended from the sky on their exhaust jets, dropping down right on top of the formation.

'Fire!' yelled Recoba. 'Open fire!'

But many of the men had no time to pull the triggers before the Black Templars were upon them, their black armour gleaming in the bright midday sun, black crosses on their white shoulder pads flashing, chainsword teeth tearing through the cultists, bolt pistols blazing.

Recoba saw one of the Marines, no, two, swamped by cultists who, having lost their weapons in the crash, threw themselves at the assault squad and dragged them down under the weight of the mob. The cultists grabbed the only thing at hand that could be used as a weapon – chunks of plascrete torn from the ground by heavy weapons fire – and set to work on the Marines. Recoba himself opened fire with his bolter, even as the two Marines' ceramite armour gave way beneath the pounding of plascrete. He heard them crack open, and felt it, too, as it gave all his men the heart not to break, to stand and fight.

The Marines were used to enemies running from them. Not this time. These were Gathalamor men. Gathalamor men could never be beaten.

The rest of the assault squad fell back towards the nearest building leaving a trail of broken bodies behind them, but ever more cultists – no, not cultists, Guardsmen once more – closed in behind them, volleys of lasgun shots sending up a wall of white-hot light around the Marines. Another fell, sparks cascading from his ruptured armour, still firing even as he died beneath the rifle butts and bare fists of the Guardsmen.

Recoba joined his men as they poured forward after the Marines, formation forgotten, some still singing, all of them eager for the fight now that blood had been tasted at last.

'All troops, rapid fire. Target saturation pattern.' Athellenas watched as incandescent death lanced down from the upper floors of the building overlooking the street, tearing a hole through the main body of cultists. Lascannon blasts gouged furrows in the broken road surface, and frag missiles burst into clouds of fire, sweeping across the road, engulfing a dozen cultists at a time. Heavy bolter shots stitched a bloody path through the cultists, and the heavy plasma blasts fell like huge drops of liquid fire that flowed as water but melted anything they touched. The noise must have been immense, a vast roar of explosive, mechanical rage, mixed with the screams of the dying and the hiss of burning flesh. But Athellenas's auto-senses filtered out the din, leaving only the communicator channels clear.

'Kytellias here. Taking fire, three men down. Counter-attacking.' The first losses, then. Now Athellenas's tactics had cost the lives of Marines. Rebellion would be an even sterner foe now.

The bolters of Athellenas's tactical squad added their own fire, each Marine picking a cultist target and spearing him with a bolt of screaming steel. The formation was nothing now and the streets were full of a swirling, burning mass of men, caught up in equal measures of panic and hate, scrambling over one another, howling, dying by the dozen. The cultists didn't fall back, but they were weak and broken.

'Kytellias, charge.'

Through a haze of static and battle-din, Kytellias's voice came over the communicator. 'Yes, sir! Squad, by sections! Charge!'

The blades of Kytellias's squad tasted blood once more as the Marines carved their way through the panicked cultists. A few of the heathens ran; others fought on half-blind, and died without ceremony. They stood their ground in knots of resistance but the Marines showed nothing but disgust for their broken enemies, cutting them down like reeds in a thunderstorm.

Kytellias's power sword accounted for most, flashing like a harnessed bolt of lightning, every stroke taking a pagan's head.

The Space Marines strode across the burning, blood-stained road, killing anything that still lived, until there was nothing there but death.

'Sir?' Valerian's voice, full of hidden tension. 'What now, sir?'

'We fall back,' replied Athellenas. 'Kytellias, cover our retreat and look out for enemy stragglers. Retreat to the spaceport–'

'Sir,' said Valerian, 'I cannot follow such an order.'

'Sergeant, fall back and maintain a defensive position.'

'I can see what you are trying to do, commander. If we fall back and destroy the cultists a wave at a time then they would be finished. But their objective is the spaceport. We cannot absorb one wave and then fall back again, or the spaceport will be taken. We must destroy them all, at once, immediately, and that objective can only be achieved if we stand and fight.'

There was silence. Athellenas could hear the gunsmoke coiling in the air and the blood running down the walls, the last licks of flame playing over the charred bodies of the cultists.

'That is why you object?' said Athellenas carefully. 'Because you believe the tactic will fail?'

Silence.

'No, sir. That is not why I object. Perhaps we can defeat this army, commander. But if we cannot, then we must sell our lives for as many heathen souls as we can.'

Valerian was almost lost, realised Athellenas. He was trying to hide it, but his whole belief system was breaking down. Everything he had been taught, as a child, as a Marine, had told him that to retreat was to die a million deaths, to give up his honour as well as his life, to betray his Emperor, his Primarch, his very species.

'Either way, we must stand and fight, commander,' Valerian continued. 'It is both our duty and our privilege.'

'Fall back, Valerian.'

'Damnation, commander, this is madness! Does this Chapter mean nothing to you? Have you no duty to the souls of your lost brothers? Already we have lost men here, do you wish to defile their memories with your cowardice? This is madness, sir, nothing but madness! I will not retreat, not ever, not for anyone or anything! I will not turn away from the fight, I will die by fire and by the sword, for if the only other option is to run like a child alongside you then I have no choice to make.'

This was where the battle was won. Athellenas knew he was right. He knew he would win. It was required of him. The enemy was nothing, he told himself. But his own men, they were the dangerous ones. They could break the back of this whole operation. If he ever had to be a leader of men, it was now.

'Valerian, you will fall back and maintain a defensive line at the spaceport. If you do not you will be shot and your name will be struck from the Liber Honarium. Your soul will have no mention at the Feast of the Departed. Your gene-seed will not be taken and given to a new initiate, because you will not be fit to have a Marine follow you into this Chapter. The faces of Rogal Dorn and of the eternal Emperor will be turned from you forever. You will not be in the Emperor's army at the end of time when the final battle is fought.

'You fear dishonour, Sergeant Valerian? If you disobey me now, if you place duty to yourself above duties to your Chapter and your Imperium, then I will show you truly what dishonour is.'

Silence again. And through the silence, Athellenas could hear the echoes of that power – the words of the Manskinner, rallying his troops. The cultists knew they had to strike as one to break through the Marine line. This wave had been a dissident group, enraged at being denied their battle.

If Athellenas could only hold his own force together in the face of the enemy of dishonour, then the Templars would win. He knew it, with every part of his soul. If he could just hold them together.

'I do this under protest, sir,' came Valerian's voice. 'When we return to Terra, if we return, I shall bring a Protest Iudicarum to the Chapter Master in person. I shall see you tried and excommunicated. But for now, I retreat.'

Even as the power of the Manskinner's heresy built up in the air, Athellenas led his Marines back through the abandoned streets of Empyrion IX, towards the spaceport. And above them hovered unseen the traitor ship, always a reminder of what would happen if the Manskinner took the spaceport.

How many would die? Billions?

But Athellenas wiped the question from his mind. Not one cultist would escape into orbit while a Black Templar still lived.

'RECOBA IS DEAD!' yelled Kireeah, his Guryan troops gathered around him. 'No more of this! The Marines may cower and deceive us but nothing can survive us! We are still four thousand strong, and they are but a handful! Now, Lord Manskinner, now we must strike!'

By the gods, the Space Marine commander was clever, thought the Manskinner. Lying and cowardly, perhaps, but clever. The Manskinner was losing his cultists. The seeds of hatred he had sown in them with the words of blood were blossoming, and their bloodlust was drowning everything else in their minds. Without battle, deprived of the joy of facing this enemy who retreated constantly and destroyed his army piece by piece, the Manskinner's men were devolving beyond his control.

The Manskinner faced his underling. Kireeah had been dangerous even before the Manskinner had found him, a young, driven officer with a reputation for savagery amongst the rest of the Guard, who had done much of the Manskinner's work beforehand in dismantling the humanity of his men. Of all of the cultists, Kireeah would be feeling that seductive hatred most keenly.

'Kireeah,' said the Manskinner darkly, 'this foe is like no other. We cannot simply charge them without a thought, for they will take us apart piece by piece. They have shown that well enough already.'

Kireeah stepped closer. The Manskinner could see the veins standing out on the side of the Guryan officer's shaven head, flecks of spittle flying as he spoke, undiluted rage filling up the darkness behind his eyes. 'Lord Manskinner, many of us may die, but we will out! Even now they cower in the space-port. If they retreat again we shall have won! They must stand or fall, and if they stand they cannot but die! No mat-ter what, we will take the spaceport, and within the hour we shall be on our way to Macharia. If we should die, then our skulls shall honour the Blood God! If we hold back, and fight with shadows and lies, like our enemy, then he will be disgusted at our weakness!'

The Manskinner knew he had only one choice. He had used the words of blood many times to turn men into ani-mals, now they had to turn animals into men. He felt their power growing within him as he spoke, his voice speaking to the very souls of Kireeah and every cultist there.

'Brothers! My brothers, this is the Blood God's final test! For we fight now not to win, or to die, but for revenge! Revenge, for Diess and Recoba and all those slain by deceit! Revenge, for the violation of the Blood God's holy rites of battle by a foe who will not face us! And revenge, like mur-der and massacre, is an aspect of His teaching – but unlike them, it is cold, fought by men purged of all emotion who fight not like animals thirsty for blood but as men acting as one, not charging blindly into the fray but marching side by side, a machine of destruction. This is the Blood God's way, to show us all the joys that bloodshed can bring, the sane alongside the savage, the cold-blooded along–'

Kireeah thrust his face close, his very breath like tongues of flame, teeth bared, heart pounding so strongly that a trickle of blood ran from one nostril and the vessels in one eye had burst into a crimson cloud spreading across the eyeball. 'Lies!' he screamed. 'This is not the Blood God's way! Now, when His worship needs him most, our lord has faltered! He has given way to cowardice! He is no better than the enemy, a coward who fights with lies instead of fists!'

Kireeah turned to the cultists. 'Charge with me, Brothers of the Blood God! Kill them! Kill them all!'

And as one, the cultists changed. The hateful loyalty the words of blood created was unpicked in a moment and the

soul of every man belonged to Khireeah, to the blood-
stained madness that was bursting across their minds.

The Manskinner didn't think, he just acted. He swung
back the shears that hulked in place of his long-dead arm
and brought them shrieking through the air, a hydraulic stab
snapping the great blades shut around Khireeah's neck, slicing his head from his shoulders so quickly the officer's
mouth still moved as it fell to the ground.

The body swayed, fountaining blood as it fell.

But it was too late. The men were already turning and
breaking away, across the plain towards the city, yelling their
homeworld's battle-cries or just keening like animals if they
were too enraged to speak, the blood on their skin gleaming
in the sun.

'Stop!' yelled the Manskinner as his entire army began to
plunge towards the ruined city. 'Damn you, stop!' The words
of blood shook the very air as he spoke but it seemed to
have no effect. These were men whose souls had been
drowned by their bloodlust, and it was to the soul that the
words spoke.

The Manskinner's claw lashed out and carved the nearest
few cultists into pieces, but the others ignored him, clam-
bering over one another to get out of the confines of the
temple and join the mad stampede.

'Stop! The Blood God commands you!'

The Manskinner strode amongst his frenzied men,
butchering any within range, taking off heads, limbs, shearing torsos in two, his skin and the metal of the shears slick
with blood. It had come to this, raged his thoughts. They
had abandoned him. The words had abandoned him. If he
could murder every single one of them, he would, if he
could bring together every single living human being and
put their necks between the blades of his claw, if he could
climb to the top of the Throne of Skulls itself and face the
God who had betrayed him...

The army was gone now, and the Manskinner was alone in
the temple, with only the bodies of the dead left under his
command.

No. His men were not the ones he hated. The enemy...

The Space Marines. They had done this. They had hidden like children and denied his men the bloodletting they lived for. Their trickery had broken even the power of the words, defiled the authority of the Manskinner, and of the Blood God above him.

'Kill them!' yelled the words, speaking to him as clearly as they had to any of his men. 'Kill them all!'

Suddenly, he was running in the thick of his men, surrounded by the bare torsos and tattered uniforms of his cultists, back with the men who owed him everything. He knew now what he must do. He must strike like a thunderbolt into the Marines, tear them limb from limb, and give him a taste of the slaughter to come.

And beyond it all, beyond the baying of his men and the thunder of their feet, the clouds of dust billowing around them and the stench of sweat and fire, drowning everything out, were the words of blood.

'Blood!' they called. 'Blood for the Blood God!'

THEY POURED THROUGH the streets, sweeping through the town like a flash flood across a plain, bringing with them the stench of sweat and blood and the din of four thousand men driven to insanity.

The cavernous, decaying spaceport loomed all around the Marines, but the vast series of half-collapsed domes offered few defensive positions amongst the debris and abandoned docking equipment. The Devastator squad had set up as best they could, shielded by a set of docking clamps corroded to lumps of rust, while Kytellias's battered Assault Marines were high up amongst the support struts of the nearest dome, looking down at the horde that charged headlong towards them. Athellenas and the tactical squad were effectively in the open, positioned at the edge of the great open expanse of smooth plascrete on which the cultists' ship would land if they took the spaceport.

This was the end, thought Athellenas. *Even if I tried to retreat, Valerian wouldn't go, and neither would most of the others. It is by our actions here that we will be judged.*

Or remembered, if we fail.

'Take aim.' Though the cultists were still out of range, the Black Templars took aim as one, ready to loose their fire-power as soon as the heathens charged too close. Through the scope of his bolter, Athellenas could see the Manskinner himself, at the front of the horde, the massive industrial shears swinging heavily as he ran, eyes no longer those of a leader, but of a fanatical follower. That was the key. No one led this horde any more.

The scream grew louder as the cultists scrambled over the remains of fallen buildings and streamed down the main road towards the spaceport, blood running from thousands of abrasions caused by their headlong, heedless charge. They had no sense of pain now. They were blind and deaf to anything other than battle. They were the true children of their god, insane and self-destructive.

'Ready to go, sir,' came Valerian's voice over the communicator.

'Hold, sergeant,' replied Athellenas. 'We wait.'

'BLOOD!' SCREAMED THE voice, over and over again, as the Manskinner's untiring limbs carried him closer and closer to where the domes of the spaceport rose above the residential blocks. There was a savage joy on the faces of his men, and in that moment he was happy, knowing that there would be a twofold slaughter ahead: the Marines first, then across the stars to Macharia.

The Manskinner was happy at last. This was why he had been born. This was why the Blood God had picked him out. To kill, to shed blood in his name.

He was at the head of the horde as it crossed the threshold of the spaceport, roaring towards the Marine lines.

'Nothing lives!' he yelled. He could see the black-armoured figures crouching amongst the debris, trying to hide, but no one could hide from the Blood God's chosen. 'No quarter! No mercy! Blood for the Blood God!'

He could see their commander, lying in wait armed with a power fist he was too cowardly to use, trying to catch them in an ambush of fire as he had done with Recoba's men. Up above them, an assault squad, under-strength, lurked – but they would drop down not onto confused weaklings but a boiling sea of men made godlike by rage. They would melt away. They all would. They were nothing.

His claw blades held open ready for the kill, the words of blood screaming in his ears to match the pounding of his heart, the Manskinner led the final charge towards the space-port.

'No quarter! No mercy! Blood for the Blood God!'

'HOLD, SERGEANT.' THEY were so close that Athellenas could feel the heat coming off them even before his auto-senses registered it. A tidal wave of men was roaring towards them, a wall of incandescent hate that would destroy anything in its way, half-naked blood-stained animals of men, with a raging daemon at their head around whom played a halo of dark power.

They were within range. He could order the Devastators to open fire but he did not. There were two battles here. The cultists must die, and along with them the stain of rebellion amongst his men.

'Hold your fire,' he ordered again. He could feel the agitation of his men, the urge to open fire on the horde battling with their respect for his command. That respect might not last much longer if Athellenas did not do everything right.

Then, it happened.

The first men across the spaceport perimeter began to falter, losing direction, eyes wild as their focus was taken off the waiting Marines. One swung his makeshift club wildly as if wishing an enemy to appear next to him – full of lust for battle, he could no longer wait to reach the enemy and sought out his nearest comrade. He struck the man across the back of the head. The victim fought back with his teeth, lunging for the first man's throat, dragging him to the ground. The violence spread like a flash fire and suddenly thrashing, kicking, biting bodies were piling up on the threshold, thick dark blood running across the plascrete, ankle-deep.

The leader tried to drag his men apart and then joined them in their carnage, his flailing shears cutting men apart, two or three at a time. The noise was awesome. None of these men felt pain any more, and they screamed not with pain, but with rage at the violence done to their bodies and the wounds they inflicted with their own hands.

This army, this river of liquid fire, foundered a pistol shot away from Athellenas's Marines, its members tearing each other apart. Denied the taste of blood for so long, they sought it in the only place they could find it: in their fellow heretics.

'BLOOD! BLOOD! NO mercy! No quarter!' The Manskinner didn't realise he was screaming. He felt nothing any more, just the thirst at the back of his throat and in the hollow at the centre of his soul, the hollow that could only be filled with death. The payment for the Blood God's favour was that they must feel his thirst, the lust for battle, the intense and all-conquering desperation that madness brought.

His claw sheared through the press of men around him. Weaklings! he thought. Idiots! To fail when they were this close! To deny the Blood God his final honour by wasting their lives! The Marines had won, their deceit denying his men battle for so long that they would butcher one another rather than wait a moment longer.

But the part of his mind that could still think was dwarfed by the boiling cauldron of rage that made up the rest of him. The Manskinner killed and killed and killed, each man slain a drop of relief in the chasm of thirst. Even as the writhing, screaming, bleeding bodies closed over him, he killed. When the press became too close for him to breathe, he killed. When night came down across his eyes and his heart finally gave up its frenzied beating, he still killed. The instinct to murder was not dulled by death alone, and the shears still snapped at the walls of flesh around him until every last scrap of the Manskinner's energy was spent.

As the life finally bled from the Manskinner, the Blood God turned his back on his champion.

WHEN THE MADNESS was over, there were perhaps three dozen that still lived, wandering dazed and battered between mounds of broken bodies. The Manskinner's army was nothing more than four thousand mangled corpses and a lake of blood that was slowly draining away between the cracks in the plascrete. Flies were beginning to descend and the heat of the cultists' rage was dissipating as the bodies turned cold. The sky above began to darken as evening fell, the lumpen shadows cast by the corpses growing longer.

'Templars, advance,' ordered Athellenas. The assault squad dropped from high up in the dome, their landings cushioned by jets from their jump packs. Chainswords flashed and surviving cultists, blind and insensible, died without a struggle. Athellenas moved forward with his tactical squad, bolters picking off the stragglers wandering in twos and threes through the human wreckage. Athellenas levelled his bolt pistol and another heretic fell.

They didn't need the Devastators. Soon the last few survivors were dead and the Manskinner's threat was truly over.

'Why didn't you tell us, sir?' asked Valerian over the communicator. 'If you knew this would happen?'

'Because, Valerian, I do not have to explain my actions to you. As your commander my word is law. I have not achieved this rank through chance. I have been judged by my Chapter to be the individual whose leadership is most likely to result in victory. My purpose is to lead you, and your purpose is to follow. If this breaks down, then all is lost. You will do what you are told, Valerian, and you will not argue. We are Marines. We are Black Templars.'

The assault squad were making a sweep of the bodies, checking for survivors. Athellenas knew even now that they would not find any.

'Some of you,' he said, 'will rise to a position where you, too, will command others from this Chapter. And then you will remember the lesson you have learned here. Above everything, above procedure and mercy, and even above the honour that Valerian held so sacred, there is victory. It is only through victory that you can truly honour the Emperor and your fellow man. To fail is the greatest shame. We have retreated in the face of the enemy, but there is no shame in that, for by doing so we have defeated them. The shame belongs to the Manskinner, for throwing away his chance of victory by fighting alongside animals, not soldiers. '

The sky above was dark now, the sun of Empyrion IX dipping below the horizon. 'Kytellias, what is the ETA of our support craft?'

'Nineteen days, sir. Two of our strike cruisers. They'll destroy the heretics' ship before they know they're there.'

Nineteen days, thought Athellenas. If they had failed, no Imperial forces would have been close enough to intercept the heathen ship. How deep a wound, in lives lost and damage to the spirit of the Imperium, had they prevented from being struck here? Deep indeed.

'Then let us bury our dead,' he said, 'and prepare their wargear and gene-seed for transport back to Terra. Valerian, you and your squad will set up a trophy here to mark our victory, so that none who set foot on this world will go ignorant of what happened here. You have your orders. Fall out.'

Athellenas's auto-senses switched automatically to night vision as the sun finally set on Empyrion IX.

RAPTOR DOWN

Gav Thorpe

THE FLIGHT DECK was a hive of activity. The murmuring of tech-priests resounded off the high gantries amongst the chatter of rivet guns and the clank of ordnance loaders. Welding torches sparked bright blue-white in the yellow glow of the standby alert lighting and figures hurried to and fro. The Marauders of Raptor and Devil squadrons were arrayed herringbone-fashion along the length of the main-tenance bay as tech-adepts and servitors crawled across them, repairing battle damage and loading new ordnance. Flight Commander Jaeger stood and watched it all with a faint sense of satisfaction. Everyone was performing well today – the pilots, their gunners and bombardiers, and the bay crews were all operating like a well-oiled machine. He cupped his hands to his mouth to shout across the din.

'Ferix, how are the repairs going?' he bellowed across the decking to the robe-swathed tech-adept monitoring the maintenance on Jaeger's own Marauder, Raptor One. Ferix hurried over with short, quick steps and nodded curtly. Over the adept's shoulder, Jaeger could read the insignia that he himself had painted onto the nose of Raptor One after their last mission. It was the Raptors' motto – Swift Justice, Sure Death – in bright white against the dark blue paint of the Navy colours. Underneath in gold was the squadron emblem, an eagle rampant in shining gold. It was reassuring to Jaeger, the familiarity he now shared with Raptor One after their bloody baptism together a year and a half ago.

'All craft are battle-worthy, Flight Commander Jaeger,' Ferix told him, his hands concealed within the voluminous sleeves of his robes. 'Raptor Three should be de-commissioned for several more hours preferably, but is operational within tolerable limits.'

'Good. Let me know as soon as weapons load and check is complete. I'll be on the bridge,' Jaeger dismissed Ferix with a wave of his hand and turned away. As he walked across the flight deck, he cast his gaze around him, looking at the bulky shapes of the Marauder bombers in the gloom and the smaller Thunderbolt interceptors in the launching alcoves on the far side of the massive chamber.

All this is my domain now, he thought, not for the first time. It had been eighteen months since Raf's death left Jaeger in charge, a year and a half of responsibility to command and lead nearly a hundred pilots and flight crewmen, to mould them into a fighting team worthy of the Imperial Navy.

He could see the men of his own squadron, the Raptors, taking a well-earned meal break at the battlestation mess tables on the starboard side of the flight deck. He saw the veterans – strong, disciplined men like Marte, Arick, Phrao and Berhandt. But there were too many new faces for the flight commander's liking, men untested in the heat of battle until today. For a year the cruiser *Divine Justice* had continued her patrol, unable to replace the losses she had suffered at the hands of the orks. Only three months ago she had returned to dock and new crews were drafted in from the flight schools. Unlike the ratings, flight crews needed to be trained professionals; you couldn't just send a press gang onto some Imperial world and see what you dredged up. For a year the *Divine Justice* had been home to only half the aircraft her holds could carry and launch. Jaeger was glad that they had seen no serious action during the rest of the patrol – a few skirmishes with outclassed pirates, the odd smuggler, but nothing like the baptism of fire and death that had been the duel with the ork hulk.

Jaeger realised he was at the lifter now, and stepped into the small chamber. He cranked the dial to 'Bridge deck' and slammed the grating shut. A moment later he was swiftly ascending amongst the clatter of chains and gears, the floor of the lifter shaking gently beneath his booted feet.

Untried boys! he cursed to himself. But for all his worries, the operation was proceeding with little difficulty. Having barely had time to refit and re-crew at Saltius, the *Divine Justice* and her three frigate escorts, the *Glorious*, the *Apollo* and the *Excellent*, had been despatched with orders to support the Imperial Guard invasion of the Mearopyis system. Even now, they were in orbit over the third world of the system, running escort to the dropships and making ground attacks against enemy supply bases and communications centres.

They were here to fight the noctal – spindly, insectoid aliens who had conquered Mearopyis and enslaved its human population several thousand years ago. Finally, the Imperium had arrived to take it back and once more bring the light of the Emperor to the people of the subjugated world. Casualties had been light so far. Admiral Veniston's rites of engagement had been very specific. The noctal fighters were incapable of orbital flight, unlike the Thunderbolts and Marauders of the *Divine Justice*. The squadrons were hitting hard and fast, dropping from orbit, bombing and strafing their targets before powering back up to the ships waiting above, safe from harm. The enemy fighters were swift and agile, but they couldn't be everywhere at once and only a single Marauder had been lost, and no Thunderbolts had yet been taken down. Jaeger had heard that the squadrons from the other ships of the fleet were having similar successes.

Perhaps this is not such a bad time to test out the new hands, Jaeger considered. No massed air battles, strict orders and a safe haven would allow his men to settle, with enough risk to keep them on their toes, but also safe enough that they'd survive to learn from the experience. Survival was the key, in Jaeger's mind. No flight commander wanted a continuous draft of newcomers flying his craft; he wanted experienced, dedicated crews who would return time and again, their mission complete.

With a thunk, the lifter reached the top of its shaft, eighteen decks up from the flight bays. Jaeger pulled back the door and stepped out, swapping a salute with a gunnery lieutenant who stepped past him. He marched up to the double doors leading to the bridge and nodded to the shotgun-wielding armsman standing guard. The armsman turned and activated the comm-set on the wall behind him, announcing Jaeger's presence. There was an affirmative and several seconds later the bridge doors swung back with a hiss of hidden pistons. Stepping through, Jaeger saw the bridge was in its normal state of organised confusion. Tech-adepts scurried to and fro, augur and surveyor servitors announced target dispositions in monotonous drones, officers snapped orders over the comm-net and flunkies and menials of every description hurried here and there taking notes, making reports or simply repeating messages from one officer to the next.

In the middle of it all stood Captain Kaurl, like a rock amidst the swirl of a rising tide.

The stocky, bearded officer had his hands clasped behind his back, his feet spread as if braced on a buffeted dropship rather than a stately cruiser. He nodded as a lieutenant passed on some piece of data and then looked at the main viewing screen. It dominated the centre of the bridge, five metres high, twice as long.

The main picture showed a duel between three Imperial cruisers and two noctal superdestroyers. Cannon-fire and missiles streaked from the Emperor's vessels, flaring into bright green flashes as they impacted on the energy shields of the alien ship.

Bright white las-fire erupted from one of the superdestroyers, a flickering coruscation of energy bolts that impacted on the void shields of one of the cruisers, their energy dissipating harmlessly.

Various sub-images charted fleet positions, drop-ship manoeuvres and sundry other details. In the bottom left, a tracker field flickered on and off in one of the *Divine Justice*'s docking bays, drawing a supply shuttle down onto the armoured deck, heat wash from its engines causing the image to waver on the screen. To the top right, a spread of torpedoes rocketed across the void. As they neared a noctal vessel the front of each peeled open, ejecting a storm of plasma and fusion warheads which rippled across its silver-grey hull in a riot of orange and red. Along the bottom of the screen, wings of Starhawk bombers manoeuvred between the las-fire of a superdestroyer's defence turrets, the armoured surface of the alien ship splintering into a shower of shrapnel as their bombs punched deep inside before exploding.

Jaeger turned his attention back to the main image and watched as retro thrusters flared into life along the length of one of the Imperial cruisers. Slowed in its course, it began to sweep to starboard, turning slowly at first but gathering pace as its forward momentum slowed. Another jet of engines halted the turn and the main engines increased to full. Its broadside opened fire again and this time the noctal shields failed, missiles and plasma blasts raking into its engine decks.

Fires blossomed and spread, burning white hot as air rushed out of the punctured hull of the enemy superdestroyer in explosive bursts.

'Jacques!' Kaurl called out, snapping Jaeger's attention from the ongoing space battle.

'Sir!' he replied crisply, saluting formally. The captain responded with an equally formal nod.

'How are things going?' Kaurl asked, taking Jaeger by the arm and leading him into his personal cabin off the main bridge. It was fitted out in wooden panelling, a deep red grain that leant an air of calm. He sat beside the captain on a long sofa whose plush covers matched the rich décor of the room.

'I have made post-mission reports, sir,' Jaeger replied with a frown. 'Everything is in there.'

'Not everything, Jaeger,' smiled Kaurl. 'Numbers, yes, but nothing else. They don't tell me how you feel the invasion is progressing.'

'Everything seems to be going smoothly, exactly to plan I would say,' Jaeger told the captain after a moment's thought. 'Better than planned.'

'And that worries you?' Kaurl seemed to read Jaeger's thoughts.

'Every plan is perfect until it makes contact with the enemy,' Jaeger recited the line from the Navy battle dogma. 'Then it usually falls apart; it doesn't exceed expectation.'

'Emperor's blood, man!' cursed Kaurl, standing up and glowering at his flight commander. 'Are you never happy?'

'No, sir, I'm not,' Jaeger replied solemnly, looking back up at Kaurl, his face impassive.

That was slightly untrue, he thought; I'm happy when I'm flying. That's the only time. A thought occurred to him then. There was someone he hadn't seen over the past twelve hours since the attack had begun. 'Where is Admiral Veniston, sir?'

'Admiral Kright has been recalled to sector command. Veniston has taken command of the fleet and transferred his flag to the battleship *Holy Dignity*,' Kaurl answered. 'I've got my own ship back, thank the Emperor,' he added with a conspiratorial grin.

'Not meaning to be rude, sir, but the Raptors will be ready to launch any minute,' Jaeger fidgeted with the collar of his flight suit and glanced at the chronometer sat on the desk behind Kaurl.

'Of course, Jacques, you get out there and bomb them to hell and back,' Kaurl nodded towards the door. Jaeger nodded thankfully and hurried out on long strides.

'I almost feel sorry for the noctal,' Kaurl muttered to himself as the door closed behind the eager flight commander. 'Almost.'

'TARGETS ALL STORED, weapons ready to go,' Berhandt announced gruffly. Jaeger glanced to his right across the cockpit towards his bombardier. He opened the comm channel to the rest of the Marauders. Both the Raptors and the Devils were in on this one, escorted by the interceptors of Arrow and Storm Squadrons.

'Everyone has their orders, let's make sure this one goes smoothly,' he told them.

++They won't know what's hit them!++ crowed Phrao's tinny voice in Jaeger's ear.

++We gonna make a fireball so big they'll see it back on board!++ chipped in Logan, squadron leader of the Devils.

'Let's cut the gossiping. Prepare for atmospheric entry. Let's not lose our heads,' Jaeger chided them. In the last twelve hours they had flown five missions with nine-tenths of their targets utterly destroyed. He wasn't about to lose a craft because some hothead forgot their procedures.

++Raptor Leader, this is Arrow Leader, moving ahead to intercept positions++ Squadron Leader Dextra's voice was quiet and distant over the comm-link.

++Raptor Leader, this is Storm Leader, taking position on your rear quarter++ Losark added as Jaeger watched the bright spark of the Arrow's engines forging ahead towards the world below.

It nearly filled the cockpit; a yellowish globe swirled with orange and red dust clouds. Down there, three quarters of a million Imperial Guardsmen were forging their way across the plains, in a massive strike determined to seize the noctal's capital within a day. The Imperial strategy relied upon a single swift hammerblow that destroyed the noctal's command before their reserves could react and bring superior numbers to bear on the Emperor's soldiers. And so far it seemed to be working – resistance was scattered, the noctal seemed to have had no warning that the Imperium had arrived. The first the aliens had known of the attack, Imperial dropships had already touched down.

The Marauder began to shudder as it entered the upper atmosphere of Mearopyis. The control stick in Jaeger's hand started to judder as the air resistance strengthened. Thermals and turbulence began to make the massive aircraft dip and weave as it streaked down towards the clouds. Ahead Jaeger watched the shapes of the Thunderbolts commanded by

Dextra disappear into the cloud cover, slipping silently from view. As air pressure built, Jaeger disengaged the attitude jets along the Marauder's wings; it would fly like a conventional aircraft now. As the first few wisps of cloud began to coalesce across the cockpit windows, Jaeger turned the comm-link dial to talk to the *Divine Justice*.

'This is Raptor Leader. Entering cloud cover now. What's the latest on enemy craft?' he reported.

There was a pause, and Jaeger could imagine the bustle on the bridge as a lieutenant sought out the information and relayed it to the comms officer.

++Raptor Leader, this is *Divine Justice*. Small enemy interceptor patrol last reported one hundred and fifty kilometres to local west. Larger concentration, approximately fifteen craft seen over target area at 0844 ship chronology.++

Jaeger absorbed this news without comment. As the air campaign had continued, the enemy had responded and now there were fewer targets left, it was inevitable that they would receive better air cover. Jaeger had argued hotly that the noctal airbases were the target of the first strikes, but Kaurl had informed him that priority had been given to targets that stood in the path of the advancing Imperial army.

'Time to target?' he asked Berhandt. The bombardier glanced at a screen to his right.

'About twenty minutes, depending on headwind,' Berhandt replied with a shrug.

Jaeger thought this over in silence. The last report had been thirty minutes old, plus another twenty minutes until they arrived. Would the enemy aircraft still be there? Would there be more of them or less?

'*Divine Justice*, this is Raptor Leader. Please inform me as soon as new data available on target's air cover.'

As he made the request, Jaeger forced himself to relax. Adaptability was one of his greatest strengths, and he felt confident he could react to whatever situation developed.

But can the others, he asked himself sourly? This invasion was the first time many of them had been under fire. So far their orders had been simple to execute and had gone by the book. How well would they react under real stress, with

Jaeger barking orders out over the comm-net; orders that might save them from being shot down if followed quickly and accurately? He had drilled them long and hard in the simulators and on training flights, mercilessly pushing them each time, berating them loudly for the smallest errors. They thought he probably didn't know, but he'd heard they called him the Iron Tyrant for his strict, disciplined approach. He didn't care; they could call him all the names in the Imperium if it meant they listened to him and learnt from his experience.

He had served under three flight commanders over nearly ten years as an Imperial Navy pilot. All three had impressed upon him the importance of duty and discipline, and it was a message he was determined to impart to his own men. He felt a responsibility to each of them, to give them the training and leadership they needed to excel, to become what the Emperor expected of them. It was why he was so hard on them, why he was the Iron Tyrant, because each small failure reflected on him in his own conscience.

'Arrow leader, move ahead and see what's waiting for us at the target,' Jaeger ordered into the comm. 'Storm Leader, remain in position ready to engage enemy from the west.'

He hated fighting blind; the memory of the attack on the space hulk was still burnt into his mind. Twenty-one men had died that day because no one had told them what they were up against.

Veniston had called it 'acceptable losses', but there was no such phrase in Jaeger's head. No loss could be tolerated and already he felt guilty for the crew of Devil Five who had been shot down by groundfire on the first mission over Mearopyis.

This time is different, he told himself, trying to build up some conviction. This time our orders are simple. We have rules of engagement written specifically to protect my men. In, attack and then out again. They were the rules and he was bound by his duty to the Navy and his men to follow them.

++Raptor Leader, this is Storm Leader. We have enemy incoming from the west. Permission to engage?++

'Go ahead, Losark,' Jaeger replied, staring out of the cockpit window towards the west for some hint of the enemy aircraft, but nothing was to be seen yet.

++Okay Storm squadron, let's chalk up some more kills++ confirmed Losark, making Jaeger smile inside his facemask. The Storm squadron leader was the best dogfighter on the *Divine Justice*, but Dextra was his senior by two years and was always just a few kills ahead in his tally. Jaeger had wagered extra drink rations to the whole of Raptor squadron that Losark would surpass his rival's total by the end of the campaign.

He watched as the Thunderbolts, eight of them, screamed overhead and banked to starboard. The squadron split into two wings of four craft each, one accelerating up towards the cloudbase, the other dipping towards the ground. Jaeger saw a sparkle in the distance – the Mearopyis star glinting off metal as the enemy fighters closed in.

'Maintain course to target,' the flight commander ordered the Marauders. 'Gunners prepare for interlocking fire, pattern omega.'

As he finished, he heard the whine of electric motors as Marte swung the fuselage gun cradle into position. Through the reinforced screen, Jaeger watched as missile trails ghosted away from Storm squadron arrowing their way across the skies towards the Noctal plains. A moment later and a bright explosion lit up the sky, an expanding star of blue created by a missile's impact. As the blast dissipated, a haze of white smoke was left drifting on the gentle wind.

'One less alien,' Berhandt muttered contentedly to himself from beside Jaeger.

The dogfight approached closer as the speedier noctal fighters burst between the two Thunderbolt formations, intent on the bombers. Jaeger saw vapour trails arcing across the sky as the Imperial interceptors banked round to follow the alien craft, but he knew they were too slow to catch them and the Marauders would have to look to their own guns for protection.

'Power up the lascannon,' Jaeger ordered Berhandt, who gave a satisfied grunt and swivelled his seat to grip hold of the nose-gun's controls. Jaeger switched the comm-link to address all of the Marauders.

'Hold your fire, wait for my order,' he steadied them, knowing that if one trigger-happy soul started firing, the rest would join in and probably waste their limited ammunition.

He could make out the noctal planes more clearly as they streaked towards him at the front of the double arrowhead of Marauders. They were racing in fast, keeping a tight formation. That was good; the closer the aliens stayed together, the more chance the firing from the turrets would hit something. Another ten seconds trickled past as Jaeger watched the bright specks turn into distinct shapes.

A bolt of green energy erupted towards the bombers as the lead craft fired its laser, the flash passing comfortably overhead.

'All crews, open fire!' Jaeger bellowed into the comm-mike. An instant later Raptor One shook with the thunder of autocannons and heavy bolters firing and a stream of tracer rounds soared across the shrinking gap between the two squadrons. More las-bolts blasted past, one so close it left a streak of after-image seared across Jaeger's eyes for a few seconds.

'Come on, up a bit… up a bit, you alien scum!' muttered Berhandt, his face pressed down into the targeting visor of the lascannon. The noctal had dipped, trying to take the Marauders from below. But there was to be no refuge there either, as the guns of the lower squadron, the Devils, opened fire and the three sleek aircraft were surrounded by a storm of tracers.

'Got yer!' cackled Berhandt, pressing the firing stud. The lascannon burst into life, a beam of white energy lancing out to pass straight through the nearest foe. The enemy craft disintegrated, its triangular wings spiralling groundward until they were out of sight, the main fuselage utterly vaporised. As the noctal planes screamed past, Jaeger got a good look at their shape. They were like blunt darts, their stubby delta wings stretching from in front of the cockpit to the rear of the plane. Four tail fins surrounded bright blue jets as

Jaeger tracked its course through the side screen, looking over his shoulder as it zoomed away.

Fire from Raptor Four, Phrao's Marauder, caught one wing of the noctal fighter, shredding it into hundreds of shrapnel fragments that scattered in its wake. Control lost, the plane went into a wild rolling spin, tumbling headlong through the rest of squadron, whose gunners easily tracked it and sent a fusillade of fire into it until finally it broke in half before exploding.

++I'll get the last one++ Losark assured him over the comm.

'How many kills behind now?' asked Jaeger, laughing softly.

++Three to go, Raptor Leader++ came the squadron leader's reply, his eagerness conveyed even across the crackling comm-net.

The Thunderbolts soared past just metres away, afterburners on full, the wash of their passing juddering the control column in Jaeger's right hand.

'Continue course to target, estimated time to attack is...' Jaeger glanced up at the chrono-display in the top left corner of the cockpit window. 'Thirteen minutes.'

'FIVE MINUTES UNTIL target in sight,' Berhandt's rough voice reported. Jaeger glanced over towards the muscled bombardier who was intent on his bomb targeter. The glowing green display underlit his face as he stared into the aiming reticule, making final adjustments to the optics with a series of switches and dials on his control panel. He never took his eyes from the reticule. Instead his fingers danced over the controls as if powered by a will of their own – in fact they were driven by a familiarity only years of experience could develop.

If they survive, all of the crews will be as good as him, thought Jaeger as he watched the bombardier at work. It's up to me to ensure that they do.

Jaeger knew that at times he was guilty of pride, but he had a dream that one day Raptor squadron and the *Divine Justice* would be recognised as the best across the whole segmentum. He wanted the admirals at Bakka to know he was there, to hear of his great work. It was a good ambition, he told himself.

The flight commander turned his attention back outside the canopy as the Marauders' altitude dropped. They were to make a low-level attack first, dropping their massive payload of incendiary explosives on an enemy bunker complex. After circling around they would make a second attack run with missiles and lascannons, picking off anything smoked out by the firebombs. It was straight out of the tactics manuals, performed in drills and simulated battles a dozen times by the pilots and bombardiers.

A subtle movement to Jaeger's right caught his attention. Something was stirring in the yellow haze to the south-west. It looked to Jaeger like a dust cloud, quite a large one, several dozen kilometres away. Checking the gauges above his head, Jaeger noted a strong headwind, which would probably blow the dust storm in their direction. Concerned, he opened up the long-range comm channel.

'*Divine Justice*, this is Raptor Leader. Any reports of storm activity on our approach?' he asked, still looking intently at the swirling cloud of ochre sand and dust.

++That is negative, Raptor Leader. Strong winds, low cloud, no storm activity++ came the reply after several seconds.

'Okay, *Divine Justice*. Please monitor this channel, I may have found something,' Jaeger told the officer in orbit, an uneasy feeling growing in the pit of his stomach.

Turning in his seat, Jaeger punched a few runes on the screen display and, after a swirl of static, a chart of the local geography was superimposed over the front canopy window. He focused the map onto his current recorded location and, glancing up again to check the direction towards the storm, placed its position. It seemed to be issuing from a long canyon complex that ran for hundreds of kilometres perpendicular to the axis of the Imperial attack, some twelve kilometres behind the forward Guard positions.

'They would have checked it out,' he muttered to himself. Berhandt looked up at him quizzically.

'Somethin' wrong?' the bombardier asked, looking out of the cockpit to follow Jaeger's gaze.

'Ferix!' Jaeger snapped, glancing over his shoulder down the length of the Marauder. The tech-adept emerged from his maintenance alcove, trailing a twist of cabling. 'Talk to one of the missile auspexes, find out if it can see anything in that dust cloud.'

Ferix nodded, and ducked through a low hatchway into the maintenance crawl space that led to the starboard wing. His voice arrived in Jaeger's ear direct through the Marauder's internal comm system.

'Initiating activation sequence, aktiva cons sequentia,' the tech-adept intoned, reciting the rites out loud. His voice took on a different timbre as his brain merged with the mechanical workings of the missile, feeling its spirit moving inside him, divorcing him from the world of the flesh. 'Librius machina auroris dei. Contact established with machine spirit of "Flail" missile, designate 14-56. Praise the Machine God. Ignis optika carta mond. Invoking surveyor sweep over target area. Calculating... Calculating... Calculating... Targets present, multiple, unknown designation.'

'Emperor's claws,' cursed Jaeger hotly. Something was inside that canyon, hiding from orbital surveillance. 'Can you be more specific, how many is "multiple"?'

'Unknown, target acquisition beyond recall capacity,' Ferix replied. His voice lost its distant edge. 'Flight commander, this missile type has a half-kilobrain of memory, capable of storing information on seventy-five separate targets.'

'So there's more than seventy-five possible targets down there?' Jaeger demanded, the clenching sensation in his stomach moving up to his throat. 'More than seventy-five armoured vehicles?'

'That is correct,' came Ferix's dispassionate reply. 'Smaller objects are disregarded.'

'In all that's holy–' came Berhandt's response, who had been listening in, eyes locked to Jaeger's.

'That's enough to cut their supplies... We have to warn the Guard!'

* * *

'YOU HAVE VERY specific orders, flight commander,' Kaurl's stern voice told Jaeger over the comms network. ++Proceed with the attack as planned.++

Jaeger glanced at the small display screen just to the left of the control stick. Ferix had re-mapped the wiring of Raptor One so that the artificial eyes of its missiles were directed towards that display. There were one hundred and twenty-three separate signals there now and still rising as they approached the canyon. Jaeger eyed the small blobs of green light with hatred. His two squadrons were enough to seriously dent the enemy force, but it would be risky. Added to that, the captain had specifically ordered him to ignore them.

If the counter-attack was allowed to continue, though, who could tell what damage it would do to the whole war effort? Speed was the basis of the assault, and if it was slowed down by an incursion into its supply lines, the whole invasion might falter. If it faltered, all would be lost as the noctal used to the time to gather their armies from across the planet. Who could tell if they had more ships in the vicinity, each now warned and powering their way to raise the orbital siege of the alien-held world? And what of the humans below?

The noctal had been so shocked there had been no time for them to bargain or use them as hostages, but millions of lives could end in torment and death if the noctal regained the upper hand.

Jaeger felt torn in several directions at once. He had his orders, they were very specific and Captain Kaurl had said as much. If he attacked the enemy column – whatever else happened – he would have to face a court of inquiry for disobeying those orders. Also, this noctal army was bound to have defences against air attack; after all they had been suffering badly from airstrikes for the last twelve hours. If this counter-attack was as important as Jaeger thought it was, it would have every available protection. And that meant a lot of added risk. Risk to himself, his planes and their crews. Risks Jaeger was loath to take. Had he not, minutes before, been ruing the day he led Raptor squadron on that deadly attack against the ork hulk? And now here he was, contemplating disobeying a direct order to lead his men down a canyon full of the enemy, into Emperor-knew-what kind of trouble and bloodshed. Jaeger swallowed hard and made his decision.

'Raptors, Devils, change of plan,' he announced to his command through gritted teeth. His duty was ultimately to the campaign as a whole, and through that to the Emperor. He had no other course of action open to him. 'Follow me to the enemy, free attack once you are in range.'

++Let's do some huntin'!++ came Gesper's reply from Devil Two.

++Behind you all the way, sir++ agreed Phrao.

'Come in low and fast, hit them with everything you've got, then make for the *Divine Justice*,' Jaeger was talking quickly now, feeling adrenaline surge through him as he banked the squadrons towards the canyon and nosed Raptor One towards the ground. 'No waiting around!'

++Raptor One, this is Storm. We are on intercept course to enemy fighters over new target.++

++Storm One, this is Arrow One, you'll have to get there before me!++

Even as the message ended, Dextra's Thunderbolt screamed across Jaeger's field of vision, its jets at full burn leaving a brief after-image in the flight commander's eyes. It was swiftly followed by the shapes of the other four Thunderbolts, spreading out in readiness for the coming dogfight. As Jaeger continued to bank, Storm squadron roared overhead, just seconds behind the Arrows.

'We'll be at the canyon in twenty-five seconds,' Berhandt reported.

Jaeger nodded and levelled the Marauder, pushing up the engines to maximum as Raptor One powered towards the enemy a mere two hundred metres above the softly undulating dunes of Mearopyis.

'Fifteen seconds to canyon,' Berhandt informed him, bent once more over the aiming reticule.

Above him, Jaeger could see the fighters duelling in and out of the rising dust cloud. A moment later and the sand

and grit was swirling around the Marauder, skittering off the windshield and obscuring everything past a couple of metres.

'I hope those engine filters hold, Ferix,' Jaeger glanced over his shoulder to the tech-adept in the maintenance bay.

'I fitted them myself, flight commander,' Ferix assured him coldly, bringing a smile to Jaeger's lips beneath his air mask.

'Ten seconds to target,' came Berhandt's countdown. 'Nine... Eight... Seven... Six... Five... Four... Three... Two... One... Target acquired!'

Jaeger felt rather than saw the ground drop away beneath him and banked the Marauder to port, heading north, and down into the canyon. Flickers of green las-fire illuminated the dust cloud ahead and to either side, but none was close yet. A hum started in Jaeger's ear as Berhandt locked-on one of the flail missiles, its warning tone rising to a screech as it became aware of its target's location.

'Fly sweet vengeance!' Berhandt spat, pressing down on the firing stud. A half-second later the missile streaked downwards and then levelled, disappearing into the dust on a trail of white fire. Jaeger felt his heart beat once, then again, then there was a bright patch in the storm and a moment later a muffled boom shook the canopy.

'Fuel carrier, I think,' Berhandt commented, not looking up from the sighting array.

The dust began to thin rapidly and soon Jaeger could see the bottom of the canyon, still half a kilometre below. *No wonder the orbital augurs didn't notice this, it's as deep as the pits of hell,* he thought. Another missile flared off towards the enemy, its vapour trail joined by eight more as the other Marauders opened fire. They jinked and wove as strong eddies in the wind, caused by the funnelling effect of the deep canyon, forced them to adjust their flight path towards their prey.

A couple of seconds later nine explosions blossomed in rapid succession in a cluster across the canyon floor, but Jaeger still couldn't make out what they were firing at. Now more ground-fire was lancing its way along the natural trench towards them. Pulses of tracer fire combined with the green las-blasts he'd seen earlier, but the enemy were aiming too high.

Looking away at the target-screen for a moment, he saw a grouping of several dozen stationary vehicles ahead.

'See that cluster?' he asked Berhandt as a shell whistled past a few metres to his left. The bombardier nodded and adjusted a couple of dials on his visor.

'Squadrons, assume formation Bravus for main payload drop,' Jaeger ordered the two squadrons into position to maximise damage from the bombing run. Without warning, he heard a detonation close from behind, and twisting in his pilot's seat he looked out the side window. A Marauder was banking off, flames engulfing its tail and rear fuselage. Its uncontrolled descent took it into the canyon wall a second later, its fuel tanks and plasma chamber exploding in a shower of flames and debris.

'Who was that? Who did we lose?' Jaeger demanded over the comm.

++Devil Three, Scairn's plane++ came the reply from Cal Logan, the Devil squadron leader.

++Dammit! We've lost two engines!++ L'stin cursed, before Jaeger could answer.

'Raptor Three, get back to orbit!' snapped Jaeger, noticing that las-bolts were streaking down towards them as well as from the ground.

'Arrow, Storm! Strafe enemy positions on the canyon walls!' Jaeger's voice was clipped, harsh, as he focussed his mind on what to do next. 'Raptor squadron continue with bombing runs. Devil Squadron use missiles and lascannons to provide covering fire.'

A series of affirmatives sounded in the flight commander's ear. Jaeger levelled out the Marauder's course to prepare for the bombing run. He couldn't afford to evade the incoming fire, it would make aiming almost impossible for Berhandt. A splintering crack appeared in the canopy between him and the bombardier as a las-bolt ricocheted off. Jaeger heard other impacts rattling along the length of the fuselage as green flashes of laser energy and yellow tracers converged on him, the lead plane.

He knew Ferix was now working at full stretch, monitoring any malfunctions, coaxing Raptor One's own systems into repairing themselves, welding, cutting and binding where that wasn't possible. He could hear the tech-adept chanting liturgies of maintenance and repair behind him. A red warning light flashed on the panel to Jaeger's right – one of the engines was leaking plasma. Without thought, the flight commander shut down power to the damaged jet and boosted up the others, stabilising the Marauder's flight path with small movements on the control stick.

++Raptor Four is down, Raptor Three is down++ reported Phrao heavily. ++Storm and Arrow have broken off, they're out of fuel.++

'Emperor damn it all to hell!' snarled Jaeger, looking back and up over his shoulder for a sign that any enemy fighters had survived the air duel. A sudden blood-curdling shriek over the inter-squadron frequency deafened him, forcing Jaeger to shut down the comm and switch off the pitiful cry. He adjusted one of the secondary view screens on his panel to display the rear camera shot. Another Marauder was tumbling groundwards, wreathed in smoke and flames, its wings spinning away on separate trajectories, trailing burning fuel. His chest tight with apprehension, he opened up the comm-link again.

'Who was that?' he demanded.

'Bombs away!' Berhandt called out, sitting up from where he'd been crouched over the bombsight. Jaeger's head whirled as so many things clamoured for his attention.

++It was Devil One, sir++ came Phrao's delayed reply.

Jaeger closed his eyes for a moment and took a deep breath, steadying himself. Opening them again, he looked at the rear view to see massive red flames bursting over the dark shapes of the enemy attack column. The fireballs continued to expand, the special incendiaries igniting the air itself with their heat, filling the canyon from wall to wall with crackling, hungry flame.

Another massive detonation followed, and then another as the other Marauders dropped their devastating payloads. Jaeger saw secondary explosions along the ground as fuel tanks expanded and burst and ammunition was set on fire. Another blossom of brighter fire, in the air this time, showed where a tailing noctal fighter had flown straight into the inferno as it had attempted to close from below.

Berhandt was firing off the remaining missiles, as were the other Marauders. In front and behind, the canyon was a blaze of destruction. Burning wrecks littered the valley floor, while the firebomb damage continued to creep along the walls and into the air, slowing now, billowing black smoke now rising thousands of metres into the clouds.

'That should give the ships in orbit something to aim at, if nothing else,' Berhandt commented gruffly, switching his attention to the lascannon controls.

Jaeger spied a group of vehicles along the east wall and banked the Marauder smoothly towards them. More ground fire sprung up to meet them, sporadic at first but building in intensity until once more Raptor One was banging and clattering with impacts, and the air became iridescent with multiple las-blasts impacting into her thick armour.

'Just another couple of seconds,' Berhandt told him, and Jaeger could hear the grind and whirr of motors as the multi-barrelled anti-tank gun swivelled in its nose mount. A movement to Jaeger's right attracted the flight commander's attention and he look across, flicking his gaze between this distraction and the approaching canyon wall. It was a bright spark of blue, growing bigger very quickly. With a start, Jaeger realised it was an incoming missile.

'Oh s–' Jaeger's curse was cut off by an explosion just to his right and behind him. He heard Marte bellow in pain and Raptor One dipped suddenly to starboard, smashing Berhandt's head against his sighting array.

'We've lost the whole wing!' screamed one of his crew, the panicked wail making their voice unrecognisable.

'Into the saviour pod!' shouted Jaeger, punching free of his harness, and releasing the dazed Berhandt as the Marauder's erratic lurch tumbled him across the bombardier's chair. He could feel Raptor One plummeting down nose first and had to almost crawl his way up the fuselage. Ferix was there, ushering the others into the armoured compartment, and he saw

Marte being bundled in by Arick, the old veteran's flight suit ripped to shreds, blood pumping from half a dozen shrapnel wounds in his chest.

Pushing Ferix and Berhandt in first, Jaeger grabbed the door. As he swung it shut he saw the ground screaming up towards him through the canopy. A las-bolt shattered the front screen and the wind howled in, almost wrenching the door from his grasp.

With a wordless, bestial snarl he grasped the handle with both hands and slammed it shut.

'Strap in, sir!' Arick pointed towards the empty seat.

'No time,' Jaeger replied, punching his fist into the release button. Explosive bolts ignited around the base of the pod, hurling it outwards from the doomed wreck of Raptor One. As it tumbled in flight, Jaeger was thrown onto the wall then the ceiling, before the pod steadied on its retro jets and he fell to the floor, dazed, his leg twisted, sending flares of pain up his spine.

'Are you—' Arick began to ask, but red filled Jaeger's vision and he heard rather than felt his head thump against the floor. The sound of his blood rushing through his ears filled his mind before unconsciousness swept through him.

JAEGER OPENED HIS eyes and winced as sunlight blinded him. He was sitting with his back to the saviour pod, out in the Mearopyis desert somewhere. Ferix was changing the bandages wrappred around Marte's chest, while Jaeger's own numb right leg was splinted, so he guessed it was broken. Arick noticed he was awake, and the young man crouched down in front of him, face solemn.

'Raptor One, there's nothing left of her.' The youthful gunner was almost in tears.

Jaeger gulped and gathered his thoughts. He pushed himself to his feet, wincing at the pain in his leg, and looked around. Just on the horizon was a massive plume of dust.

'Don't worry, it's the Guard advancing on the capital,' Arick reassured him.

'Other... other losses?' Jaeger asked quietly, keeping his eyes on Arick's.

'Two thirds of the Marauders are destroyed,' Arick's reply was hoarse, and this time there really was a glint of moisture in his eyes. 'Half the Thunderbolts. Seven pilots dead. Losark won't be getting any more kills, I'm afraid. Thirty-three other crew members dead. Fourteen wounded, including Marte who has shrapnel lodged in his spine, and you.'

'So, almost the entirety of the *Divine Justice*'s flight complement destroyed,' sighed Jaeger bitterly. 'Was it worth it, Arick?'

'I think so, sir. You saved thousands of lives, by my reckoning,' Arick replied with a fleeting grin.

'I doubt the Imperial Navy will see it that way,' Jaeger answered with a heavy heart, already picturing his court martial. He sat down again and rested his chin against his chest for a moment, eyes closed against the harsh light. With another sigh he looked up at Arick, into his fresh, grey eyes. 'They'll hang me for this disaster.'

He gazed out at the distant army, rumbling towards the enemy capital, intent on recapturing this world. Was it worth it, Jaeger asked himself? He honestly didn't know.

CHAINS OF COMMAND
An Ultramarines story
Graham McNeill

CONCEALED AT THE edge of the jungle, Veteran Sergeant Uriel Ventris stared through the pouring rain at the grey, rockcrete bunker at the end of the bridge and tallied off the number of sentries he could see. There were four rebel troopers in the open, but they were sloppy, unconcerned, and that was going to kill them. They sheltered in the lee of the bunker's armoured door, smoking and talking. It was unforgivable stupidity, but Uriel always gave thanks whenever his enemies displayed such foolishness. The hissing of the warm rain falling through the canopy of thick, drooping fronds and bouncing from the rocks muffled all sounds. The roaring of the mighty river in the gorge below only added to the noise.

Moisture glistened on his blue shoulder guards, dripping from the inlaid Chapter insignia of the Ultramarines. He slipped from his hidden position and ghosted through the drizzle, the actuators in his powered armour hissing as the fibre-bundle muscles enhanced his every movement. Uriel slid clear his combat knife and tested its edge, even though he knew it was unnecessary. The gesture was force of habit,

55

learned at the earliest age by the people of Calth. The long blade was triangular in section, its edges lethally sharp and designed to slip easily between a victim's ribs, breaking them as it penetrated.

It was a tool for killing, nothing more.

Thanks to the heavy rain, the visibility of the guards was cut to less than thirty metres. Uriel's eyesight was far superior to a normal human's; he could clearly see the outline of the men he was about to kill.

He felt no remorse at the thought. The enemies of the Emperor deserved no mercy. These men had made their choice and would now pay the price for making the wrong one. Uriel slipped behind one of the bridge's adamantium stanchions, moving incredibly quietly for such a bulky figure. He was close enough to his victims for his enhanced hearing to pick out the individual sounds of their voices.

As was typical with soldiers, they were bemoaning their current assignment and superior officers. Uriel knew they would not complain for much longer. He was close enough for his superior senses to pick out the smell of their unwashed bodies and the foetid dampness of stale sweat ingrained into their flesh after weeks of fighting. His muscles tensed and relaxed, preparing for action. The rune on his visor display that represented Captain Idaeus flashed twice and with a whispered acknowledgement Uriel confirmed his readiness to strike. He waited until he heard the scraping footfall of his first target turning away and twisted around the stanchion, sprinting for the bunker.

The first guard died without a sound, Uriel's knife hammering through the base of his skull. He dropped and Uriel wrenched the blade clear, spinning low and driving it into the second guard's groin. Blood sprayed and the man shrieked in horrified agony. A lasgun was raised and Uriel lunged forwards, smashing his fist into his foe's face, the augmented muscles of his power armour smashing the man's head to shards. Uriel spun on his heel, dodging a thrusting bayonet, and thundered his elbow into the last guard's chin, taking the base of his skull off. Teeth and blood splattered the bunker door.

He dropped into a defensive crouch, dragging his knife clear of the corpse beside him and cleaning the blade on the dead man's overalls. The killing of the guards had taken less than three seconds. He glanced quickly around the corner of the bunker to the sandbagged gun positions further down the bridge. There were two, set in a staggered pattern to provide overlapping fields of fire. The dull glint of metal protruded from the glistening, tarpaulin covered positions and Uriel counted three heavy bolters in each emplacement. The rain and thundering river noise had covered his stealthy approach to the bunker, but there was nothing but open ground before the gun nests.

'Position secure,' he whispered into the vox-com, removing shaped, breaching charges from his grenade dispenser. He worked quickly and purposefully, fastening the explosive around the locking mechanism of the bunker's armoured door.

'Confirmed,' acknowledged Captain Idaeus. 'Good work, Uriel. Squads Lucius and Daedalus are in position. We go on your signal.'

Uriel grinned and crawled around to the front of the bunker, making sure to keep out of sight below the firing slit. He drew his bolt pistol and spun his knife, holding it in a reverse grip. He took a deep breath, readying himself for action, and detonated the charges on the door.

The bunker's door blasted inwards, ripped from the frame by the powerful explosion. Choking smoke billowed outwards and Uriel was in motion even before the concussion of the detonation had faded. He heard the crack of bolter fire from the jungle and knew that the remainder of the Ultramarines detachment was attacking. By now the enemies of the Emperor would be dying.

Uriel dived through the blackened doorway, rolling to a firing crouch, his pistol sweeping left and right. He saw two heads silhouetted by the light at the firing slit and squeezed the trigger twice. Both men jerked backwards, their heads exploding. Another soldier was screaming on his knees, blood flooding from his ruined body. His torso was almost severed at the waist, razor-edged metal from the door's explosion protruding from his body. A las-blast impacted on Uriel's armour, and he twisted, kicking backwards in the direction the shot had come from. His booted foot hammered into a rebel guardsman's knee, the joint shattering. The man shrieked and fell, losing his grip on his weapon and clutching his ruined knee. The remainder of the bunker's complement crowded around Uriel, screaming and stabbing with bayonets.

Uriel spun and twisted, punching and kicking with lethal ferocity. Wherever he struck, bones crunched and men died. The stink of blood and voided bowels filled his senses as the last soldier fell. Blood streaked his shoulders and breastplate. His eyes scanned the dimness of the bunker, but all was silent. Everyone was dead.

He heard sounds of fighting and gunfire from outside and moved to the door, ducking back as heavy bolter shells raked the inside face of the doorway. He glanced round the edge of the bullet-pocked wall, watching with pride as the Ultramarines assault squad now joined the fray, their jump packs carrying them high over the bunker.

They dropped from above, like flaming angels of death, their chainswords chopping heads and limbs from bodies with shimmering, steel slashes. The first gun emplacement was in tatters, sandbags ripped apart by bolter fire and tossed aside by the attacking Space Marines. The poorly trained defence troopers broke in the face of such savagery, but the Ultramarines were in amongst them and there was no escape.

The assault troopers hacked them down with giant, disembowelling strokes of their swords. The battle became a slaughter.

The staccato chatter of massed bolter fire echoed from the sides of the gorge, explosions of dirt rippling from the bullet-ridden sandbags of the second gun emplacement. But even under the constant volley, Uriel could see the gunners within were realigning their heavy bolters. Hurriedly, he voxed a warning.

'Ventris to Idaeus. The second gun position has re-sited its weapons. You will be under fire in a matter of moments!'

Idaeus's rune on Uriel's visor blinked twice as the captain acknowledged the warning.

Uriel watched as the captain of Fourth Company barked a command and began sprinting towards the second gun position. Idaeus charged at the head of five blue-armoured warriors, and Uriel swore, leaping forwards himself. Without support, the assault troops would be prime targets! Tongues of fire blasted from the heavy bolters, reaching out towards the charging Ultramarines. Uriel saw the shells impact, bursting amongst the charging Space Marines, but not a single man fell, the blessed suits of powered armour withstanding the traitors' fire. Idaeus triggered his jump pack and the rest of his squad followed suit, streaking forward with giant powered leaps.

Las-blasts filled the air, but the Ultramarines were too quick. Idaeus smashed down through the timber roof of the gun nest, a fearsome war cry bursting from his lips. He swung his power sword, decapitating a rebel trooper, and backhanded his pistol into another's chest, smashing his ribcage to splinters.

Uriel's long strides had carried him to the edge of the gun nest and he leapt, feet first, into the sandbagged position. He felt bone shatter under the impact and rolled to his feet, lashing out with his armoured gauntlet. Another rebel died screaming. The sound of gunshots was deafening. Uriel felt a shot impact on his shoulder, the bullet ricocheting skywards. He turned and fired a bolt into his attacker's face, destroying the man's head. He sensed movement and spun, pistol raised.

Captain Idaeus stood before him, hands in the air and a broad grin on his face. Uriel exhaled slowly and lowered his weapon. Idaeus slapped his hands on Uriel's shoulder plates.

'Battle's over, sergeant,' he laughed.

Idaeus's grizzled face was lined with experience and his shaven skull ran with moisture and blood. Four gold studs glittered on his forehead, each one representing a half century of service, but his piercing grey eyes had lost none of the sparkle of youth. Uriel nodded, scowling.

'It is, yes, but the Codex Astartes tells us you should have waited for support before charging that gun nest, captain,' he said.

'Perhaps,' agreed Idaeus, 'but I wanted this done quickly, before any of them could vox a warning.'

'We have heavy weapons with us, captain. We could have jammed their vox units and blasted them apart from the cover of the bunker. They sited these gun positions poorly and would not have been able to target us. The Codex Astartes says–'

'Uriel,' interrupted Idaeus, leading him from the charnel house of the gun nest. 'You know I respect you, and, despite what others say, I believe you will soon command your own company. But you must accept that sometimes it is necessary for us to do things a little differently. Yes, the Codex Astartes teaches us the way of war, but it does not teach the hearts of men. Look around you. See the faces of our warriors. Their blood sings with righteousness and their faith is strong because they have seen me walk through the fire with them, leading them in glorious battle. Is not a little risk to me worth such reward?'

'I think I would call charging through the fire of three heavy bolters more than a "little risk",' pointed out Uriel.

'Had you been where I was, would you have done it differently?' asked Idaeus.

'No,' admitted Uriel with a smile, 'but then I am a sergeant, it's my lot in life to get all the dirty jobs.'

Idaeus laughed. 'I'll make a captain out of you yet, Uriel. Come, we have work to do. This bridge is not going to blow up on its own.'

As the assault troopers secured the bridge, the remainder of Captain Idaeus's detachment advanced from the jungle to reinforce them. Two tactical squads occupied the bunkers at either end of the bridge while Uriel organised the third repairing the sandbagged gun nests. In accordance with the Codex Astartes, he ordered them re-sited in order to cover every approach to the crossing, rebuilding and strengthening their defences.

Uriel watched as Idaeus deployed their scouts into the hills on the far side of the ridge above the gorge. They wouldn't make the same mistake the rebels had made. If the traitors launched a counter-attack, the Ultramarines would know of it. He stepped over a dead guardsman, noting with professional pride the bullet hole in the centre of his forehead. Such was the price of defeat. The Ultramarines' victory here had been absurdly easy, barely even qualifying as a battle, and Uriel felt curiously little pleasure at their success.

Since the age of six, he had been trained to bring death to the Emperor's enemies and normally felt a surge of justifiable pride in his lethal skills. But against such poorly trained opposition, there was no satisfaction to be gained. These soldiers were not worthy of the name and would not have survived a single month in the Agiselus Barracks on Macragge where Uriel had trained so many years ago. He pushed aside such gloomy thoughts and reached up to remove his helmet, setting it on the wide parapet of the bridge. Thousands of metres below, a wide river thundered through the gorge, the dark water foaming white over the rocks. Uriel ran a hand over his skull, the hair close cropped and jet black. His eyes were the colour of storm clouds, dark and threatening, his face serious. Two gold studs were set into his brow above his left eye.

The bridges were the key to the whole campaign. The Emperor's warriors had driven the poorly armed and trained planetary defence troopers of Thracia back at every turn and now the rebel-held capital, Mercia, was within their grasp. Despite horrendous losses, they still had the advantage of numbers and, given time, they could pose a serious threat to the crusade. The right flank of the Imperial Guard's push towards Mercia was exposed to attack across a series of bridges, one of which Uriel now stood upon. It was imperative the bridges were destroyed, but the Imperial Navy had demanded days of planning for the missions to destroy the bridges, days the crusade could ill afford to waste. Therefore the task of destroying the bridges had fallen to the Ultramarines. Thunderhawk gunships had inserted the assault teams under cover of darkness, half a day's march from the bridges, and now awaited their signal to extract them after the crossings had been destroyed.

The rebellion on Thracia was insignificant but for one thing: reports had filtered back to the crusade's High Command that Traitor Space Marines of the Night Lords legion were present. So far, Uriel had seen nothing of these heretics and, privately, believed that they were phantoms conjured by the over-active imagination of guardsmen. Still, it never paid to be complacent and Uriel fervently hoped the reports would prove to be true. The chance to bring the wrath of the Emperor down on such abominable foes could not be passed up.

He watched a Techmarine wiring the bridge supports for destruction. Melta charges would blast the bridge to pieces, denying the traitors any way of moving their armoured units across the river and flanking the Imperial attack. Uriel knew that the same scene was being repeated up and down the enormous gorge as other Ultramarine detachments prepared to destroy their own targets. He scooped up his helmet and marched towards a mud-stained Techmarine hauling himself over the parapet and unwinding a long length of cable from his equipment pack. The man looked up as he heard Uriel approach and nodded respectfully.

'I suppose you're going to tell me to hurry up,' he grumbled, bending awkwardly to hook the cable into a battery pack.

'Not at all, Sevano. As though I would rush the work of a master craftsman like yourself.'

Sevano Tomasin glowered at Uriel, searching his face for any trace of sarcasm. Finding none, the Techmarine nodded as he continued wiring the explosives, moving with a lopsided, mechanical gait as both his legs and right arm were heavier, bionic replacements.

The apothecaries had grafted these on after recovering his body from the interior of a wrecked Land Raider on Ichar IV after a rampaging carnifex had ripped it apart. The horrifying creature's bio-plasma had flooded the interior of the armoured fighting vehicle, detonating its ammo spectacularly. The carnifex was killed in the blast, but the explosion sheared Tomasin to the bone and, rather than lose his centuries of wisdom, the Chapter's artisans had designed a completely new, artificial body around the bloody rags of his remains.

'How long until you and the servitors are finished?' asked Uriel.

Tomasin wiped the mud from his face and glanced up the length of the bridge. 'Another hour, Ventris. Possibly less if this damned rain would ease up and I didn't have to stop to talk to you.'

Uriel bit back a retort and turned away, leaving the Techmarine to his work and striding to the nearest gun nest. Captain Idaeus was sitting on the sandbags and speaking animatedly into the vox-com.

'Well make sure, damn you!' he snapped. 'I don't want to be left sitting here facing half the rebel army with only thirty men.'

Idaeus listened to the words that only he could hear through the comm-bead in his ear and cursed, snapping the vox unit back to his belt.

'Trouble?' asked Uriel.

'Maybe,' sighed Idaeus. 'Orbital surveyors on the *Vae Victus* say they think they detected something large moving through the jungle in our direction, but this damned weather's interfering with the auguries and they can't bring them on-line again. It's probably nothing.'

'You don't sound too convinced.'

'I'm not,' admitted Idaeus. 'If the Night Lords are on this world, then this is just the kind of thing they would try.'

'I have our scouts watching the approaches to the bridge. Nothing is going to get close without us knowing about it.'

'Good. How is Tomasin getting on?'

'There's a lot of bridge to blow, captain, but Tomasin thinks he'll have it done within the hour. I believe he will have it rigged sooner though.'

Idaeus nodded and rose to his feet, staring into the mist and rain shrouded hills on the enemy side of the bridge. His face creased in a frown and Uriel followed his gaze. Dusk was fast approaching and with luck they would be on

their way to rejoin the main assault on Mercia before night-
fall.

'Something wrong?'

'I'm not sure. Every time I look across the bridge I get a
bad feeling.'

'A bad feeling?'

'Aye, like someone is watching us,' whispered Idaeus.

Uriel checked his vox-com. 'The scouts haven't reported
anything.'

Idaeus shook his head. 'No, this is more like instinct. This
whole place feels wrong somehow. I can't describe it.'

Uriel was puzzled. Idaeus was a man he trusted implicitly,
they had fought and bled together for over fifty years, forming a bond of friendship that Uriel found all too rarely. Yet
he could never claim to truly understand Idaeus. The captain
relied on instinct and feelings more than the holy Codex
Astartes, that great work of military thinking penned ten
thousand years ago by their own Primarch, Roboute Guilliman.

The Codex formed the basis of virtually every Space
Marine Chapter's tactical doctrine and laid the foundations
for the military might of the entire Imperium. Its words were
sanctified by the Emperor himself and the Ultramarines had
not deviated from its teachings since it had been written following the dark days of the Horus Heresy.

But Idaeus tended to regard the wisdom of the Codex as
advice rather than holy instruction and this was a constant
source of amazement to Uriel. He had been Idaeus's second-
in-command for nearly thirty years and, despite the
captain's successes, Uriel still found it hard to accept his
methods.

'I want to go and check those hills,' said Idaeus suddenly.

Uriel sighed and pointed out, 'The scouts will inform us
of anything that approaches.'

'I know, and I have every faith in them. I just need to see
for myself. Come on, let's go and take a look.'

Uriel took out his vox unit, informing the scouts they
would be approaching from the rear and followed Idaeus as
he strode purposefully to the end of the bridge. They passed

the far bunker, the one the rebels should have occupied, noting the glint of bolters from within. The two Space Marines marched up the wide road that led into the high hills either side of the gorge and for the next thirty minutes inspected the locations Uriel had deployed the scouts to watch from. The rain deadened sounds and kept visibility low and there was enough tree cover to almost completely obscure the jungle floor. There could be an army out there and they wouldn't see it until it was right on top of them.

'Satisfied?' asked Uriel.

Idaeus nodded, but did not reply and together they began the trek back to the far bunker where they could see Sevano Tomasin.

The warning came just as the first artillery shell screamed overhead.

Almost as soon as Uriel heard the incoming shell, the comm-net exploded with voices; reports of artillery flashes in the distance and multiple sightings of armoured personnel carriers and tanks. A blinding explosion in the centre of the bridge, followed by half a dozen more in quick succession, split the dusk apart. Uriel shouted as he saw the servitors and two Space Marines blasted from the bridge, tumbling downwards to the rocks below.

The two officers sprinted down towards the bridge.

Uriel dialled into the vox-net of the Scouts as he ran and yelled, 'Scout team Alpha! Where in the warp did they come from? Report!'

'Contacts at three kilometres and closing, sergeant! The rain held down the dust, we couldn't see them through the dead ground.'

'Understood,' snapped Uriel, cursing the weather. 'What can you see?'

'Can't get an accurate count, but it looks like a battalion-sized assault. Chimeras mainly, but there's a lot of heavy armour mixed in – Leman Russ, Griffons and Hellhounds.'

Uriel swore and exchanged glances with Idaeus. If the scouts were correct, they were facing in excess of a thousand men with artillery and armoured support. Both knew that this must be the contact the auguries on the *Vae Victus* had detected then lost. They had to get everyone back across the bridge and blow it right now.

'Stay as long as you can Alpha and keep reporting, then get back here!'

'Aye, sir,' responded the scout and signed off.

More shells dropped on the bridge, the echoes of their detonations deafening in the enclosed gorge. Each blast threw up chunks of the roadway and vast geysers of rainwater. Some were air-bursting above the bridge, showering the roadway with deadly fragments.

Uriel recognised the distinctive whine of Griffon mortar shells and gave thanks to Guilliman that the PDF obviously did not have access to the heavier artillery pieces of the Imperial Guard.

Either that, or they realised that to use such weapons would probably destroy the bridge.

Most of the Space Marines who had been caught in the open were in cover now and Uriel knew they were lucky not to have lost more men. He cursed as he saw the lumbering shape of Sevano Tomasin still fixing explosive charges and unwinding lengths of cable back towards the last bunker. The Techmarine's movements were painfully slow, but he was undaunted by the shelling. Uriel willed him to work faster.

'One and a half kilometres and closing. Closing rapidly! Dismounted enemy infantry visible!' shouted the scout sergeant in Uriel's comm-bead.

'Acknowledged,' shouted Uriel over the crash of falling mortar shells and explosions. 'Get back here now; there's nothing more you can do from there. Sword squad is waiting at the first bunker to give you covering fire. Ventris out.'

Uriel and Idaeus reached the bunker and splashed to a halt behind its reassuringly thick walls. Idaeus snatched up his vox-com and shouted, 'Guard command net, this is Captain Idaeus, Ultramarines Fourth Company. Be advised that hostiles are attacking across Bridge Two-Four in division strength, possibly stronger. We are falling back and preparing to destroy the bridge. I say again, hostiles are attacking across Bridge Two-Four!'

As Idaeus voxed the warning to the Imperial Guard commanders, Uriel patched into the frequency of the Thunderhawk that had dropped them in position.

'Thunderhawk Six, this is Uriel Ventris. We are under attack and request immediate extraction. Mission order Omega-Seven-Four. Acknowledge please.'

For long seconds, all Uriel could hear was the hiss of static and he feared something terrible had happened to the gunship. Then a voice, heavily distorted said, 'Acknowledged, Sergeant Ventris. Mission order Omega-Seven-Four received. We'll be overhead in ten minutes. Signal your position with green smoke.'

'Affirmative,' replied Uriel. 'Be advised the landing zone will in all likelihood be extremely hot when you arrive.'

'Don't worry,' chuckled the pilot of the gunship. 'We're fully loaded. We'll keep their heads down while we extract you. Thunderhawk Six out.'

Uriel snapped the vox-unit to his belt and hammered on the bunker's door. He and Idaeus ducked inside as it slid open. The five Space Marines within were positioned at the bunker's firing step, bolters and a lascannon pointed at the hills above, ready to cover their brothers' retreat. Uriel stared through the anti-grenade netting, watching the scouts falling back in good order towards the bridge.

'As soon as the scouts are past you, fall back to the first gun nest and take up firing positions,' ordered Idaeus. 'The other squads are already in position and they'll cover you. Understood?'

The Space Marines nodded, but did not take their eyes from the ridge above the approaching scouts. Idaeus turned to Uriel and said, 'Get across and see how close Tomasin is to blowing this damned bridge. We'll join you as soon as we can.'

Uriel opened his mouth to protest, but Idaeus cut him off, 'Stow it, sergeant. Go! I'll join you as soon as Alpha Team are safe.'

Without another word, Uriel slipped from the bunker. Another series of thunderous detonations cascaded across the bridge and impacted on the sides of the gorge. Uriel waited until he detected a lull in the firing then began sprinting across the bridge, weaving around piles of rubble, debris and water filled craters left by the explosions. He could still see Sevano Tomasin behind the sandbagged gun nests, working on the detonators.

He heard gunfire behind him, the distinctive, dull crack of bolter fire and the snapping hiss of lasguns. He glanced over his shoulder as a terrible sense of premonition struck him.

Twin streaks of shrieking projectiles flashed overhead, one landing behind him and another before him with earth shaking detonations. The first shell exploded less than four metres above the men of Alpha team, shredding their bodies through the lighter scout armour leaving only a bloody mist and scraps of ripped flesh. The shockwave of the blast threw Uriel to the ground. He coughed mud and spat rainwater, rising in time to see Sevano Tomasin engulfed in blinding white phosphorescent fire.

The Techmarine collapsed, his metal limbs liquefying and the flesh searing from his bones. A second melta charge ignited in his equipment pack, also cooked off by the mortar shell's detonation. Tomasin vanished in a white-hot explosion, the rain forming a steam cloud around his molten remains.

Uriel pushed himself upright and charged towards the fallen Space Marine. Tomasin was dead, there could be no doubt about that. But Uriel needed to see if the detonator mechanism had gone up with him. If it had, they were in deep, deep trouble.

IDAEUS WATCHED THE first squadron of enemy vehicles crest the ridge above, hatred burning in his heart. Even in the fading light, he could clearly make out the silhouette of three Salamander scout vehicles and Idaeus vowed he would see them dead.

He could smell the acrid stench of scorched human flesh from the blasted remains of the scouts. They had died only ten metres from the safety of the bunker. Idaeus knew he should fall back to the prepared gun positions further along the bridge; if they stayed here much longer, they'd be trapped. But his thirst for retribution was a fire in his heart, and he was damned if he would yield a millimetre to these bastards without exacting some measure of vengeance for his fallen warriors.

'Nivaneus,' hissed Idaeus to the Space Marine carrying the lascannon. 'Do you have a target?'

'Aye, sir,' confirmed Nivaneus.

'Then fire at will. Take down those traitorous dogs!'

A blinding streak of las-fire punched from the massive weapon. A Salamander slewed from the road, its hull blazing and smoke boiling from its interior. The vehicles' supporting infantry squads fired their lasguns before the Space Marines' bolter fire blasted them apart with uncompromising accuracy. But Idaeus knew they were inconsequential. Killing the tanks was all that mattered.

Nivaneus calmly switched targets and another Salamander died, its crew tumbling from the burning escape hatches. The last tank ground to a halt, stuttering blasts from its autocannon stitching across the bunker's face. Idaeus felt the vibrations of shell impacts. He smiled grimly as the Salamander's driver desperately attempted to reverse back uphill. Its tracks spun ineffectually, throwing up huge sprays of mud, unable to find purchase. Dust and an acrid, electric stench filled the air as Nivaneus lined up a shot on the struggling tank.

Before he could fire, a missile speared through the rain and smashed into the immobilised tank's turret. It exploded from within, wracked by secondary detonations as its ammo cooked off.

'Captain Idaeus!' shouted Uriel over the vox-net. 'Get out of there! There will be more tanks coming over that ridge any moment and you will be cut off if you do not leave now! We have you covered, now get back here!'

'I think he's got a point, men,' said Idaeus calmly. 'We've given them a bloody nose, but it's time we were going.'

The Ultramarines fired a last volley of shots before hefting their weapons and making for the door.

'Uriel!' called Idaeus. 'We are ready to go, now give me some fire.'

Seconds later a withering salvo of bolter fire and missiles swept the ridge top, wreathing it in smoke and flames. Idaeus shouted, 'Go, go, go!' to the Space Marines and followed as they sprinted through the rain. The mortar fire had ceased; probably due to the Griffon tanks being moved up into a direct firing position, thought Idaeus. Whatever the reason, he was grateful for it.

He heard a teeth-loosening rumble and a squeal of tracks, knowing without looking that heavy tanks had spread out across the ridge, moving into a firing position behind them. He saw two missile contrails flashing overhead and heard the ringing clang of their impact. A crashing detonation told him that at least one enemy tank was out of action, but only one.

'Incoming!' he yelled and dived over a pile of debris into a crater as the thunder of two battle cannons echoed across the gorge. He felt the awesome force of the impacts behind him, even through the ceramite of his power armour. His auto-senses shut down momentarily to preserve his sight and hearing as the massive shell exploded, the pressure of the blast almost crushing him flat. Red runes winked into life on his visor as his armour was torn open in half a dozen places. He felt searing pain and cursed as he yanked a plate-sized piece of sizzling shrapnel from his leg. Almost instantly, he could feel the Larraman cells clotting his blood and forming a protective layer of scar tissue over the wound. He had suffered much worse and shut out the pain.

The two surviving Leman Russ tanks rumbled downhill, smashing the smoking remains of the Salamanders aside with giant dozer blades. Furious gunfire spat from their hull-mounted heavy bolters, sweeping across the bunker's face and the bridge, throwing up spouts of water and rock. None hit the Ultramarines and Idaeus shouted, 'Up! Come on, keep moving!'

The Space Marines rose and continued running towards the comparative safety of the far side of the bridge. More tanks and infantry spilled over the ridge, following in the wake of the Leman Russ battle tanks. Las-blasts fired at the Space Marines, but the range was too great.

Then, at the edge of his hearing, Idaeus heard the welcome boom of a Thunderhawk gunship's engines and saw the angular form of the aerial transport sweep from above the jungle canopy. Rockets streaked from its wing pylons, rippling off in salvoes of three and the ridge vanished in a wall of flames. Heavy cannons mounted on the hull and wings fired thousands of shells into the rebels, obliterating tanks and men in a heartbeat.

Idaeus punched the air in triumph as the Thunderhawk swept over the ridge and circled around for another strafing run. He jogged leisurely into the sandbagged gun nest, the Space Marines who had followed him taking up firing positions.

'Uriel,' voxed Idaeus. 'Are you ready to get out of here?'

'More than ready,' replied Uriel from the bunker behind Idaeus. 'But we have a problem. Tomasin was killed in the shelling and he had the detonators. We can't blow the bridge.'

Idaeus slammed his fist into a sandbag. 'Damn it!' he swore, teeth bared. He paced the interior of the gun nest like a caged grox before saying, 'Then we're going to have to hold here for as long as possible and pray the Guard can realign their flank in time.'

'Agreed. The Emperor guide your aim, captain.'

'And yours. May He watch over you.'

URIEL SHUT OFF the vox-com and slid a fresh magazine into his bolt pistol, staring out at the flame wreathed hillside. The distant Thunderhawk had circled around, guns blazing at something Uriel could not see. Fresh explosions blossomed from behind the ridge as more traitors died.

Suddenly shells burst around the gunship and streams of fire, bright against the dark sky, licked up from the ground. Uriel swore as he realised the traitors were equipped with anti-aircraft weapons. The gunship jinked to avoid the incoming fire, but another stream of shells spat skyward and seconds later the gunners had the Thunderhawk bracketed. Thousands of shells ripped through the gunship's armour, tearing the port wing off. The engine exploded in a brilliant fireball. The pilot struggled to hold the aircraft aloft, banking to avoid the flak, but the gunship continued to lose altitude, spewing black smoke from its stricken frame.

Uriel watched with horror as the Thunderhawk spiralled lower and lower, its wobbling form growing larger by the second.

'By the Emperor, no!' whispered Uriel as the gunship smashed into the ground just before the bridge, skidding forwards and trailing a brilliant halo of sparks and flames. The wreckage crashed into the unoccupied bunker, demolishing it instantly, and slewing across the bridge towards the Ultramarines with the sound of shrieking metal. The remaining wing sheared off, spinning the flaming gunship upside down and tearing up the roadway. The gunship ground onwards, finally coming to a halt less than two hundred metres from the gun nests.

Uriel let out the breath he had been holding. Movement caught his eye and he saw more enemy vehicles rumbling through the swirling black smoke towards the bridge.

'Targets sighted!' he shouted. 'Enemy tanks inbound. Mark your targets and fire when you have a clear shot!'

The lead rebel armoured column consisted of dozens of Chimeras, daubed in blasphemous runes. Uriel snarled as he recognised the winged skull motif of the Night Lords crudely copied onto the Chimeras' hulls. There could be no doubt now. The taint of Chaos had come to Thracia. Each vehicle mounted a powerful searchlight, sweeping blindingly back and forth in random patterns across the bridge as they charged. Missiles and lascannon blasts pierced the darkness, and the night was illuminated by scores of exploding tanks. No matter how many the Ultramarines killed, there were more to take their place. Soon the bridge was choked with burning wrecks. Hundreds of screaming soldiers dismounted from their transports, working their way forward through the tanks' graveyard.

Uriel fired shot after shot from his pistol. It was impossible to miss, there were so many. The darkness of the gorge echoed to the sounds of screams and gunfire. But Uriel was not fooled by the slaughter they were wreaking amongst the ranks of the traitors. Their ammunition was finite and soon the battle would degenerate into bloody close quarter fighting and, though they would kill many hundreds, they would eventually fall. It was simply a question of numbers.

He reloaded again and wished there was something else he could do, cursing Sevano Tomasin for dying and condemning them to this ignoble end. He pictured again the image of the Techmarine incinerated by the chain-reacting melta charge in his equipment pack.

Something clicked in Uriel's head and he stopped.

No, it was insane, utterly insane and suicidal. But it could work. He tried to remember a precedent in the Codex Astartes, but came up with nothing. Could it be done? A frag wouldn't do it and only the assault troops had been issued with kraks. He checked his grenade dispenser. He had one breaching charge left.

His mind made up, he grabbed a Space Marine from the firing step, shouting to be heard over the bolter fire. 'I'm heading for the captain's position. Give me covering fire!'

The man nodded and passed on his order. Uriel ducked out the ragged doorway and crouched at the corner of the bunker. Streams of las-blasts and bolter rounds criss-crossed the darkness causing a weirdly stroboscopic effect.

Volleys of sustained bolter fire blasted from the bunker and Uriel leapt from cover, sprinting towards Idaeus's position. Instantly, lasgun fire erupted from amongst the burning tanks. Each shooter was silenced by a devastatingly accurate bolter shot.

Uriel dived behind the gun nest and crawled inside on his belly.

Idaeus, bleeding from a score of gouges in his armour, directed disciplined bolter fire into the traitors' ranks. Two Space Marines lay dead, the backs of their helmets blasted clear, and Uriel was suddenly very aware of how much less protection there was in the gun nest than in the bunker.

Idaeus spared Uriel a glance, shouting, 'What are you doing here, Uriel?'

'I have an idea how we can blow the bridge!'

'How?'

'The assault troops have krak grenades. If we can attach some to one of the melta charges on the bridge supports it could set of a chain reaction with the others!'

Idaeus considered the idea for a second then shrugged. 'It's not much of a plan, but what choice do we have?'

'None,' said Uriel bluntly. Idaeus nodded and hunkered down in the sandbags, snatching out his battered vox. Hurriedly, he explained Uriel's plan to the sergeant of the assault troopers, receiving confirmation as to its feasibility of execution.

Idaeus raised his head and locked his gaze with Uriel. 'You picked a hell of a time to start thinking outside the Codex, sergeant.'

'Better late than never, captain.'

Idaeus smiled and nodded. 'We'll have about thirty seconds from the first detonation to get clear. If we're not off the bridge by then, we're dead. I've already called for another Thunderhawk, but it will not arrive before morning at the earliest.'

The captain opened a channel to the remaining Space Marines in his detachment and said, 'All squads, as soon as the assault troops move, I want enough firepower laid down on these bastards to blow apart a Titan. Understood?'

Shouted confirmations greeted Idaeus's order. He reloaded his pistol and motioned for Uriel to join him at the edge of the gun nest.

From the second gun nest, flaring jets of light erupted as the assault squad fired their jump packs.

'NOW!' yelled Idaeus and the Ultramarines fired everything they had. Volley after volley of bolter shells, missiles and lascannon shots decimated the rebel troopers. The swiftness of death was unbelievable. The Space Marines pumped shot after shot into their reeling mass.

It began with a single rebel turning his back and fleeing into the night. An officer shot him dead, but it was already too late. Others began turning and fleeing through the maze of wrecked tanks, their resolve broken in the face of the Emperor's finest.

And then it was over.

Uriel could not recall how long they had fought for, but it must have been many hours. He checked his visor chronometer and was surprised to find it had been less than two. He knelt and counted his ammo: six clips, not good. Risking a glance over the top level of sandbags, their outer surfaces vitrified to glass by the intense heat of repeated laser impacts, Uriel saw the bridge littered with hundreds of corpses.

The tension was palpable, every Space Marine ready to move the instant they heard the first detonation of a krak grenade. Long minutes passed with nothing but the hiss of the vox, the crackle of flames and moans of the dying outside. Everyone in the gun nest flinched as they heard the crack of rapid bolt pistol fire. The shooting continued for several minutes before dying away.

Uriel and Idaeus exchanged worried glances. Both sides were using bolt pistols.

Uriel shook his head sadly. 'They failed.'

'We don't know that,' snapped Idaeus, but Uriel could tell the captain did not believe his own words.

WEAK SUNLIGHT SHONE from the carcasses of the crashed Thunderhawk and smashed tanks on the bridge, their black shells smouldering fitfully. The rain had continued throughout the night. Thankfully, the rebels' attacks had not. There was no detonation of krak grenades and Idaeus was forced to admit that the assault squad had been thwarted in their mission.

Uriel scanned the skies to their rear, watching for another Thunderhawk or perhaps Lightning strike craft of the Imperial Navy. Either would be a welcome sight just now, but the skies remained empty.

A sudden shout from one of the forward observers roused Uriel from his melancholy thoughts and he swiftly took his position next to Idaeus.

He saw movement through the burnt out shell of the Thunderhawk, flashes of blue and gold and heard a throaty grinding noise. The sound of heavy vehicles crushing bone and armour beneath their iron tracks. Darting figures, also in blue and gold, slipped through the wrecks, their movements furtive.

With a roar of primal ferocity that spoke of millennia of hate, the Night Lords Chaos Space Marines finally revealed themselves. Battering through the wreckage came five ornately carved Rhino armoured personnel carriers, coruscating azure flames writhing within their flanks. Uriel was speechless.

They resembled Rhinos in name only. Bloody spikes festooned every surface and leering gargoyles thrashed across the undulating armour, gibbering eldritch incantations that made Uriel's skin crawl.

But the supreme horror was mounted on the tanks' frontal sections.

The still-living bodies of the Ultramarine assault squad were crucified on crude iron crosses bolted to the hulls. Their armour had been torn off, their ribcages sawn open then spread wide like obscene angels' wings. Glistening ropes of entrails hung from their opened bellies and they wept blood from blackened, empty eye sockets and tongueless mouths. That they could still be alive was impossible, yet Uriel could see their hearts still beat with life, could see the abject horror of pain in their contorted features.

The Rhinos continued forwards, closely followed by gigantic figures in midnight blue power armour. Their armour was edged in bronze and their helmets moulded into daemonic visages with blood streaked horns. Red winged skull icons pulsed with unnatural life on their shoulder plates.

Idaeus was the first to overcome his shock, lifting his bolter and pumping shots into the advancing Night Lords. 'Kill them!' he bellowed. 'Kill them all!'

Uriel shook his head, throwing off the spell of horror the spectacle of the mutilated Ultramarines had placed upon him and he levelled his pistol. Two missiles and a lascannon shot punched towards the Night Lords. Uriel prayed the tortured souls crucified on the Rhinos would forgive them, as two of the tanks exploded, veering off and crashing into the side of the bridge. The prisoners burned in the flames of their destruction and Uriel could feel his fury rising to a level where all he could feel was the urge to kill.

The Space Marine next to Uriel fell, a bolter shell detonating within his chest cavity. He collapsed without a sound, and Uriel swept up his boltgun, emptying the magazine into the traitor legionnaires. A handful of Night Lords were dead, but the rest were closing the gap rapidly. Two more Rhinos died in fiery blasts. Disciplined volleys of bolter and lascannon fire from the Ultramarines in the bunker kept hammering the ranks of Night Lords as they attempted to overrun the gun nests. But few were falling and it was only a matter of time until the traitors reached them.

The Space Marines across the bridge from Uriel and Idaeus perished in a searing ball of white-hot fire as Night Lord warriors unloaded plasma guns through the firing slit of their gun nest. The backblast of the resultant explosion mushroomed into the dawn, incinerating the killers. Still they came on.

Uriel yelled in fury, killing and killing.

An armoured gauntlet smashed into the gun nest.

Idaeus chopped with his power sword and blood sprayed.

Uriel yelled, 'Grenade!' as he saw what was clutched in the severed hand. He kicked the hand into the gun nest's grenade pit and rolled a dead Space Marine on top. The frag blew with a muffled thump, the corpse's ceramite back-plate absorbing the full force of the blast.

'Thank you, brother,' muttered Uriel in relief.

Another Night Lord kicked his way into the gun nest, a screaming axe gripped in one massive fist. His blue armour seemed to ripple with inner fires and the brass edging was dazzling in its brightness. The winged skull icon hissed blasphemous oaths and Uriel could feel the axe's obscene hunger for blood.

Idaeus slashed his sword across his chest, but the blade slid clear. The warrior lunged, slashing his axe across Idaeus's shoulder and blood sprayed through the rent in his armour. Idaeus slammed his elbow into his foe's belly and spun inside his guard, hammering his sword through the Night Lord's neck.

He kicked him back outside as more enemies pushed themselves in. Uriel fired his pistol and rolled beneath a crackling power fist. He drove his combat knife into the gap between his enemy's breastplate and helmet, wrenching the blade upwards. Blood fountained and he yelled in sudden pain as the warrior fired his bolter at point blank range. The shell penetrated Uriel's armour and blasted a fist-sized chunk of his hip clear. He stabbed his opponent's neck again and again, stopping only when his struggles ceased completely.

Idaeus and the last Space Marine in the gun nest fought back to back, desperately fighting for their lives against four Night Lords. Uriel leapt into the combat, wrapping his powerful arms around one Chaos Space Marine's neck. He twisted hard, snapping his spine.

Everything was blood and violence. The Space Marine fighting alongside Idaeus fell, his body pulverised by a power fist. Uriel dragged his blade free from the Night Lord's helmet and beheaded the killer, blowing out another foe's helmet with a bolter shell. Idaeus drove his sword through the last Night Lord's belly, kicking the corpse from his blood-sheathed blade. The two Space Marines snatched up their bolters and began firing again. The gun nest stank of blood and smoke. The last Rhino was a blazing wreck, the prisoner on its hull cooking in the fires.

He tossed aside the bolter as its slide racked back empty and grabbed Idaeus by the shoulder.

'We need to get back to the bunker. We can't hold them here!'

'Agreed,' grimaced Idaeus. Grabbing what ammo they could carry, the two warriors ducked outside into the grey morning and ran back towards the bullet scarred bunker. The attack appeared to be over for now.

As they ran, Idaeus's vox crackled and a voice said, 'Captain Idaeus, do you copy? This is Thunderhawk Two. We are inbound on your position and will be overhead in less than a minute. Do you copy?'

Idaeus snatched up the vox and shouted, 'I copy, Thunderhawk Two, but do not over-fly our position! The enemy has at least two, but probably more, anti-aircraft tanks covering the bridge. We already lost Thunderhawk Six.'

'Understood. We will set down half a kilometre south of the bridge,' replied the pilot.

Uriel and Idaeus limped inside the bunker and dropped the bolter magazines on the floor.

'Load up. This is all we have left,' ordered Idaeus.

The Ultramarines began sharing out the magazines and Uriel offered another bolter to Idaeus, but the captain shook his head.

'I don't need it. Give me a pistol and a couple of clips. And that last breaching charge of yours, Uriel.'

Uriel quickly grasped the significance of Idaeus's words. 'No, let me do it, captain,' he pleaded.

Idaeus shook his head, 'Not this time, Uriel. This is my mission, I won't let it end like this. The seven of us can't hold the Night Lords if they attack again, so I'm ordering you to get the rest of the men back to that Thunderhawk.'

'Besides,' he said with a wry smile. 'You don't have a jump pack to get down there.'

Uriel could see there was no arguing with the captain. He dispensed the last breaching charge and reverently offered it to Idaeus. The captain took the charge and unbuckled his sword belt. He reversed the scabbard and handed the elaborately tooled sword to Uriel.

'Take this,' he said. 'I know it will serve you as well as it has served me. A weapon this fine should not end its days like this, and you will have more need of it than I.'

Uriel could not speak. Idaeus himself had forged the magnificent blade before the Corinthian Crusade and had carried it in battle ever since. The honour was overwhelming.

Idaeus gripped Uriel's wrist tightly in the warrior's grip and said, 'Go now, old friend. Make me proud.'

Uriel nodded. 'I will, captain,' he promised, and saluted. The five remaining Space Marines in the bunker followed Uriel's lead and came to attention, bolters held tightly across their chests.

Idaeus smiled. 'The Emperor watch over you all,' he said and slipped outside into the rain.

Uriel was gripped by a terrible sense of loss, but suppressed it viciously. He would ensure that Idaeus's last command was carried out.

He loaded a bolter and racked the slide.

'Come on, we have to go.'

IDAEUS WAITED UNTIL he saw Uriel lead the five Space Marines from the bunker towards the jungle's edge before moving. He had a chance to do this stealthily, but knew it wouldn't be long before the Night Lords realised the bridge was now undefended and the rebels drove their forces across. He would not allow that to happen.

He crawled through the mud and rubble, keeping out of sight of the enemy lines, eventually reaching the pitted face of the rockcrete sides of the bridge. He grabbed a handful of mud and ash, smearing it over the blue of his armour, then slithered onto the parapet. The river was thousands of metres below and Idaeus experienced a momentary surge of vertigo as he looked down. He scanned the bridge supports, searching for one of the box-like melta charges Tomasin had placed only the day before. He grinned as he spotted one fixed to the central span. Muttering a prayer to the Emperor and Guilliman, Idaeus pushed himself over the edge.

He dropped quickly, then fired the twin jets of his jump pack, angling for the central span. The noise of the rockets' burn seemed incredibly loud to Idaeus, but he could do nothing about it. It was all or nothing now.

He cursed as he saw his trajectory was too short. He landed on a wide beam, some twenty metres from the central span and crouched, waiting to see if he had been detected. He heard nothing and clambered through the multitude of stanchions, beams and tension bars towards the central column.

Suddenly, a shadow passed over the captain and he spun in time to see dark winged creatures in midnight black power armour swoop down alongside him. Their helmets were moulded in the form of screaming daemons and ululating howls shrieked from their vox units. They carried stubby pistols and serrated black swords that smoked as

though fresh from the furnace. Idaeus knew the foul creatures as Raptors, and fired into their midst, blasting one of
the abominable warriors from the sky. Another crashed into
him, stabbing with a black bladed sword. Idaeus grunted as
he felt the blade pierce one of his lungs, and broke the Raptor's neck with a blow from his free hand. He staggered
back, the sword still embedded in his chest, taking refuge in
the tangle of metal beneath the bridge to avoid the howling
Raptors. Two landed between him and the melta charge as
dozens more descended from the bridge. Three more
swooped in behind him, their wings folding behind them
and they landed on the girders. Idaeus snarled and raised his
pistol as they charged.

Idaeus killed the first with his pistol. A second shot killed
another, but he couldn't move quick enough to avoid the
third. White heat exploded in his face, searing the flesh from
the side of his skull as the Raptor fired its plasma pistol. He
fell back, blind with pain, and didn't see the crackling sword
blow that hacked his left arm from his body. He bellowed
with rage as he watched his arm tumble down towards the
river, Uriel's last breaching charge still clutched in the
armoured fist.

The Raptor closed for the kill, but Idaeus was ready for it.
He dragged the smoking sword from his chest and howled
with battle fury as he hammered the sword through the Raptor's neck. He collapsed next to the headless corpse,
releasing his grip on the sword hilt. Dizziness and pain
swamped him. He tried to stand, but his strength was gone.
He saw the Raptors standing between him and the melta
charge, their daemon-carved helmets alight with the
promise of victory.

He felt his lifeblood pumping from his body, the Larraman cells powerless to halt his demise and bitterness arose
in his throat.

He reached out with his arm, propping himself upright as
weariness flooded his limbs. He felt a textured pistol grip
beneath his hand and grasped the unfamiliar weapon
tightly. If he was to die, it would be with a weapon in his
hand.

More Raptors hovered in the air, screeching in triumph and Idaeus could feel a bone-rattling vibration as hundreds of armoured vehicles began crossing the bridge. He had failed. He looked down at the pistol in his hand and hope flared. The flying abominations raised their weapons, ready to blow him away.

Then the Raptors exploded in a series of massive detonations and Idaeus heard a thunderous boom echo back and forth from the sides of the gorge. He twisted his dying body around in time to see the beautiful form of Thunderhawk Two roaring through the gorge towards the bridge, its wing mounted guns blasting the Raptors to atoms.

He smiled through the pain, guessing the fight Uriel must have had with the pilot to get him to fly through the flak of the Hydras and down the gorge. He raised his head to the two Raptors who still stood between him and his goal. They drew their swords as Thunderhawk Two screamed below the bridge. Lascannon fire chased the gunship, but nothing could touch it.

Idaeus slumped against a black stanchion and turned his melted face back towards the two Raptors. Between them, he could see the melta charge. He smiled painfully.

He would only get one shot at this.

Idaeus raised the plasma pistol he had taken from the dead Raptor, relishing the look of terror on his enemy's faces as they realised what must happen next.

'Mission accomplished,' snarled Idaeus and pulled the trigger.

URIEL WATCHED THE unbearably bright streak of plasma flashing towards the central span of the bridge and explode like a miniature sun directly upon the melta charge. The searing white heat ignited the bomb with a thunderclap and it detonated in a gigantic, blinding fireball, spraying molten tendrils of liquid fire.

The central support of the bridge was instantly vaporised in the nuclear heat, and Uriel had a fleeting glimpse of Idaeus before he too was engulfed in the expanding firestorm.

The echoes of the first blast still rang from the gorge sides as the remaining charges detonated in the intense heat. A heartbeat later, the bridge vanished as explosions blossomed along its length and blasted its supports to destruction. Thunderous, grinding cracks heralded its demise as giant sections of the bridge sagged, the shriek of tortured metal and cracking rockcrete filling Uriel's senses. Whole sections plummeted downwards, carrying hundreds of rebel tanks and soldiers to their deaths as the bridge tore itself apart under stresses it was never meant to endure.

Thick smoke and flames obscured the final death of Bridge Two-Four, its twisted remains crashing into the river below. Thunderhawk Two pulled out of the gorge, gaining altitude and banking round on a course for the Imperial lines. Even as the bridge shrank in the distance, Uriel could see there was almost nothing left of it.

The main supports were gone, the sections of roadway they had supported choking the river far below. There was now no way to cross the gorge for hundreds of miles in either direction.

He slid down the armoured interior of the Thunderhawk and wearily removed his helmet, cradling Idaeus's sword in his lap. He thought of Idaeus's sacrifice, wondering again how a warrior of the Ultramarines could command without immediate recourse to the Codex Astartes. It was a mystery to him, yet one he now felt able to explore.

He ran a gauntleted hand along the length of the masterfully inscribed scabbard, feeling the full weight of responsibility the weapon represented. Captain Idaeus of the Fourth Company was dead, but as long as Uriel Ventris wielded this blade, his memory would remain. He looked into the blood-stained faces of the Space Marines who had survived the mission and realised that the duty of command now fell to him.

Uriel vowed he would do it honour.

LOYALTY'S REWARD

Simon Jowett

THE VOX-ENHANCED BELLS of the nearby Ecclesiarchy chapel
were sounding vespers when Kleist spotted them. They had
only just stepped into the bar. There were three of them –
well-dressed, but not ostentatiously so. They wouldn't have
looked out of place among the crowds in one of the uptown
bars or restaurants, but here, close to the landing fields, they
stood out among the off-duty loaders and packers who
made up the regular clientele at the Split Pig.

Several heads turned as the newcomers made their way
slowly towards the bar – then turned quickly back to stare
into drinks or strike up conversations with companions. The
strangers' expensive suits couldn't hide the heavy muscles
beneath their fabric or the air of suppressed violence that
hung around them like a dark cloud. Even Ernst, the bar's
permanently-stewed mascot, didn't try to tap the newcomers for a free drink.

The walls shook and a dull roar filled the bar as a heavy
cargo shuttle passed overhead, drowning out the sound of
the call to worship as it made its way from the landing fields
to the Merchants' Guild transport barge that waited for it in

low orbit. The fields were busy day and night; Equus III was
the most ore-rich world in this edge of the segmentum and
Praxis its most prosperous city. The Split Pig was not a place
to go if you wanted peace and quiet.

From his booth at the rear of the room, Leon Kleist
scanned the bar's dimly-lit interior, hoping to spot a group
of Imperial Guard troopers on shore leave from their orbit-
ing transport. The Split Pig was a favourite among
guardsmen in transit with only a few hours of furlough
before their next journey through the warp. No luck.

Kleist looked back towards the bar and saw one of the
newcomers beckon to the bartender. The young man
stopped stacking glasses and sauntered towards the stranger,
wiping his hands on his apron, ready to take his order. Kleist
knew that the stranger didn't want a drink; he and his companions wanted information.

While he talked to the bartender, the stranger's companions surveyed the room. Kleist slid as far back into his booth
as possible, while still keeping the three of them just in view.
He felt the beginnings of panic swirl in his gut. What had he
been thinking? He should have kept his mouth shut! His
eyes darted nervously towards the rest room door. All he
needed was a chance to...

The ascending shuttle's sonic boom rattled the glasses on
their shelves. None of the regulars took any notice. The bartender continued talking; Kleist saw him point towards his
booth. But all three strangers glanced upwards, surprised by
the aerial concussion. One of them slid a hand inside his
jacket, unconsciously reaching for a concealed weapon.

Kleist ran for the door.

From behind him came the sound of chairs being over-
turned, shouts and the sound of glasses breaking. He
slammed through the door and raced down the short,
poorly-lit passageway towards the rest room. The door
swung shut behind him, cutting off the noise.

Before it reached the latrines, the passageway branched
right. Kleist took the turn and sprinted towards the door
that led to the alley behind the bar. He knew that it would
be a matter of seconds before the three strangers were on

his tail – there wasn't enough of a crowd in the bar to slow them down for very long – but, once he was outside, he stood a better chance of losing them.

Kleist cursed himself as he ran. If he hadn't stayed for that last drink. If the drunken conversation hadn't turned to old man Gaudi's death.

And if he hadn't started shooting his mouth off.

He straight-armed the door at the end of the passage and found himself in the garbage-strewn alley. From here he could go left, across the main street and head home – though only the Emperor knew what he would tell his wife – or right and take the back way towards the landing fields. There was a local Arbites sub-station at the field gates, but Kleist couldn't risk the planetary representatives of Imperial law probing too deeply into his business dealings. Right now the idea of being on some distant world felt very appealing. Unfortunately, he was not alone.

'Hey, Leon, I've been looking all over for you.'

The man was tall, well dressed in the same unobtrusive style as the strangers in the bar and carried himself with the confidence of someone who knew that, in this case, a one-on-one confrontation meant the odds were already stacked in his favour. A thin scar ran the length of the right side of his face, from the hairline of his slicked-back, sandy-coloured hair, almost to the point of his narrow chin. He was not a stranger.

'Mister... Mister Kravi...' Kleist managed to stammer. And then his world exploded.

HE DIDN'T REMEMBER landing in the filth at the foot of the wall. He rolled painfully onto his front and pushed himself up onto all fours. His mouth was full – it felt as if he had swallowed as much of the muck as now covered his clothes. He spat. A large gobbet of blood hit the back of his left hand. As he stared at it, blinking away the tears that had inexplicably appeared, fogging his vision, another joined it, this time falling from his nose. He raised an unsteady hand to the centre of his face, pressed gently and felt the grinding of cartilage against bone. Fresh tears welled up in his eyes.

'That hurt, Leon?' Someone was standing over him. A pair of expensive-looking shoes stood in the muck a short way from him. Kleist craned his neck to look up at the man who spoke.

The fist slammed into the side of his face. Stars exploded behind his eyes and his supporting arm gave way. Gasping with pain and surprise, he inhaled a mouthful of filth.

A hand reached for his shoulder, turned him onto his back. Coughing, fighting down the urge to vomit, he stared up at Mikhail Kravi, right arm of Aldo Graumann, the Protektor, or local boss, for the Haus Gaudi, which had run this part of the hive for as long as anyone could remember.

'I... I'm sorry!' Kleist stuttered. Feet sliding in the slime that coated the alley's flagstones, he began to push himself away from Kravi, towards the rear wall of the bar, expecting every heartbeat to be his last.

'Sorry for what, Leon? Sorry for shooting your mouth off to your buddies in the Transport Confederation, or sorry for making me come down here and bruise my knuckles on your face?'

Kravi seemed amused to watch him slide along the ground, then push himself up into a half-seated position against the wall. Only now did Kleist dare to shift his gaze from Kravi's face.

He noticed that the three strangers from the bar now stood a short way behind their leader, hands clasped, mute witnesses to his humiliation.

Kravi dropped to his haunches in front of Kleist, and locked eyes with him.

'You see, Leon, word reached Mister Graumann that you'd been telling your pals that now Graf Gaudi was dead, Emperor bless his departed soul, you didn't see why you should keep on paying tribute to... what did you call him... "his whore-hopping whelp"? Was that it?'

Kleist started shaking his head in a feeble, pointless attempt at denial. Kravi reached out, caught his chin in one large hand and held his head still.

'That's the Graf's grandson you were calling a whelp, Leon. The new Graf. You think that, just because he's young and likes to have a good time, that he's not going to be interested in taking care of business?'

'N–no,' Kleist spluttered. A mixture of blood and alley-filth dribbled down his chin. He wanted to say something, anything that would prevent Kravi from hitting him again. 'It... it was the drink.'

'You know, that's what I thought, when Mister Graumann told me what he'd heard. You meet up with some friends and colleagues, you eat, drink a little too much wine, it goes to your head and you say some crazy things.' Kravi's voice was soft, reasonable. 'I knew you wouldn't have forgotten all the help the old Graf had given you, all the contracts he put your way, the competitors he persuaded not to bid for runs along your routes. He gave you the route from the refineries to the landing fields and I knew you respected him for that.'

Kleist tried to nod, but Kravi's hand was like a iron glove clamped around his jaw.

'And I knew, once you'd had time to think about it, you'd respect the new Graf in just the same way. More, even. I guess that's why you came to this toilet, instead of one of the nicer places near your home: to think things through. Am I right?' He released his grip on Kleist's jaw and the older, fatter man nodded like a chastened child.

'That's good.' Kravi stood, smoothed back some strands of hair that had fallen about his face. 'Now there's going to be a gathering in honour of the new Graf's accession. Everyone's going to be there, paying tribute. And I know whose tribute is going to be the biggest of all, don't I, Leon?'

Kleist nodded again. He had noticed a clammy sensation between his legs and realised that, at some point, he had wet himself like a newborn. Hot tears – not of pain, but of humiliation – rolled down his cheeks.

'I'm glad we had this little talk.' Kravi beckoned to his men and they moved forward, passing Kravi as he stepped away from Kleist. 'My associates here are going to tidy you up and get you home safely to your lovely wife and that very pretty daughter of yours. The gathering is the day after tomorrow at the compound. That gives you time to organise your tribute in the proper manner. If you look out your window before then and happen to see one of my men outside your home, don't worry. He'll be there to make sure nothing interferes with your preparations.

'After all,' Kravi added as two of his men hauled Kleist to his feet, 'you know we only have your best interests at heart.'

THE LAYOUT OF the Haus Gaudi compound had changed little since its construction at the end of the First Age of Vendetta, the blood-soaked decades that followed the founding of Equus III's first industrial colonies. This was a rich world; the opportunities for profit – legitimate or otherwise – were boundless. The houses that would one day control the black economy of Equus III grew out of loose-knit gangs of street thugs, entrepreneurs who had failed to prosper in legitimate trade, crewmen who had grown tired of life aboard the Merchant Guild's ships, and discharged members of the Imperial Guard regiments which had accompanied the first settlers.

The First Age of Vendetta saw allegiances harden into blood loyalty as the gangs jockeyed for position and power. The weaker houses were absorbed by the more powerful, the better organised, or else they were eliminated. An observer who looked only at the spires and towers of Equus III's rapidly expanding cities, or at the vast wealth generated by the burgeoning trade in refined ores, would be unaware of the war being fought in the shadows.

Franz Gaudi, the first Graf, had seen his house come close to extinction during this time. He was determined that it should not happen again. The compound, set on the banks of a lake on the outskirts of Praxis, beyond the curtain wall that marked the boundary of the hive proper, most of it constructed below ground level and surrounded by a high, hexagonal wall, was the result.

The Second Age of Vendetta was a quieter, less blood-soaked affair, marked by assassinations and the occasional skirmish over territory. Like the players of some abstruse intellectual game, the Grafs of the remaining houses directed their street-soldiers against their rivals, gaining control of the illegal interests in one territory, only to lose control of another. Where the First Age had lasted decades, the Second lasted centuries.

Bruno Gaudi had been young and ambitious when he became Graf. Over time, he saw both his sons die – one by an assassin's blade, the other gunned down on a street corner – and came to the conclusion that, during the whole of the Second Age of Vendetta, there had been only one real casualty: profit.

From its unpromising position at the end of the First Age of Vendetta, Haus Gaudi had grown to become one of the most influential criminal entities in Praxis. When its Graf spoke, people listened. For Bruno, the only real surprise was how readily the other Grafs agreed with him. Endless vendettas had got in the way of doing business, had depleted the houses' funds and wasted their manpower. Peace, they agreed, was the only answer. Ritual and respect should replace the blade and the gun. Each house could then concentrate on exacting tribute from those who operated within their agreed territories; violence would be directed only against those who refused to pay. After lengthy negotiations, the Second Age of Vendetta came to an end around the long table in the subterranean sanctum of the Gaudi compound.

'GRAF GAUDI, IN honour of your grandfather's memory – may the Emperor bless his soul – and of your accession, I offer this in tribute.'

With a trembling hand, Leon Kleist placed the data slate on the polished surface of the long table. Viktor Gaudi, pale-skinned and sharp-featured, clad in a high-collared suit of crimson velvet, reached forward, picked up the slate in one slim, elegantly-manicured hand and thumbed its screen into life.

The room was panelled with dark wood and discreetly lit; the back-lit screen cast a pale green glow over his face. Gaudi raised an eyebrow as he read the display, then passed it back to the slightly older man who stood at his left shoulder – Filip Brek, formerly a minor member of the dead Graf's inner circle and Viktor's companion on his visits to the

fleshpots of Praxis, now elevated to the major role of Grafsberator, the Graf's most valued advisor.

'You have been most generous,' Gaudi said quietly. 'Excep-
tionally so. In memory of my beloved grandfather, I thank
you.'

'The honour is mine,' Kleist replied, more loudly than was
necessary, in an attempt to disguise his nerves. Kravi and his
boss, Graumann, stood behind him, flanking the door, over-
seeing the tributes from their part of the hive. Kleist was the
last; he could feel their gaze burning into his back. Before
ushering Kleist and the others down the long corridor to the
sanctum, Kravi had checked the slate, then shown it to Graumann.

The older man had whistled appreciatively – and so he
should. Kleist had liquidated over a third of his assets to
ensure that this tribute was sufficiently extravagant for him
to escape another beating.

'The Haus Gaudi does not forget its friends.' Gaudi nodded towards the door, ending the interview. 'Aldo, stay a
while,' he added as Kleist took an unsteady step backwards,
then turned. Ahead of him, Kravi stepped forward to open
the door. As Kleist passed, Kravi nodded and smiled a self-
satisfied, predator's smile before following him into the
corridor and closing the door behind them.

'You did well in there, Leon,' Kravi said as they walked
along the corridor. Panelled with the same warm, dark wood
as the sanctum, it was lined with niches, in which busts of
long-dead Grafs stood atop stone plinths. Kravi kept pace
with Kleist, one or two steps behind him, a menacing voice
at his shoulder. 'There's just one more thing I wanted to ask
you.'

'Your daughter – what does she like to do?'

'THE GRAF'S PLEASED with you, boy,' Graumann blinked as his
eyes adjusted to the afternoon sunlight. The second of
Equus III's twin suns was dipping towards the tops of the
trees that ringed the lake. He had found Kravi standing at
the battlements atop the hexagonal wall that surrounded the
compound. In all the years since its construction, no one

had ever tried to breach the wall, but its rock-and-plasteel
bulk, metres thick, looked capable of withstanding any
assault short of orbital bombardment.

'Yeah?' Kravi might sound relaxed, unconcerned, but
Graumann knew that was an act. He remembered the hot-
tempered young street hustler who had been caught
boosting liquor from a vehicle owned by a trader under
Haus Gaudi protection. He had already been given a work-
ing-over by Graumann's men, but he still stared defiantly
out at Graumann from a swollen, bruised face. Normally,
his men wouldn't bother their boss with such an incident,
but Kravi was the son of another trader under Gaudi protection. Apparently, the kid had seen Graumann's men, their
expensive clothes and cars, and decided that their line of
business was more appealing. Graumann had found himself
admiring the boy's guts and decided to give him a chance to
learn the business from the inside.

'You won't regret it,' Kravi had slurred through split lips.
Graumann had laughed out loud at that – even then, when
most people would simply be grateful to still be alive, this
kid was trying to hustle him! But Kravi had made good on
his promise; Graumann did not regret taking him on.

'The Graf asked about Kleist's tribute,' Graumann said.
Taking a silk kerchief from his pocket, he dabbed at the
sweat that beaded his forehead after the climb to the battlements. He was getting old, older than he liked to admit,
even to himself. 'I told him that you'd prevailed upon Leon's
better nature. He liked that. He's got something in mind, I
can tell. Now the old Graf's gone – Emperor bless him – he's
looking to stir things up.'

'Stir things up how?' This time, there was no mistaking the
interest in Kravi's voice.

'He didn't say. But, as I was leaving, someone came into
the sanctum through another door. Not a Haus man.
Seemed pretty friendly with Brek.' He patted the broad
expanse of jacket that covered his midriff.

'Something in here tells me things are going to get interesting.'

* * *

THERE WAS NO recoil when he triggered the alien weapon. For a moment, Kravi feared that the firing mechanism had malfunctioned. If this was so, and if all of the weapons the Graf had delivered to the Graumann crew were defective, then he and his men would die here, in a storage depot under the protection of Haus Reisiger.

And then his target – a heavily-built Reisiger enforcer – dropped suddenly to his knees, his features pulped, the top third of his skull sheared off. The laspistol he had been in the process of drawing from a shoulder holster concealed inside his jacket clattered to the floor from nerveless fingers, then the corpse pitched forward and lay still.

The corpse's companions – four of them, foot-soldiers making their regular circuit of Reisiger turf, collecting tribute from the businesses under their Haus's control – reacted with shouts of anger and surprise as they reached for their own concealed weapons.

Kravi and the three men who flanked him cut them down with short, silent bursts from the elegantly-crafted rifles they each held. Their smooth curving lines and long tapering barrels made them look more like pieces of sculpture than weapons; their pistol grips, set behind curved magazines that jutted forward like the teeth of some huge sea-beast, had been designed for slimmer hands, possessed of longer, more delicate fingers. This, combined with their weight – much less than an autogun or bolter – gave Kravi the impression that he might be holding a child's toy, rather than a firearm, but the bloody chunks that now lay scattered across the depot floor bore mute witness to their deadly capabilities.

Kravi poked the air with a finger, directing his men to take up positions on either side of the open doorway, then ran forward, weapon held at hip-height. As he had expected, two of the Reisiger crew had remained outside the covered warehouse section of the depot, guarding their vehicle. The first appeared in the doorway, pistol drawn, coming to investigate the cries from within. Kravi fired and the thug fell back, his chest a ruin. The second, seeing his comrade fall, ducked to one side, away from the doorway.

'The wall – there!' Kravi pointed to the metal wall to one side of the door. His men stared at him for a moment, puzzled. 'Shoot the damn wall!' he repeated. According to Graumann, Brek claimed these fragile-looking things could punch through light armour plate.

Kravi's men each fired a sustained burst at the wall. By the time they released their triggers, the metal hung in shreds and the man behind it lay in pieces. Two of Kravi's men – Gregor and Rudy – stared down at their rifles, wearing comical expressions of almost religious awe.

The squeal of protesting vulcanite came from outside the warehouse. Kravi ran through the door in time to see the Reisiger crew's vehicle tearing away from them, on a swerving, barely-controlled course towards the depot gates. Depot workers in the auto's path scattered to avoid being run down. Those in the clear had turned from the wagons and tractors they were working on to stare at the carnage.

Gregor had followed Kravi through the door. He raised his rifle, sighting after the speeding vehicle. Kravi put out a hand, pressing the barrel down.

'Let him go,' Kravi said. 'He'll be our messenger. He's seen what we can do with these.' Kravi hefted his rifle. In the sunlight, an iridescent sheen swirled just beneath the surface of the weapon's carapace. The metal of which it was composed – if indeed it was metal – had not been mined on Equus III, or any other world in the Imperium. Looking down at the shifting pattern, Kravi felt a thrill run through him – a mixture of fear and elation.

'He'll tell his Protektor and his Protektor will tell Reisiger: Haus Gaudi is taking over.'

IN THE SANCTUM beneath the family compound, Viktor Gaudi listened to the reports. Haus Volpone was losing its hold on the docks as Protektor Seynitz's men moved in. Graf Malenko's men had taken a beating in the smelting districts – it remained to be seen whether they would attempt a reprisal on Gaudi territory. Viktor doubted it – word would already have reached them of the death of Graf Reisiger, gunned down while presiding over a council-of-war in his favourite restaurant. According to that report, there was barely enough left of Reisiger, his closest advisors and their bodyguards to make one of the stews the old Graf loved so much. Since then, large numbers of Reisiger men, protektors as well as foot-soldiers, had been defecting to Haus Gaudi.

An audacious move, the assassination had been planned and led by Graumann's protege, Mikhail Kravi. Kravi's hand-picked crew hijacked a pantechnicon on its way to make a delivery to the restaurant and, disguised in the coveralls of the delivery firm, had strode unopposed through the kitchens and into Reisiger's private dining room. By the time the Graf's bodyguards realised anything was amiss, the air was thick with high-velocity mono-molecular disks. At a stroke, Graumann's young lieutenant had torn the heart from Haus Reisiger. Grown soft during the years of the truce, none of Reisiger's remaining heirs had the experience or the will to rally their house against Haus Gaudi's annexation of their territory. Viktor had already sent word that Kravi was to be acknowledged as a Protektor in his own right and given control of the depot district that had formerly been under Haus Reisiger protection.

'I take it that our merchandise has met with your approval, Graf.' The merchant stood before the long table, looking down at Viktor with dark, heavy-lidded eyes. He wore the same bland, neutral expression as he had when Filip had introduced him to Viktor in the salon of the Leather Venus, one of the more salubrious establishments in Praxis's pleasure district. Using the most polite, convoluted form of High Gothic, he had requested an audience. Viktor, tired from the night's exertions and more than a little drunk, had agreed and left Filip to make the arrangements. He had arrived on the day of the gathering, alone, carrying a long, slim case made from what appeared to be some kind of wood, inlaid with ornate icons. It had reminded Viktor of the case in which his grandfather stored his favourite antique hunting rifle. Its contents, however, could not have been more different.

'We'd be happier if we knew where those unholy relics came from,' growled Friedrik Engel, before Viktor had a chance to speak. From his seat on Viktor's left, Brek shot a look along the table at the old man who sat on the Graf's right. He opened his mouth to speak, but Viktor held up a hand to quiet him. His grandfather's Grafsberator, Viktor only kept Engel by his side to appease the old Graf's retainers – and to make it easier to dispose of him when Viktor's position was secure. Engel didn't approve of Viktor's plans, or the means by which he had set about achieving them, but his sense of loyalty to the family had kept him in line thus far.

'As I explained to your new Graf,' the merchant replied smoothly, as if unaware of the sudden tension in the room, 'I am merely a representative of a larger concern, one that specialises in supplying – shall we say unusual – material to those who might make best use of it.' Though he was addressing Engel, he was still looking at Viktor. His tone was polite, emollient, but the implication was clear: his business was with the new Graf, not an ageing subordinate. Viktor felt the old man bristle and smiled.

'Our ships came upon a drifting hulk. Its exact location is of no concern. Within its hold were certain artefacts. When the news reached us of Graf Gaudi's accession, it occurred to us that others might seek to take advantage of the situation – to move against the family before the new leader had settled into his position – and so we offered our services. From what I have heard, things are going well for Haus Gaudi.'

'They are indeed,' Viktor agreed. 'Though the words of the Divine Emperor rightly teach us to be wary of the work of alien hands, the fact is that a gun is a gun, nothing more. Better that such weapons should be in the hands of our men, rather than those of our rivals.' Viktor directed his words at Engel and now it was Brek's turn to smile. The younger man had just repeated, almost verbatim, the reasoning Brek had used to quell Viktor's misgivings at the sight of the curved, shimmering surface of the shuriken catapult nestling within the merchant's case.

'When you contacted me to request this audience, you said that you had more merchandise that would be of use to us?' Brek addressed the merchant, who nodded.

'Oh yes,' the merchant replied. Viktor thought that, for the first time, the flicker of a smile played across his thin lips. 'There is so much more that we can show you.'

KRAVI HAD BEEN at prayer when he received the summons. Kneeling in the dark, incense-heavy atmosphere of the Ecclesiarchy sub-chapel, he had been giving thanks for his recent elevation to Protektor of the first district he and his crew had wrested from Reisiger control. That it was the Emperor's will that he should have achieved this was beyond doubt. Was it not written in the Holy Books of Terra that the Emperor of Man would help those who helped themselves?

Any doubts he did have centred around the means by which he had achieved so much in so short a time. After Graf Reisiger's death, merely the sight of the shuriken catapults was enough to un-man the Reisiger crews Kravi and his men had faced. He smiled at the memory of the Protektor of a neighbouring district who, upon his first sight of the weapon in Kravi's hands, immediately pledged his stammering allegiance to the Haus Gaudi without a shot being fired.

Be not tempted by the works of the Alien, for they are abominations. Equus III was a loyal world and Praxis its most devout city. Like all of its inhabitants, Kravi knew large sections of the Books of the Emperor by heart. Regular chapel attendance was taken for granted by the members of every Haus on the planet. It was not unusual for a Gaudi, Reisiger or Malenko foot-soldier to kneel in prayer beside a member of a rival family, or a judge from the Arbites. Whatever happened on the streets outside, the sacred ground on which Ecclesiarchy buildings stood was neutral territory.

There was no denying that the weapon he had used to carve Graf Reisiger into bloody slivers had been created by alien minds to be used by alien hands, perhaps against the loyal human servants of the Imperium. As he knelt in the chapel, Kravi had taken a breath before offering thanks for their delivery into the hands of Haus Gaudi. Then he waited, head bowed and heart hammering, for judgement, for some sign that he was damned.

Instead, he had felt a hand on his shoulder, followed by a familiar voice, whispering. 'You're wanted at the compound.'

As they walked briskly down the chapel steps in the fading evening light, Gregor had told him that every Protektor had been summoned to attend upon the Graf immediately. Gregor had driven to the chapel in Kravi's personal vehicle – a sleek, powerful two-seater which Kravi had accepted in lieu of tribute from a trader whose depots fell within his newly-acquired territory – so that he might drive out to the compound directly. Before slipping behind the wheel, Kravi had instructed his lieutenant to let Maria Kleist know that he would be late for tonight's assignation.

As he drove towards the compound, the canyons of the city's streets giving way to fields and woodland, he laughed at his earlier doubts. There had been no bolt from the chapel's rafters, sent by the Emperor in retribution for his daring to use the alien weapons. None of the chapel's priests had denounced him from the high altar as marked by abomination. For all their gleaming strangeness, these 'works of the Alien' were no different to a laspistol or a bolter.

Equus III's second sun was setting as he approached the compound, casting a crimson glow across the high wall. Sentries stood atop the battlements; the curving metal stocks and thin, tapering barrels of their weapons glittered in the fading light.

The compound beyond the wall resembled a vehicle bay at the landing fields. Kravi was one of the last of the Gaudi Protektors to arrive. Graumann was already below ground, a sentry informed him as he hurried towards the low, bunker-like structure that was the only part of the sanctum to protrude above ground. As he stepped between the bunker's heavy doors, Kravi felt – as he had in the frozen heartbeat that preceded the assassination of Reisiger – that he was taking another decisive step towards his destiny.

THE HIGH-PITCHED SQUEALING threatened to burst his skull as he crashed into the bathroom. The side of his head connected with the door-frame and stars shot across his already-blurred vision as he groped his way towards the sink.

He made it just in time. His cramping guts contracted in a spasm that almost dropped him to his knees and shot a column of vomit into the metal bowl. Elbows locked, he supported himself against the sink and gagged for air. He managed a brief glimpse of his reflection in the ornately-engraved mirror set above the sink – long enough to take in blood-shot eyes set in a puffy, blotched face framed by hair that was dishevelled and lank with sweat – before his stomach clenched again and another yellow and green stream splashed into the bowl.

This time he was able to draw enough breath to let out a low, animal moan. The squealing had subsided, but his knees were trembling almost as violently as his guts. If he threw up for a third time, he feared that his arms would give way and he'd end up lying on the bathroom floor in a pool of his own waste.

He retched, then coughed and spat out a last gobbet of bile. Nothing else left, it seemed. Kravi closed his eyes and took a deep, shuddering breath.

That must have been some party, he told himself. Wish I could remember some of it.

There was a shape in the star-flecked darkness behind his eyelids. A darker shape against the darkness. Its outline was regular, many-sided. There was something written across its surface...

Kravi's knees felt strong enough to support him, so he eased himself upright and lifted an experimental hand to the side of his head that had collided with the door-frame. A bruise was already rising, but the skin hadn't been broken. He took another deep breath and opened his eyes.

The light was like slivers of glass pressed against his eyeballs. Kravi gasped, blinked rapidly and raised a hand to shade them before focusing, with some difficulty, on the image in the mirror.

It was no prettier than before. He looked like someone who had just risen from his bed after a week-long fever. As he struggled to recollect the events of the previous night, he peered more closely at his reflection. He noticed what looked like an elongated teardrop, rust-brown in colour, at the corner of one eye. He prodded at it with a finger and it flaked away at his touch. Blood?

There was blood caked around his nostrils too, he noticed. Alarmed, he turned his head to one side. There, running in a thin line from his ear to the corner of his jaw, was more. He turned his head in the opposite direction. His ear-lobe was caked in what looked like an enormous brown scab.

What, in the Emperor's Name, had happened at the compound last night? Had there been some kind of drunken brawl? Kravi remembered the squealing, the pressure inside his skull, as if something was trying to force its way inside his head.

There had been something in the room. Not the sanctum, but one of its annexes. The furniture had been cleared to make way for it. A solid shape, carved from a single block of black stone: a polyhedron. There had been markings on its surface – shapes, sigils of some kind – but they had been almost impossible to make out because the stone, though highly polished, reflected hardly any of the light cast by the candles that had been set around the room's perimeter. All of the other Protektors had been there; Graumann had nodded a greeting from the far side of the room. The Graf had been there, too, and Brek, but he didn't remember seeing Engel, the old Grafsberator. There had been someone else standing beside Gaudi, a face Kravi hadn't recognised, with hooded eyes and thin lips curled in an unpleasant smile.

Kravi groaned as another cramp rippled through him. Despite their violent evacuation, his guts felt heavy, bloated. It occurred to him that a drink might calm them down – and immediately discounted the idea as they clenched and rolled again.

Looking down into the sink, he saw that the yellow and green vomit was draining slowly and glutinously away. He thumbed the faucet and splashed his face with cold water, cupping his hands over his eyes to ease their aching.

Hangover or not, you've got work to do, he told himself. As the new Protektor he had to show his face, prove to his men, and to those who owed him tribute, that he was in control.

But he didn't feel as if he was in control. He didn't feel as if he had a hangover. His bowels rolled over yet again. It felt as if they were moving of their own accord, settling into a more comfortable position. He looked down at his flat, muscled abdomen and realised for the first time that he was naked. He didn't remember getting home last night; he didn't remember undressing. He had jolted awake to find himself sprawled on the couch in his new apartment's living room, wood-panelled and softly-lit in imitation of the Gaudi sanctum.

As he looked down at himself, he half-expected to see evidence that something was moving beneath his skin.

'Like it or not, I need a drink,' he muttered. The first mouthful of liquor came back up almost as quickly as he swallowed it. His guts cramped and twisted, but he persisted. The second mouthful burnt its way down his bruised throat, but didn't return. By the time he took his fifth and sixth pulls on the bottle, a pleasant numbness had spread through him and he felt ready to face the day. He showered, dressed, then called Gregor to pick him up.

When Gregor arrived, Kravi took the half-empty bottle with him.

'SORRY, MIKHAIL, BUT the old man ain't takin' any calls.' Grisha Volk's voice came from the vox-unit's handset. 'He's cancelled all his tribute meetings, too. Didn't say why. He ain't looking too good, though.'

Sitting in the back of the armoured limousine he had 'inherited' from Graf Reisiger, Kravi knew what Volk – his replacement as Graumann's chief lieutenant, a stolid, loyal soldier – was talking about. He had seen Gregor's look of surprise when he had opened his apartment's front door.

'He really tied one on last night – we all did,' Kravi replied – the same answer he gave to Gregor's unspoken question.

'That's what I figured,' Volk said with a chuckle.

'Tell him I'll be in touch tomorrow,' Kravi said, then cut the line and sat in silence for a while, looking out at the city streets – his streets – that flowed past the vehicle's darkened windows. Something was nagging at his memory: the Graf's words from the previous evening, about how the shining alien weapons were just the beginning, and that he was going to show the assembled Protektors the means by which Haus Gaudi's hold over the city would be made secure for years to come.

And then what? There had been chanting, first in High Gothic, then in a language Kravi couldn't properly recall. Not so much words as noises: clicks and squeals...

With the memory of the squealing came that of the pressure, building inside his head. With suddenly unsteady hands, he unstopped the bottle and lifted it to his lips.

'Where to, Mikhail?' Gregor asked via the inter-vox from the driver's cab, separated from the passenger compartment by another sheet of black glass. Kravi swallowed twice, draining the bottle, before he replied.

'Home.'

GRAUMANN WASN'T TAKING calls the following day, or the next. Neither were any of the other Protektors. Several had not emerged from their homes since the evening at the compound. For those whose territories had been in Gaudi hands for generations, that was not a problem. For Kravi, however, it was vital that he showed his face – however blotchy and blood-shot it might still be – to those traders, shopkeepers and bar and restaurant owners who until recently paid tribute to the Reisigers.

The drink helped. It steadied his hands and eased the cramps that still woke him early each morning. Not that his sleep was undisturbed, either. The memories of ghoulish, lurid dreams hung about him when he woke, too indistinct to remember clearly, though fragments would suddenly jump into unnaturally-sharp focus at odd times during the day: the Gaudi sanctum, the assembled faces of the other Protektors, subtly but monstrously changed, voices chanting in deep, immeasurably ancient voices, offering power in exchange for obedience. At such moments, Kravi would reach for the bottle again.

The liquor had another benefit: by clouding his mind, it allowed him to ignore the questions that nagged at him when sober. How did the alien weapons reach Equus III? Where did the black stone polyhedron come from and what did the sigils etched into its surface mean? These were questions that Kravi feared to face, because he already knew the answers.

Guns were one thing. The Dark Gods were another.

On the day he received the summons, he waited until dark before travelling alone to the Palace of the Ecclesiarchy.

As he stood at the foot of the broad marble steps, looking up at the vast double doors, decorated with an intricate bas-relief carving of the Emperor's triumph over the heretic Horus, he surprised himself by thinking of his father. Woyzek Kravi was a devout man, who raised his sons to trust in the Emperor's all-knowing wisdom and who never bothered to hide from them his distaste for the men who came to collect tribute in the name of Haus Gaudi.

To their faces, however, he was always unfailingly courteous and respectful and this, Mikhail, his eldest son, saw as proof that they and the people they served had power over his father.

That power fascinated him, grew into a desire to become one of them. He kept his early adventures into petty crime a secret from his father but, when Graumann accepted him into his crew, Mikhail could not resist visiting his father's office, dressed in a fine new suit and the newly-adopted arrogance of a Gaudi foot-soldier.

He had expected rage, but all he saw in his father's eyes was disappointment. Whenever they met during the years that followed, always as a result of Gaudi business, neither father nor son acknowledged their blood-tie. Only once did Mikhail ask after Emile, his younger brother, who had harboured ambitions to join the ranks of the Ecclesiarchy. Woyzek Kravi fixed his son with a steady gaze and informed him that Emile had been accepted as a student in the seminarium attached to the palace.

Two brass censers, each taller than two men, stood inside the main doors. Kravi walked between them, wisps of their pungent incense clinging to him as he passed. Ranks of pews spread out to either side as he walked down the nave's long central aisle. Supplicants sat or kneeled in prayer, just as many hundreds of thousands of others knelt in the subordinate chapels located throughout the city. A low, almost sub-sonic hum filled the air. It came from the choir stalls at the far end of the aisle, ranged before the high altar: invocations of the Emperor's goodness and might, chanted and repeated endlessly by rotating shifts of priests and students. The hymns of praise never ceased, day or night.

Kravi scanned the vast space until he spotted what he was looking for: a priest, stepping through the iron gate set in the grille separating a side-chapel intended for private worship from the rest of the palace. The priest closed the gate, drew a ritual sigil of protection in the air before it, then moved off along a side-aisle. Quickening his pace, Kravi hurried after him.

'Father.' Kravi's voice was little more than a whisper. The priest turned. Kravi half-expected to see his brother's face framed by the hood of the priest's robe. Thankfully, a stranger returned his gaze.

'My name is Mikhail Kravi,' he told the priest, then paused. On Graumann's turf and now on his own, mention of his name usually produced some reaction. This time there was none. The priest remained silent, his gaze steady.

'I am a... a businessman and a loyal follower of the Emperor, blessed be His name,' Kravi continued, now doubting his wisdom in coming here. Fear had driven him to the palace, fear of what might await him at the Gaudi compound, to which he had been summoned in three days' time. That fear had been replaced by a cold, appalling sense of what he was about to do: break the first rule that any footsoldier was expected to learn, the only rule he would carry in his heart until the day he died. Never speak of Haus business to an outsider.

'That is as it should be,' the priest replied. Kravi thought he saw a flash of impatience cross the other man's features. 'The

Emperor watches over us that we may live secure from the works of the unholy, the blasphemous and the alien. If you have come to reaffirm your faith in his righteousness, take a seat. I am required to be elsewhere, but I will send a novitiate to guide you in the Litany of Renewal.'

'No!'

The priest took a surprised step back. Kravi hadn't meant to raise his voice, but he knew that, if he didn't speak now, he would not have the will to speak again. 'My faith is strong. I'd not be here if it wasn't. There's... there's something you must know. The Dark Gods. They're here–' His guts spasmed, cutting him off. He gasped, forced down the urge to retch, then continued, 'They're here. In Praxis. And I have seen them.'

THE CEREMONY HAD begun. The confined space of the sanctum annexe was filled with the sound of thirty voices, chanting in unison. Viktor stood at the centre of the candle-lit room, flanked by Brek and the merchant, basking in the palpable sense of power that had already begun to permeate the atmosphere.

All but one of the Protektors had answered the summons. As they arrived, Viktor had detected a nervousness, but also a sense of anticipation. He understood the mixture of feelings – he had felt the same when Brek and the merchant had brought him before the polyhedron that now stood, altar like, at his back. There had been pain, uncertainty, but that had passed. When he now gazed upon the stone-set sigils, he saw only his future: more wealth and power than could have been imagined by the Grafs who had come before him and, if the rasping voices that spoke to him from the depths of the black monolith were to be believed, immortality.

Only Kravi, the newest Protektor, had failed to answer the summons. He would have to be removed, replaced. Viktor had decided to send Graumann, the boy's mentor, to do the job. As the chanting grew in volume, now underscored by a deeper, resonating tone that seemed to emanate from a past beyond reckoning, from a dimension beyond that through which mere humans moved, Viktor felt a vague sadness that Kravi would not share in the riches to come.

The sudden rush of ecstasy swept the thought from his mind. His spine popped as he arched backwards, energy racing along the vertebrae, then igniting within his skull. Colours blossomed behind his eyes – a spectrum the human brain was never meant to perceive. With a strangled half-moan of blasphemous pleasure, he dropped first to his knees, then forward onto all-fours. The thing inside him thrashed against his ribs, coiling about itself in a voluptuous frenzy.

His head snapped up as another jolt ran through him and he saw that he was not alone. Most of the Protektors were also on their knees; several lay on the polished wood floor, writhing and groaning.

He caught sight of Graumann, trembling like some palsied beast. As he watched, the older man's face began to melt, the skin running like tallow, remoulding itself into a series of new countenances, each more impossible than the last, as the power of the Lord of Change coursed through him.

At first, Viktor thought the series of dull, muffled concussions came from within him, another manifestation of the power that was being channelled into the room through the monolith. Only when he heard the merchant's curse did he suspect that something was wrong. Fighting against the fog of delirium that clouded his mind, he looked around the room. Several of the others had noticed it as well. The walls and floor vibrated as impact followed impact – the sounds of an attack, transmitted through the earth from the compound above.

THE THUNDERHAWK DROPPED vertically out of the night sky above the Gaudi compound, its bay doors already open. Its armour-clad cargo launched themselves into space, flares of exhaust from their jump packs slowing their vertiginous descent. Bolt pistols coughing throatily, they fired as they fell, clearing most of the guards from the compound wall before their ceramite-booted feet touched earth.

The more quick-witted of those left guarding the vehicles parked in the compound managed to loose off volleys of shuriken fire at their attackers. Most of the shots went wide, but one, at least, found its target, cutting through a jump pack's fuel line. Suddenly engulfed in a ball of flame, the armoured figure plummeted to earth, ploughing through the roof of a limousine. A number of the foot-soldiers let out a small cheer of triumph, which was quickly extinguished as the still-blazing figure tore its way out of the vehicle, pumping round after round across the courtyard as the fuel that covered its power-assisted carapace burned harmlessly away.

The Gaudi foot-soldiers knew the battle was already lost, but trapped within the walls which were intended to keep them safe, they now had no choice but to fight back against the killers who had fallen into their midst. They were huge, half as tall again as any normal man and almost twice as broad, clad as they were in dull grey armour, emblazoned with the Imperial seal. Shuriken fire spattered against their breastplates like summer rain as they moved across the compound with deadly, implacable purpose. Those who threw down their alien weapons fared no better than those who died fighting. The Grey Knights of the Ordo Malleus had their orders: none who had dared lay hands on the works of the alien were to live.

By the time the gate exploded inwards in a shower of fire and debris, the compound was quiet. The Rhino transport that nosed through the ragged gap had been set down by the Thunderhawk far enough away to avoid detection and had sped towards the compound while the drop-ship delivered the rest of its cargo. Grinding to a halt in the centre of the courtyard, its tracks smeared with the pulped remains of fallen Gaudi foot-soldiers, the vehicle's side and rear hatches swung open and ten more grey-armoured figures emerged and immediately moved to set up a secure perimeter.

The Rhino's last passenger was far less physically imposing than his travelling companions. In contrast to the ceramite and plasteel wargear of the figures who now moved about the compound, gathering up the alien weapons and stowing them within the Rhino, the suit he wore would not have looked out of place on the streets of Praxis's business district. A tall man, he still only reached the shoulder of the Grey Knight who greeted him.

'The compound is secure. We await your orders,' the Space Marine's voice emerged, electronically-filtered, from his helmet grille. Although he no longer wore his jump pack and his armour bore a patina of sooty scorch marks, the insignia on his armour's shoulder plates marked him out as a sergeant of the 4th Company, the Pax Mortuus. His name was Alexos, the leader of the airborne assault team.

'So I see.' Inquisitor Belael gestured towards the low, bunker-like structure that was the only visible sign that the compound comprised more than the shattered courtyard in which they stood. 'The informer provided us with a detailed description of the chambers that lie below ground. Take your men. Clear every room. Inform me when you have located the abomination.'

'In the Emperor's name.' The Grey Knight nodded and turned away. As he marched across the compound, his assault team formed up behind him. Some had exchanged their bolt pistols for bolters, others for meltas. A krak grenade took care of the single door set into one face of the bunker and they filed cautiously inside.

Almost immediately, the sound of gunfire burst from the open doorway. The Grey Knights who had remained above ground turned, weapons held ready. As was suspected at least some of the compound's defenders had waited in hiding, while their fellows died. Judging by the way the sounds of combat grew fainter, they were able to offer little resistance to the downward progress of the sergeant's team.

Standing by the Rhino, Belael yawned. He had slept very little over the three days since the Palace of the Ecclesiarchy here on Equus III had alerted the Inquisition to the presence of a newly-formed cabal of Chaos worshippers in Praxis. He never slept well when travelling and, immediately upon his arrival in the city, had conducted his own interrogation of the informer. The company of Grey Knights, in transit after the successful completion of another operation against the followers of Chaos, had arrived while he was interviewing Kravi.

He had found Kravi to be a dullard, barely able to comprehend the forces in which he had unwittingly become enmeshed. But even the most slow-witted may do his duty in the war that was raging across the Imperium and beyond. Belael smiled as he remembered the look of almost childlike gratitude that spread across the informer's face when he told him that his loyalty to the Emperor and to Mankind would be rewarded.

Oh, yes, Belael had assured him, he would see that he was appropriately rewarded.

THE ANNEXE WAS a scorched ruin. The stench of cooked flesh hung thickly in the air as Belael stared at the sigils etched into the surface of the black stone monolith: blasphemous names, among which one stood out – Tzeentch, the Lord of Change. The polyhedron had operated as a channel for his unholy energies, but that channel was now closed. One of the crisped bodies that lay about the floor of the room would have been its human attendant. He must have warned his masters soon after the attack began. To all intents and purposes, the monolith was nothing more than an inert lump of rock. Soon it would not even be that.

'Set the charges,' Belael instructed Alexos. 'Then mine the entire compound. I have summoned the Thunderhawk. I will perform the Rite of Exorcism from the air.'

'In the Emperor's name,' the Grey Knight replied.

'Indeed,' Belael nodded. 'And once this place is little more than an unholy memory, I shall have one more job to do. In the Emperor's name.'

SITTING ALONE ON the low, hard cot in the bare cell, Mikhail had lost track of time and of how many times he had repeated his story – first to the priest in the vast nave of the palace, then to the priest's superiors, in a series of smaller chambers set high in one of the palace's spires, and then, in the cell in which he now sat, to the inquisitor. With each telling, the reality of the events he described seemed to become more distant, less real. Had he misunderstood the events at the compound? Had he broken his vow of silence for nothing? If this were the case, he could expect swift and deadly retribution from Haus Gaudi. If he wanted to avoid that, he would need protection – the kind of protection even the Haus would recognise.

'Your loyalty to the Emperor and his works shall be remembered – and rewarded,' the inquisitor had told him.

Mikhail now knew what kind of reward he most desired: induction into the priesthood. No Haus in Praxis, or any of the other cities on Equus III, would harm a member of the Ecclesiarchy. That his brother was already a priest would surely stand his request in good stead. Of course, it would mean starting over, back at the bottom of the heap, but he had done that with Graumann's crew and the Ecclesiarchy was just another organisation, like the Haus. He was smart, he would learn how to get things done, catch the eyes of his superiors and rise through the ranks. Perhaps he would be sent off-world, where the opportunities for advancement would be limitless.

'Preacher Kravi' – the title had a nice ring to it.

The thud of heavy footsteps sounded on the other side of the cell door. His guts cramped and spasmed. Just nerves, he told himself as he pressed a hand against his abdomen. Just nerves.

The door swung inwards and the inquisitor stepped into the room, followed by a towering figure: a living statue, cast from a dull grey metal that seemed to absorb the light from the cell's single ceiling light. The Imperial eagle spread its wings across the figure's chest and a human head sat atop its shoulders, whose eyes regarded Mikhail with a coldness he imagined to exist only in the gulfs between the stars.

'Did you find them?' Mikhail managed to tear his eyes from the grey apparition and turned to the inquisitor. 'Was I right? I have been waiting...'

He paused, searching for the right words to begin his petition for acceptance into the Ecclesiarchy. If an Imperial inquisitor was to lend his approval to Mikhail's request, surely none would argue.

'I have been praying that you found the blasphemers before their power grew stronger,' he continued, the words coming out in a rush. 'I... I know that I've not lived a conventional life. I have done things others would consider wrong, but... but I have always loved the Emperor. I have always been loyal. My one hope is that I may make amends for my past, prove my loyalty even further...'

Belael smiled, raised a hand to halt Mikhail's flow.

'We found them. As you suspected, they had assembled to perform another of their unholy rites. We brought it to a premature end and wiped their stain from this world. Had the stain been allowed to spread, it would have necessary to sacrifice this city, perhaps this world in the process of their annihilation.'

'Emperor be praised!' Mikhail, anxious to prove his piety, blurted out. 'I sought only to be of service to the Golden Throne. My greatest wish is to be of yet more service. Perhaps if...' He faltered as he saw the smile drop from the inquisitor's face.

'There is indeed one more service you can render to the Emperor.' In his eyes, Mikhail now saw something of the coldness he had noticed in the eyes of the grey-clad hulk that stood behind him. 'There remains one last fragment of the unholy seed your former employers sought to sow on Equus III. It must be eradicated.'

'Of course!' Mikhail gushed. 'If you need a guide, someone who knows his way around Praxis, I–' Then the meaning behind the inquisitor's words slammed home, cutting off his words.

'No!' he gasped, wincing as something inside him began to twist and thrash, claws scraping against the cage of his ribs. Belael only nodded. Taking this as a signal, the Grey Knight stepped forward, raised one massive gloved hand. Seeing that hand held a bolt pistol, emblazoned with the Imperial seal and sigils of power, Mikhail tried to say something, anything that would delay the inevitable. But all that emerged from his throat was a low, guttural snarl, as if the thrashing thing within him had seized control of his voice.

'I call upon the cleansing fire of the Emperor's gaze to purify this tainted vessel.' For the second time that day, Belael began to intone the Rite of Exorcism. Ignoring his words, Mikhail scrambled backwards across the narrow cot until his back pressed against the wall of the cell.

'As the Emperor sacrificed Himself into the eternal embrace of the Golden Throne, so it is right and proper that all those tainted by the unholy and the blasphemous should submit themselves to his judgement.' Belael's words bored into Mikhail's mind. Legs still kicking in a futile attempt to get further away from the mouth of the bolt pistol and the steady, cold gaze of the figure who held it, he raised his hands in a final pleading gesture. Absurdly, he found himself thinking of Leon Kleist, grovelling in the filth outside the Split Pig.

'By fire and shell shall they become clean. Through sacrifice shall they receive their reward.'

The bolt pistol coughed once and Mikhail Kravi, loyal servant of the Emperor, received his reward.

DEUS EX MECHANICUS

Andy Chambers

THE SCREAM OF the engines fought against the howling winds in a terrifying crescendo of doom. Hyper-velocity mica particles skittered across the hull of the ship like skeletal fingers as it wallowed in the storm, shuddering and dropping by steps as the pilot struggled for control. In the midst of the tumult, Lakius Danzager, tech-priest engineer, Votaris Laudare, illuminant of Mars, adept of the Cult Mechanicus was struggling to open up the skull of that failing pilot, and cursing in a distinctly un-priestly fashion as he struggled to find the right tools for the job.

'Dammit! Osil, find me a hydro coupling, my boy. We'll need one if I can free these accursed fasteners. Look in the vestibule.' He tried to keep his voice calm so as not to frighten his acolyte, but Osil's face was pallid in his cowl as he nodded and hurried out through the rusty bulkhead hatch.

The ship's rattling, brassbound altimeter showed them at a height of nearly seven kilometres above the planet. They had already been dropping out of control for twelve. As Lakius turned back to the rune-etched panel enclosing the ship's pilot, another violent lurch smashed his shaven skull against it, triggering an emgram patch he had only recently divined from his auto-shrine. It was about their too-rapidly approaching destination, and ran in confusing counterpoint through his right optic viewer as he tried to focus on repairing the nav-spirit.

NAOGEDDON IS A DEAD WORLD.

The ringing impact of Lakius's metal-shod head had partially freed the rusting key-bolts. With a whispered prayer for forgiveness from the already distraught machine-spirit, he bent to the task. He carefully unscrewed the panel, murmuring the rite of unbinding and ensuring that he removed the keys in the correct cardinal directions. The ghostly image of a dun-coloured sphere hovered in his right eye. Red text scrolled past it.

Orbital distance: 0.78 AU.

Equatorial Diameter: 9,749 km.

Rotation: 34.6 hours.

Axial Tilt: 0.00.

As he'd feared, the coupling between the augur spike and the pilot-stone had ruptured, blinding the pilot to its landing beacon. He checked the altimeter as he began the ritual of dislocation to remove the charred remnants. Less than two kilometres of howling winds now lay beneath their rocking hull.

Weather: See storms*.

'Osil! Where's that coupling, boy?'

'Here, father. The first one was faulty and I had to go back for another.'

0% Precipitation. Wind speed: Constant 24 kts, Variance 76 kts.

Lakius took the twist of hydro-plastic without comment but silently gave praise to the Omnissiah that the lad had been attentive enough to spot the difference. Under current circumstances, a normally forgivable sin of oversight could prove fatal. Lakius took a breath to steady himself before beginning the ritual of insertion.

Lifeforms: Autochthonic: None.

   Introduced: None.

Less than a league of free air remained before they would hurtle into solid rock. His servo-hand shook as he tried to apply the proscribed number of half-turns to the coupling mounts. He yearned to simply call the rite finished and resurrect the pilot. But years of discipline and doctrine drove him on as he completed the benediction against failure, applied the sacred unguents and retrieved the panel so he could begin the final rites of protection and sealing.

Archaeotech Resource: Limited/Xeno artifacts*/@ 600,000,000 yrs (pre.GA) Class: Omega.

'Father, I can see dust dunes below us. I think we're going to crash.'

Notes:

First Catalogued: 7/243.751.M32, Rogue trader Xiatal Parnevue. Orbital Augury Only*. Annexus Imperialus.

'Mechanism, I restore thy spirit! Let the God-Machine breathe half-life unto thy veins and render thee functional.' Lakius firmly depressed the activation rune on the pilot's casing and prayed.

Landed: 6/832.021.M35. Explorator Magos Dural Lavank. Expedition Lost.

Landed: 7/362.238.M37. Explorator Magos Prime Holisen Zi. Expedition Lost.

The ship's engines rose in a triumphant scream to drown out the rushing winds and skittering dust. Lakius and Osil felt the heavy weight of high-G deceleration as the ungainly craft steadied itself and slowed. Lakius could see dust dunes too now, through the curving port in the ship's prow, but the dunes with their trailing streamers of blowing dust were dwarfed by the serried ranks of sharp-angled black monoliths which rose up around the ship as it dipped between them. Osil let out an involuntary gasp as the scale of the structures became apparent. The monoliths were mountain-sized edifices of harsh, alien rock cutting the horizon into sawtooth edge, or a predator's maw.

Landed: 6/839.641.M41. Explorator magos Prime Reston Egal. Surface Survey*. Xeno Structures Catalogued*.

The ship changed course, angling towards a vast dark triangle which blotted out half the sky. The pilot-spirit was faithfully following the beacon now, bringing them in towards a tiny ring of light in the shadows below it. There lay the Explorators' camp.

GRITTY SAND CRUNCHED underfoot and a cold, stinging wind blew more of it into their faces as they stepped down to the landing ground. Patchwork figures of steel and flesh were rolling towards them on armoured treads; Lakius and Osil waited by the ship and made no sudden moves.

'See there, Osil: the Explorators have invoked a laser mesh for the protection of the camp. How powerful would you say it is?'

'I see three transformation engines on this side of camp. Assuming the same number on the far side I would estimate 10 to 20 gigawatts, father.'

The figures came closer. They were Praetorians, bionically reconstructed warrior-servitors of the Machine God. Their cadaverous faces gazed stonily from a nest of targeting scopes and data-wires, gun barrels and energy tubes tracked Lakius and Osil until they halted. A chest-mounted speaker on one crackled into life.

'Two lifeforms identified. Classified non-hostile. Please follow, Father Lakius, Acolyte Osil.'

They followed a pair of the heavy servitors between low buildings of pre-fabricated armourplas panelling towards a central command sphere. Osil pointed to one of the smaller structures which had its panels folded back to create a workshop lit from within by welding arcs and showers of sparks.

'What works are being undertaken here, father?'

Lakius repressed a chill sensation of foreboding 'They are re-initiating servitors, Osil. Evidently there has been some accident or mishap which has rendered the units non-functional.' He forbore to comment on the row of ready caskets outside the workshop, containers for tech-priests whose biological components were fit only for incorporation into new servitors. Several priests must have died here already.

The Praetorians motioned them into the command-sphere and remained on guard outside. Inside was a scene of barely organised chaos. Wiring cascaded from panels and conduits, devices of a hundred types thrummed, buzzed and sparked, screenplates flickered and scrolled through endless lines of scripture. A robed priest detached himself from a group clustering around the central dais and addressed Lakius.

'Adept Danzager, your arrival has been greatly anticipated. I am Adept Noam, Lexmechanic Magos Tertius. I have the honour of analysing and compiling data on this expedition.' Noam was gaunt and emotionless, only his lack of bionic enhancement and priestly robes marking him apart from the servitors. Two other priests gathered behind him. Noam pointed to each in turn and pronounced their roles with toneless efficiency.

'Adept Santos, artisan, responsible for camp construction and maintenance.' A rotund man nodded. He was heavily rebuilt with a subsidiary lifting arm at his shoulder and a mass of diagnostic probes in place of his left hand and eye.

'Adept Borr, rune priest, extrapolation and theory.' Borr was slight and nervous-looking, and seemed to be on the edge of speaking when Noam cut him off. Noam and Borr evidently didn't get along. Noam gestured to the other robed figures within the chamber.

'Adepts Renallaird, Kostas and Adso are engineers like yourself, their areas of expertise covering the mysteries of generation, augury and metriculation. Adept Virtinnian is absentia, attending to the servitors at present.' Renaillard, Kostas and Adso looked up briefly as their names were mentioned and gave a perfunctory nod before bending back to their work.

'Blessings of the Omnissiah be upon you all,' Lakius said. 'Am I to assume that you are the leader of this expedition, Adept Noam?'

'No, Explorator Magos Prime Reston Egal has that blessing. He will be joining us shortly.'

'Can you tell me why I have been summoned here then? I know that this is an important undertaking; after all, it has already made me late for my own funeral.'

If Noam understood the joke he made no sign, but Borr grinned behind his hand. Noam replied, 'Yes, you were scheduled for dissemination at the termination of your last assignment. A post with the Officio Assassinorum, I understand. You must be disappointed that your emgrams cannot yet be joined with the Machine-God.'

'In truth, it is my belief that I serve better as a living being than a collection of memories and servitor wetware.'

'Understandable, and very biological.' Something close to disdain was passed across Noam's features when he said biological. 'I see that you have never considered undertaking the unction of clear thought.'

'The unction of clear thought? What is that, father?' blurted Osil, forgetting that he should be seen and not heard amongst such adepts.

Noam replied smoothly, apparently not troubled by the acolyte's gaucheness. 'The full utilisation of cerebral mass is a simple matter of isolating our thoughts from the rigours and distractions of emotion – hunger, fear, joy, boredom and so forth. This we know as the unction of clear thought.'

'A common surgical practice among lexmechanics,' Lakius told Osil, 'whose renowned cognitive abilities are enhanced thereby.' At the price of becoming an emotionless automaton he thought to himself, before adding more diplomatically, 'In my own role as engineer I have always found crude emotions such as "fear" and "pain" to be useful motivators under the right circumstances.'

'Indeed?' Noam said, warming to his subject matter. 'Studies of stress–'

'Splendid! This must be our new expert in cryo-stasis!'

Noam was cut off by a newcomer who had lurched into the chamber like an animated scarecrow, all gangling arms and legs. His narrow, vulpine head, scrawny neck and thin body conspired to complete the illusion. He grinned voraciously at Lakius. 'Now you're finally here, we can get on with it! Splendid!'

Lakius bowed deeply. 'Magos Egal, I presume.'

'That's right. I see you've met the others and Noam's about to treat you to a sermon!' Magos Egal winked conspiratorially at Lakius, bouncing up and down on his heels as if he couldn't contain his delight. Lakius was astonished. He was used to a certain amount of... eccentricity among senior members of the Mechanicus, Explorators in particular, but Egal seemed to be verging on the edge of lunacy. 'You come highly commended, you know! Highly commended! Two centuries of experience!'

'Almost fifty aboard a single craft, servicing a single sarcophagus, magos. Admittedly, that was of alien design and its failure would have brought about my immediate dissemination – but I cannot imagine how I may be of service here.' In truth, Lakius had a strong and unpleasant suspicion exactly why cryo-stasis was of interest to this famed Explorator, but he wished to hear it said out loud.

'You can't guess? I bet you can, but you want to hear it anyway! You're a sharp one! I like that.' Egal grinned lopsidedly, 'Do you know what this place is?' Egal thrust his arms outwards to encompass the whole world.

'Naogeddon... a dead world.'

'No!' Egal thrust up a finger to make his point. 'Not dead, sleeping! Sleeping these six hundred million years!' Lakius's stomach underwent a queasy lurch.

Egal composed himself a little and went on. 'Let me begin at the beginning. Over six hundred million years ago, a race we know as the necrontyr arose and spread across the galaxy. What little we know of these giants of prehistory has been learned from a handful of so-called dead worlds, like this one, scattered at the very fringes of the galaxy. On each world stand vast, monolithic structures which have remained all but impenetrable to every device at the hand of Man. The level of technology evident in their construction is almost incomprehensible to us and many Explorators have been lost winning the fragmentary knowledge we do have.

'On my first expedition to Naogeddon, we gained certain measurements and calibrations which are singular to the dead worlds of the outer rim, these ancient seats of the necrontyr. These have enabled myself and Adept Borr to fashion a device... a key, if you will, which can unlock these structures without awakening their occupants.'

Adept Borr had grown increasingly agitated as Magos Egal spoke and now he interjected, 'Magos, the last attempt caused an exponential jump in attacks–'

Noam cut him off smoothly. 'Adept Borr, those projections have not been verified. Adept Santos has confirmed the current threat is well within the capacity of our defences to contain.'

'The current threat, yes, but if things go wrong–'

Adept Santos seemed affronted by Borr's implied criticism. 'We have a fifteen gigawatt laser mesh, twenty armed servitors and storm-bunkers built out of cubit thick, Titan grade armourplas panels. What could possibly go wrong?'

Egal had passively watched the exchange with fatherly humour and a slight grin, but now he became animated again. 'Ah yes! Speaking of which, I believe they're due to attack any time now. Stations, everyone!'

Lakius's queasy stomach lurched up towards his mouth. Sirens wailed a second later.

'You mean they attack at the same time every day?'

'Well, every dusk. Strictly speaking.'

Lakius, Osil and Borr were in an observation gallery at the top of the command sphere. As a rune priest adept, Borr was trained to piece together fragmentary information and make speculative theorem, something akin to black magic to most tech-priests. As such, Borr had explained, he was detailed to make observations of their attackers, try to understand their tactics, strengths and weaknesses and then feed effective protocols to the Praetorians.

'I thought it was already night,' Osil said.

'No, Osil, it's always this dark because of the dust in the atmosphere, most of the suns' light is reflected back into the void,' Lakius replied. 'Adept Borr, what are these attackers? Despite Adept Santos's reassurances, I note a number of casualties have already been incurred.'

'They appear to be mechanisms: humanoid, skeletal, most assuredly armed. We have not been able to secure one for study, despite strenuous efforts.'

'And I did not note an astropath adept among those spoken of so far.'

Hesitantly, Borr looked up at Lakius. His tattooed face was underlit by the greenly glowing glass of the augurs before him, but to Lakius the sickly pallor was underwritten by a deeper fear. 'Adept Arraius... disappeared prior to the very first attack. I–I fear Magos Egal has not fully thought through the implications of this site. There are machine spirits here which have functioned continuously for six hundred million years.'

Borr would have continued but an alarm began chiming, quietly but insistently.

The augur screen flashed and displayed a grid with moving icons, Borr glanced down and said, 'The Praetorians have spotted something. We should have it at any moment. There, eight energy sources, six hundred metres out on the west side. We'll have visual soon.' Another glass flashed and displayed icons. Borr was all business now, his fears forgotten in his devotion to his work. 'Eight more, at six hundred and closing from the south-east. They're tempting us to split our fire, I expect... yes here it is, a third group at six hundred metres north waiting to see which way we go.'

Outside, the dark skies had deepened to an impenetrable, inky blackness which the powerful arc lights of the camp barely kept at bay. Borr fed attack vectors and co-ordinates to the Praetorians while Lakius and Osil clustered around an augur glass. The laser mesh was shown as a ragged line of X's representing the ground based refraction spines. Red triangles approached in serried lines from two directions and held back on another angle. The Praetorians were represented by cog-shapes, in respect for their selfless devotion to the Machine-God. The Praetorians were moving southwest and an exchange of fire soon took place across the laser mesh. The tiny bolts flying back and forth on the glass was eerily echoed by the flashes visible through the observation ports. More frightening were the snaps and booms like distant lightning that came rolling across the compound.

The massed fire of the Praetorians was overwhelming the south-west group, the red triangles dimmed in quick succession, some disappearing altogether. Only two of the Praetorian-cogs showed the solid black of non-function, but even as Lakius watched one of the red triangles brightened momentarily and its shot turned another icon solid black. On the west the enemy was at the laser mesh, advancing through it in a tight wedge and destroying the spines with tightly controlled salvoes. Red lines flickered across the interloper's progress as detection beams were broken and the continuous energy flow of the mesh jumped to full output, searing through the ranks. Time and again the icons dimmed but recovered, they would soon break through. The northern group began to move.

'The north group are coming,' Lakius said.

'I see them.'

Most of the Praetorians turned west, leaving a small group to finish off the tattered southern group.

The artificial lightning storm was getting closer. Osil was not paying attention the glass any more. The scenes unfolding outside in plain sight froze him. Stray shots flashed into the camp, exploding in sparks or gouging glittering welts in Santos's storm-bunkers. Several Praetorians were in view, driving parallel with the laser mesh and firing at something out of view. More came into view from the camp, closing in around the spectral alien cohort forcing its way in from the west. The foe was terrible to see, their shining metal skulls and skeletons too symbolic to be missed. *Here is Death*, they had been built to communicate, in any language, across any gulf of time and to any race.

That was not the worst of them. These harbingers seemed in some horrible sense to live. Each was a mechanism, to be sure, but one with a fierce anime, like the idol of some ferocious, primitive god. Not only were they death, but they manifested a horrible sense of passion, even joy in their work. As machine spirits they were the most obscene perversions Lakius had ever seen, and inwardly part of him wept to see such things could still exist.

'Father,' Osil said, 'the northern group...'

Lakius couldn't tear his eyes away from the battle between the Praetorians and death machines below. The energy weapons of the aliens were frightening in their potency, their actinic bolts visibly flaying through whatever they struck layer by layer like some obscene medical scan compressed into a heart beat. The warrior-servitors fought back with plasma fire and armour piercing missiles, cutting down the skeletal apparitions one by one, but four more servitors had been cut down by the enemies' deadly accurate fire.

Borr used the same tactic again, the bulk of Praetorians broke off and wheeled north. A small group was left to finish off the alien machines which kept stubbornly rising after hits that would have stopped a dreadnought. Lakius was grateful for Borr's obvious tactical skill. If either the western or southern groups were not completely eliminated the foe would undoubtedly get a foothold inside the camp. The trouble was the Praetorians moving north to parry the third thrust numbered only six; for the first time they would not outnumber the enemy.

'Borr, set the northern face of the mesh to maximum sensitivity,' Lakius said.

'But the spines will fire continuously, dissipate into the windblown dust!'

'Mica dust,' Lakius corrected.

Borr grinned and began a rite of supplication.

THE PRAETORIANS FOUGHT well on the northern side. They used a storm bunker to narrow the angles so they only fought part of the enemy at once. Clattering forward on armoured treads, a salvo of missiles scorched across the void-black sky and cut down two enemy machines as they emerged from the las-mesh. Lightning-crack discharges of plasma burned another, but a critical overheat damaged one of the servitors as his shoulder-mounted plasma cannon suffered meltdown. Five faced five. The storm bunker was being torn to pieces, its adamantium sheath impossibly burning with metal-fires. With a groan it collapsed in on itself, revealing more of the foe at the inner edge of the mesh. The Praetorians lost two of their number for only one of the enemy. Three armoured servitors were left against four skull-faced killers. The aliens grinned their hideous, fixed grins as they stepped forward.

Without warning the laser mesh crackled into frenzy of discharges. Gigawatts of energy were dissipated into the swirling dust particles, pointlessly scattering their power in flashes of heat and light.

The flashes were harmless, but powerful enough to temporarily blind the optics of the nearby skeleto-machines. Their fire slackened momentarily and the Praetorians used the opportunity to halt and let rip with every weapon in their arsenals; bolter shells, missiles and plasma carved through the silhouetted enemy.

Osil gaped at the scopes. A moment ago he had thought he was going to be killed, but instead they had won.

They had won.

LAKIUS STOOD LOOKING at Magos Egal's 'key', a fifteen metre-long phase field generator, poised like some giant, complex syringe of steel and brass over the unyielding black stone of the alien structure. The smooth, blank wall sloped away to giddying heights, making an artificial horizon of solid black against the grey sky. Adept Renaillard was connecting power couplings at the nether region of the key-machine, quietly reciting catechisms as he anointed each socket and clamped the cables in place. Noam stood nearby, arguing with Borr about something. Four paces further along the key the magos himself was making fine adjustments to the key's controls. Four Praetorians were arrayed nearby, their torsos swivelling back and forth as they scanned for danger.

Lakius had just completed a long shift restoring what Praetorians and servitors they could from the casualties sustained in the attack. The unseen Adept Virtinnian, whose duty it was to undertake such blessings, had been crushed to death along with Adept Adso and six servitors in one of Santos's Titan grade storm bunkers. Adept Santos himself had lost an arm when he attempted to secure an alien machine which had reactivated.

If the alien machine-spirits kept to their rigid timetable the next attack was due in six hours. The thought of it crawled at the back of Lakius's mind constantly, a nagging fear which grew minute by minute, hour by hour. He wished he could find some reason to dissuade the magos, stop him pursuing this patently dangerous study, but his authority was beyond question on an expedition like this. The doctrine of the Mechanicus was clear – entire planetary populations of tech-priests could be sacrificed in pursuit of sacred knowledge; the individual weighed nothing against the Cult Mechanicus. But was this sacred knowledge or something ancient and tainted?

'All set?' Magos Egal trilled to Renaillard, who nodded his assent. 'Places everyone! Lakius, you stand with me and we can all chant the liturgy of activation together.'

Chanting in choral tones, Egal made a series of connections and static started to jump from the generator, accompanied by a rising humming noise and the reek of ozone. The black stone shimmered, glittering like quicksilver as it started to deform away from the spiralled needle of the generator. An arch was appearing, tall and tapering, of perfect dimensions and straightness. Within its angles the stone writhed and coiled like a living thing before fading away like mist to reveal the mouth of a corridor. The perfect alien symmetry of it was marred only by the head and shoulder of a Praetorian which appeared to be sunk into the wall on the left hand side – mute testimony to the previously failed attempt to penetrate the structure.

Unperturbed by its silent brother, the first Praetorian moved into the corridor, its powerful floodlights piercing the darkness within. Osil gasped, the outer shell of the structure had made him imagine the inside to be the same, unadorned stone. But the lights picked out complex traceries of silvery metal set into every surface; walls, floor and ceiling twinkled with captured starlight. A murmur of wonder rose from the gathered tech-priests. Magos Egal grinned with delight.

'You see! A simple adjustment of three degrees was all it took! Quite, quite fascinating! I haven't seen anything quite like this since the moons of Proxima Hydratica!' he chuckled. Lakius felt relieved; the Magos was evidently more accomplished than he appeared. One by one, trailing sensor cables and power threads behind, the techno-magi entered the alien structure.

The corridor with its rich silver filigrees sloped down and away. After a dozen metres it dropped down in knee-high steps for another hundred. The Praetorians struggled to negotiate the giant steps, laboriously lowering themselves over each one. The slow progress gave Lakius ample time to examine the silver-traced corridor walls. They were undoubtedly depicting script in a language of some form. Spines and whorls marched in lines apparently formed from continuous individual strands. The lines and strands of script crossed and re-crossed up and down the walls, across the floor and on high in frozen sine waves, creating the sensation that the alien language was somehow conveyed by the totality of what was before him, rather than its individual elements.

Adept Noam was taking input from a cadaverous-looking scanning servitor, a long umbilical connecting its oversized eye-lenses to a socket in the lexmechanic's chest. Borr was nearby, puzzling over a hand-held auspex.

'Can you make anything of it, Adept Borr?' Lakius whispered to the rune priest. The sepulchral quiet of the necrontyr monolith seemed to demand silence, as if noise would manifest all of its invisible, crushing weight to punish the impudent interlopers.

By unspoken agreement none of the party had broken that brooding silence with more than a harsh whisper since they had entered.

'No, I'm not sure that it's supposed to be read in the human optic range. Set your view-piece to read magnetic resonance and you'll see what I mean.'

Lakius fumbled with the focusing knob on the rim of his artificial eye, tuning it to scan electromagnetic frequencies. The corridor was bathed in it, every whorl and spine was a tiny energy source which glowed with magnetic force. The overall effect was dizzying, like walking through a glass corridor over an infinite gulf full of stars. After a time Lakius had to reset his vision to blank it out.

After an hour of descent the corridor flattened out and then twisted sharply to the right before being blocked by a portal of black metal. The two lead Praetorians halted before it, their floodlights darkly reflected in the glossy metal of the obstacle. Three geometric symbols were marked on it at knee, waist and shoulder height.

'Should we use weapons fire, magos?' One of the Praetorians asked, its plasma cannon eagerly swivelling into the ready position. Magos Egal shook his head, stepping up to the door with Noam faithfully shadowing him with his trailing servitor.

'No, no,' Egal muttered 'I'm sure it's a simple matter of–' He touched the metal of the portal. Lakius flinched slightly, fearing some ancient necrontyr death trap. Nothing happened. 'Understanding how to trigger these symbols.'

A pregnant silence fell behind Egal's words. Noam began analysing the symbols, cross-referencing with all the data he stored in his machine-enhanced brain.

Lakius softly let out a breath he been holding until he heard a new sound, a low buzz which rose quickly to a high pitched whine. It sounded horribly like a weapon charging up, its capacitors being filled to maximum before it unleashed an atomising blast. Hairs rose on Lakius's neck. The sigils were flickering with their own light now; their ghostly fingers of energy could be felt tangibly. The Praetorians sensed it too and went to a threat response, readying and charging their own weapons with a hiss of servos and whine of capacitors.

Lakius felt a surge of panic, as if he stood beneath a giant hammer which would smash down at any second. He wanted to run back up the corridor but his way was blocked by the two rearmost Praetorians. They were agitatedly swivelling back and forth with their baleful targeting eyes lit as they searched for enemies. One of them turned far enough to spot its companion and its ruby eye irised down into a pinpoint as it locked on target. The Praetorian's plasma cannon crackled up to a full charge, a compressed lightning bolt which would annihilate anything within metres of its impact point.

Osil was gibbering with fear.

Lakius was shouting out command dogma: 'Praetorians! Audio primus command! Deus ex Terminus est.'

The cannon fired, a searing flash and thunderclap which tore through the other Praetorian and sent white-hot shrapnel scything down the corridor. Osil bravely shouldered Lakius to one side, saving the old engineer from a fiery demise. Shouts and another roar echoed from near the portal, a wave front of scorching heat washed back up the corridor. The nearby Praetorian swivelled round and trained its plasma cannon on Lakius and Osil, its eye glowed with single-minded determination to destroy as it narrowed at them.

'Ergos Veriat excommen!' Lakius shouted hoarsely. 'Shut down!'

The Praetorian sagged down on its chassis like a puppet with its strings cut and the crisis was over as suddenly as it had begun. The eerie silence fell like a curtain which was broken by the crackle of tiny fires, the plink of cooling metal and the groans of Osil as he writhed on the blood slick slabs. Metal splinters had struck him in his side when he saved Lakius. By the blessings of the Omnissiah, the wounds were not too deep and Adept Borr shrived them with a somatic welder.

Adept Renaillard had not been so lucky and a shard of smouldering casing had struck him in the throat, almost shearing his head off. Smoke rose from the smouldering remains of the two Praetorians nearest the portal. Noam's servitor had been destroyed in the exchange of fire as the two destroyed each other, but Magos Egal and the lexmechanic were unharmed.

'A sophisticated form of faeran field,' Noam explained dispassionately. 'It was cut off when I completed decryption of the portal locks.' A faeran field interfered with brain functions, inducing, among other things, extreme fear responses and seizures. Lakius couldn't help but think the lexmechanic sounded a little smug. Clear thought indeed.

Beyond the portal the corridor appeared to continue as before. Osil was sorely hurt in spite of Borr's ministration, and Lakius undertook the rituals to reboot the solitary remaining Praetorian so that it could carry him back to the surface. Osil protested weakly, but Lakius spoke a few quiet

words to him before sending him on his way. The young
acolyte looked very much like a child clinging to the Praetorian's wide back and Lakius prayed that nothing was
waiting back there in the darkness for them. With only four
tech-priests left in the expedition it seemed dangerous to
Lakius to push on, but the Magos insisted, convinced they
were at the verge of a breakthrough.

EGAL'S BREAKTHROUGH PROVED to be a labyrinth. The corridor
split and then split again and again to become many. The
different ways sloped sharply up and down, some narrowing
to slits too small for even a servomat to enter. Within three
turns Lakius felt thoroughly disorientated. The marching
hieroglyphs on the walls seemed to hint at other corridors
lying just out of sight, showing outlines of other labyrinths,
turnings, dead ends which were just out of phase with themselves. In the Mechanicus doctrine the faeran portal alone
would have been the subject of months of careful study
before further advance was made. The twistings of this alien
maze would constitute a lifetime's work with studies of
geometry and numerology.

Magos Egal was in no mood to linger, though, and he set
Noam and Borr to calculating a path through. Adept Noam's
vast analytic power was directed entirely onto building an
accurate map of the interweaving passages they moved
through using direct observation, phasic scanning, micro-
pressure evaluation and tactile interrogation. Adept Borr
used his carefully learned arts conjecture and intuition to
understand the underlying structure of the maze, and to
determine what kind of xenomorphic logic would guide
them through it.

Lakius was reduced to doing the work of a servitor, spool-
ing out power thread and invoking marker-points at each
junction so that Noam could tick them off on his mental
plan.

The spool's metriculator showed less than a thousand
metres left of its five kilometre length when they found
another portal, though the term seemed inappropriate for
the gargantuan metal slabs confronting them.

The gleaming, baroquely etched metal stretched up into the darkness further than their hand lights could reach. The corridor angled away in either direction, following some inner wall but leaving a sizeable vestibule that the four Explorators now occupied. They were dwarfed by the new barrier, rendered so insignificant that the opening of those titanic gates could only foretell their doom at the hand of something ancient and monstrous. Adept Noam did not even flinch as he stepped forward to begin deciphering the locking-glyphs.

Lakius's mouth was dry with fear as the adept began tracing the first glyph. He looked back along the corridor, sure he had heard some scuttling noise. The twinkling silver traceries hurt his eyes, mechanical and organic. It took him a moment to realise that shapes were moving across them. Silvery, glittering shapes.

'Watch the rear!' Lakius shouted and hefted his personal weapon, an ancient and beautifully crafted laser made by Ortisian of Arkeness, whose spirit he had long tended to. Its angry red lash was sharp and true: it caught a shape, which blew apart in a blinding flash which spoke of minor atomics. The others crouched on their spindly legs and then leapt forward, buzzing down the corridor like a swarm of metallic insects.

Each was the size of a man's torso, flattened at the edges like scarabs and fringed with vicious looking hooks and claws. They were fast but so aggressive that they impeded each other's progress as they rattled and bounced over one another. Borr's bolt launcher joined its roaring song to the hiss of Lakius's laser. Their combined fire clawed down three more of the steely scarabs. Nonetheless, Lakius and Borr had to back towards the doors to keep their distance as more swarmed forward.

'Keep them back!' shouted Egal. 'Noam almost has it!'

Their backs were almost against the doors already. Lakius focused all his attention on tracking and eliminating the machine-scarabs, his laser flickering from one to another in a deadly dance of destruction. But they were still getting closer. One scarab ducked between two of its fellows at the point of their destruction, and surged forward while the tech-priests were half-blinded by the explosions. The machine's scrabbling claws ripped Borr's bolter from his hands before its momentum carried it over Lakius's head. It bounced off a wall and arrowed down amongst the priests. Lakius flinched away and saw it clamp on to Adept Noam's back even as he completed the last sigil. Surgical-sharp hooks ripped into the lexmechanic as the twin portals began to slowly separate.

'Could someone remove this?' Noam asked calmly, like a man being troubled by a wasp on a summer's day. 'I–'

The scarab exploded like a miniature nova and Adept Noam was gone, consumed in an actinic fireball which knocked Lakius flat. He rolled desperately, purple after-images flashing in his vision, ears filled with the roar of detonation. He expected to feel the dread weight of one of the machines landing on him at any second.

OSIL LAY GRIPPED to an operating table by steel bands, the arms of an auto chirurgeon delicately sliced at his skin, pulling forth steel splinters and suturing his torn flesh together. Pain blockers numbed his body but his mind was racing. Father Lakius had told him to prepare their sacred cargo for release. Such a dangerous undertaking was normally only made in response to a signal from the Adeptus Terra on distant Earth.

To begin the investiture of the living weapon the ship carried in cryo-stasis without the initiation code was tantamount to suicide. If the assassin's crypt was opened without receiving the preparatory mnemonics and engrams specifying its target it would kill everything it found until it was destroyed.

Father Lakius, he concluded, must privately believe things had gone very, very wrong indeed.

LAKIUS FLINCHED AS something gripped his shoulder and started dragging him backwards. He realised someone was trying to pull him to safety and kicked his legs to scramble across the floor.

Moments later, Lakius's vision cleared enough to see that he was beyond the doors and that they were closing. The dark slit of the corridor outside narrowed rapidly as they smoothly swept together. He pointed the laser still gripped in his shaking hand but no scarab-machines came through the gap before it sealed.

'Splendid! They are without and we are within,' Magos Egal's voice said, close to Lakius's ear.

He scrambled to his feet as quickly as he could, fearfully looking around. Egal stood nearby and beyond him the chamber they had entered could be seen in its full majesty. Huge, angular buttresses marched away down either wall, the floor sloped gently downward. Frosty pillars of greenish light shone down from an unseen roof to reveal row upon row of tall blocks covered in angular alien script. The air held a chill and the silence of the labyrinth outside had given way to a gentle susurration like waves against distant shore.

'Where's Adept Borr?' Lakius demanded. Egal turned away from his accusing gaze, looking off down the cyclopean chamber.

'I'm sorry, I had to shut the portal or the scarabs would have killed all of us,' Egal seemed genuinely repentant. He could not even meet Lakius's gaze.

'You just left him outside!' Lakius's angry words rang hollow even to him. The young rune priest was dead and recriminations would not bring him back. They were trapped at the centre of the monolith now, the heart of the ancient structure. The Mechanicus-trained academic in him was already studying the chamber, too awed by the storehouse of alien archaeotech to give thought to the cost already incurred. The rows of man-high blocks seemed familiar, something about them... understanding blossomed with a now-familiar tang of fear.

'These are cryo-stasis machines,' he whispered. Metriculation memo-chips in his optic viewer calmly extrapolated that the chamber held over a million of them.

'It's what I brought you to see. They resemble the cryo-crypt of the Assassinorum vessel you arrived in, do they not?

The best is at the centre, these are just… servants. Come and we may look upon a sight no living thing has seen in six hundred million years.'

Egal moved off down the slope and Lakius numbly followed. They passed block after block, each glittering with a rime of ancient frost. The floor got steeper until they had to crawl on hands and knees, gripping the blocks to lower themselves down to a flat circular section dominated by an immense stasis crypt. It was a sarcophagus in form, its top moulded into a representation of what lay within. Lakius expected to see a mask of death like the machine warriors, but instead found vivid life rendered in polished metal, beautiful but inhuman and cruel. Rows of sigils around the lid shone with an inner light, and it felt warm to the touch.

'Its already been opened,' said Lakius. 'Help me move the lid. I need to see inside.'

Between them they managed to turn the huge, heavy lid, swivelling it to reveal the interior. The sarcophagus was empty.

Egal seemed unsurprised; in fact, he was delighted. 'Splendid! Just as I had hoped.' He reached a gangling arm into the sarcophagus and brought out a silvery, metallic staff.

'Lakonius described an artefact like this in the Apocrypha of Skarros. He spoke of a symbol of mastery born by the lords of the necrontyr, called the "staff of light".' He hefted the ornate device in both hands. As he did so, an intense blue-white light flared in the symbol at the top of the staff. 'With this, we need fear no denizen of this edifice; with time they can even be tamed and made to serve.'

'But what of the occupant of the crypt?' Lakius asked, nervously noting the maniacal gleam in Egal's eye. 'The lord and master of this place that we're plundering from? I fear in our current circumstances we could scarcely fend off any kind of attack and that artefact is more likely to draw one to us. We should go while we still can.'

'Very well, but the staff of light could be our salvation. It would be madness to leave it behind.'

* * *

OSIL LIMPED TOWARDS the landing field where their ship lay. He had agonised greatly about whether to accede to his mentor's request. By Imperial and Mechanicus law, the activation of one of the lethal members of the Officio Assassinorum without proper authorisation was treason of the highest order. Death of the flesh would be a secondary consideration beside the terrible punishments that would entail.

But Osil had spent almost twenty Terran years in the company of Lakius Danzager, studying the tasks he would one day continue when the father was gathered to the Librarium Omnissiah. He had imagined he would spend the rest of his life aboard the ageing cutter, maintaining its systems and preparing its cargo of Imperial vengeance when it was required. That was not going to be the case now. Osil had learned enough of Lakius's clarity to understand that the Explorator's expedition was woefully inadequate in the face of the alien terrors of Naogeddon. Father Lakius feared the worst, that they were about to unwittingly unleash something so terrible that he believed only an adept of the Eversor temple would have a chance of stopping it. And so the assassin must be prepared.

MAGOS EGAL STRODE ahead confidently through the labyrinth, thrusting out the staff like a torch, its fierce light burning back the shadows and setting the hieroglyphs aflame with blue-white flashes. Lakius scuttled along behind him, jumping at each new scraping, slithering noise, jabbing his pistol towards each new vagrant glitter of steel as it flicked out of sight behind a corner. The denizens of the labyrinth were dogging their heels, giving back before the circle of light from the staff and closing in behind.

After what seemed like an eternity they reached the first portal where they had fallen foul of the faeran field. The melted wreckage of the Praetorians and Renaillard's body were gone, the corridor clear except for the power threads trailing off into the darkness. Magos Egal wanted to stop and investigate but Lakius feared some assault would take place if they lingered, and urged him to press on. The soft scrapes and scratches of movement were behind them now, but following closely all the time. As they started to climb the steps Lakius looked back and caught sight of dozens of tiny lights floating in the gloom. They looked like blue fires, seemingly cold and distant, but drifting forward in pairs, the twin eye-lights of murder-machines on their trail.

The cool grey light of the outside seemed blinding after the blackness within. The edges of the phasic rift in the structure's outer sheath were wavering alarmingly and they ran past the entombed Praetorian to stumble out onto the gritty dust of the surface. It took Lakius a moment to gain his breath and he looked up to see Egal making adjustments to the phase generator.

'You're shutting it down, I trust,' said Lakius.

'Quite the contrary; I'm stabilising it so we can use the same entryway to go back in.'

'That's what I thought,' Lakius said, and fired his laser.

OSIL'S KNEES ALMOST failed him when he saw their ship. A living sheath of machines covered it, their silvery bodies shifting over one another as they sought a way inside. The ship carried a great many devices to prevent tampering, as Osil knew all too well. If the machines found a way in, or worse still tried to breach the hull, the results could be devastating. He turned and forced his torn legs to start back to the command sphere.

EGAL DARTED AWAY from Lakius's laser with inhuman quickness. But Lakius had been aiming at the phase generator's power couplings, and the hit was more spectacular than he had imagined. The key-machine detonated and then imploded, a halo of white-hot flame flashing outwards for a moment before it was dragged back. A ragged distortion-veil skated erratically over the machine, crushing it smaller and smaller as it tried to suck everything nearby into it. Egal had been blown clear, but was left wrestling to hold onto the alien staff of light as it was drawn inexorably towards the rift.

'Help me, Lakius. I can't hold it!' Egal shouted over the piercing shriek of air being annihilated in the void. Lakius levelled his laser at the magos and shot him in the head without replying. Egal fell back clutching his face. The staff plunged into the rift and exploded with a crack like lightning. Ozone hung heavy in the air as Lakius backed away through the laser mesh spines towards the camp. He spared a glance for his treasured weapon's indicator jewel, and saw it was dim. His last shot had been at full strength, enough to punch through plasteel. Magos Egal was still moving, standing up.

'Have you any idea how hard it was to get this texture right?' he demanded indignantly, indicating the side of his face that had been caressed by a steel-burning laser. Charred welts revealed glittering metal beneath, quicksilver curves that betrayed an inhuman, yet familiar, anatomy. Lakius kept moving back, the figure of the thing that had pretended to be Egal was getting reassuringly distant, dwarfed by the solid black base of the alien structure. A pair of Praetorians came rattling forward from amidst the stormbunkers, balefully scanning Lakius with their targeters.

'One life form identified. Classified non-hostile,' one concluded.

The magos-thing was at the laser mesh. It leapt suddenly, astoundingly covering the hundred metres to Lakius and the Praetorians in a single somersaulting bound.

'One life form identified. Classified non-hostile,' the other Praetorian stated.

'Surely you didn't believe these clattering toys would be able to identify me?' the Egal-thing smiled. 'I had thought you one of the more intelligent specimens.'

Lakius's mouth was dry with fear, but he managed a curt nod of acceptance before crying out 'Praetorians! Audio primus command! Overwatch!' The Praetorians locked their weapons onto the alien with eye-blurring speed, their simple brains entirely devoted to obliterating the first rapid movement they sensed.

'You forget that I spent time repairing servitors after the last battle. I took the liberty of updating their command protocols at the same time,' Lakius said with more courage than he felt.

The thing smiled more broadly still, and slowly cocked its head to one side. The Praetorians' weapons tracked the minute movement faithfully.

'Good for you, Lakius Danzager. You really are a clever one. How did you know I wasn't human?'

Lakius hesitated for a moment. The thing before him exuded an almost primal sense of power. It was at his mercy for the present, but his instincts told him it could pounce on him at any moment. The Mechanicus in him yearned to learn what he could about it while his humanity screamed out to destroy it. His curiosity overpowered his instincts for a moment.

'I wasn't sure, but either you were the thing from the crypt or an insane Explorator who was bent on unleashing something unspeakable upon the world. When I understood that, my choices became clear. How did you replace Egal? Did he wake you in there?' Icy daggers caressed Lakius's back as he talked to the thing. Its silver and flesh smile widened even further.

'What makes you think I replaced him at all? I have travelled a great distance since my first waking, walked in many places that have changed so very much since I saw them last.'

'What were you seeking?' whispered Lakius.

The thing's ferocious smile was spread almost ear to ear. 'Knowledge, mostly. I wanted to know how the galaxy had fared; who was left after the plague. You can't imagine my surprise on finding your kind and the krork scattered everywhere. I've seen you humans trying to forge an empire in the name of a corpse; I have seen your churches to the machine. Racially, your fear and superstition are most gratifying. You make excellent subjects.'

'You are necrontyr, then. You went into stasis to escape a disease.'

'No, your language is inefficient. The plague was not a disease and it couldn't harm us, but…' The necrontyr tilted its head back as if dreaming of long lost times. 'It was killing everything else.' It looked back at Lakius. 'And no, I am not a necron. You mistake the slave for the master. You'll understand better when I take you back inside.'

It leapt. The Praetorians blazed into it with lasers and plasma, their bolts lashing at the thin form. Lakius was momentarily blinded by the orgy of destruction, and he fled towards the command centre in the hope of finding reinforcements. He looked back to see a silvery figure ripping pieces out of one the Praetorians. The other battle-servitor was smouldering nearby. The figure waved a piece of carapace jauntily at Lakius.

'Sorry, Lakius, I couldn't resist it,' the thing called 'My race raised what you call "melodrama" to a high art form before you were even evolved.' It chuckled and returned to eviscerating the Praetorian.

LAKIUS WAS SPINNING the locks shut on the command centre hatch when he sensed a presence behind him. He turned, too terrified and weary to fight but wanting to see his nemesis. He almost died of relief when he saw it was Osil.

'Osil, it's–'

'I know, father, I was watching on the monitor.'

'The assassin?' Lakius gasped as he sagged to the ground.

'I couldn't reach the ship, it was covered by a swarm of insect machines. I'm afraid they'll trigger its anti-tampering protocols sooner or later. I searched for something we could use to protect ourselves but there are only components, nothing complete.'

'I fear the thing out there may survive the blast anyway. If so it would be better to–'

A ringing blow sounded against the hatch, making both Osil and Lakius jump. Then another blow slammed into it, then a third. At the third blow a bulge appeared in the Titan-grade adamantium plate. Silence fell.

'I think we'd better look at those components, Osil.' Lakius said, struggling to his feet. Osil fussed around him, his fears assuaged by having someone else to think about. He showed Lakius the ready-caskets and crates he had brought.

'I've performed the rites of preparation on these pieces, and anointed the calibrators,' Osil said hopefully. A hissing, popping noise came from the hatch, and a bright heat-spot formed at its centre.

Lakius looked at the mass of unconnected components and despaired.

THE HEAT SPOT had made a complete orbit of the door, leaving a trail of molten fire behind it. As the circle was closed the metal fell inward of its own weight, clanging to the ground and sending up a cloud of reeking fumes. A tall, inhuman figure stepped through the gap.

'Mechanism, I restore thy spirit. Let the God-Machine breathe half-life unto thy veins and render thee functional,' muttered Lakius, scarcely looking up. Osil gaped at the apparition, sure that his life was over.

'Ah, splendid, both of you,' it grinned. 'Don't tell me you've been trying to make something to stop me? With all your chanting and bone-rattling it would take days, years!'

There was a flash outside, and seconds later a titanic roar. The blast wave from the assassinorum vessel's plasma reactor going critical was a second behind that.

'Don't worry, I can save you.' The thing grinned again.

'No need,' grated Lakius and closed the last connection.

A dome of shimmering, bluish light sprang into being. It filled the hatchway with the necron-master frozen at its centre. It was a charcoal-black silhouette in the glare of the plasma-flash beyond the field. The rest of the armoured command centre shook and rattled alarmingly but held, its vulnerable hatch protected by Lakius's improvised stasis bubble.

After the blast wave had passed there was a long moment of silence before Osil asked. 'Father, won't the Omnissiah be angry that you mistreated all those Machine Spirits making the field?'

'Let it be our secret, Osil. Deus Ex Mechanicus. The Emperor watches over us.'

BARATHRUM

Jonathan Curren

NIGHT, AND THE site is quiet as a morgue. The only sound is the gentle clink clink of chains rustling from the high ceiling, connected to the crane mechanisms running from gantries the length of the hangar. Machines hum silently, a faint disturbance of the air the only sign that they are active. The occasional light pierces the twilight walkways and balconies, stairways and alcoves. Archaeo-site R347 is the inside of a great hive, its workers and machines the silent insects, termites in the service of the Machine-God.

Tech-Brother Crans stands bent over a workbench, a tray of thick viscous fluid in front of him. Immersed in the unguents is an array of fine machinery, tiny metal plates and wires meshed together in intricate fractal patterns. Crans murmurs prayers, manipulator gloves caressing the fine wires, divining rods following the paths of energy locked in the device.

He straightens up, stretching his sore back. Removing the manipulators, he lays them down on the workbench and raises the optical enhancers from in front of his eyes. Balancing them on his forehead, he rubs his tired eyes with his fingers. He's worked with mechanical optics all his life, yet has steadfastly refused bio-implants of his own, maintaining that the optics he was born with would see him to the grave.

Something. A noise, almost inaudible.

Crans turns round.

'Hello,' he calls, quietly, almost so as not to disturb the tranquillity of the place.

He appreciates the silence and solitude, it's why he chooses to work at night. He doesn't want to disturb it. 'Is anybody there?'

Nothing.

He turns back to the workbench, flipping the opticals back down in front of his eyes. The component swings back into view, large as a fist. He picks up the manipulators.

A crash, as something falls behind him.

He spins round, and something fills his vision, the opticals fighting to make sense of the image, magnified hundreds of times.

Then his sight fills with red mist as something hard and sharp shatters the opticals, plunges into the flesh around his eyes, driving through bone and filling his head with fiery pain.

The last thing he hears before the darkness of death overwhelms him is the soft shuffle of slippered feet walking quickly towards him.

ECHO TWELVE BEARING *three three zero, range forty clicks and counting. Requesting landing permission, code blue seven zero seven. Over.*

A burst of static. Then.

Echo Twelve, landing permission granted. Proceed to landing bay seven zero seven.

The Imperial shuttle drifted slowly through the cloud cover, its wings jostled by the heavy thick air. Red dust thrown up by the industrial exchange outlets down on the surface swirled into the engines, causing the rotor-blades to shudder. Wind howled around the tiny craft, as if daemons of the air competed to swallow it.

Inquisitor Anselm watched the red crosshairs of the nav-com playing across the face of the pilot as he struggled to keep the shuttle on its computer-assisted course. The pilot's right hand was jacked into the shuttle's controls and his bio-eye scanned the clouds for the first lights of the landing bay. Technobabble issued from the cabin speakers as the cogitators spoke to the pilot at a rate of several thousand words mixed with binary codes a minute.

Looking into the swirling maelstrom outside the shuttle's forward screens, he was surprised to see his own reflection staring back at him. A craggy face, weathered by long tours of duty in the Emperor's service made him look older than his years. Long-service studs embedded above his eyes glinted in the winking lights from the console. A shock of close-cropped white hair, dark, hooded eyes, an imperious nose added to his imposing figure, made people think carefully before crossing him. He knew full well the advantage it gave him.

Gazing at himself like this made him uncomfortable, and he turned away. He felt impatience grip him, and he forced himself to stay calm. It was a long time since he'd last seen Cantor, many years, and he freely admitted that he was looking forward to seeing his old friend. But that wasn't the only reason he was pleased to have been assigned this investigation. There was something else, the opportunity to investigate a crime at the very limits of Imperial jurisdiction. Only a short hop from unexplored space itself. He'd never travelled this far before, and now he was entering the atmosphere of Barathrum, a planet that despite years of extensive archaeological investigation, was still a mystery to Imperium scholars. Who knew what may happen this far from the centre of Imperial space? Not that this sort of thing meant anything to an Imperial inquisitor, but at the back of his mind, he knew that heading such an investigation could propel him along the road leading to the highest echelons of the Inquisition.

The shuttle docked, and the pilot unplugged himself from the console, pale from the concentration needed for their landing. Anselm unbuckled himself, and felt his seat relax, its shape melting away from his body. The shuttle's hatch opened with a hiss of compressed air, and as he walked down the rampway, his senses were assaulted with the smells of ozone, oil, metal and industrial solvents. His enhanced olfactory system idly recognised a dozen different chemical compounds, but before his brain had time to register them, he heard his name being called.

'Anselm! Anselm! I'm so glad you've made it.'

He looked over to the double doors facing the shuttle hangar. A tall thin man approached, dressed in brown robes with a leather apron from which hung tools, calibrating instruments and various optical measures. His face was flushed, and he was sweating slightly. They gripped each other's forearms in an old comradely gesture. Cantor indicated that they should walk, and they boarded the enclosed monorail pod that he'd just emerged from.

As the monorail slowly accelerated, Anselm was the first to voice what he was thinking.

'Cantor, it's good to see you. It has been a long time. It saddens me that after all these years, we only get the chance to meet on such an ominous occasion.'

'You've read the transcripts? There is something unnatural happening. I'm glad you are here.'

'It's affected you deeply.' It was a statement, not a question. 'You look flushed. Have you not been sleeping? You look uneasy.'

'No, my sleep is fine. You always were an apothecary first and foremost. But that is not why I am uneasy.'

Cantor reached out and stabbed a finger at the panel of buttons by the door. The monorail slowed, and a light started flashing on the console.

Anselm looked at him. 'What is it? Is there something you need to tell me? Remember that I am the Emperor's ear here. Speak freely.'

Cantor lowered his voice. 'There is something you should know. You are not the only member of the Emperor's Inquisition here on Barathrum.'

Anselm felt something clench in his stomach. 'What do you mean?' he demanded.

His friend paused, and at that moment, the pod slowed to a stop, the doors sliding gently open on a waft of pneumatic air.

The inquisitor stepped out into a long room. At one end was a huge window, filling the whole wall. Silhouetted against the setting sun were two figures, one bulky, the other slight. Anselm strode towards the figures, and as he approached, the pair turned round.

Surprise stopped Anselm in his tracks, but he made an effort to steady himself.

'Grogan! What in the Emperor's name are you doing here?'

The tall man smiled a smile that made Anselm's blood boil. His smaller companion looked confused. He recovered himself quickly, and bowed to Anselm in greeting, a half bow of respect to an equal. Anselm returned the gesture, never taking his eyes off Grogan.

Inquisitor Grogan was tall, taller than Anselm and many years older. His eyes were cold, and seemed fixed on the middle distance, as if permanently watching out across the broad expanse of tundra that comprised his home planet had fixed his gaze far away; a long moustache drooped on either side of his lips, giving him a permanently sour expression. He wore rough clothes tied together with an immense belt from which hung a myriad of tools, knives and weapons, along with devices best left unrecognised. It was if he wanted to make it clear that he would brook no nonsense of the kind that flourished in courts and palaces across the galaxy. He had a reputation for harshness and inflexibility that Anselm could attest to and that reputation had no doubt preceded his arrival on Barathrum. No wonder Cantor was nervous.

'So,' the smaller man started, 'you two know each other?'

Grogan turned to his companion. 'Anselm was a pupil of mine. When he was first elevated to the rank of inquisitor adept, he was entrusted into my care.'

'That was many years ago,' Anselm cut in, and then stopped, angry with himself. It was a long time ago, long enough for him to have worked through the anger that his time under Grogan's tutelage had left him. He continued. 'The inquisitor and I have worked together before. We know each other's methods well. Our differing approaches will no doubt cover all the possibilities in this situation.' He gave Grogan a meaningful look and was relieved to see him back down. The man merely grunted in reply and indicated the man standing at his side. 'Anselm, this is Eremet. He is the master explorer in charge of the work here on Barathrum.'

Eremet bowed, and extended one hand to Anselm. His grip was strong, the skin rough and weathered. The explorer's face was open, friendly. 'The holy Inquisition is most welcome on Barathrum,' he said. 'You've read Cantor's report?'

'I have,' Anselm replied. 'But I would hear it from your mouth. There are many ways to tell the same story.'

'Follow me then. Perhaps when you see, you will understand more than if you simply listen.'

Eremet led them through a set of double doors and down a short flight of stairs. He pushed open a plain door and they entered a clean bright room that smelled of antiseptic. Racks of surgical instruments lined the walls, and an operating table stood under bright theatre lights. Behind a green cloth screen, just visible from the doorway, stood a row of gurneys, each holding a shrouded figure.

The master explorer moved the screen aside and stood beside the first body.

With a flick of his hand, he removed the shroud from the figure. Despite himself, Anselm felt his stomach heave. He was no stranger to battle and the hideous wounds that resulted from close combat, but this was no war-wound. The face had been mutilated almost beyond recognition, great gouging marks like those of a wild beast scoured the face from top to bottom. The jaw had been broken by the violence of the attack, and the mouth hung open, making it look like the corpse had been interrupted in the process of screaming. One eye had been destroyed, the socket torn across, but the other stared out between curtains of ragged flesh.

Eremet's voice was matter of fact. 'We have lost six of our company in the past eight work cycles. The first to go missing, Aleuk, was found in sector four, one of the mid-city areas, then one by one we lost the others, each one deeper and further in towards the heart of the city. And now, Crans, he was working at the furthest point that we have excavated...'

'How big is the city?' asked Anselm. 'All I saw on the flight in was the bunker and the landing bay.'

Eremet laughed. 'That is all you would see. The bunker is in fact the highest part, the spire if you like, for a great city that has sunk beneath the sands of this planet. It once stood proud above the ground, but something in ages past made it sink through the sand, and now all that lies above the earth is this part.'

'How far does the city extend?'

'The city stretches underneath us for over five kilometres. We've only mapped the core. The deeper we get, the more spread out it is – we estimate up to ten kilometres in diameter at the deepest points – and the less we know. The city is incredibly complex in design, but Cantor is the best tech-priest explorator there is. Every time we were halted in our efforts, Cantor advised us where to dig next, and, each time, we made such progress that we were able to carry on.

'As I was saying, Aleuk was in sector four, about three kilometres down. Our servitors had just cut into a new area – a lot of the work here involves cutting or digging through debris to reach a new level – and this level was much older. There was less concrete and steel, much of the building was formed from great blocks of hewn stone.

'The standard of masonry is extraordinarily high, there's hardly a gap between any of the blocks. It's quite astonishing.

'One of our adepts was taking geochron readings, trying to gauge how old the area was. How it happened we haven't been able to discover but one of the blocks from the ceiling must have been loose. It fell, blocking the corridor he was in and cutting the man off from the rest of the team. It was then it happened. He was attacked. The sound of him screaming in pain and fear could be heard from the other side. It was horrible.'

'You were there?' asked Grogan.

'No, I wasn't. I was here in the medi-bay.'

'Alone?'

'Yes.'

What about the other corpses?' asked Grogan.

Silently, Eremet moved from trolley to trolley, pulling back the sheets that covered the forms, until all the corpses lay exposed, side by side in death like a roll-call of the slain. Each of them was terribly torn, the flesh of each flayed back from their musculature and in places bones, cracked and splintered, appeared through the tattered muscles.

'The others disappeared and were found, each one deeper down in the structure of the city. I had to order the complete shutdown of all our operations until you came.'

Anselm cast a critical eye over the display.

'Has the cause of death been established for each?' he asked Eremet.

Grogan snorted. 'I think the cause of death is pretty self-evident. Attack by some sort of wild beast, could be a 'stealer or some other species of 'nid. Something big and dangerous. Look at that one – his arms have been ripped off. Complication of the simple always was one of your…'

He broke off, and turned to Eremet. 'Master explorator, I think this is a clear-cut case of xeno-infestation, type unknown. Unless there's some other evidence to the contrary, I would say this is not a crime-scene. I suggest that, as we're here, we find your missing tech-priest, hunt whatever's running loose here and move on.'

He turned to Anselm. 'Cantor's already explained to me that the missing tech-priest was scheduled to work on some newly discovered archaeotech, in a recently excavated area, sector twenty-eight. I suggest we start looking for him there. Eremet, do you have weapons here?'

'No – this site has been active for years and we've never had any problems with hostiles. It's away from the main trade routes, we have no trouble from pirates or xenomorphs. The Imperial zoologians who surveyed the planet found no indigenous life that posed a threat, and the planet itself has a green security rating.'

'Well, we have,' Grogan countered. 'So soon there won't be any indigenous life forms around to threaten anyone!' Then he added, as if to himself, 'The Inquisition is a tool of cleansing fire. It's time to light the flame.'

He turned and stalked out of the medi-bay.

'Follow me,' Anselm said and moved swiftly after the inquisitor. They caught up with him in the control room, where he was waiting for Cantor to guide them. The tech-priest handed each of them a torch from a rack, then led the way out of the control room and towards a pair of lifts. Stopping only to pull his combat shotgun from his kit bag, Anselm followed him. Once inside, they stood silently while Cantor jabbed at buttons with his finger. The lift doors closed and a gentle humming sound filled the small room. There was a barely perceptible shift as the lift started to descend. There was almost no sensation of falling but Anselm felt his ears popping before the lift came to a gentle halt about a minute later. The doors opened and they moved out into a vast space.

The room was a hall of some kind. It seemed as if it were once some sort of meeting area or place of worship. There had once been fine paintings on the walls, but age and water damage had destroyed them, leaving only mouldering frames. What had once been furniture was now nothing more than splintered timbers and broken masonry, pushed to one side. The dust lay heavy at the edges of the room, but the middle had been worn clean by the countless feet of the archaeotech priests over the years.

They moved down through the hall, Grogan leading, his great strides kicking up dust. Cantor followed, his soft shoes shuffling, and Anselm brought up the rear. They went through a door and found themselves in a broad corridor, almost a road, leading downwards. On either side of them, doors and corridors led off into different directions. Burnt out machinery, some of it looking incredibly old, was scattered haphazardly around the area. Doors, broken and hanging off their hinges, sometimes blocked a doorway.

Every now and again, they passed some dark staining on the walls or floors. It looked as if oil or some carbonised matter had been spilt there.

They came to a crossroads of sorts, lit by the harsh lights of the exploratory team who had set up permanent illumination across the dig area. High pillars held up the roof, now hung with webs of what looked like the spinnings of some long gone creatures. He could see balconies, mezzanine levels, bridges spanning the void above them. Anselm shuddered. He suddenly realised that they were moving through the heart of what had been a great city, a city to rival in splendour any that he had seen, but now ruined and desolate. In his mind's eye he could see shops, warehouses, palaces, gardens, roads and walkways, once splendid, now ruined and empty. He noticed marks in the walls from small arms fire, bolter marks and scorches from lasguns. All was quiet and beyond the perimeter of light afforded by the arc-lamps, he could see nothing. He gripped the comforting bulk of his shotgun, holding it ready as he scanned the darkness. The beam from his torch wavered as he settled the gun's stock into his hip.

Great loops of black cabling snaked back the way they had come, no doubt supplying power to those digging deeper in the bowels of the city. Arc lamps threw stark shadows, and as they passed each lamp, Anselm saw the silhouette of Grogan rear up the wall towards him and then sink down again as the inquisitor strode past, his powerful bulk seeming to leap at him.

His skin prickled. Out of the corner of his eye, he thought he saw movement. He turned his head, shining the strong beam of his torch into the blackness, but there was nothing there, only an empty hole where one part of a wall had collapsed. He turned his attention back to the group.

'Do we know anything about the city, its people?' Anselm asked Cantor.

'Nothing at all,' he replied. 'The city itself is very old, but apart from the buildings themselves, which you can see around you, there is very little that it has revealed to us. It is a bit of a mystery – there is nothing in the ancient chronicles about a city or even a civilisation this far away from the galactic core. Whatever was here was either well hidden from the main routes or kept itself to itself. I would have posited some sort of pirate community or frontier world but the size and complexity of this city denies that. There is almost no evidence of how they lived other than the buildings. There is much damage, it looks like a heavy battle was fought here but over what we cannot tell. The centuries hide a lot of evidence – we found bones but they'd almost worn away to nothing, clothes had rotted, even metal had rusted away.'

Anselm shuddered. He couldn't get rid of the feeling that they were being watched but he could see no sign of anything nearby. The dark windows of buildings seemed to gaze at him blankly but every now and then he felt that something was watching him from behind stone buttresses or broken walls. He shook his head, clearing the visions. He wouldn't allow himself to start imagining that he could see back into the city's living past. He looked ahead. They were coming to a narrowing of the way, almost a tunnel.

He concentrated on Cantor's monologue.

'Much of this part of the city was sealed off by rockfall. We had to excavate heavily in order to get past it, as sensors indicated that the city continued for some way beyond it. Took some doing, I can tell you. This rock's hard as adamantium. Wore away hundreds of drillbits, but in the end... Ah, here we are. As you can see, what we found was well worth the effort.'

They had come to the end of the tunnel. In front of them stood a wall, carved from massive blocks of stone, fitted together with such precision that only the thinnest line separated the blocks from one another. At the base of the wall was an opening, barely two metres high, and only half the width. Surrounding the opening was an inscription in a language they could not read.

'The translation has defeated us so far; it was sent to the Ecclesiarchy for translation but we heard nothing back,' Cantor said, rather sheepishly. 'There was a stone blocking the doorway. I'm afraid we had to use compact charges to remove it. The interesting thing, you'll notice, is that none of the other blocks were scarred by the explosion. The door-block was made of a softer stone than the wall. Why, we've no idea, but we sent the fragments back for analysis all the same.'

Anselm had to stoop to get through the doorway, and when he lifted his head on the other side, he felt his breath catch in amazement. Ahead of him, sloping down, illuminated in the soft light of hundreds of glow-globes, the corridor stretched ahead for what seemed like kilometres. The passageway was barely wider than the door they had entered it by, but the roof stretched hundreds of metres above him. On the floor was a soft fine dust that stirred as he stepped through it.

Grogan grunted. 'Impressive,' he conceded, striding forward, his cloak billowing behind him, throwing up miniature dust-storms. 'But we've no time for sightseeing. My work is fighting heretics, not playing historian. This stuff should all be left underground where it belongs. The Imperium is best guarded with the Emperor's word and a hellgun, not with ancient trinkets. In the meantime I want to find your missing priest as quickly as possible. Or the corpse,' he added darkly. 'If there is something alive down here, I want it hunted down and exterminated so that we can get off this rock.'

Cantor huffed. 'Come on,' Anselm said. 'Until we find whatever's out there, it may strike again.' Cantor led the way down the immense corridor. Anselm gazed up in wonder. The roof soared away into darkness above him. About halfway along, there was a dark strip of rock all the way across the floor and reaching high up the walls on either side.

Cantor noticed him looking at it. 'That's hardened basalt,' he commented. 'It cut the corridor in half. Our cogitators have surmised that at one time a wall of molten lava bisected this corridor, held in place by the Emperor knows what. In time it cooled and hardened into a perfect wall of basalt. We had to cut through it with high intensity laser drills. The basalt extends for hundreds of metres in every direction as if the wall stretched far into the rock like a protective barrier.

We knew once we passed it that we were reaching the heart of what had been the city – we think it may have acted as some sort of heat sink or repository for their energy needs. What we do know is that there is still much molten magma near this part of the dig, held in check by the great weight of rock.'

They passed the ring of basalt and after some time, the passageway levelled out. Soon afterwards, it opened up into a room, perhaps ten metres wide. Machinery lay on wheeled trolleys, cables and unlit glow-globes were stacked in piles around the room, and there was the noise of humming. Anselm guessed that the machinery was pumping fresh air into the room and taking away spent air. Above them, balconies overlooked the room, and there was the faint sound of chains swinging in an imperceptible breeze.

Cantor said 'This is the heart of Barathrum. It is the deepest our excavations have brought us.' Then he stopped.

The body lay slumped face down against workbench. There was a pool of blood around his head, and his hair was matted with it. Blood and brain matter was spattered against the walls. Grogan motioned Anselm forwards.

'Anselm,' he said. 'You're the chirugeon, if I remember correctly. What can you tell us?'

Anselm moved forwards, stepping over the outstretched legs of the corpse. He leaned forward and gently pulled the body round. As it slumped over onto its back, he gasped in horror. The man's front had been torn apart, the chest a gaping cavity, arms hanging limply from sleeves of lacerated skin. Dark holes gazed into nothingness where his eyes had been, and blood had oozed from the sockets, drying into black crusted rivulets across his cheeks.

'I can tell little from here,' he said. 'We must take him to the medi-bay. I will examine him there.'

He turned his face away from the shattered corpse and examined the room in which they had found him. The walls were made of small mud bricks stacked one on top the other and sealed with some sort of rough cement. There was a glow-globe in the corner and he played it over the wall, the flickering light tracing daemonic patterns on the rough brickwork. Apart from the blood spray near the corpse, there were no other marks on the wall.

Except...

'What's this?' Anselm ran his fingers over one part of the wall. The bricks seemed to be rougher here, the finish less clean. His fingertips found a line, near the floor, almost imperceptible, and followed it up until it was about half a metre above his head. Then it turned sharply, at ninety degrees and continued horizontally for about a metre.

'A door,' he breathed. 'Cantor, look at this.' The tech-priest came close and peered at the line.

'You're right,' he said. 'A door. We'd have never have seen this if you hadn't noticed it.'

Grogan barked at Eremet. 'Get servitors down here. I want this area sealed off and I want to know what's behind this wall.'

Eremet nodded. 'I will see to it, inquisitor.'

Anselm made a circuit of the room, remembering everything in case a clue came to him later. Then, reluctantly, they lifted the corpse and wrapped it in a length of tarpaulin, before placing it on one of the machinery trolleys that stood to one side. Anselm, his mind already on the work ahead, guided the trolley as its internal suspensors moved it forwards.

As they passed once more though the labyrinthine passages of the dead city, Anselm again felt the hairs on the back of his neck begin to rise. Out of the corner of his eye, in the dark passages and openings that they passed, he could swear he saw eyes glinting at him, hundreds of eyes staring, unblinking. But each time he turned his head, his torch illuminating the darkness, he saw nothing, only the empty blackness of the tunnels. He was sure it was only his imagination, but he thought he could hear laughter; laughter dusty, dry and alien. He shook his head and the sound disappeared.

The tension must be getting to him, the horrific corpse they had found and the knowledge that Grogan was once again watching him. What if this was some sort of test? What if Grogan had been sent to report back on how he was handling this enquiry, whether he was showing sufficient zeal and devotion?

What if... What if, he told himself angrily, you concentrate on the task at hand and leave the worries for another time. He had a post-mortem to carry out and despite the gruesome nature of the task, he was looking forward to it; a chance to pit his keen intelligence against something that would eventually yield up its secrets.

It took some time before they reached the apothecary's bay. They placed the body on the operating table and unwrapped the tarpaulin. Cantor and Eremet stood back against the wall, trying not to watch, and Grogan pulled a high lab stool up close.

Donning a pair of transparent surgical gloves, Anselm began to work, cutting the shredded remains of the man's clothing away from the body.

He muttered to himself as he did so, a habit from the days when he had a med-servitor to record the results of the post-mortem. 'Hmm, number of deep incisions on the torso, mostly vertical... some bruising of the solar plexus... let's see, ribs cracked on left hand side, heavy blow to the shoulder, no bruising. Most interesting...' His voice died away as he reached across to pick up a pair of oculators and a small surgical pick. He leaned across the body and tentatively lifted up a flap of skin on the corpse's chest. 'Most interesting,' he confirmed as he squinted through the oculators.

'What is it?' demanded Grogan.

'Not ready to say... I just need to...' Anselm mumbled half to himself. He transferred his attention to the man's ruined face. Taking a pad of cotton, he soaked it in surgical alcohol and began to wipe the dried blood from the skin. Under the blood, the slashes were livid, purple and swollen. Cantor looked away and made a strangled gargling sound in his throat. Eremet looked pale. Grogan watched stoically, occasionally rubbing the vein at his temple. In the now clean face, the corpse's empty eye sockets glared evilly and despite their lack of occupants, Grogan felt they were watching them.

It was some time before Anselm spoke again: 'Now this is most interesting...'

This time, Grogan lost his patience. He stood up and leaned over the body on the table. 'For Emperor's sake, what are you muttering about?'

Anselm pulled of the oculators and stripped the gloves from his fingers.

'This is not the work of a zoomorph, a beast, at least not in the way we thought. These slash marks are certainly caused by claws of some kind, though the exact identity of the creature that caused them is beyond my knowledge. However, they are not the cause of death, nor the most interesting part of the examination. Look at the man's head, the area around the eyes, and tell me what you see.'

'This is insufferable,' Grogan declared, but bent his head until his nose was almost touching the ripped nasal cavity of the dead man.

'Throne of Earth!' he exclaimed. Cantor and Eremet jumped up as if they had been stung and crowded round.

'What is it?' the explorator demanded.

Grogan jumped in before Anselm could open his mouth. 'Don't you see?' he said. 'Look at the eye sockets. It seems like the eyes have been ripped out, but look more closely. It's not just the eyes that have gone, it's the bone around the eye socket too.'

'And if you look through the oculator,' continued Anselm, 'the eyes weren't torn out. They were removed. Something, or someone, removed those eyes with great precision, using some kind of device that removed them at high speed and with great accuracy. There are hardly any radial injury marks on the rest of the skull round the wound – this was done with something incredibly sharp – whatever else, I would say this man's eyes were intact when they were removed. But what kind of creature takes the eyes and leaves the rest of the body?'

Anselm ran his fingers through his cropped hair and started to pace the room. He suddenly stopped. 'What about the eyes on the other bodies?' he suddenly exclaimed. He strode to the screen behind which the bodies lay on their gurneys. He rapidly pulled back the sheets and then stopped in disappointment. Whatever the extent of their injuries and cause of death, it was clear to see that the eyes of the other bodies were either intact or at least extant.

He turned to face the others. 'I need to be alone,' he said. 'I need to think about this. I will examine the other bodies. There may be some clue as to how they died that may help us.'

Cantor and Eremet bowed towards the inquisitor and left. Grogan remained.

'Inquisitor,' Anselm asserted. 'I must do this alone. I need to deliver these souls into the Emperor's care and ask their spirits to guide me in finding their killer. To do that I must be alone.'

Grogan looked suspiciously at him. 'What is this? Is this some sort of ritual?'

'No, it is merely that I must examine the other bodies, but I need to have my mind clear to accept whatever the results tell me, no matter how strange or confusing they may seem to my brain. I just need quiet.'

Grogan seemed to consider this. 'Very well,' he said. 'But I want a full debrief.'

'Before you speak to the others,' he added, as he turned and strode out of the room.

It was some hours later that Grogan heard a knock on the door of the hab-mod that had been assigned to him. He put away the documents he had been reading and opened the door. Anselm stood there, looking tired but alert.

'May I enter?' he asked. Grogan stood aside and Anselm entered, seating himself at the table strewn with transcripts and documents. Grogan swept them up into a pile and sat down opposite him.

'Well, what have you found?' he asked.

'This is a lot darker than you or I suspected,' the inquisitor began.

Grogan's face twitched and Anselm could have sworn he saw the flicker of a smile pass across the older man's craggy features. Nothing gave Grogan more pleasure,

Anselm remembered, than having an enemy, preferably a self-confessed heretic, that he could pin all his fiery, destructive, righteous energies on.

'I've examined all the bodies. Apart from Crans, they all seem to have died in a savage and frenzied attack. They were literally torn apart. Whatever it was that killed them, it was hugely strong, fast as a tyranid, but man-sized, bipedal, with only two arms, and legs for locomotion, not attack. The attack was frenzied, as I say, but I would say from the pattern of the lacerations, it was carried out by someone who was not. In other words, this is not the work of a beast, nor of a deranged madman, but a madman who is cold, calculated and very cunning.'

'I don't follow. How can a killer be mad and yet not mad? You're not making sense?'

'There is something strange about the bodies. They are each missing part of their anatomy. This is something that had been missed in all previous examinations but I made the connection after examining Crans. Even in the case of the body that was missing its arms, while the fact of the missing arm was obvious, what was less so was that the arm had been removed, carefully and surgically, after death. It was amputated, not ripped off.'

Grogan had become still, his jaw twitching slightly as Anselm spoke.

'We are missing a heart, brain, eyes, a number of bones and many kilos of muscle tissue from various parts of the body. In one case the face had been torn away, but in such a way that it would have been undamaged by the removal. The question I put to myself was, why?'

'And what did you come up with?'

'I wasn't able to come up with an answer, until I made a final discovery which meant that the answer to the riddle became secondary to the real truth about what's happening here on Barathrum. This mark was burned into the back of the eye socket of Tech-priest Crans.'

Anselm leaned over and thrust a thin data-slate towards Grogan. The older inquisitor took it and thumbed the activation button. The data-slate glowed pale and illuminated the man's face from below as he gazed at it. Anselm watched as an image, upside down from his perspective at the other side of the table, began to coalesce on the slate's screen. It was a symbol, dark and clear-edged, yet hard to see, as if it was being inspected under ultraviolet light, or another wavelength just beyond the limits of human eyesight. He knew that he wouldn't have been able to describe it if asked. The symbol seemed to twist and turn in on itself like a writhing creature, yet Anselm knew that logically it could not move; it was a snapshot captured on the data-slate, yet it was an image with both meaning and power. Despite himself, he shivered.

'So,' Grogan stated, the word slow and ponderous, hanging in the air between them. 'Chaos has come to Barathrum.'

THERE WAS A knock at the door. Grogan thumbed the slate clear and slipped the inert machine into the voluminous sleeve of his robe and called out: 'Enter.' The door opened a crack and the anxious face of Eremet appeared.

'Your eminences,' he began. 'I think you had better come with me.'

'Has there been another death?' Grogan asked, standing up.

'No, but there has been a discovery. Please follow me.'

'Where are we going?' Grogan asked. Out of the corner of his eye, Anselm could see his companion's right hand wandering towards the holster where he kept his hellgun strapped tight to his thigh.

'Inquisitor Anselm's discovery of the door was followed up, as per orders.' The Excavator seemed nervous now, as if the whole investigation was starting to take on a life of its own and was running away from his control. Anselm felt for him. The man's job was risky, but the kinds of risks he faced were ones he could normally tackle – here he was now, faced with an investigation with not one but two of the Emperor's finest inquisitors, one of whom was evidently getting increasingly trigger-happy.

Eremet led them quickly through the pathways and tunnels towards the area where they had discovered the body of

the unfortunate tech-priest. This time Anselm felt no eyes
upon him and he was glad. He felt a rising excitement: they
were starting to make some headway. He had done well to
put together the clues held in the bodies of the slain. It was
a difficult conclusion to have come to but it held up. If
things worked out on Barathrum, there would be nothing
standing in his way. Barathrum would be simply the beginning. He would be elevated through the ranks of his
brothers and he would lead them. Those who stood in his
way would be quashed...

He shook his head to clear it and forced his mind back to
the present. He was tired. He had not slept since leaving
Atrium two days ago. After they saw whatever it was that
Eremet was bringing them to, he would rest for a couple of
hours. Or at least take some stim to keep him going and risk
the attendant headaches.

THE ROOM WHERE they had found the body was unchanged
since they removed the corpse. Anselm could still see the
spatters of blood and the dark shadow where the body of
the tech-priest had lain in a pool of its own blood. Now,
however the single glow-globe had been replaced by an
array of harsh arc-lamps, casting their stark light on the
scene. To his left stood a doorway, in the place where his fingers had traced out the line in the mud bricks. The doorway
led into a room that was filled with lambent light that
seemed to create, and then chase away, shadows on the
walls. Eremet stood at the side of the doorway and extended
his arm, almost as if he were inviting them in.

Anselm took a deep breath, almost without knowing why,
and stepped through the doorway, Grogan close behind
him.

The first thing he noticed was Cantor, locked in conversation with a recorder, the servitor a mass of audio-visual
feeds, spectrometers and devices for measuring humidity
and air density. Cantor looked up as the inquisitors entered
and ushered the servitor away. It bowed briefly and then
went back to its work. Cantor's face was aglow with excitement as he faced his old friend.

'I would say congratulations if you had been a member of my team,' he said. 'You seem to have stumbled onto some sort of heart of our enterprise, I would say, no?' He gestured expansively around him.

Anselm gazed around him in wonder. The room was huge, a great pillared hall, the trunks of the pillars like a forest of great trees. The ceiling was high and seemed to glow with an angry red light, almost as if it were some sort of burning sea. It was this ceiling that lit the room and the waves of light washing across it had caused the play of light and shadow that Anselm had noticed when he had entered. Suddenly, he realised what it was – lava, molten rock, swirling above them, held in place by who knew what artifice. They stood under a lake of fire that swirled in the air above them.

Ahead of him there were great double doors, almost twenty metres tall, each door perhaps five or six metres wide. It seemed to be made from what looked like beaten copper, or perhaps bronze – it glowed dully in the reflection of the ceiling. Around the door were carved great hieroglyphics in a language that was unfamiliar to him. The glyphs were mainly pictoral, with lines and circles making up the remainder. Although he couldn't read them, they didn't look alien and he was relieved.

He noticed other tech-priests in the room, some directing servitors who lugged great chests of instruments, trailing wires, struggling under the immense weight. Others were taking notes on data-slates, still others appeared to be transcribing some of the hieroglyphics. He watched idly as one of them approached the great copper doors and reached out to touch them.

There was a high pitched hum and a beam of intense red light erupted from a point above the doors and focused on the tech-priest. The luminescence washing over the ceiling darkened momentarily as if someone had thrown ink into a bowl of bright liquid. The tech-priest writhed as he was caught in the beam of light, a silent scream forced from his lips. Then the light was gone and the man collapsed, like a puppet Anselm had once seen on Darcia that had had its strings cut. Grogan ran over to the man and prodded him

with the toe of his boot. Nothing happened. He knelt down
and pressed his finger to the man's neck.

'Dead!' he announced.

He raised his voice so that all could hear him. 'I want no
one to touch this door. I want these glyphs read and deci-
phered and delivered to me in my quarters within the hour.
Anselm, I want to speak with you. Privately.' He turned to
Eremet. 'Get this place sealed off.'

Cantor faced him, apoplectic with rage.

'Inquisitor! This area is under the jurisdiction of the Adeptus Mechanicus. There is so much to learn here, from the
inscriptions, from the structures here. You cannot make such
an order. We must lose no time.'

Grogan refused to be countermanded. 'On pain of death,
tech-priest, I order you to stay away from here. And that
applies to everyone.' He whirled on his heels and stalked out
of the room.

ANSELM FACED GROGAN across the table in the younger man's
hab-mod. The senior inquisitor looked as if he was barely
containing his anger. Anselm knew that look. It meant that
Grogan smelled the stink of corruption and knew exactly
how to deal with it. It also meant that he was not prepared
to discuss any alternative.

'I'm ordering immediate evacuation of Barathrum and
requesting back up from an Astartes kill-team. I want Termi-
nator squads to scour this place and if they find nothing I
will be recommending full Exterminatus. Barathrum is a
threat to the Imperium. The Imperium is a city built behind
high walls and these frontier systems are the unknown
beyond. It is our job to defend those walls and what shelters
behind them, whatever the cost. If there is the influence of
Chaos at work here, then I will stamp it out. It is unfortunate
but necessary – I will be demanding that the explorator mission here be relieved of its duties and subjected to rigorous
review.'

Anselm knew full well what that meant. He had been
party to Grogan's reviews before, when he was an acolyte.
It meant death for those who confessed, and torture for

those who did not. Until they did. They all confessed in the end.

'Grogan, we must investigate further. If there is a manifestation of Chaos here, we must get to the bottom of it, certainly, but we should root out its heart, not destroy the body just to get at the tumour. There is something unspeakably evil here but there is also great good in what we can learn from this planet. You heard Cantor – the archaeotech finds are immeasurable, there may be standard template devices that the Adeptus Mechanicus have only dreamed about. You cannot take the decision to destroy all that these men have worked and died for simply because we have only just begun to understand what has been happening here.'

'That is weakness, Anselm. Everything contrary to the rule of the Imperium is heresy and there can be no exceptions. I'm surprised you do not remember that after what happened on Tantalus. That is what happens when you show weakness.'

Anselm looked into the dark eyes of Grogan. His voice shook with anger.

'I did not show weakness, Grogan, as you well know. It is not weakness to show restraint. What you did on Tantalus was unprecedented and unnecessary. To destroy a planet because of an insurrection that was limited to one city was arrogant, and typical of your approach.'

Grogan's eyes remained enigmatic, unreadable. 'I seem to recall, Anselm, that you were in charge of suppressing that insurrection. A charge you expressly failed to carry out. I did what I did only when the rebellion threatened the stability of the whole star system.'

Anselm kept his voice calm. There was no point in getting angry with Grogan. The man's icy manner would never crack, and Anselm knew from bitter experience that if he lost his temper, he would be the loser. He took a deep breath, and when he spoke, his voice was again calm. 'May I remind you, Grogan, that I had only been on Tantalus for four days when your agents had me pulled out. Of course I failed to halt the insurrection; I hardly had time to open my office.'

'Tantalus was under your jurisdiction. The insurrection should have been crushed. Instantly. Diplomacy is only useful after force has driven the other side to the table. Alone, it is a tool for the weak, for effete Imperial ambassadors. The Inquisition is not a tool, it is a force in itself. As I'm sure you remember.' Grogan breathed in deeply.

Anselm forced a tight smile to his lips. 'I remember only too well, inquisitor; your classes made a great impression on us all. But perhaps we should concentrate less on what happened in the past, and more on the present.'

There was a shuffle of robes as Grogan stood up. He checked his chronometer. 'I have ordered that no one leave their quarters tonight. Barathrum has moved into its night cycle. There is nothing we can do until light, when the planet has turned its face once more towards the core systems and we can send word back to the Ecclesiarchy.'

'Yes.' Anselm's silence swallowed up the end of the word, and dismissed his erstwhile tutor. The old man gathered up his robes and left, closing the door after him, leaving Anselm exhausted. Why was it that every time he spoke to Grogan, he felt himself back in the Scholarium, being tested on Imperial ethics or some obscure matter from a legal codex?

He moved his weapons case from his bunk and set it on the table. He lay back on the sleeping pallet and closed his eyes, allowing his mind to clear, leaving it open to thought.

ANSELM AWOKE AND looked at the glowing chronometer next to his pallet. He had been asleep for only a matter of minutes but something had woken him. There was a strange scratching sound, almost at the edge of his hearing. No, not scratching, more like a shuffling, soft fabric being drawn across polished stone. He shook his head and sat up. The sound wasn't coming from inside his hab-mod, it was coming from outside, in the corridor.

He moved across to the door, silent on bare feet, rubbing his eyes with tiredness. Opening the door a crack, he looked out into the corridor. There was nothing there. The corridor was empty. He closed the door again, but this time he locked it. He lay back on his pallet and closed his eyes.

ANSELM WAS DREAMING. In his dream, he was gliding through the labyrinth below the dig site. Again, he felt eyes on him, many eyes watching him as he moved through the darkness. Although he had no torch with him, he could see as if it were day, and in his dream, the darkness and complexity of the labyrinth held no fear for him. He came at last to the room where they had found the body. It sat slumped against the wall, its front stained with blood and the empty hollow eye sockets seeming to watch him, a dark fire burning within them.

To his left was the doorway cleared by the servitors and he felt himself being drawn towards it. He passed through, but instead of the great hall with its brass doors and pillars, he found himself in a throne room. Warm light streamed over him. Before him stood a dais with a throne on it. The throne was enormous, bigger then a building, and on the throne sat a great figure, haloed in golden light. In his dream, Anselm knew that this was – praise be the holy throne of Terra – the Emperor himself, great father of mankind.

His heart soared and he felt himself sink to his knees. He looked up into the ancient wise face of the saviour of mankind… and saw it swim before his eyes, seem to melt and flow, and there on the throne sat a beast, the face of a hyena, eyes glowing red with immeasurable evil, the muzzle long, creased in a bestial snarl or smile, he couldn't tell which. The creature stood, its rich robes sweeping the floor. It held out one arm and Anselm could see fine rings glittering on dark fingers. The creature gazed at him.

'Anselm!' it said, the voice deep, dark, rich, evil. 'Anselm, my servant, you have come to me. Anselm!' The voice drove into his skull and his heart began hammering as if it would burst from his ribcage. And then the scene faded and the hammering of his heart became the hammering of someone banging on his door and calling 'Anselm, Anselm! Open the door!'

* * *

HE LEAPT UP, dazed with sleep, his fingers instinctively reaching for his shotgun.

'Who is it?' he called.

'Eremet,' came the reply. 'A transmission has arrived from the Ecclesiarchy with the translation of the hieroglyphs.'

Anselm opened the door cautiously.

'Come in. What does it say?' Eremet came in, looking behind him before he closed the door. Silently, he handed a data-slate over to Anselm.

'The transmission was coded and bears the highest seal of your Ordo. I cannot read it.'

Anselm thumbed the power rune and the screen lit up. There was a brief moment while the slate read the print of his thumb and verified his identity. He entered his personal code number, then a jumble of hieroglyphics swam across the screen, resolving themselves into neat rows. Slowly, starting at the top, the glyphs began to change into the regular characters of High Gothic text.

He read: 'Inquisitor Anselm, this transcription is for your eyes only. What it contains is reserved for the highest level of the Ordo and the Ecclesiarchy. The information cannot be revealed to any outside our order.

'The hieroglyphs of Barathrum have been translated as follows:

> 'Let it be known that we, the Mugati, humans, descendants of the tribes of the Ilatrum, claimed this world for our people in the name of the Holy Emperor. The land was cultivated and great cities we built in his name. We grew strong, our people were brave; many journeyed beyond the stars amongst their brothers in the armies of the Imperium. Our trade stretched beyond this system. We were a proud people. That pride was our downfall. The eye of the Evil One turned its gaze upon us.
>
> 'When the warp storms came, we were cut off from our brothers who had left to protect other parts of the galaxy. For years, we trembled in fear as foul raiders came out of the Immaterium to attack us. Our cities fell, one by one and we drew back to our capital. Here was the scene of our last battle.

'We fought hard and pushed the foe back, but then it called up Szarach'il, foul servant of their gods, and terrible was the destruction he wrought. Our city could not stand against such a foe, and so it was that our world teetered on the brink of oblivion.

'The final battle took place deep in the catacombs beneath the city. Our finest warriors fought a desperate battle, until at last Szarach'il himself stood face to face against Amaril, leader of all our people, brother of the Holy Inquisition.

'Amaril knew that Szarach'il could not be killed, nor banished by his powers, diminished as they were by the months of battle. Instead, in a final act that destroyed his mortal body, he bound Szarach'il behind great doors of promethium, sealing them with words of great power such that he should never be released.

'Our planet is destroyed, our people no more. I, Dramul, last of the Mugati, have caused these words to be carved on the prison walls that any who read them will know.'

Anselm felt his heart grow cold. What have we uncovered here, he thought?

Then he suddenly realised why he was here. The Ecclesiarchy had already sent one inquisitor to investigate the events on Barathrum. Why send another? Unless his Ordo had known, somehow, what Barathrum meant. Their archives were endless and ancient beyond memory. Did they send him to Barathrum to prevent Grogan, staunch puritan that he was, from destroying all trace of the daemon from existence? And in the process banish to nothingness all that the Mugati had learnt from their battle, the ancient powers that had bound the daemon in its abyssal prison?

'Where is Grogan?' he demanded.

'He is not in his mod, excellency,' replied Eremet.

Anselm turned and opened his weapons case. Inset in red velvet was an ancient sword. The handle was made from fine wood wound with hand-tooled leather. He released it from its cradle, held it up in front of his face, depressing a button on the handle to test the blade. The metal of the blade hummed and the cutting edge shimmered. He released the button and the humming stopped, the blade inert.

'Come on!' he said to the terrified explorer. 'Let's go and find them. I know where he is.'

As ANSELM DREAMED, Grogan paced his room, trying to wear off his impatience at having to wait until he could call down divine retribution on Barathrum.

He stopped, hearing a soft shuffling sound outside his mod. He opened the door a crack and saw Cantor as he faded into the darkness at the end of the corridor.

He called after him, but there was no answer. Where was the fool going? And after he had specifically forbidden anyone from venturing forth tonight. Grogan turned back to grab his hellgun, and snatched up his chainsword at the same time.

By the time he reached the end of the corridor, Cantor had disappeared. But Grogan knew where he would be heading. The damn fool scholar was going to go and investigate the glyphs.

He followed the footprints they had made earlier until he came to the long straight passage. As he approached the room with the door, he heard the sound of soft chanting. Alarmed, he gripped his hellgun tightly in his left hand, the right fingering release on his chainsword. Silently, it began to whirr, the light from the glow-globes flickering off its spinning serrated surface.

He stood at the side of the doorway and cautiously peered in.

Inside he could see the great pillars reaching up, their surfaces shifting in the light from the ceiling. Shadows pooled around their bases, anchoring each pillar in its own plot of darkness. The light caressed the carven script set into the walls surrounding the door.

And settled on the figure of Cantor, tech-priest and disciple of the Adeptus Mechanicus as he stood in front of the great copper doors, his arms raised in a gesture of welcome, ancient words spilling from his throat.

'El'ach mihar, cun malaas, an ach! Szarach'il cun malaas!'

The words hung in the air like incense in a temple, and the sound of them hurt Grogan's ears. They were unholy words,

words of summoning, words of power. Words of evil. The voice of Chaos.

In front of Cantor the glyphs carved into the great beaten copper doors began to glow, tendrils of luminescence flickering over the images and jumping from rune to rune. The lighted ceiling began to darken, storm clouds the colour of bruised flesh forming in the artificial sky. A tremor shook the earth and the dust rose on the floor at Grogan's feet. Cantor's chanting grew louder.

Grogan stepped out from behind the door, his hellgun pointed straight at the tech-priest's back and bellowed: 'In the name of the Emperor, foul hell fiend, cease your chanting or die.'

What happened next was the very last thing he expected. Cantor ceased his chanting and turned round. His eyes were black pits of darkness, the pupils enlarged hugely, filling his sockets. The face was a rictus of concentration, his mouth wide in the midst of a chant. Then Grogan saw his hands. Where his fingers should be, claws that gleamed like metal had burst from his hands. He could see the tips, glistening with blood.

Cantor lowered his arms, and held them out towards Grogan.

'Welcome, inquisitor!' the mouth hissed but the voice was not Cantor's. It was dark, dry, dusty, the voice of one imprisoned for aeons and not used to forming words aloud. 'You are just in time to welcome me at the moment of my release. But there is still the final invocation, and you cannot be allowed to prevent that.'

The creature gestured to one side and Grogan turned to look in the direction.

From the shadow of one of the pillars emerged a monstrosity from the very pit of hell.

It resembled a man only in as much as it had a head, torso and four limbs but that was where the resemblance ended. The thing lurched towards him, arms outstretched, hands ending in claws that looked like metal spikes driven into flesh. Its limbs were red muscle, flayed raw, dripping with plasma and ichor. The creature's face was seemingly stitched to a skull of sorts, hanging oddly so that the features were drooped and rucked into each other, ending in a gash where a jaw had been secured to the upper skull. Bits of metal and what looked like machinery were attached to the thing at odd intervals, making up part of a leg here, part of its sternum there. It limped towards Grogan, a bloodcurdling hiss issuing from its broken mouth.

Grogan leapt back, hearing as he did so the sound of chanting resume. He had no time to think about it before the foul creature was on him. He thumbed the switch on his chainsword, hearing the reassuring whirr as its teeth carved the air.

The beast covered the ground between itself and the inquisitor in two strides. He could smell the putrid smell of rotting flesh as it reached out for him. The metal claws on its hands raked Grogan's chest, the armour there sparking from the force of the attack. The inquisitor lashed out with his boot and connected with the thing's kneecap, knocking it back. It fell onto one knee but then rose again. Grogan could see the white sheen of bone where his boot had broken the thing's knee but it didn't seem to notice, ignoring any pain it may have felt and lurched back towards the fray.

Grogan cut the air with his chainsword, slashing the creature across one shoulder. No blood spurted from the wound, instead the flesh separated and the pink muscle tissue gleamed wetly.

The thing roared with anger and jumped at Grogan. It landed on his chest, the weight of it knocking the wind out of him. He fell on his back, his right arm up against the creature's chest, trying to stop the slavering jaws from ripping his throat out, foul breath choking him. Held away from his face, the creature began to pound against Grogan's belly with its feet. Pain wracked the inquisitor. Slowly, he pressed the muzzle of his hellgun against the belly of the creature and fired.

There was a roar as the creature was hurled up in the air, and then it landed down on Grogan, the stench of suppurating flesh making him gag. He scrambled to his feet.

And froze...

In front of him the great doors stood ajar. Between them, Cantor stood, outlined in shimmering light.

No, not stood, floated. Suspended in a nimbus of light, the old tech-priest hung, like a heretic on a rack, writhing in pain. Tendrils of light wrapped themselves round his body and spun it round.

The dark voice came again, this time appearing inside Grogan's head without Cantor speaking. At the same time, it reverberated around the room, causing the pillars to shake.

Inquisitor! You are most welcome!

The inquisitor raised his weapon. 'Die, hellspawn!' he spat. He pressed the trigger.

The gun recoiled, there was a flash of light and he saw the shell hurtle towards Cantor. Before it could impact, there was a shimmer in the air as if the very fabric of reality had turned to glue. The bullet slowed, stopped, then clattered to the floor, inert. Then the handle of the hellgun jumped in his hand. Then his chainsword too jumped from his grasp and the two weapons clattered to the ground.

'Really, inquisitor, that showed no imagination.' The voice was soothing, paternal, chuckling as if at a disappointing but much loved child. 'I have called to you across time and space and this is how you welcome me.'

'Who... who are you?' Grogan's voice was shaky.

'I am Szarach'il, the Great Destroyer, Devourer of Souls, daemon, world defiler. Endless was the torment I inflicted on the galaxy. Whole systems fell before me. Then my great crusade brought me to this accursed planet. Nothing could stop me, until I came face to face with one man, an inquisitor from the dawning of your order, who rallied his men. He had studied my kind, he knew he could not destroy me. Instead, coward that he was, he wrought a dungeon for me here and incarcerated me. For an eternity I have languished here in this pit, this abyss, until the scratchings of these Mechanicus slaves woke me from my slumber. They had no idea that this whole planet was my prison, buried as I was at its heart.

'When they broke through the city limits into the prison's outer chambers I knew that my time was once more drawing nigh. This one, this tech-priest, he burned for knowledge and delved deep into the planet. Weak though I was after my imprisonment, I was able to control him for certain periods. With each hour, the day of my release grew closer, but what then? I was trapped on the planet with old men and half machine creatures. Their spirits were slight. I would perish without souls, without strength to feed me.

'Then I realised how to live, to thrive and to use the very instrument of the Imperium to release me from this planet and be the instrument of my revenge. Through this man, I stalked the city once more, killing his fellows. How I relished the spilling of blood again after all these centuries. How I laughed at their feeble cries as I ripped the still beating heart from one, the very flesh from the bones of another. I felt free again. And under my instruction, this human constructed the creature you have vanquished. It would protect him from any threat until the doors were discovered and the runes imprisoning me read and broken.

'And I knew that he would be horrified at the killings that he had no memory of carrying out, for by day, he was his own man with no recollection of what he had done while I controlled him. I read his mind and saw his old friendship with the inquisitor. He would seek help from his old friend and that man would come. A man strong, resolute, full of power and ambition, and then, I would have the body that would allow me to escape this planet and cut a swathe of revenge through the ranks of the Imperium. A fitting irony, don't you agree?'

Grogan stood, staggered at this revelation. He took a step backwards.

'Not so fast, human. I have been kept talking too long but it has been many ages since I heard my own voice. Now is the time for action.'

Cantor held out a hand. A tendril of light flickered from it and snaked through the air towards Grogan. It reached him and his body writhed in the coruscating light as the daemon took possession. The moment the tendril touched Grogan, the light that had surrounded Cantor disappeared. The tech-priest fell from the air, and crashed in a crumpled heap on the floor. He raised his head and looked at Grogan, his eyes

normal again, his body his own. 'I'm sorry,' he whispered
and his head fell back. His eyes went blank and he was still.

Szarach'il stretched his new arms and Grogan's features
twitched in a parody of a smile. He whirled round at a noise
and came face to face with Anselm. The daemon could tell
from the look on the inquisitor's face that he had seen everything that had taken place in the last few moments. The
daemon raised one hand and Grogan's discarded
chainsword flew into his hand. He activated it and waved it
experimentally at Anselm.

Anselm raised his own sword and sidled into the room,
giving himself some space as he activated the blade. Grogan
leapt at him, the sword a blur of whirling teeth. Anselm
raised his own in a parry and the two blades met in mid air,
sparks flying from the discharged energy. Anselm's arm rang
with the force of the blow. Even before, Grogan had been far
stronger physically and now the daemon within him added
the force of his own infernal strength to that of the inquisitor. Anselm's sword slid down the length of his opponent's
and as they broke contact, he spun, swinging the blade
down low in a sweeping arc. Grogan jumped, easily evading
the blade and a bellow of pleasure issued from his mouth.

'You humans are not as puny as I remembered. This one
is strong and I see that you too are skilled with a blade. The
contest is pleasing to me.' As Anselm looked at his old master, the man's face seemed to change, and for a second
Anselm saw the bestial face of the daemon, his hyena smile,
the long teeth; then the vision changed and Grogan's face
reasserted itself.

Anselm tried not to think of Grogan as a human any
longer; he was a creature of darkness, a vessel for infernal
power. That was how Grogan would have thought about it if
the roles had been reversed. His former tutor would have
had no trouble in executing him if it had been he who had
succumbed to daemonic power, no matter how unfortunate
it may have been.

He lunged at Grogan, feinted, then pulled back. Grogan
bellowed again, and thrust forward. Anselm dodged the
thrust, putting out his boot and tripping his former tutor.

The creature stumbled and rammed his head against the wall. It turned and for a moment, the eyes changed, and Anselm could see the deep wells of darkness clear and Grogan's own eyes gaze out at him.

'Anselm, my pupil,' he croaked. 'Remember that the path of the inquisitor... is one of holy fire. One must... fight fire... with fire.'

The eyes darkened briefly, then lightened. Grogan made a gesture. His hellgun, lying unnoticed against the wall, flew into his hand. He raised it, towards Anselm... then slowly, shakingly, upwards until it pointed towards the ceiling.

'Get.... out!' Grogan croaked and pulled the trigger. The shell flew upwards and hit the ceiling. There was a moment of awful silence and then a tremendous roar. The ceiling shattered above the daemon and an instant later, a cascade of molten lava fell, obliterating Grogan in a waterfall of glowing heat. It hissed as it hit the floor and immediately began to harden, the solid rock being covered with more lava that flowed endlessly from the ceiling, a stalactite of solid fire with Grogan at its core.

Anselm jumped back, scrambling to get away from the river of magma that began to flow towards him. He stumbled and his boots smoked as spraying droplets of lava touched them. The flow was relentless and he felt his eyebrows singeing from the intense heat. Gathering his strength, he ran from the room. Looking behind him, he could see the room beginning to fill with the fiery molten stone. At the doorway, he passed Eremet standing in horror watching the scene unfold, and pulled the speechless explorator along with him.

They ran until they reached the long passageway. Behind them, at the mouth of the passage, there was a wall of glowing rock that was slowly, relentlessly moving towards them. Fear lent them strength and, lungs screaming with the effort, they ran. Behind them, the magma, rose, solidifying as it did so, sealing off the body of his former tutor with its daemon intruder forever.

They reached the command module and Eremet gave the evacuation order. The archaeotech site at Barathrum was no more. There would be no more digging after eldritch knowledge here. Barathrum's secrets would remain locked under countless tonnes of stone, sealed forever.

Later, as he sat, strapped into the seat of the Imperial shuttle that carried them from the planet, Anselm looked back at the archaeosite as it disappeared under the fury of a newly born volcano. He found himself pondering Grogan's final words, and for the first time since he was received as a noviciate amongst the ranks of the Inquisition, he found he could agree with his old tutor and erstwhile foe. In a universe full of Chaos and darkness sometimes it was necessary to fight fire with fire.

MISSING IN ACTION

An Eisenhorn story
Dan Abnett

I LOST MY left hand on Sameter. This is how it occurred.

On the thirteenth day of Sagittar (local calendar), three days before the solstice, in the mid-rise district of the city of Urbitane, an itinerant evangelist called Lazlo Mombril was found shuffling aimlessly around the flat roof of a disused tannery lacking his eyes, his tongue, his nose and both of his hands.

Urbitane is the second city of Sameter, a declining agrochemical planet in the Helican subsector, and it is no stranger to crimes of cruelty and spite brought on by the vicissitudes of neglect and social deprivation afflicting its tightly packed population. But this act of barbarity stood out for two reasons. First, it was no hot-blooded assault or alcohol-fuelled manslaughter but a deliberate and systematic act of brutal, almost ritual mutilation.

Second, it was the fourth such crime discovered that month.

I had been on Sameter for just three weeks, investigating the links between a bonded trade federation and a secessionist movement on Hesperus at the request of Lord

Inquisitor Rorken. The links proved to be nothing – Urbitane's economic slough had forced the federation to chase
unwise business with unscrupulous ship masters, and the
real meat of the case lay on Hesperus – but I believe this was
the lord inquisitor's way of gently easing me back into active
duties following the long and arduous affair of the Necro-
teuch.

By the Imperial calendar it was 241.M41, late in that year.
I had just finished several self-imposed months of recupera-
tion, meditation and study on Thracian Primaris. The eyes
of the daemonhost Cherubael still woke me some nights,
and I wore permanent scars from torture at the hands of the
sadist Gorgone Locke. His strousine neural scourge had
damaged my nervous system and paralysed my face. I would
not smile again for the rest of my life. But the battle wounds
sustained on KCX-1288 and 56-Izar had healed, and I was
now itching to renew my work.

This idle task on Sameter had suited me, so I had taken it
and closed the dossier after a swift and efficient investigation. But latterly, as I prepared to leave, officials of the
Munitorium unexpectedly requested an audience.

I was staying with my associates in a suite of rooms in the
Urbitane Excelsior, a shabby but well-appointed establish-
ment in the high-rise district of the city. Through
soot-stained, armoured roundels of glass twenty metres
across, the suite looked out across the filthy grey towers of
the city to the brackish waters of the polluted bay twenty
kilometres away.

Ornithopters and biplanes buzzed between the massive
city structures, and the running lights of freighters and
orbitals glowed in the smog as they swung down towards
the landing port. Out on the isthmus, through a haze of yellow, stagnant air, promethium refineries belched brown
smoke into the perpetual twilight.

'They're here,' said Bequin, entering the suite's lounge
from the outer lobby. She had dressed in a demure gown of
blue damask and a silk pashmeena, perfectly in keeping
with my instruction that we should present a muted but
powerful image.

I myself was clad in a suit of soft black linen with a waist-coat of grey velvet and a hip length black leather storm-coat.

'Do you need me for this?' asked Midas Betancore, my pilot and confidante.

I shook my head. 'I don't intend to be delayed here. I just have to be polite. Go on to the landing port and make sure the gun-cutter's readied for departure.'

He nodded and left. Bequin showed the visitors in.

I had felt it necessary to be polite because Eskeen Hansaard, Urbitane's Minister of Security, had come to see me himself. He was a massive man in a double-breasted brown tunic, his big frame offset oddly by his finely featured, boyish face.

He was escorted by two bodyguards in grey, armour-ribbed uniforms and a short but handsome, black-haired woman in a dark blue bodyglove.

I had made sure I was sitting in an armchair when Bequin showed them in so I could rise in a measured, respectful way. I wanted them to be in no doubt who was really in charge here.

'Minister Hansaard,' I said, shaking his hand. 'I am Inquisitor Gregor Eisenhorn of the Ordo Xenos. These are my associates Alizebeth Bequin, Arbites Chastener Godwyn Fischig and savant Uber Aemos. How may I help you?'

'I have no wish to waste your time, inquisitor,' he said, apparently nervous in my presence. That was good, just as I had intended it. 'A case has been brought to my attention that I believe is beyond the immediate purview of the city arbites. Frankly, it smacks of warp-corruption, and cries out for the attention of the Inquisition.'

He was direct. That impressed me. A ranking official of the Imperium, anxious to be seen to be doing the right thing. Nevertheless, I still expected his business might be a mere nothing, like the affair of the trade federation, a local crime requiring only my nod of approval that it was fine for him to continue and close. Men like Hansaard are often over-careful, in my experience.

'There have been four deaths in the city during the last month that we believe to be linked. I would appreciate your advice on them. They are connected by merit of the ritual mutilation involved.'

'Show me,' I said.

'Captain?' he responded.

Arbites Captain Hurlie Wrex was the handsome woman with the short black hair. She stepped forward, nodded respectfully, and gave me a data-slate with the gold crest of the Adeptus Arbites on it.

'I have prepared a digested summary of the facts,' she said.

I began to speed-read the slate, already preparing the gentle knock-back I was expecting to give to his case. Then I stopped, slowed, read back.

I felt a curious mix of elation and frustration. Even from this cursorial glance, there was no doubt this case required the immediate attention of the Imperial Inquisition. I could feel my instincts stiffen and my appetites whetten, for the first time in months. In bothering me with this, Minister Hansaard was not being over careful at all. At the same time, my heart sank with the realisation that my departure from this miserable city would be delayed.

ALL FOUR VICTIMS had been blinded and had their noses, tongues and hands removed. At the very least.

The evangelist, Mombril, had been the only one found alive. He had died from his injuries eight minutes after arriving at Urbitane Mid-rise Sector Infirmary. It seemed to me likely that he had escaped his ritual tormentors somehow before they could finish their work.

The other three were a different story.

Poul Grevan, a machinesmith; Luthar Hewall, a rugmaker; Idilane Fasple, a midwife.

Hewall had been found a week before by city sanitation servitors during routine maintenance to a soil stack in the mid-rise district.

Someone had attempted to burn his remains and then flush them into the city's ancient waste system, but the human body is remarkably durable. The post could not prove his missing body parts had not simply succumbed to decay and been flushed away, but the damage to the ends of the forearm bones seemed to speak convincingly of a saw or chain-blade.

When Idilane Fasple's body was recovered from a crawl-space under the roof of a mid-rise tenement hab, it threw more light on the extent of Hewall's injuries. Not only had Fasple been mutilated in the manner of the evangelist Mombril, but her brain, brainstem and heart had been excised. The injuries were hideous. One of the roof workers who discovered her had subsequently committed suicide. Her bloodless, almost dessicated body, dried out – smoked, if you will – by the tenement's heating vents, had been wrapped in a dark green cloth similar to the material of an Imperial Guard-issue bedroll and stapled to the underside of the rafters with an industrial nail gun.

Cross-reference between her and Hewall convinced the arbites that the rug-maker had very probably suffered the removal of his brainstem and heart too. Until that point, they had ascribed the identifiable lack of those soft organs to the almost toxic levels of organic decay in the liquescent filth of the soil stack.

Graven, actually the first victim found, had been dredged from the waters of the bay by salvage ship. He had been presumed to be a suicide dismembered by the screws of a passing boat until Wrex's careful cross-checking had flagged up too many points of similarity.

Because of the peculiar circumstances of their various post mortem locations, it was pathologically impossible to determine any exact date or time of death. But Wrex could be certain of a window. Graven had been last seen on the nineteenth of Aquiarae, three days before his body had been dredged up. Hewall had delivered a finished rug to a high-rise customer on the twenty-fourth, and had dined that same evening with friends at a charcute in mid-rise. Fasple had failed to report for work on the fifth of Sagittar, although the night before she had seemed happy and looking forward to her next shift, according to friends.

'I thought at first we might have a serial predator loose in mid-rise,' said Wrex, 'but the pattern of mutilation seems to me more extreme than that. This is not feral murder, or even psychopathic, post-slaying depravity. This is specific, purposeful ritual.'

'How do you arrive at that?' asked my colleague, Fischig. Fischig was a senior arbites from Hubris, with plenty of experience in murder cases. Indeed, it was his fluency with procedure and familiarity with modus operandi that had convinced me to make him a part of my band. That, and his ferocious strength in a fight.

Wrex looked sidelong at him, as if he was questioning her ability.

'Because of the nature of the dismemberment. Because of the way the remains were disposed of.' She looked at me. 'In my experience, inquisitor, a serial killer secretly wants to be found, and certainly wants to be known. It will display its kills with wanton openness, declaring its power over the community. It thrives on the terror and fear it generates. Great efforts were made to hide these bodies. That suggest to me the killer was far more interested in the deaths themselves than in the reaction to the deaths.'

'Well put, captain,' I said. 'That has been my experience too. Cult killings are often hidden so that the cult can continue its work without fear of discovery.'

'Suggesting that there are other victims still to find...' said Bequin casually, a chilling prophecy as it now seems to me.

'Cult killings?' said the minister. 'I brought this to your attention because I feared as much, but do you really think–'

'On Alphex, the warp-cult removed their victims' hands and tongues because they were organs of communication,' Aemos began. 'On Brettaria, the brains were scooped out in order for the cult to ingest the spiritual matter – the anima, as you might say – of their prey. A number of other worlds have suffered cult predations where the eyes have been forfeit... Gulinglas, Pentari, Hesperus, Messina... windows of the soul, you see. The Heretics of Saint Scarif, in fact, severed their ritual victims' hands and then made them write out their last confessions using ink quills rammed into the stumps of–'

'Enough information, Aemos,' I said. The minister was looking pale.

'These are clearly cult killings, sir,' I said. 'There is a noxious cell of Chaos at liberty in your city. And I will find it.'

I WENT AT once to the mid-rise district. Grevan, Hewall and Fasple had all been residents of that part of Urbitane, and Mombril, though a visitor to the metropolis, had been found there too. Aemos went to the Munitorium records spire in high-rise to search the local archives. I was particularly interested in historical cult activity on Sameter, and on date significance. Fischig, Bequin and Wrex accompanied me.

The genius loci of a place can often say much about the crimes committed therein. So far, my stay on Sameter had only introduced me to the cleaner, high-altitude regions of Urbitane's high-rise, up above the smog-cover.

Mid-rise was a dismal, wretched place of neglect and poverty. A tarry resin of pollution coated every surface, and acid rain poured down unremittingly. Raw-engined traffic crawled nose to tail down the poorly lit streets, and the very stone of the buildings seemed to be rotting. The smoggy darkness of mid-rise had a red, firelit quality, the backwash of the flares from giant gas processors. It reminded me of picture-slate engravings of the Inferno.

We stepped from Wrex's armoured speeder at the corner of Shearing Street and Pentecost. The captain pulled on her arbites helmet and a quilted flak-coat. I began to wish for a hat of my own, or a rebreather mask. The rain stank like urine. Every thirty seconds or so an express flashed past on the elevated trackway, shaking the street.

'In here,' Wrex called, and led us through a shutter off the thoroughfare into the dank hallway of a tenement hab. Everything was stained with centuries of grime. The heating had been set too high, perhaps to combat the murky wetness outside, but the result was simply an overwhelming humidity and a smell like the fur of a mangy canine.

This was Idilane Fasple's last resting place. She'd been found in the roof.

'Where did she live?' asked Fischig.

'Two streets away. She had a parlour on one of the old court-habs.'

'Hewall?'

'His hab is about a kilometre west. His remains were found five blocks east.'

I looked at the data-slate. The tannery where Mombril had been found was less than thirty minutes' walk from here, and Graven's home a short tram ride. The only thing that broke the geographical focus of these lives and deaths was the fact that Graven had been dumped in the bay.

'It hasn't escaped my notice that they all inhabited a remarkably specific area,' Wrex smiled.

'I never thought it had. But "remarkably" is the word. It isn't just the same quarter or district. It's an intensely close network of streets, a neighbourhood.'

'Suggesting?' asked Bequin.

'The killer or killers are local too,' said Fischig.

'Or someone from elsewhere has a particular hatred of this neighbourhood and comes into it to do his or her killing,' said Wrex.

'Like a hunting ground?' noted Fischig.

I nodded. Both possibilities had merit.

'Look around,' I told Fischig and Bequin, well aware that Wrex's officers had already been all over the building. But she said nothing. Our expert appraisal might turn up something different.

I found a small office at the end of the entrance hall. It was clearly the cubbyhole of the habitat's superintendent. Sheaves of paper were pinned to the flak-board wall: rental dockets, maintenance rosters, notes of residents' complaints. There was a box-tray of lost property, a partially disassembled mini-servitor in a tub of oil, a stale stink of cheap liquor. A faded ribbon and paper rosette from an Imperial shrine was pinned over the door with a regimental rank stud.

'What you doing in here?'

I looked round. The superintendent was a middle-aged man in a dirty overall suit. Details. I always look for details. The gold signet ring with the wheatear symbol. The row of permanent metal sutures closing the scar on his scalp where the hair had never grown back. The prematurely weathered skin. The guarded look in his eyes.

I told him who I was and he didn't seem impressed. Then I asked him who he was and he said, 'The super. What you doing in here?'

I use my will sparingly. The psychic gift sometimes closes as many doors as it opens. But there was something about this man. He needed a jolt. *What is your name?* I asked, modulating my voice to carry the full weight of the psychic probe.

He rocked backwards, and his pupils dilated in surprise.

'Quater Traves,' he mumbled.

'Did you know the midwife Fasple?'

'I sin her around.'

'To speak to?'

He shook his head. His eyes never left mine.

'Did she have friends?'

He shrugged.

'What about strangers? Anyone been hanging around the hab?'

His eyes narrowed. A sullen, mocking look, as if I hadn't seen the streets outside.

'Who has access to the roofspace where her body was found?'

'Ain't nobody bin up there. Not since the place bin built. Then the heating packs in and the contractors has to break through the roof to get up there. They found her.'

'There isn't a hatch?'

'Shutter. Locked, and no one has a key. Easier to go through the plasterboard.'

OUTSIDE, WE SHELTERED from the rain under the elevated railway.

'That's what Traves told me too,' Wrex confirmed. 'No one had been into the roof for years until the contractors broke their way in.'

'Someone had. Someone with the keys to the shutter. The killer.'

The soil stack where Hewall had been found was behind a row of commercial properties built into an ancient skin of scaffolding that cased the outside of a toolfitters' workshop like a cobweb. There was what seemed to be a bar two stages up, where a neon signed flicked between an Imperial eagle and a fleur-de-lys. Fischig and Wrex continued up to the next scaffolding level to peer in through the stained windows of the habs there. Bequin and I went into the bar.

The light was grey inside. At a high bar, four or five drinkers sat on ratchet-stools and ignored us. The scent of obscura smoke was in the air.

There was a woman behind the counter who took exception to us from the moment we came in. She was in her forties, with a powerful, almost masculine build. Her vest was cut off at the armpits and her arms were as muscular as Fischig's. There was the small tattoo of a skull and cross-bones on her bicep. The skin of her face was weathered and coarse.

'Help you?' she asked, wiping the counter with a glass-cloth. As she did so I saw that her right arm, from the elbow down, was a prosthetic.

'Information,' I said.

She flicked her cloth at the row of bottles on the shelves behind her.

'Not a brand I know.'

'You know a man called Hewall?'

'No.'

'The guy they found in the waste pipes behind here.'

'Oh. Didn't know he had a name.'

Now I was closer I could see the tattoo on her arm wasn't a skull and crossbones. It was a wheatear.

'We all have names. What's yours?'

'Omin Lund.'

'You live around here?'

'Live is too strong a word.' She turned away to serve some-one else.

'Scary bitch,' said Bequin as we went outside. 'Everyone acts like they've got something to hide.'

'Everyone does, even if it's simply how much they hate this town.'

The heart had gone out of Urbitane, out of Sameter itself, about seventy years before. The mill-hives of Thracian Primaris had eclipsed Sameter's production, and export profits fell away. In an effort to compete, the authorities freed the refineries to escalate production by stripping away the legal restrictions on atmospheric pollution levels. For hundreds of years, Urbitane had had problems controlling its smog and air-pollutants. For the last few decades, it hadn't bothered any more.

My vox-earplug chimed. It was Aemos.

'What have you found?'

'It's most perturbatory. Sameter has been clear of taint for a goodly while. The last Inquisitorial investigation was thirty-one years ago standard, and that wasn't here in Urbitane but in Aquitane, the capital. A rogue psyker. The planet has its fair share of criminal activity, usually narcotics trafficking and the consequential mob-fighting. But nothing really markedly heretical.'

'Nothing with similarities to the ritual methods?'

'No, and I've gone back two centuries.'

'What about the dates?'

'Sagittar thirteenth is just shy of the solstice, but I can't make any meaning out of that. The Purge of the Sarpetal Hives is usually commemorated by upswings of cult activity in the subsector, but that's six weeks away. The only other thing I can find is that this Sagittar fifth was the twenty-first anniversary of the Battle of Klodeshi Heights.'

'I don't know it.'

'The sixth of seven full-scale engagements during the sixteen month Imperial campaign on Surealis Six.'

'Surealis... that's in the next damn subsector! Aemos, every day of the year is the anniversary of an Imperial action somewhere. What connection are you making?'

'The Ninth Sameter Infantry saw service in the war on Surealis.'

Fischig and Wrex had rejoined us from their prowl around the upper stages of the scaffolding. Wrex was talking on her own vox-set.

She signed off and looked at me, rain drizzling off her visor.

'They've found another one, inquisitor,' she said.

* * *

IT WASN'T ONE. It was three, and their discovery threw the affair wide open. An old warehouse in the mill zone, ten streets away from Fasple's hab, had been damaged by fire two months before, and now the municipal work-crews had moved in to tear it down and reuse the lot as a site for cheap, prefab habitat blocks. They'd found the bodies behind the wall insulation in a mouldering section untouched by the fire. A woman and two men, systematically mutilated in the manner of the other victims.

But these were much older. I could tell that even at a glance.

I crunched across the debris littering the floorspace of the warehouse shell. Rain streamed in through the roof holes, illuminated as a blizzard of white specks by the cold blue beams of the arbites' floodlights shining into the place.

Arbites officers were all around, but they hadn't touched the discovery itself.

Mummified and shrivelled, these foetally curled, pitiful husks had been in the wall a long time.

'What's that?' I asked.

Fischig leaned forward for a closer look. 'Adhesive tape, wrapped around them to hold them against the partition. Old. The gum's decayed.'

'That pattern on it. The silver flecks.'

'I think it's military issue stuff. Matt-silver coating, you know the sort? The coating's coming off with age.'

'These bodies are different ages,' I said.

'I thought so too,' said Fischig.

WE HAD TO wait six hours for a preliminary report from the district Examiner Medicae, but it confirmed our guess. All three bodies had been in the wall for at least eight years, and then for different lengths of time. Decompositional anom-alies showed that one of the males had been in position for as much as twelve years, the other two added subsequently, at different occasions. No identifications had yet been made.

'The warehouse was last used six years ago,' Wrex told me.

'I want a roster of workers employed there before it went out of business.'

Someone using the same m.o. and the same spools of adhesive tape had hidden bodies there over a period of years.

THE DISUSED TANNERY where poor Mombril had been found stood at the junction between Xerxes Street and a row of slum tenements known as the Pilings. It was a foetid place, with the stink of the lye and coroscutum used in the tanning process still pungent in the air. No amount of acid rain could wash that smell out.

There were no stairs. Fischig, Bequin and I climbed up to the roof via a metal fire-ladder.

'How long does a man survive mutilated like that?'

'From the severed wrists alone, he'd bleed out in twenty minutes, perhaps,' Fischig estimated. 'Clearly, if he had made an escape, he'd have the adrenalin of terror sustaining him a little.'

'So when he was found up here, he can have been no more than twenty minutes from the scene of his brutalisation.'

We looked around. The wretched city looked back at us, close packed and dense. There were hundreds of possibilities. It might take days to search them all.

But we could narrow it down. 'How did he get on the roof?' I asked.

'I was wondering that,' said Fischig.

'The ladder we came up by...' Bequin trailed off as she realised her gaffe.

'Without hands?' Fischig smirked.

'Or sight,' I finished. 'Perhaps he didn't escape. Perhaps his abusers put him here.'

'Or perhaps he fell,' Bequin said, pointing.

The back of a tall warehouse over-shadowed the tannery to the east. Ten metres up there were shattered windows.

'If he was in there somewhere, fled blindly, and fell through onto this roof...'

'Well reasoned, Alizebeth,' I said.

The arbites had done decent work, but not even Wrex had thought to consider this inconsistency.

We went round to the side entrance of the warehouse. The battered metal shutters were locked. A notice pasted to the wall told would-be intruders to stay out of the property of Hundlemas Agricultural Stowage.

I took out my multi-key and disengaged the padlock. I saw Fischig had drawn his sidearm.

'What's the matter?'

'I had a feeling just then... like we were being watched.'

We went inside. The air was cold and still and smelled of chemicals. Rows of storage vats filled with chemical fertilisers lined the echoing warehall.

The second floor was bare-boarded and hadn't been used in years. Wiremesh had been stapled over a doorway to the next floor, and rainwater dripped down. Fischig pulled at the mesh. It was cosmetic only, and folded aside neatly.

Now I drew my autopistol too.

On the street side of the third floor, which was divided into smaller rooms, we found a chamber ten metres by ten, on the floor of which was spread a sheet of plastic smeared with old blood and other organic deposits. There was a stink of fear.

'This is where they did him,' Fischig said with certainty.

'No sign of cult markings or Chaos symbology,' I mused.

'Maybe not,' said Bequin, crossing the room, being careful not to step on the smeared plastic sheet. For the sake of her shoes, not the crime scene, I was sure. 'What's this? Something was hung here.'

Two rusty hooks in the wall, scraped enough to show something had been hanging there recently. On the floor below was a curious cross drawn in yellow chalk.

'I've seen that before somewhere,' I said. My vox bleeped. It was Wrex.

'I've got that worker roster you asked for.'

'Good. Where are you?'

'Coming to find you at the tannery, if you're still there.'

'We'll meet you on the corner of Xerxes Street. Tell your staff we have a crime scene here in the agricultural warehouse.'

We walked out of the killing room towards the stairwell.

Fischig froze, and brought up his gun.

'Again?' I whispered.

He nodded, and pushed Bequin into the cover of a door jamb. Silence, apart from the rain and the scurry of vermin. Gun braced, Fischig looked up at the derelict roof. It may have been my imagination, but it seemed as if a shadow had moved across the bare rafters.

I moved forward, scanning the shadows with my pistol.

Something creaked. A floorboard.

Fischig pointed to the stairs. I nodded I understood, but the last thing I wanted was a mistaken shooting. I carefully keyed my vox and whispered, 'Wrex. You're not coming into the warehouse to find us, are you?'

'Negative, inquisitor.'

'Standby.'

Fischig had reached the top of the staircase. He peered down, aiming his weapon.

Las-fire erupted through the floorboards next to him and he threw himself flat.

I put a trio of shots into the mouth of the staircase, but my angle was bad.

Two hard round shots spat back up the stairs and then the roar and flash of the las came again, raking the floor.

From above, I realised belatedly. Whoever was on the stairs had a hard-slug side arm, but the las-fire was coming down from the roof.

I heard steps running on the floor below. Fischig scrambled up to give chase but another salvo of las-fire sent him ducking again.

I raised my aim and fired up into the roof tiles, blowing out holes through which the pale light poked.

Something slithered and scrambled on the roof.

Fischig was on the stairs now, running after the second assailant.

I hurried across the third floor, following the sounds of the man on the roof.

I saw a silhouette against the sky through a hole in the tiles and fired again. Las-fire replied in a bright burst, but then there was a thump and further slithering.

'Cease fire! Give yourself up! Inquisition!' I bellowed, using the will.

There came a much more substantial crash sounding like a whole portion of the roof had come down. Tiles avalanched down and smashed in a room nearby.

I slammed into the doorway, gun aimed, about to yell out a further will command. But there was no one in the room. Piles of shattered roofslates and bricks covered the floor beneath a gaping hole in the roof itself, and a battered lasrifle lay amongst the debris. On the far side of the room were some of the broken windows that Bequin had pointed out as overlooking the tannery roof.

I ran to one. Down below, a powerful figure in dark overalls was running for cover. The killer, escaping from me in just the same way his last victim had escaped him – through the windows onto the tannery roof.

The distance was too far to use the will again with any effect, but my aim and angle were good. I lined up on the back of the head a second before it disappeared, began to apply pressure–

–and the world exploded behind me.

I CAME ROUND cradled in Bequin's arms. 'Don't move, Eisenhorn. The medics are coming.'

'What happened?' I asked.

'Booby trap. The gun that guy left behind? It exploded behind you. Powercell overload.'

'Did Fischig get his man?'

'Of course he did.'

He hadn't, in fact. He'd chased the man hard down two flights of stairs and through the main floor of the warehall. At the outer door onto the street, the man had wheeled around and emptied his autopistol's clip at the chastener, forcing him into cover.

Then Captain Wrex, approaching from outside, had gunned the man down in the doorway.

WE ASSEMBLED IN Wrex's crowded office in the busy Arbites Mid-Rise Sector-house. Aemos joined us, laden down with

papers and data-slates, and brought Midas Betancore with
him.

'You all right?' Midas asked me. In his jacket of embroi-
dered cerise silk, he was a vivid splash of colour in the
muted gloom of mid-rise.

'Minor abrasions. I'm fine.'

'I thought we were leaving, and here you are having all the
fun without me.'

'I thought we were leaving too until I saw this case. Review
Bequin's notes. I need you up to speed.'

Aemos shuffled his ancient, augmetically assisted bulk
over to Wrex's desk and dropped his books and papers in an
unceremonious pile.

'I've been busy,' he said.

'Busy with results?' Bequin asked.

He looked at her sourly. 'No, actually. But I have gathered
a commendable resource of information. As the discussion
advances, I may be able to fill in blanks.'

'No results, Aemos? Most perturbatory,' grinned Midas, his
white teeth gleaming against his dark skin. He was mocking
the old savant by using Aemos's favourite phrase.

I had before me the work roster of the warehouse where
the three bodies had been found, and another for the agricultural store where our fight had occurred. Quick
comparison brought up two coincident names.

'Brell Sodakis. Vim Venik. Both worked as warehousemen
before the place closed down. Now they're employed by
Hundlemas Agricultural Stowage.'

'Backgrounds? Addresses?' I asked Wrex.

'I'll run checks,' she said.

'So... we have a cult here, eh?' Midas asked. 'You've got a
series of ritual killings, at least one murder site, and now the
names of two possible cultists.'

'Perhaps.' I wasn't convinced. There seemed both more
and less to this than had first appeared. Inquisitorial hunch.

The remains of the lasrifle discarded by my assailant lay
on an evidence tray. Even with the damage done by the over-
loading powercell, it was apparent that this was an old
model.

'Did the powercell overload because it was dropped? It fell through the roof, didn't it?' Bequin asked.

'They're pretty solid,' Fischig answered.

'Forced overload,' I said. 'An old Imperial Guard trick. I've heard they learn how to set one off. As a last ditch in tight spots. Cornered. About to die anyway.'

'That's not standard,' said Fischig, poking at the trigger guard of the twisted weapon. His knowledge of guns was sometimes unseemly. 'See this modification? It's been machine-tooled to widen the guard around the trigger.'

'Why?' I asked.

Fischig shrugged. 'Access? For an augmetic hand with rudimentary digits?'

We went through to a morgue room down the hall where the man Wrex had gunned down was lying on a slab. He was middle-aged, with a powerful frame going to seed. His skin was weatherbeaten and lined.

'Identity?'

'We're working on it.'

The body had been stripped by the morgue attendants. Fischig scrutinised it, rolling it with Wrex's help to study the back.

The man's clothes and effects were in plasteen bags in a tray at his feet. I lifted the bag of effects and held it up to the light.

'Tattoo,' reported Fischig. 'Imperial eagle, left shoulder. Crude, old. Letters underneath it... capital S period, capital I period, capital I, capital X.'

I'd just found the signet ring in the bag. Gold, with a wheatear motif.

'S.I. IX,' said Aemos. 'Sameter Infantry Nine.'

THE NINTH SAMETER Infantry had been founded in Urbitane twenty-three years before, and had served, as Aemos had already told me, in the brutal liberation war on Surealis Six. According to city records, five hundred and nineteen veterans of that war and that regiment had been repatriated to Sameter after mustering out thirteen years ago, coming back from the horrors of war to an increasingly depressed world beset by the blight of poverty and urban collapse. Their regimental emblem, as befitted a world once dominated by agriculture, was the wheatear.

'They came back thirteen years ago. The oldest victim we have dates from that time,' said Fischig.

'Surealis Six was a hard campaign, wasn't it?' I asked.

Aemos nodded. 'The enemy was dug in. It was ferocious, brutal. Brutalising. And the climate. Two white dwarf suns, no cloud cover. The most punishing heat and light, not to mention ultraviolet burning.'

'Ruins the skin,' I murmured. 'Makes it weatherbeaten and prematurely aged.'

Everyone looked at the taut, lined face of the body on the slab.

'I'll get a list of the veterans,' volunteered Wrex.

'I already have one,' said Aemos.

'I'm betting you find the names Brell Sodakis and Vim Venik on it,' I said.

Aemos paused as he scanned. 'I do,' he agreed.

'What about Quater Traves?'

'Yes, he's here. Master Gunnery Sergeant Quater Traves.'

'What about Omin Lund?'

'Ummm... yes. Sniper first class. Invalided out of service.'

'The Sameter Ninth were a mixed unit, then?' asked Bequin.

'All our Guard foundings are,' Wrex said proudly.

'So, these men... and women...' Midas mused. 'Soldiers, been through hell. Fighting the corruption... your idea is they brought it back here with them? Some taint? You think they were infected by the touch of the warp on Surealis and have been ritually killing as a way of worship back here ever since?'

'No,' I said. 'I think they're still fighting the war.'

IT REMAINS A sad truth of the Imperium that virtually no veteran ever comes back from fighting its wars intact. Combat alone shreds nerves and shatters bodies. But the horrors of the warp, and of foul xenos forms like the tyranid, steal sanity forever, and leave veterans fearing the shadows, and the

night and, sometimes, the nature of their friends and neigh-
bours, for the rest of their lives.

The guards of the Ninth Sameter Infantry had come home
thirteen years before, broken by a savage war against
mankind's arch-enemy and, through their scars and their
fear, brought their war back with them.

The arbites mounted raids at once on the addresses of all
the veterans on the list, those that could be traced, those that
were still alive. It appeared that skin cancer had taken over
two hundred of them in the years since their repatriation.
Surealis had claimed them as surely as if they had fallen
there in combat.

A number were rounded up. Bewildered drunks, cripples,
addicts, a few honest men and women trying diligently to
carry on with their lives. For those latter I felt especially
sorry.

But about seventy could not be traced. Many may well
have disappeared, moved on, or died without it coming to
the attention of the authorities. But some had clearly fled.
Lund, Traves, Sodakis, Venik for starters. Their habs were
found abandoned, strewn with possessions as if the occupant had left in a hurry. So were the habs of twenty more
belonging to names on the list.

The arbites arrived at the hab of one, ex-corporal Geffin
Sancto, in time to catch him in the act of flight. Sancto had
been a flamer operator in the guard, and like so many of his
kind, had managed to keep his weapon as a memento.
Screaming the battlecry of the Sameter Ninth, he torched
four arbites in the stairwell of his building before the tactical squads of the judiciary vaporised him in a hail of
gunshots.

'WHY ARE THEY killing?' Bequin asked me. 'All these years, in
secret ritual?'

'I don't know.'

'You do, Eisenhorn. You so do!'

'Very well. I can guess. The fellow worker who jokes at the
Emperor's expense and makes your fragile sanity imagine
he is tainted with the warp. The rug-maker whose patterns

suggest to you the secret encoding of Chaos symbols. The midwife you decide is spawning the offspring of the arch-enemy in the mid-rise maternity hall. The travelling evangelist who seems just too damn fired up to be safe.'

She looked down at the floor of the land speeder. 'They see daemons everywhere.'

'In everything. In every one. And, so help them, they believe they are doing the Emperor's work by killing. They trust no one, so they daren't alert the authorities. They take the eyes, the hands and the tongue... all the organs of communication, any way the arch-enemy might transmit his foul lies. And then they destroy the brain and heart, the organs which common soldier myth declares must harbour daemons.'

'So where are we going now?' she asked.

'Another hunch.'

THE GUILDHALL OF the Sameter Agricultural Fraternity was a massive ragstone building on Furnace Street, its facade decaying from the ministrations of smog and acid rain. It had been disused for over two decades.

Its last duty had been to serve as a recruitment post of the Sameter Ninth during the founding. In its long hallways, the men and women of the Ninth had signed their names, collected their starchy new fatigues, and pledged their battle oath to the God-Emperor of mankind.

At certain times, under certain circumstances, when a proper altar to the Emperor is not available, guard officers improvise in order to conduct their ceremonies. An Imperial eagle, an aquila standard, is suspended from a wall, and a sacred spot is marked on the floor beneath in yellow chalk.

The guildhall was not a consecrated building. The founding must have been the first time the young volunteers of Urbitane had seen that done. They'd made their vows to a yellow chalk cross and a dangling aquila.

Wrex was leading three fireteams of armed arbites, but I went in with Midas and Fischig first, quietly. Bequin and Aemos stayed by our vehicle.

Midas was carrying his matched needle pistols, and Fischig an auto shotgun. I clipped a slab-pattern magazine full of fresh rounds into the precious bolt pistol given to me by Librarian Brytnoth of the Adeptus Astartes Deathwatch Chapter.

We pushed open the boarded doors of the decaying structure and edged down the dank corridors. Rainwater pattered from the roof and the marble floor was spotted and eaten by collected acid.

We could hear the singing. A couple of dozen voices voicing up the Battle Hymn of the Golden Throne.

I led my companions forward, hunched low. Through the crazed windows of an inner door we looked through into the main hall. Twenty-three dishevelled veterans in ragged clothes were knelt down in ranks on the filthy floor, their heads bowed to the rusty Imperial eagle hanging on the wall as they sang. There was a yellow chalk cross on the floor under the aquila. Each veteran had a backpack or rucksack and a weapon by their feet.

My heart ached. This was how it had gone over two decades before, when they came to the service, young and fresh and eager. Before the war. Before the horror.

'Let me try... try to give them a chance,' I said.

'Gregor!' Midas hissed.

'Let me try, for their sake. Cover me.'

I slipped into the back of the hall, my gun lowered at my side, and joined in the verse.

One by one, the voices died away and bowed heads turned sideways to look at me. Down the aisle, at the chalk cross of the altar, Lund, Traves and a bearded man I didn't know stood gazing at me.

In the absence of other voices, I finished the hymn.

'It's over,' I said. 'The war is over and you have all done your duty. Above and beyond the call.'

Silence.

'I am Inquisitor Eisenhorn. I'm here to relieve you. The careful war against the blight of Chaos that you have waged through Urbitane in secret is now over. The Inquisition is here to take over. You can stand down.'

Two or three of the hunched veterans began to weep.

'You lie,' said Lund, stepping forward.

'I do not. Surrender your weapons and I promise you will be treated fairly and with respect.'

'Will... will we get medals?' the bearded man asked, in a quavering voice.

'The gratitude of the God-Emperor will be with you always.'

More were weeping now. Out of fear, anxiety or plain relief.

'Don't trust him!' said Traves. 'It's another trick!'

'I saw you in my bar,' said Lund, stepping forward. 'You came in looking.' Her voice was empty, distant.

'I saw you on the tannery roof, Omin Lund. You're still a fine shot, despite the hand.'

She looked down at her prosthetic with a wince of shame.

'Will we get medals?' the bearded man repeated, eagerly. Traves turned on him. 'Of course we won't, Spake, you cretin! He's here to kill us!'

'I'm not–' I began.

'I want medals!' the bearded man, Spake, screamed suddenly, sliding his laspistol up from his belt with the fluid speed only a trained soldier can manage.

I had no choice.

His shot tore through the shoulder padding of my storm coat. My bolt exploded his head, spraying blood across the rusty metal eagle on the wall.

Pandemonium.

The veterans leapt to their feet firing wildly, scattering, running.

I threw myself flat as shots tore out the wall plaster behind me. At some point Fischig and Midas burst in, weapons blazing. I saw three or four veterans drop, sliced through by silent needles and another six tumble as shotgun rounds blew them apart.

Traves came down the aisle, blasting his old service-issue lasrifle at me. I rolled and fired, but my shot went wide. His face distorted as a needle round punched through it and he fell in a crumpled heap.

Wrex and her fireteams exploded in. Flames from some spilled accelerants billowed up the wall.

I got up, and then was throw back by a las shot that blew off my left hand.

Spinning, falling, I saw Lund, struggling to make her prosthetic fingers work the unmodified trigger of Traves's lasgun.

My bolt round hit her with such force she flew back down the aisle, hit the wall, and tore the Imperial aquila down.

NOT A SINGLE veteran escaped the guildhall alive. The firefight raged for two hours. Wrex lost five men to the experienced guns of the Sameter Ninth veterans. They stood to the last. No more can be said of any Imperial Guard unit.

THE WHOLE AFFAIR left me sour and troubled. I have devoted my life to the service of the Imperium, to protect it against its manifold foes, inside and out.

But not against its servants. However misguided, they were loyal and true. However wrong, they were shaped that way by the service they had endured in the Emperor's name.

Lund cost me my hand. A hand for a hand. They gave me a prosthetic on Sameter. I never used it. For two years, I made do with a fused stump. Surgeons on Messina finally gave me a fully functional graft.

I consider it still a small price to pay for them.

I have never been back to Sameter. Even today, they are still finding the secreted, hidden bodies. So very many, dead in the Emperor's name.

LIBERTY

A Kage story
Gav Thorpe

PRISON GUARD Serpival Lance suppressed a yawn and withdrew into the sentry alcove a little further to get out of the driving wind and dust. The permanent tempest howled around the roof of the tower, all but obscuring the ruddy lights that shone from the edge of the landing pad only a dozen metres away. He had been on duty for three hours and still had three to go, and he glanced enviously at the light shining beneath the door of the guardhouse to his left. Here he was, wrapped up in his heavy weather coat, hood pulled tight around his face, while the others laughed and played cards inside. It wasn't right for a man of his age. He had served the Emperor on this prison planet for thirty years, and still he was stuck out here on Emperor-forsaken nights like this.

His misanthropic musings were interrupted when the internal comm-speaker squawked behind him. He pressed the receiver rune and bent his aching back to listen closely.

'He's come back. Due to land in a few minutes,' the guard captain's voice crackled over the comm-set. Serpival grunted an acknowledgement and cast his eye into the cloud-covered skies. It wasn't long before the landing beacon sprung to life, a guiding low energy laser piercing the gloom from the centre of the landing pad. Shortly after, answering lights could be seen glimmering in the darkness as the shuttle descended, the howl of its engines growing clearer and clearer as they drew closer and blotted out the noise of the wind.

With a clang of metal landing feet on the mesh surface of the roof, the shuttle settled, its engines at a roar which kicked up the dust into even more violent swirls before cutting out. An erratically wobbling entry gantry extended out from the docking area and connected with the shuttle's hatchway. The door opened and banged against the shuttle fuselage and a tall uniformed figure stepped out. The three guards in the tower spilled out and stood to attention by the doorway into the interior. The Imperial Guard officer said something to them and pointed inside the shuttle. The guards saluted and hurried past to emerge a moment later carrying a heavy bundle.

Curious, and knowing that it was a breach of regulations but unable to stop himself, Serpival ducked out of the sentry post and hurried across the rooftop to the others. They were carrying a man, slumped unconscious in their arms, dressed in full combat fatigues and camouflaged in black and dark blues. As they bundled him into the room, his head lolled towards Serpival and the guard suppressed a shudder at the sight of the man's face. It was horrifically scarred, criss-crossed by weals and cuts, bullet grazes and burns.

'The governor has all of the official notification. Lock him up with the rest,' the officer said curtly before turning on his heel and walking back towards the shuttle.

At that moment the new prisoner groaned and came round, shaking his head. The others lowered him to the floor, glancing at the retreating back of the officer. Groggily, the Imperial Guardsman stood up, blinking his eyes to clear them.

'Where the frag?' he asked, still slightly disorientated.

'Ghovul vincularum,' Serpival told him.

'A prison planet?' the man asked for confirmation, his eyes suddenly focussing on Serpival, all dizziness gone, making the guard squirm as if he were looking down the barrel of a lasgun.

'Yes, a prison,' the guard repeated himself, nervous under the evil stare of the newcomer.

It was then that the prisoner followed the gaze of the others. The officer was just climbing through the hatchway.

'Come back here, you bastard! Schaeffer, you sump sucking piece of crap!' the newly arrived inmate screamed, roughly shoving Serpival aside and taking a step out onto the docking gantry. The officer turned, looked once and then slammed the hatch shut without a word. The prisoner broke into a run, yelling incoherently, and the other guards sprinted after him.

It was Shrank who caught him first, grappling the man's left arm. The prisoner stumbled, recovered his footing and then smashed the extended fingers of his right hand into Shrank's face, who fell away screaming, clutching at his eyes. Frentz swung a right-handed punch, but the guardsman easily swayed to his left, delivering a short kick to the prison officer's knee that made it snap the wrong way, tumbling him to the ground with shrieks of agony.

The shuttle engines roared back into full life, bathing the rooftop in their white glare, the prisoner silhouetted against them, his fist raised, his words of hatred drowned out by the noise.

Serpival and the remaining guard, Jannsen, drew their heavy pistols and took aim at the prisoner, who stood there, fist still raised, watching the departing shuttle.

'Try any more of that and I'll plug you, you vicious scumbag!' Jannsen called out.

The prisoner turned around slowly, his face lit by the lights of the landing pad, bathing his scarred features in a hellish red glow. Slowly the man walked back towards them, and Serpival had to fight to remain calm and his grip on his pistol steady as the stranger slowly strode towards them, murderous intent on his face. He stopped a couple of metres away.

'Just take me to my fraggin' cell before I take that pistol off you,' the man growled, nodding towards the gun in Jannsen's shaking grip.

'The prisoner will lie face down and do as he is told,' Jannsen said, without much confidence.

'Kage,' the prisoner replied, glancing at each of them in turn and then stepping easily between them, looking back over his shoulder at Serpival. 'Call me Kage.'

I'M STANDING THERE wishing this repetitive, idiotic man would just shut the hell up. The prison governor is a sour, hatchet-faced man, crouched like a malevolent rodent behind his massive desk. That desk says volumes on its own – three metres wide, two metres deep, an Imperial eagle burnt into the surface but otherwise empty. He sits there behind it, elbows resting on the deep red wood, his chin resting on the knuckles of his clasped hands as he drones on and on and on. Behind him are two guards with shotguns, and I know there are two more behind me, similarly armed. They really don't trust me in here with their commander.

'Which is why you will adhere by these rules at all times,' Governor Skandlegrist is saying, peering at me over a pair of half-moon glasses. He is dressed in layered robes of black and deep red, strangely matching the desk in colour. 'Punishment for infractions will vary depending on the severity of the offence. I have had special instructions from Colonel Schaeffer to keep an eye on you, Kage, and I will do so. I will be watching you like a hawk, and if you step out of line the full force of my authority here will fall upon you. Be warned, you are under close observation, so don't think you can get away with anything, anything at all.'

'Right, I get the picture,' I butt in desperately, taking a step forward which causes the guards to pull up their shotguns. At least they're paying attention, which is more than I am. 'Can I just get to my cell now?'

'Your disrespect for a commanding officer is shocking, Kage, as is your disregard for the laws and regulations of the Imperial Guard,' Skandlegrist replies. 'You are a bad seed, Kage, and I have no idea why Colonel Schaeffer wants you to be detained at this facility instead of being on the gallows like you should be, no idea at all. But, unlike you, I have my orders and I follow them, and follow them I will, mark my words. Yes, I'll be watching you, Kage, very closely, very closely indeed.'

With a gesture from thin, crabby fingers he orders the guards to escort me out. We're near the top of the tower, maybe just a couple of floors down from the landing pad on the roof. The whole tower is a broad cylinder, with just a single elevator shaft linking all the floors at the circle's centre. We stand there while the lift cranks and rattles up from the depths of the tower, the guards still nervous and agitated.

When the conveyor arrives, one of the guards opens the doors, which squeal on rusting hinges with an ear-grinding shriek. A shotgun butt in my back propels me into the interior of the open ironwork cage, and they follow me in, not standing too close, guns lowered at my belly. One of them pulls the lever, to the eighteenth storey I note, and we start to judder our way down the shaft.

'Shrank was my friend, you piece of filth,' one of the guards hisses in my ear over the sound of grinding gears. 'I'm gonna make you pay for blinding him, one of these days.'

I turn and look at him with a patronising smile.

'You try anything, I'll rip your arm off and shove it down that big mouth of yours,' I tell him, meeting his gaze and causing him to flinch.

'I bet,' he says, recovering well. Before I realise what he's doing, he slams the shotgun in his hands straight into my chin, smacking my head against the iron grillwork of the elevator cage. Another one steps up and puts a boot into my gut, winding me badly, while the first jabs the shotgun into my face again, bruising my right cheek. Another three or four blows rain down on me. I take the brunt of it on my shoulders, before they step back, panting.

I crouch there for a moment before straightening up, feeling my right eye begin to swell and close. I roll my neck with an audible clicking and look at each of them in turn through my good eye. I take a good look at them, memorising the names on the tags on their uniforms.

'I'm gonna kill all of you meatheads, and I'm gonna do it slowly,' I warn them, meaning every word of it.

As I step into the cell, the door clangs behind me. There's a rough ironwork bunk on either side of the room; the left one has an occupant. He snorts and wakes, sitting up. He's a huge bear of a man. As the crudely spun woollen blanket falls from his torso, it reveals a mass of hair across his broad chest, shoulders and back. He looks at me in the dim light of the glow-globe set behind a grille in the ceiling, his dark eyes almost invisible under a bushy brow. His hair is cropped short on top, as is his full beard, and over his right eye he has a tattoo of a pair of dice, mirrored on his left cheek. He gives a wheezing grunt and swivels further around.

'Welcome to Ghovul,' he says, his voice a hoarse whisper. I ignore him for the moment, sitting myself down on the other bed, nursing the growing bruises on my chest and ribs.

'Guards don't like you then, man,' my cellmate comments, and I look up at him.

'Nobody likes me,' I say quietly. 'I prefer it that way. Puts everybody in the same place. Me and everyone else. Frag, even I don't like me.'

'Thor's teeth, man, I can see you're gonna cheer me up with your witty banter,' the other man grumbles, his fat lips twisted into a sour grimace. 'Name's Marn.'

'Kage,' I say, offering him my hand to shake. As he leans forward, I see he really is hairy pretty much all over. He takes my hand in his massive paw, giving it a firm squeeze which I return. We sit there for a couple of seconds, measuring each other up.

'You're not gonna give me any trouble, man, are you?' he asks, letting go. 'I keep myself to myself, and if you do the same then we'll get along fine.'

'I'm not much for gabbling and gossip,' I reassure him. 'In fact, if these are the last words we say to each other, that wouldn't bother me for a moment.'

'Well,' he replies, rubbing his hand across his head and lying back down again. 'You don't have to go that far, man, but we're cellmates, not friends.'

'Damn right,' I reply, unlacing my boots and placing them neatly under the bed. 'All my friends are long dead.'

I strip off my socks and shirt, slide under the blanket and close my eyes. I'm weary as a poor infantry footslogger after a week's marching, but sleep won't come. My mind is whirling with recent events. After the Colonel picked me up again, I've been in a holding cell aboard the *Pride of Lothos*. Must have been several weeks travelling, crossed quite a few systems I reckon. I didn't see hide nor hair of the Colonel until I got here, and he was leaving me to rot in this cell.

Emperor knows what he's got in store for me. After all, the last words I heard him say were, 'I can shoot you right now, or I can give you one more Last Chance.' I bloody said yes of course, considering he was pointing a pistol at me at the time. But that's all I know. I've got one more Last Chance. I figure that's another spell in the Colonel's suicide squad, the 13th Penal Legion. Another suicide mission or two, another chance to get my arse blown off and back again on some hellhole or other, fighting some poxy aliens or heretics who should know better than to try their luck fighting the Emperor's armies. Maybe I'll be blowing up another city, who can tell?

All I know is that if the Colonel wanted me to just rot in a cell, he would have left to rot on that prison planet he first picked me up from. And if he wanted me dead, well then he would have just pulled the trigger and blown my head to bits. He's got something in store, I'm certain of that. But I don't really plan on hanging around for it to happen.

With that in mind, and the droning noise of Marn's snoring, I begin to drift asleep.

THE CLATTER OF bowls and plates fills the mess halls as the inmates sit down with their food. I'm sat on a bench at a long wooden table, twenty of us to each side, the bowl of soup, the hunk of dark bread and the plate of what may once have been meat but now resembles boot leather in front of me. We sit there patiently, waiting. It's about half a minute before Preacher Cleator starts his sermon. He keeps it short, like he normally does, Emperor bless the doddering old fart, and mumbles something about the bounties of faith and the punishments of sin. Just like he has done for the last sixteen days I've been here. He finishes.

'Praise the Emperor,' we all intone solemnly before grabbing up our knives and spoons and tucking in with gusto. The food tastes like crap, but when you only get cold gruel for breakfast and this sump filth twelve hours later, you'll eat whatever they dump in front of you. It's quite varied, to tell the truth. Sometimes the unidentifiable carcass is seared beyond recognition into charcoal, other times it's so bloody and raw I'd swear the fragging thing is probably still breathing. Never somewhere in between though, never nicely cooked. And the thin, watery spew that passes for soup, well, it probably came out the same animal is all I can say. Doesn't stop me soaking up every last drop with the fist-sized hunk of mud that passes for bread. Better than going hungry, as I learnt from two years of protein chunks on my last tour out with the Last Chancers.

Marn is sat opposite me, wolfing his food down. Thor's blood, but he eats fast. Not an ounce wasted though, it all gets crammed into that maw of his with ruthless efficiency. It's like watching a well-oiled machine at work, both hands working simultaneously, his jaws chewing constantly, barely pausing for split second for him to open his lips and shove another quivering spoonful into his mouth. Thirty seconds and he's done, while I'm barely halfway through the soup, which is piping hot if nothing else. Emperor knows how he stays so big on such meagre rations, because he must weigh at least half as much again as I do.

We all eat in silence; nobody really has anything to say. It's odd, comparing this prison with life on the *Pride of Lothos*. There was upward of two hundred of us in each of those converted holds, and we pretty much hated each other's guts. But we were a fighting unit, we were in squads and platoons, and had some kind of unity from that. We all had our little groups which we kept to, who we talked to stop ourselves going mental and slashing our own throats or blowing our brains out the next time we went into battle. Well, after a while, I remember when we first got to Ichar IV, the first war-zone we were deployed on, there was a good eighty, ninety soldiers topped themselves in the first week. I don't know if that was the effect of fighting the tyranids, or the realisation that they were gonna be stuck in one long war until they died, with no respite and no pardons. Well, no pardons back then, at least.

Here, it's every man for himself. There's you, and a vague bond with your cellmate, and that's it. It's driving me nuts, and no mistaking. I wake up at first light, well, when the glow-globes on the landing outside the cells come on any-way. I never have been a heavy sleeper, I'll wake up at a gnat's cough. I lie there for maybe three hours before break-fast call. Then we're roused out, herded to the hose rooms to get washed down, then we come down here, to the mess hall at the bottom of the tower. It takes forever, only a handful of prisoners and twice as many guards in the lift at one time. It's a really inefficient system for moving large numbers of prisoners around. Perhaps I'll make a complaint to the gov-ernor. Anyway, it takes the best part of an hour to get the two hundred or so prisoners into the hall and then we all queue up again for our slop. We sit there while the guards hand out the knives and spoons and the preacher totters about, wav-ing incense around in the rusty old burner that usually hangs from his belt, staining his white robes browny-orange down his left leg. Then it's five minutes to eat up, another wait while they count the knives back in, and gather up the spoons and dishes. Then back in groups of twenty up in the exercise hall on one of the middle levels, for two hours. After that, back to Marn's quiet company for nine hours until the whole meal ordeal is repeated for dinner. Then it's lock up and shut up.

Deacis's holy arse, but I'm bored out of my wits. All my bitching about suicide missions and getting my face blown off aside, I'd much rather be out there with the Colonel doing whatever insane thing it is he's doing, than stuck in here slowly getting older, with my brain dribbling out of my

ears. My resolve hardens. Another month here and I'm going
to be smashing my grey matter out on the walls of that cell,
standing over Marn's ragged corpse, screaming and damning
Schaeffer's name to the Abyssal Chaos and back. I have to
get out of this fragging tower.

DAY EIGHTEEN, AND my desperation is beginning to grow. Last
night, Marn's snoring was driving me insane. I can't sleep as
it is, even pushing myself to the limits in the two hours of
exercise I'm allowed is nowhere near enough to tire me out.
I feel so lethargic and tired; this inactivity is slowly killing
me. If the Colonel does come back for me, which I'm starting to doubt more and more with each passing day, I'll be a
flabby, useless piece of filth, rather than the fit, lean soldier
I was when he brought me in here. Surely he wouldn't let
such a good fighter go to waste like that. Anyway, Marn's
snoring like a fire klaxon, his wheezing breaths echoing off
the walls, driving through my ears right into my brain. I got
up, and my fingers were within centimetres of his throat.
Hell, he wouldn't have known a thing, my thumbs would've
crushed his windpipe before he even woke up. I'd probably
be doing him a favour. I must have been stood over him like
that for over an hour, resisting that murderous urge.

  I work out what anger I can on the sand-filled punch bag,
pounding my bare fists into the poorly tanned leather, alter-
nating between imagining Marn's hairy face there and the
Colonel's chiselled features. There's just me and them, and I
work and work, throwing jabs and crosses, bone-breaking
uppercuts, organ splitting body blows, kicks that would
burst men's intestines and shatter ribs into dozens of pieces.
I picture all this in my mind, and it's easy, because I've done
it to real men and seen the effects. I imagine the blood
flooding from Marn's nostrils as I drive my elbow into what
would be the bridge of his nose. I imagine the Colonel collapsing breathless as the middle knuckle of my left hand
slams into his abdomen. Over and over, punishing them
with my fists and feet, until even my callused knuckles are
raw and bleeding, the thick skin scraped off on the clumsily
made punchbag. Sweat pours off me in rivulets, I can feel it

rolling down my back, splashing all around me as I wallop Marn with a right roundhouse to his bushy eyebrow. My heart's hammering in my chest, the blood coursing through my body, fuelling the destruction of these two hated men.

Suddenly I'm aware of someone stood behind me. I spin on my right heel, fists raised. There's another prisoner there, I've seen him here every day, obviously, but I don't know his name. Marn's the only person here whose name I know. He's a little taller than me, with muscles bulging out of his ragged vest like boulders. He looks like he was carved rather than grown. His bald head is tattooed with blue flames, as are his massive chest muscles and biceps.

'You've been on that for ages. My turn, trooper,' he says, nodding towards the bloodied punch bag. 'I think it realises you don't like it.'

'I'm not finished yet,' I tell him, turning away and taking up my stance again.

'I wasn't asking,' he barks, shoving me to one side, almost knocking me off my feet.

'Frag off, or I'll kill you,' I warn him, squaring up.

'Go play with the others, pretty boy,' he laughs.

He stops laughing when the extended fingers of my right hand slam into his throat. He reels back and I follow up immediately, slamming a left hook into his jaw, his face already reddening from choking, and then catching him under the chin with the heel of my right hand. I hear shouting and chanting start up around me, but don't listen, focussing on this bastard in front of me instead. He flails madly, forcing me to duck, and as I rise, my right fist drives straight into his nose, ripping open a nostril and crunching cartilage. He stumbles back against the bare stone wall and I feel rather than see the other prisoners and the guards forming up around us. Their noise is blocked out by the roar of blood in my ears.

A spinning kick to his midriff hurls him back against the wall as he rebounds towards me, and I get my whole body weight behind the next punch, driving it between his eyes and smashing his head back against the unforgiving stone, leaving a bloody stain as he slumps to one side.

'That's enough,' I hear someone shout and a guard's gloved hand closes around my right wrist. With a simple twist of my hands, I snap his arm at the elbow, not even turning around, and drive the heel of my left boot into the other prisoner's face again, crushing his jaw and cheek, and pounding his head against the wall once more. He flops to the ground and I stamp on his neck for good measure, feeling the crack of his spine snapping like a twig. Then something hard smacks across the back of my neck, stunning me and forcing me to my knees. I see the baton swing across my face and feel a sharp pain across my forehead before I fall unconscious.

I'M STOOD TO attention in the governor's office again, nursing a bump on my head the size of Terra and still feeling groggy. There's six armsmen in here with me this time, I figure that the governor's not one to take chances.

'I am sure I don't have to tell you that this kind of behaviour is wholly inappropriate, wholly inappropriate to a military facility, whether it be a garrison or a prison,' he tells me.

'I understand well the pressures placed upon our inmates, and that occasionally tempers will flare. In fact, given our population, I expect instances of this kind now and then. We have highly trained, aggressive soldiers penned up here, and fuses can be short on occasion with no outlet for that professional aggression. In most cases, I am lenient and understanding.'

'That's very broad-minded of you, sir,' I say, resisting the urge to rub the bruise on my forehead.

'However,' Skandlegrist continues, with a scowl of annoyance, 'I cannot tolerate the death of another prisoner at your hands. Fighting and brawling I consider an unpleasant but necessary evil of running a vincularum. Murder I do not. Murder, cold-blooded or otherwise, is not an option, and an example will be made of you.'

'That's ridiculous,' I snort, earning another stare from the governor. 'I've been trained to kill. That's what I do. What do you expect? It's the whole point of fighting, isn't it?'

'You are trained to fight and kill under orders, Kage,' snaps the prison governor, standing up, his expression hard. 'You were trained to be a disciplined killer, to exterminate the enemies of the Emperor as ordered by your superior officers. You were not trained to kill every man or woman who happens to disagree with you. You are so far out of line, Kage, and you do not even see it. If I cannot convince you, perhaps the whip can. As the authority of the Imperial Commissariat on this world, I sentence you to two dozen lashes, to be carried out before breakfast tomorrow in front of the other inmates. I could, and would, normally order you executed for this heinous, malicious act, but given the specific orders I received from Colonel Schaeffer that is not an option available to me. Take him away!'

He spins on his heel and clasps his hands behind him, ignoring me as the armsmen grab me by the arms and roughly bundle me out of the room.

'Costaz should get the honour,' one of them says to the others. I remember that name; it was the guard who attacked me in the elevator.

The solemn beat of a drum echoes around the exercise hall, whose walls are lined with the assembled prisoners and guards. At one end, a wooden slab with two chains hanging from thick rings is propped up against the wall, the governor stood next to it. Two guards walk in front of me, with four others behind, my punishment escort. At a slow march, we pace across the hall in time to the drum. I look at the sea of faces, recognising none of them; they're just a blur of different coloured flesh all wrapped up in the same drab grey prison fatigues.

'Prisoner and escort, halt!' commands the governor, his voice surprisingly loud and strong. We all halt, our boots clashing in unity on the bare boards of the floor.

'Prisoner, advance!' the governor orders me forward and I step out sharply, my chin high, looking at the chains on the wooden board. I spread-eagle myself against the board, and two guards step forward and clasp the manacles around my wrists, before pulling the chains up, stretching me out, and fastening them to bolts screwed into the top edge of the slab. One of them offers me a leather strap, and I open my mouth and he places it between my teeth. This isn't the first time I've taken a whipping. I know the routine. I bite down hard, vaguely wondering who else's mouth the leather bit has been in.

I hear the clump of the guards' boots as they withdraw and focus my attention on the grain of the wood in front of me. The wood is quite pale, but dark red stains the grooves between the planks, and the deeper areas of grain. There's no mistaking that it's blood, the blood of those who've been punished like this. There are a few score marks above my right shoulder, though I can't think what could have caused them.

It's then that I realise the governor is talking again.

'...in accordance with Imperial Guard regulations,' I hear him finish.

There's a hiss behind me and a short crack a moment before searing pain tears across my shoulder blades as the whip's end opens up a furrow in my skin. I bite harder on the leather, my eyes going wide as agony wracks my back. There'll be no blood trickling down yet, it'll be five or six more before the weals split into cuts and gashes. Another hiss and crack and more pain, this time further down, across the small of my back. It's fleshier down there and the pain seems to spread further around to my sides. I block it out, it's easy at the moment. It was more painful when a tyranid warrior stuck its bonesword through my thigh on Deliverance. It was a hell of a lot more painful when a spore mine exploded in my face, hideously scarring me for the rest of my life and making one side of my face almost totally numb. Another hiss and crack, and pain explodes across my shoulders again. I don't know if it is the guard who attacked me holding the whip, but whoever he is, he knows his stuff. Four more times the lash rips across my spine before I can feel the trickle of my blood oozing out of the lacerated flesh.

I close my eyes until they water as he carries on, methodically, relentless tearing strips of skin and fat from my back. I lose count and open my eyes again, staring deep into the wood, pretending I'm elsewhere as hot pain burns across the whole of my body. In the short pause between blows, I glance up and see blood leaking out of my clenched fists and on to the chain, from where I'm clenching my hands so hard my nails have broken the skin. I relax them, only to tighten my grip even more when the next lash strikes me.

And that's how it goes on until the sentence is carried out. My eyes are watering, my throat is constricted and my heart is hammering in my chest, but not once do I cry out. I take the pain, and I take it deep inside. Storing it away, using it as fuel for myself. My life has been built on pain, pain that I'll throw back at my enemies. Pain and agony that I'm saving up for the Colonel. As the guards unfasten the manacles, I give a grunt, the only noise to have passed my lips. It's a grunt of satisfaction, because deep inside that pain is boiling around, and it'll come out one day. One day when the Colonel's throat is in my grip. This is just another episode of pain and hate in the life he's created for me, and I'll pay every second of it back to him. Every second.

IT'S FOUR DAYS of agony before I can even start thinking straight again, laid up in the tower's infirmary, my back swathed in saltwater-soaked bandages. It hurts like a bastard, but the salt will help my tattered back knit itself together. The prison surgeon, some inmate called Stroniberg, had to put a few stitches into the worst of the cuts, but my back was so numb by then I didn't feel a thing. The day after I'm out of the infirmary, I begin to plot my escape.

There's only one way out of the tower, and that's the roof. If I can get up there, perhaps with a rope or something, I'll be able to scale the outside wall and get to safety. There's one problem. The only way up to the roof is the elevator. I have to find some way of gaining control of the elevator long enough to reach the top. I'm not sure yet how to do that, but I know a weapon of some kind will be needed. I have to work out a way of making a weapon, easily concealed but deadly.

The answer comes to me during dinner the next day. As they've always done, the guards clear away the knives first, keeping careful count of them. I'd never get away with one of them. However, the spoons on the other hand are just cleared away with the rest of the dishes, without too much attention paid to them. At breakfast the day after, I make my move.

Everybody's finishing their gruel, well everybody except my gluttonous cellmate who wolfs his down without taking a breath. Next to me is a slim man, with tawny hair and a drawn face. To be honest I've never noticed him before, I've always sat fixated watching the eating machine on the opposite side of the bench from me. Today, however, he becomes the object of my attention.

I rise to my feet with a roar, smashing his dishes and mine across him.

'What did you say about my mother?' I bellow at him, grabbing him by the collar of his prison vest. He snarls wordlessly at me, and swings a punch which I put my head down into so his fist cracks against the hard part of my brow. I heave him upwards and slam him down onto the table, scattering more bowls and spoons and cold gruel over those nearby. The prisoner opposite and to my right lunges at me across the table, but I drag the skinny guy upward, so the other inmate's punch slams squarely across his face. Letting go of him, I turn to the man on my left, seeing out of the corner of my eye that Marn is starting to lay into the guy who tried to attack me.

Pretty soon, there's seven or eight of them brawling around me. One of them punches me on the chin and I roll with the blow, hurling myself over the bench and rolling under the table. Quickly, I snatch up one of the discarded spoons and shove it into my boot, pulling my fatigues out of them to hide the long handle. I shelter there for about half a minute more, and then emerge as the guards break up the fight. One of them grabs me and pushes me to one side.

'Clear this mess up, troublemaker,' he growls at me, pointing to the broken dishes and scattered cutlery.

'Of course, sir, sorry about that,' I mumble, dropping to my knees and picking up the pieces of cracked pottery and gathering up the spoons. I stand there holding the jumbled mess until another guard turns up with a metal basin and tells me to drop it all in.

'No dinner tonight, Kage,' the guard with the basin tells me. 'If you can't eat without acting like an animal, then you can't eat.'

'Sorry, sir,' I apologise again. 'I'll watch my temper in future.' Inside I'm grinning like a fool. The plan's starting to work.

It takes three nights of furtive labour to file the edge of the spoon's bowl into a sharper blade. The scraping hidden by Marn's snoring, I spend my night hours rasping the spoon back and forth across the bricks of the wall, under my bed so a casual inspection won't see the score marks. Another four days of rubbing, my hands cramping on occasion with holding the thin handle of the spoon, allows me to sharpen the end of the handle into a point. Perfect for piercing throats, lungs and windpipes. With my weapon sorted out, albeit a bit of a crude one, I turn my attention to what I have to do next.

The elevator only stops at a floor when it's time for meals, ablutions or exercise period, and at those times, there's always a bunch of guards and other prisoners around. Certainly too many people for an efficient escape attempt. I need to think of some way to get the guards to make a special visit, only one or two of them preferably, and somehow get them to open the cell door at the same time.

It's two sleepless nights listening to Marn's incessant droning snore before the answer comes to me. It brings an ironic smile to my face when I think about it. I rise up in the dim glow through the vision slit in the door and pull my pillow clear from my bed. I stand over Marn, considering my options, and decide this is the best one. I lean down and place the pillow over his face, pushing ever so slightly harder and harder so as not to startle him. He wakes up briefly, eyes staring wide at me in accusation, but lack of breath pushes him into unconsciousness a few seconds later. I pull the pillow off, and check that he's still breathing, but only

shallowly. I don't want him dead yet. Taking my makeshift
knife from where it's concealed under my mattress, I roll
Marn onto his side. I count down his ribs and probe the
sharp end of the spoon between the fifth and sixth one,
almost effortlessly sliding the point back, puncturing his
lung. I let him flop back and then sit on my bed and wait.

It's several minutes before his breathing gets more and
more laboured, and then flecks of blood start appearing on
his lips. Soon, more is bubbling up into his mouth and I
decide it's time to act.

Running to the door I shout through the grille at the
guard stationed a few doors down.

'Quick!' I call to him. 'Something's wrong with Marn. I
think he's got a pox or something, lungrot maybe.'

The guard stride over towards me, his expression full of
suspicion.

'Look for yourself,' I say, backing away from the door. He
shines a handlamp through the grille onto Marn, the small
circle of light settling on his face and the trickle of crimson
from the corner of his mouth. The guard swears and I hear
him pound off across the landing. A couple of minutes pass
before the clank of the elevator sounds from the shaft, followed by the rusty creaking of the guard opening the doors.
It's another tense three or four minutes before the elevator
returns.

'Back into the far corner, Kage,' I hear the guard order me,
and I do as he says, my hands behind my back concealing
the sharpened spoon.

There's a rattle of keys and the door opens. There are three
guards stood there, and between them a medical orderly.
He's dressed as a trustee, one of the sycophantic inmates
who's got extra responsibilities by behaving himself and
toadying to the governor or guards. They step inside, and the
orderly bends over Marn, checking his breathing. I wait,
poised to act, until the guards are looking at my dying cellmate.

Three steps and I've crossed the cell, slashing the blade
across the jugular of the guard closest to me, blood fountaining through the gloom. I kick the next guard hard in the

chest, hurling him against the wall, and wrap my arm around the startled trustee's throat, the point of the spoon hovering next to his right eyeball. The third freezes where he is, hand hovering over the pistol at his belt.

'One wrong move and he dies,' I snarl as the winded guard clambers to his feet, his face aghast under a thick mop of black hair.

'What the hell are you doing, Kage?' he asks quietly, his eyes straying to the corpse of his comrade.

'Back out onto the landing, meatheads,' I tell them, tightening my grip on the orderly, who squeals on cue.

'You can't go anywhere,' the dark-haired guard continues, trying to circle to my right, but I swivel on my heel, dragging the trustee with me, to keep him in view.

'I said to stay still!' I snap, ramming the spoon into the orderly's eye, who screeches briefly before collapsing. I hurl the body at the circling guard and dive at the other, who pulls his pistol free a moment before my hands close on his wrist and snap upwards, cracking open the bones in his arm. I snatch the gun from him as he collapses backwards cradling his arm and round on the remaining warden.

'Don't,' I warn him, the muzzle of the pistol aimed squarely between his eyes.

'Drop your weapons,' I say, and he does as he's told, unbuckling his belt and letting it clatter to the ground. 'Now out through the door.' I wave him on his way, darting a glance at the guard with the broken arm, but he's slumped on the floor, whimpering. Hooking his weapons belt over my shoulder, I follow the guard on to the landing.

We make our way over to the elevator and I push him inside before swinging the doors closed behind us. Switching the pistol to my left hand to keep him covered, I crank the lever fully to the right, and the conveyor begins to rumble into motion.

Floor by agonising floor we slowly crawl our way up the centre of the tower, the progress of the elevator marked out by an illuminated dial set above the door way. We're twenty floors short when a klaxon starts to sound out, an escape warning.

'They're onto you,' the guard says with satisfaction. 'They've got orders to kill you if you resist. Give yourself up or you'll die.'

'You won't see it,' I tell him, pulling the trigger of the pistol and blowing half his face away. As the gunshot's retort still echoes around me, the elevator creaks to a halt, and then begins to descend again. I try the lever desperately, but there must be some kind of external override. I glance around the conveyor and notice the maintenance access panel in the roof.

Ramming the pistol into my belt, I jump up and smash the panel open. Leaping again, I get a grip on the edge and pull myself on to the elevator roof. Above me, dimly lit by sparsely placed glow-globes, the shaft stretches upwards out of sight. I see the doors to other levels passing me, and walking to the edge, I look down and see light pouring from several entrances not far below me, where the guards have forced the doors open. I can't stay where I am, too much of an easy target.

There's a ladder running the length of the elevator shaft, up the wall just across a small gap. It's no big matter to grab one rung as I slowly descend, and pull myself on to it. Dragging the pistol free, I aim at the receding shape of the elevator's braking block and fire two shots. There's a hiss of hydraulic fluid spraying into the gloom, and the elevator picks up pace, accelerating down the shaft. I've been climbing for several seconds before there's an ear-shattering crash from below as the lift hits the bottom of the shaft.

I haul myself upwards as fast as I can, more light pours into the shaft from opened doors above and below me. Something ricochets off the wall next to me, accompanied by the sharp crack of a pistol. Soon more bullets are flying, tracers amongst them, some of them passing close by, others way off. The guards can't really see me, they're aiming blind. I pull myself up a few more floors, the fire pinging and screaming around me, and then pause for breath. At that moment, the door on the opposite side swings open, and I hang there face to face with two trustees and a couple of guards.

I react first, bringing up the pistol and emptying the clip into them, punching them off their feet in a hail of bullets. The shots at me intensify from above, and I swing off the ladder into a small maintenance alcove just to my left. Crouched there, I discard the empty pistol and pull the other free from the belt, throwing that down the shaft as well.

I crouch at the edge of the alcove, and fire a few shots upwards, aiming for the rectangles of light that indicate the open doors above me. There's a scream and a guard comes toppling out, falling past me. Realising that it's only a matter of time before they get me if I stay here, I jump back on to the ladder and carry on climbing.

My shoulders and arms burn as I drag myself up rung by rung, the wounds in my back opening again and causing blood to trickle down onto my fatigues and soaking my vest. I pause occasionally to fire at the shapes of guards I see peering and shooting from the open doors above, and by keeping their heads down in this way make good progress.

I've climbed perhaps two dozen floors when the elevator chain begins to grind into action once more, so I figure the crash didn't take it out of commission permanently. I redouble my efforts, pulling myself up rung by rung, trying to outrun the approaching lift whilst also firing up at the opening above me.

More shots flare around me from below, and I glance down and see firing through the open work elevator roof, about ten storeys below me. I fire back down at them, trapped in a horrid crossfire. Swinging desperately from the ladder, I wait until the elevator is just a few floors below, before jumping off the ladder, firing down as I leap on to the roof. I land with a clang of boots and roll automatically, falling through the open maintenance hatch into the midst of the guards inside.

I fire the pistol point-blank into the gut of one and twist, bringing the butt of the pistol smashing across the face of another. I punch a third in the throat, crippling his breathing. Another already lies on the floor, holes stitched across his chest. I stand there panting as the lift grinds its way upward, taking me to the top of the tower.

Just before I reach the last level, I ram the lever into the halt position and the brakes squeal in protest before the elevator comes to a stop. Climbing out on to the lift's roof once more, I pull myself up to the doors to the roof. Now with two more pistols claimed from the guards lying dead and unconscious in the lift, I brace myself on the inside of the door, trying to detect any movement on the far side. I hear and see nothing.

I crash my shoulder against the doors and they fly open, a guard on the far side giving a startled yelp as one of them smashes into him. I roll through the opening, arms crossed, firing the pistols to either side of me, before coming to my feet and spinning around, the guns blazing in my hands. Three more corpses litter the floor behind me as I sprint out onto the roof.

There's a massive storm raging, lightning flickers all around and thunder rolls. The wind howls across the tower, stinging my flesh and whipping up a cloud of dust and grit. Behind me I hear more shouts, and realise that there are more wardens spilling from the guardhouse. I pay no heed, and run for the edge. I'll climb down by hand if I have to.

I JUMP UP onto the parapet that runs around the tower roof and stop. In the light of the storm, I look out over Ghovul. Far below me, the tower stretches down onto a rocky mesa. Beyond that is a flat, featureless plain. Everything is grey and rocky, with no shelter from the elements, no cover to hide in, nothing to drink from, nothing to eat, just barren rock and gravel. As far as the eye can see. Distant lightning shows me that the plain stretches on far into the distance. There are no hills, no mountains, nothing, just a massive expanse of desolation.

There's nowhere to go.

I hear shouts from behind me and shots whine past. I raise my hands above my head and let the pistols fall from my fingertips, feeling numb.

Nowhere to go, nothing to do except wait here for the Colonel.

The Colonel. As I think about him, the pain flares up inside me, the burning anger builds in my gut and chest. I clench my fists above me as the guards close in, and scream into the storm.

'Schaeffer!' I shriek. 'Come back here, you bastard!'

ORK HUNTER
Dan Abnett

KEYSER, WHO THEY call the sergeant but who wears no rank
pins I can see, calls a halt. He gets up on the limed trunk of
a massive fallen cypress and stands, sniffing the air.

We wait, thigh deep in the stinking soup below.

The wet air seems to fill my lungs with steam, and I want
to cough, but the Skinner nearest me, a lean brute with char-
coal-blackened eye-sockets and piercings down his ears,
fixes me with a savage glare as if he can tell what I'm thinking. Keyser waves three scouts ahead, and that leaves thirty
of us, twenty-two Skinners and eight Jopall Indentured. I'm
halfway down the file, the swamp water bubbling and oozing around my legs, dust flies swirling round me.

The silent halt seems to last an eternity. There are spiders
in my hair. I can feel them.

Captain Lorit, looking as out of place as the rest of us
Jopall in his white-flecked, jade green fatigues and white
peaked cap, wades forward. 'What are we–' he begins.

The Skinner they call Pig, standing to the captain's left,
surges forward and takes my commander in a choke hold,
clamping one greasy paw across his mouth. The captain

227

struggles, wild-eyed, and Pig tightens his grip. The reason for Pig's nickname is self-evident – slabby and fat, with vastly developed muscle groups stretching his tattered tunic, he has a face ruined by scars and a ragged snout of flesh where his nose was bitten off.

Pig's muscles tighten further and the captain begins to turn blue. We Jopall look on in silent disbelief.

Keyser drops his hand and the Skinners un-freeze and move again. Pig releases the captain and throws him, gagging, face down into the water.

Keyser's jumped down off the cypress by then, and drags the captain up with one hand.

'He assaulted me! That man assaulted me! Put him on a charge!' The captain spits out weed and slime, indignant. Keyser doesn't put Pig on a charge. He punches the captain in the throat and silences him. The Skinners laugh, an ugly sound. Pig snorts, a far, far uglier noise.

'I thought we covered this in basic back at Cerbera. When I signal silence out here in the Green, I mean *silence.*' Keyser's voice is as sharp and taut as a wire. He says this to the captain, who is too busy grovelling and vomiting in the liquid mud to listen attentively.

HE TURNS TO the rest of us. 'We've got a scent of the 'skins. Close by, no more than a kilometre. Arm, load and follow. No noise. Especially you skinbait.'

That's what we are to them. Not Imperial Guard, not fellow troopers, not noble soldiers from the Jopall Indentured Squadrons. No matter most of us are from good, up-hive stock, no matter our comrades are even now defending the walls of Tartarus Hive against the Invasion.

We are skinbait. Nothing. Lower than scum.

For these Skinners set the value of scum. There are juvegangs from the Tarterus underhive I'd have more respect for.

It is my considerable misfortune, mine and the other members of my squad, to have been sent to Cerbera Base to undergo jungle warfare training with the ork hunters just as the war for beloved Armageddon began. There is no hope of rejoining our company or hive. We are stuck for the duration, seconded to one of the most notorious units of 'skull-takers', the so-called Keyser's Skinners.

Once in a while, from very far away, we hear the thump of artillery or the scream of ram-jets. Open war is being waged in the lands beyond the jungle, far away. It may as well be on another world. Word is Yarrick himself had returned. Oh to be part of that!

Oh to not be part of this... I believe the Skull-takers have been fighting the feral greenskins for so long, they have begun to mirror what they fight. The least of them are painted and pierced, the worst have implanted tusks jutting from their jawlines. All have ork finger-bones, teeth and ears dangling from them as grisly trophies. They have no official chain of command. They respect no rank or authority other than their own. I have been told they *elect* their leaders. Think of that!

We edge forward now, slopping through the pools of mire; thick, sticky fluid like mucus. Dragonflies, with stained-glass wings as wide as a man's arm span, cross the glades, beating the air louder than the blade-fans of the air-cars in Tartarus's elite district. Skaters as big as my hand skitter across the sheened water.

Pig tells us we're wading through sap, sap drooled out of the fleshy cycads and root-ferns all around. He snorts again. It's hard to catch my breath, the air is so humid. The Skinners though... they move so silently. They disturb nothing. They make no ripples, leave no trace. Their damn boots never get stuck in the mud-pools. Their sleeves never catch on thorns. Fronds never whip back as they pass. Bark doesn't snap as they climb over it. Even cobwebs remain miraculously intact, as if the Skinners were never there.

For coarse brutes, they move with unimaginable care and enviable skill. We Jopall blunder like fools amongst them. I spent four weeks last summer on a covert training course at the Hades Hive Guard Academy. I did well. I thought I was good. How... how in the name of the Emperor who watches us all do you not make a ripple when you wade through water?

We stop once more, and I lean against the bole of a giant ginkgo. Something has laid a clutch of wet, yellow eggs in the fabric of my jacket cuff. The size of rice grains, they glisten. I shudder and make to wipe them off.

A dirty hand grabs mine and stops me. It is the Skinner with the blackened eye sockets.

'Don't touch them. Rot-wasp eggs. Be thankful they chose your fancy jacket to lay in and not your ear, or your genitals, or your tear-ducts.'

He scrapes the eggs off me with the blade of a rusty shear-knife.

I look at him, bewildered.

'You wanna wake up with larvae munching out of your nose? Eating out your brain?'

I shake my head. Who would?

He chuckles.

'What's your name?' I ask.

'Deadhead.'

'No... your real name.'

'Er... Rickles,' he replies, as if he has to think about it. Then he turns away.

'Don't you want to know my name?' I call after him.

He turns back with a shrug. 'No point remembering the name of a skinbait who'll be dead by tonight. I'll never use your name anyway.'

Anger puffs up inside me, dry and fire-hot despite my sweat. 'I'm Corporal Ondy Scalber of the Jopall Indentured, you scum-sucker! Remember it! Emperor help you that you do ever have to use it!'

He grins, as if my forthright attitude has impressed him.

But he punches me in the mouth anyway.

We press on, the ever-quiet Skinners silently punishing every clumsy stumble of us Jopall. We reach a glade where the vast upper canopy is broken and sunlight streams down bright as lasers. There are flowers here, floating on the frothy, weed-choked water, huge flowers with shocking pink heads. Vast insects too, slow and drowsy, buzzing the air like chainswords and dripping nectar from each hideously limp proboscis. A pallid white serpent with vestigial limbs slides through the murk between my legs. My friend, Trooper Rokar, starts to whimper. He has just discovered that something unseen and submerged has gnawed off the cap of his boot... along with two of his smaller toes.

I was in a scholam with Rokar. I pity him. His injury. His weakness.

The scouts come back, two of them. We never see the third again. They confer with Keyser for a while. Then he tells us, low and mean, there's a nest nearby and we must fan out.

Rokar is whimpering even more now, and begins to climb up into a tree. The captain tries to call him down. Rokar shakes his head, refusing, terrified.

Keyser gets him out of the tree. He throws a stab-knife and impales my old friend through the sternum. Rokar drops and hits the ooze with a wet slap. His body sinks.

'He was no use to us anyway. A liability. Worse than a liability,' Keyser tells the captain.

The captain is speechless with rage and horror. We all are. I don't know what to think or feel any more.

I am sent on the right hand side of the fan advance, with Deadhead and Pig, and another Skinner called Toaster who hefts a heavy flamer unit. Trooper Flinder of the Jopall is with us.

Pig stops us under the shade of a horsetail and smears foul smelling grease over our skin from a dirty pot. Now we smell as bad as the Skinners, and I notice for the first time that they are caked in the stuff. It isn't just dirt. It's deliberate.

'It's skin tallow,' Toaster sneers as he explains while checking the hoses of his sooty flamer. 'Now you won't smell of soap and humans.'

Pig has just daubed us with ork grease, blubber fat from their pestilent bodies. My stomach turns over.

We edge onwards. Flinder and I try to be as silent as the Skinners. Our efforts seem laughable. Then Deadhead stops me again, and points down at the gossamer skein my shin was about to break. He traces it back to a clump of flowering moss and gently exhumes a clutch of stik-bombs, wired to the cord.

Keyser appears.

'Good work, Deadhead. Good eye.'

'Wasn't me who found it, sir. It was Ondy there.'

I look round, delighted to hear my name used.

'His shin, anyway,' Deadhead adds, and he and the Skinner boss laugh out loud. Curse their filthy hides.

WE CROUCH IN sap-water for half an hour, not daring to breathe. Bird calls and insect chirrups wing through the air. Some of them are natural, some are disguised signals. I can't tell them apart.

Deadhead waves us on.

As we cross a deep culvert of mud and slime, I see movement in the far tree-line. I've always had a good eye. It's the one skill I'm still proud of. I make something pustular and green amid the Green.

So I don't hesitate. I raise my lasrifle, and fire a stuttered burst.

Something big and green and tusked and monstrous slumps out of the foliage, its chest cavity exploded, and drops into the mere.

Then hell breaks loose. There are 'skins all around us, throwing themselves up out of the ooze, spitting out the hollow reeds they were breathing through. They are lean, malnourished, pale things, with jutting teeth like anthracite and deep-set eyes like diamonds. They howl and whoop. They stink. They wield heavy cleavers, cudgels and crude sidearms.

We're all firing. Gunfire explodes from the other elements of our formation. The wet air becomes cinder dry with ozone from the laser discharge. Las-rounds pepper through the leaf cover and fill the air with sap-vapour.

Toaster triggers his flamer and wastes the curtain of foliage before us. Swine-shrieks issue from the raging fire, piercingly harsh.

I fire, on full auto now, dropping 'skins around him. A rusty cleaver takes Flinder's head off his shoulders in a welter of blood and frayed tissue. I see Captain Lorit lifted right up out of the water on a primitive spear that transfixes his gut. He screams, piteously, flailing his limbs.

I had fixed my bayonet hours before, as per the Skinners' briefing. Now, with las-rounds expended and no time to change the clip, I stab and gut and slash.

Deadhead is nearby. He has wrested an ork lance from some dead grip, and is splitting skulls and whooping like a 'skin. Toaster fires again, his belch of flamer vaporising a tide of charging 'skins so that nothing but their fused skeletons slump in the steaming water, dribbling molten fat.

I impale a charging 'skin on my rifle-blade. It howls and pulls towards me, dragging the weapon out of my grasp. There is a plate-metal hatchet in its massive paw already wet with human brain tissue.

I pull my autopistol and blow its face apart.

'Throw! Throw!' yells Deadhead, tossing me a clutch of stik-bombs.

We hurl them together into the densest part of the 'skin press. In the flash-wash, slivers of shrapnel flutter back, stippling the water with a million separate impacts.

The orks turn and melt away, as if they were never there.

We regroup. Five Skinners are dead. I am one of only three Jopall left alive. I slump, hollowed by shock, against a lichen-covered rock with the others of my hive as the Skinners lock down the perimeter and take the spoils.

'What do you want?' Pig asks, and I turn.

He is sawing the head off an ork corpse with a serrated knife.

'What?'

'An ear? A tooth? You earned it.'

My gut tosses in revulsion. 'Skin ichor is leaking from the sawed incision he is working and forms a stinking slick on the water's surface.

'Don't make a mistake now, Ondy Scalber.' It is Deadhead. His voice is low.

'A mistake?'

'Pig's offering you a trophy. Can't remember the last time Pig did that for skinbait. It's an honour. Don't refuse it.'

'A tooth then,' says I, turning back to see the butchery.

'Yeah,' agrees Deadhead. 'He had a good eye back there. Saw them first.'

Pig nods, snorts, and digs his blade in.

'A good eye? Then that's what he'll get. A good eye for Good Eye!' Pig and Deadhead laugh.

Pig hands me the trophy. It dangles like a pendant on its long rope of blood-black optic nerve.

I can't refuse. I take it, tie it to my dog-tags. It thumps against my chest like a rubber ball at every move I make. As soon as Pig is gone, I'll lose it.

The Skinners build what they call warning shrines. Ork skulls and limbs spiked on posts or nailed to trunks. The idea is the 'skins will now shun this area because it stinks of murder and defeat. But the Skinners wire up the remnants to grenades anyway, in case the 'skins decide to recover their dead.

It's what Keyser calls a win-win situation.

Keyser. I see him across the clearing as the Skinners raise the ork heads on display all around us. He is bent over the eviscerated body of Captain Lorit, who is cruelly still alive. Toaster says Keyser is giving the captain last rites. I see the sudden twist of Keyser's hand. That wasn't last rites as we know it.

The nest is close. We move in, forming small groups. I find myself with Pig, Toaster, and two other Skinners called Slip-knot and Buck.

In the glade ahead, swathed in vapour, rises a great, ghostly tree. I sense it is not one tree but several that have become wrapped around each other over time. Hundreds of metres tall and thousands of years old, the great, entwined trunks are lifted clear of the water by a vast raft of winding roots. Birds flitter in the upper canopy. Beetles crawl and gnaw on the exposed roots.

We enter the root system, finding a tunnel half-filled with rank water. The roots coil and interlock above our stooped heads, reminding me of the interlocking arch vaults of the glorious Ecclesiarchy chapel back home on Jopall.

Toaster leads the way. We can smell the leaking prome-thium of his blackened flamer.

Buck shows me how to take a strip of field dressing and soak it in the swamp water to make a breath mask. Already, the pungent smoke of fires deliberately lit by the scouts on the far side of the nest is creeping back to us.

I breathe through wet gauze.

They're on us a moment later. Toaster scours the tunnel with his flamer, but they're pouring out of side turnings we didn't even see. I'm killing them even as I realise these are youngsters, small ork spawn no taller than my waist, weeping and shrieking as they run from the smoke.

Children. That's what we'd call them.

I don't care any more. Slipknot and I push down a side-vent, clawing our way through the tangles of black roots, and engage fierce 'skin youths, who jab at us with short spears and broken blades.

No match for las-fire.

'This way, Good Eye!' I hear Slipknot shout.

Then I'm into a larger root cavity, with Buck and Slipknot on my heels. We can still hear the rasp of Toaster's flamer nearby, and smell the burning promethium.

Feral orks are all around us now, many full-grown and massive. Some have guns. Slipknot is blown apart by a bolt round. His left hand slaps against my shoulder as it is blown clear of his carcass.

I kill the ork with the bolter. Then Buck and I pepper the cavity with random automatic fire. Green blood splats and sprays in the close air.

An ork is right on top of me, howling, raising a blade in a meaty paw bigger then my head. My gun is out. I fumble. It sees the eye bouncing across my chest and it seems to make it pause. I need no further urging. I slam the bayonet up into its jutting chin so the blade-end punches out through the back of its skull. Its huge jaws, spasming shut as it dies, bite the end off my lasgun.

I take up its blade in my right hand, holding my autopistol in my left. With the blade I dash out 'skin brains. With the pistol I wound and cripple and kill. I am plastered with 'skin blood now, as feral as the things I slay, murderous, wanton, out of my mind.

Jopall seems a long, long way away. Further than ever before.

And I know now I can't go back there.

Not now.

Not after this.

Toaster comes in behind us and yells for us to drop. Buck does, and I pull my head down as the flamer wash gusts like a sun's heat over our heads, incinerating the rest of the chamber.

We're all laughing as we clamber out of the nest. Golder and Spaff, the remaining Indentured Squadrons, look as me as if I have run mad. I know how I must look to them, singed and filthy and covered in 'skin blood that is baked like treacle. I don't care. I don't care what they thought. I don't care for anything any more.

KEYSER IS FIGHTING the boss. Driven out by the smoke and carrying a ragged stomach wound, the massive 'skin has found himself cornered in a sap-pool east of the nest. Keyser confronts him. We all group around to watch. No one interferes. We just watch and whoop and chant.

Like orks.

The 'skin boss is one hundred kilos heavier than Keyser, and massively muscled, with molars like daggers and tusks like bayonets. It wears turtle-shell breast plate, and carries a hooked bill on one paw and a gutting knife in the other. Its torn belly oozes foul-smelling ichor, making the thing crouch.

Keyser, lank and lean in tattered camo-fatigues and webbing, his skin white with paint, has only a shear-knife. They circle and jab. We stand around the clearing, clapping and cheering, chanting 'Key-ser! Key-ser!' like animals. The boss circles in, sidestepping Keyser's blade and taking a decent cut of meat from Keyser's left thigh with its bill. In return, Keyser swings and kicks the monster square in its wounded abdomen, throwing it back into the water in a spray of slime.

The boss rises to its feet awkwardly. Keyser is now limping from the ragged slice in the meat of his thigh, a slice that has flapped the skin open to show pink meat and gleaming white bone.

BUSINESS AS USUAL

Graham McNeill

RIGHT AWAY, SNOWDOG could tell that these six, deadhead Jackboys were trying to pull one over on him. Sure, they talked the talk, walked the walk and apparently had some real heavy connections with the High Hive gangs, but his gut told him that this deal was going to hell. He couldn't put his finger on it, but something was definitely wrong. Maybe it was the location the Jackboys had chosen for the deal, too close to the tyranid nests for Snowdog's liking. Or maybe it was their attitude. They were too cocky, acting like he was some dumb squarejohn who didn't know the score and Snowdog didn't like that. Not one bit. It meant they thought they were holding all the cards.

Like all Jackboys, they wore plain grey boiler suits, pulled in at the waist with a broad leather belt. Every one of them had shaven heads, tattooed with crosses, guns and gang symbols. They wore knee-length, shining jackboots and two carried arbites combat shotguns, no doubt looted from a couple of dead Bronzes. They looked a bit too ready to use them and if this deal did go ballistic, then he'd have to put those two down first.

'Well?' said one of the Jackboys. 'It's good stuff, yeah? Your boy looks like he's pretty happy with it.'

Snowdog had to agree, the Kalma was top notch. Lex was smacked out of his damn eyeballs, sedated by the euphoric drug and grinning inanely, thick, ropes of drool dangling from his chin. If some shooting action went down here, Lex would be frag all use in the fight. Thank the Hive Spirit he'd decided to bring Silver and Tigerlily with him. The girls could take on any hard case and make him wish he'd never been born. He'd seen their handiwork many times and was eternally grateful they ran with his gang.

Both were clad in dark catsuits and pistol belts. Tigerlily kept her red hair cropped close to her skull in shaven stripes and wore a baldric of assorted throwing knives and daggers across her chest. Silver's albino-white hair was tied in a long ponytail and she was armed with two gleaming autopistols, holstered beneath a long, leather coat. The kind of firepower the Jackboys were packing was beginning to make him wish he'd brought Trask or Jonny Stomp along as well, but he'd wanted to make a point. He'd wanted the Jackboys to know he didn't need big guns to prove how much of a player he was.

'Yeah,' nodded Snowdog, conceding the point, 'it looks like good stuff, but Lex trips out on coffee and ain't payin' for it neither.'

'Hey, a free sample only goes so far, you know? You wanna deal or what?' said a second Jackboy, irritation in his voice. Snowdog's suspicions racked up a notch. They were too eager to deal. Jackboys usually felt the need to strut like damn peacocks before getting down to the dealing.

They sat in a junked out factory unit, on the northern edge of the Stank, one of the lowest and most dangerous bad-zones in Erebus Hive. Not even the Arbites Enforcers would come here without damn good reason. A hab unit had col-lapsed on the factory a couple of months back, killing all the workers and flattening most of the machinery. It had been abandoned and left to rot; another stinking, sedimentary layer of metal and flesh. There were still tunnels and cham-bers left in the unit, areas that had escaped the violence of the hab's collapse. The area they now sat in was low ceilinged and strewn with broken glass and twisted metal girders. The flattened hulk of a milling machine served as their business table.

A large, sealed petri dish sat on the machine, filled with tiny red capsules. Six hundred Kalma drops, worth a small fortune – enough to get some real heavy ordnance, haul themselves upwards and carve out some more stamping grounds.

'So, you wanna deal?' repeated the Jackboy.

'Maybe,' said Snowdog, nodding imperceptibly to Silver.

'Don't be givin' me no "maybe". Yes or no, that's all I wanna hear. I don't give out nothing for nothing. Understand, boy? You take our Kalma, we want something back.'

'Hey, I didn't say I wasn't gonna deal,' soothed Snowdog, 'Let's all just flatline and be cool. We all here to do a little business, not bag 'n' tag each other.'

The Jackboys seemed to relax at this and moved their hands away from their pistols. They might be hard cases in the High Hive, but they didn't know jack about how negotiations were handled down here in the badzones.

Snowdog glanced at the petri dish again. Six hundred Kalma drops. It looked pure as well, the best, not cut with chalk or rock powder. This stuff would make you feel like the inside of your brain had been dipped in honey.

The cares of the world could all go to hell while you were on Kalma, at least for a while.

But the good stuff didn't come cheap.

No. These boys were setting him up for something and he sure as hell didn't like the feeling. He'd stayed alive in the Stank this long by trusting his instincts and right now there was a four alarm fire going off in his head. The Jackboys knew he had the connections and the hard cash to pay for this and he also knew they would probably try to keep the drugs and the money. Which meant they wouldn't let him leave here alive.

Snowdog was not an especially tall man, but his compact body was rangy and muscled and he could fight like a cornered hellcat. His skin had an unhealthy pallor to it, the result of living in the darkness of the underhive and his full features were rugged and careworn. His head was crowned with short, bleached blond hair that was backcombed in short spikes and his brown eyes suspiciously checked out the Jackboys. He wore a pair of black, tiger striped trousers, tucked into a pair of enforcer's combat boots he'd pulled from a dead Bronze. At his belt hung a long bladed knife and a wire garrotte. His white shirt was printed with a faded holo-patch depicting a rippling explosion that expanded and contracted as he moved. Over this he wore a black leather waistcoat and shoulder holster containing a battered autopistol.

'Look, how much you want for this?' asked Snowdog, 'You got a lot of stuff here, probably more'n I can take in one go.'

'Hey, man. It's cool. We know we got a lot. But we need to get rid of it quick, you know?' said the lead Jackboy, his pitted face right in Snowdog's. Out of the corner of his eye, he saw the Jackboys with the shotguns quietly ease the safeties off their weapons.

Snowdog sat back, folded his arms and, unnoticed, loosened the catch on his autopistol's shoulder holster. He noticed Silver and Tigerlily tensing, readying their muscles for instant action. They knew the drill.

He locked eyes with the Jackboy and shrugged, 'Like I said, how much you want?'

'Ten thousand,' snapped the Jackboy without hesitation.

'Ten thousand–' said Snowdog, knowing what the next question would be.

'You got that kinda cash?'

'Yeah,' said Snowdog, sliding his hand towards his holster.

'Then I guess we'll take all you got!' shouted the Jackboy, snatching for his gun.

Snowdog was quicker.

He whipped out his autopistol and squeezed off a round full in the Jackboy's face. The ganger screamed foully, tumbling backwards, the top of his head blasted clear.

The Jackboys with the shotguns were moving. Chambering shells, they aimed and fired. Snowdog dropped, hitting the deck hard and rolling, firing off an entire clip of wild shots. Tigerlily leapt towards the second Jackboy and rammed her elbow into his throat. She spun low and hammered a slender-bladed dagger into his belly, slicing upwards in one fluid motion. The Jackboy gurgled and fell to the factory floor, dropping his shotgun and grasping his crushed larynx.

Silver calmly fired her pistols, double tapping the second shotgun-wielding Jackboy in the head. Snowdog slid another clip into the grip of his pistol and rose from behind his shelter.

Bullets stitched a path towards him. He spun quickly and fired twice towards a crouching Jackboy. The man grunted, shot in the chest and fell back, blood pouring from his wounds.

Snowdog felt a whipcrack sting to his cheek and dived forwards, reaching for the fallen shotgun. He scooped it up on the roll and rose smoothly to a crouch, firing off a succession of shots. The noise was tremendous and he whooped with excitement as the Jackboy who'd fired at him went down, his chest punched clean through by the close range blasts.

Silver and Tigerlily worked their way towards him, using every bit of cover available. Neither had even broken sweat. He smiled at them as silence descended on the factory.

'Time to split, girls,' he said.

'Damn straight.' said Silver, 'Bound to be some more Jackboys nearby waitin' for us.'

'Figured as much.'

'Only way outa here that ain't gonna take us into more of these guys is down past the 'nid nests,' pointed out Tigerlily, 'and that ain't gonna be a barrel of laughs.'

'Nope,' Silver agreed. She glanced over the debris they sheltered behind and said, 'What about Lex? We just gonna leave him for the Jackboys? They'll bag'n'tag him for sure, man.'

'Damn!' said Snowdog. He'd forgotten about Lex. He'd still be lying there thinking that this was some Kalma related trip-out. He could hear the Jackboy talking on a comm-unit. More would be here soon, that was for damn sure. He

checked his pistol and took Silver's gun also, handing her
the Arbites shotgun.

'I'll get Lex. You cover me with this. We'll be out of here
and high n' dry before you know it.'

THE STANK DARKENED at their passing. The black, armour-clad
warriors charged down the twisting halls, combat shotguns
held at the ready across their broad chests. Dark cloaks
trailed behind them, gusted by the sputtering oxy-recyc
units. The six man Adeptus Arbites Enforcer squad, grim
men in fully enclosed suits of carapace armour, cast a pall of
fear as they passed the stinking hovels and battered habs of
the lower hive.

The leader of the squad, Captain Jakob Gunderson,
scanned from side to side, alert for a Skum sniper, Wyldern
snuff gang or any one of the many other dangers that lurked
in this place. Travelling in such numbers and at this speed
made such an attack unlikely, but in the Stank, if you wanted
to stay alive, you never took things like that for granted.

The Wall of the Dead in the Precinct House was carved
with the names of those who had.

Gunderson was a feared man. His name was spoken in
whispers by the denizens of the Stank. It was a name to
quell the worst of riots, a reputation to tell over flickering
fires by older, wiser heads which nonetheless glanced
furtively over their shoulders as though the mere mention of
his name would somehow conjure him from thin air.

At well over two metres, Gunderson was a giant of a man,
radiating his authority and power like a threat. He was
broad and powerfully built, with muscles like slabs of iron
beneath his midnight blue carapace armour. He wore his
non-reflective bronze captain's badge over his left breast and
was helmetless, tiny vox-comm beads attached to his larynx
and the canal of his ear. A black, protective eye visor
shielded his vision.

The ragged residents ducked out of sight of the Enforcers,
pulling rusted iron doors shut and hauling tattered strips of
cloth over tears that served as windows in their prefabri-
cated steel shacks. Children were dragged indoors, the

adults fearing the soldiers of the Adeptus Arbites as much as the feral Stank gangs and tyranid monsters that roamed these regions of Erebus Hive.

They'd intercepted a radio call on an unlicensed frequency moments earlier as they patrolled the outskirts of District Quintus, almost half a kilometre away. Strictly speaking, this area wasn't within their patrol envelope, but a chance to nail that punk Snowdog was too good to pass up.

Snowdog had been a thorn in Jakob Gunderson's side for longer than he cared to remember. Several times Gunderson had almost had the diminutive ganger in his sights, but each time the slippery little fragger had managed to escape him.

He was known to front for a couple of heavy hitters up in the refinery city of Desirata who synthesised Kalma, Spook, Slaught and Throne knew what else in secret factories, shipped it to every hive on the planet and, it was rumoured, off-world.

Snowdog was a major player in the odious underworld of Erebus Hive. He ran a fair sized piece of turf with his gang, the Nightcrawlers, and supplied drugs and guns to the ever-hungry population of the hive. What was even more of an affront to Gunderson was that they knew portions of Snowdog's territory included his own Precinct House 13.

As well as being immensely satisfying, a bullet in his head would put a sizeable dent in the drug traffic entering the lower hive from Desirata.

From the garbled communication his men had intercepted, it appeared that some kind of drug deal had gone wrong and there was a chance Snowdog was involved.

Gunderson carried his shotgun as though it were part of his own flesh, gripping it tight in a vice-like grip. It was set to fire Executioner rounds, hunting shells that would zero in on their target's location. He was taking no chances that Snowdog would get away this time.

He and his squad of five Enforcers reached the collapsed factory their vox-comms had identified as the source of the signal and began climbing the rugged, metal slope of girders and debris towards the entrance, no more than a rusted iron cave mouth.

From inside he could hear screams and gunfire, heavy shotgun blasts and the smaller crack of pistol fire. He racked the slide of his own shotgun, turned to face his men and said, 'No one kills Snowdog but me.'

SNOWDOG HOLLERED AND hurdled the crate, firing wildly. Silver rose with him and began pumping shells from the shotgun at the surviving Jackboy. He was well under cover and hopefully the fire she was laying down would keep it that way.

He'd almost reached Lex when he saw he'd made a mistake. A big mistake.

From his left, the light at the entrance to the factory was suddenly blocked as a team of Bronzes pushed their way inside. He swore to himself as he recognised the bulky form of their leader and twisted to snap off a couple of shots at him.

He saw them hit, but cursed as they were deflected by the Bronze's heavy carapace armour. Gunderson turned at the sound of the shots and a feral grin spread across his face as he recognised his prey before him. Snowdog veered off to find cover.

Gunderson lifted the shotgun to his shoulder and squeezed the trigger twice.

Snowdog saw the distinctive flashes of Body-Chaser shells as their tiny motors ignited. He knew he was a goner. Bagged 'n' tagged for sure. He kept running anyway, suddenly changing direction as an idea came to him.

He dived forwards, pulling Lex's doped-up body around and over him.

Sorry, Lex, it's you or me, buddy.

And let's face it. It's you.

He felt the double thump as the 'Chasers slammed into his human shield, blasting a plate sized-hole in him. Lex didn't even make a sound, and Snowdog knew he was so doped up that he probably hadn't even felt the shells hit. Snowdog winced, thinking that if Lex lived, it was going to hurt like a cast-iron bitch when the Kalma wore off. He pulled Lex's body closer as he heard more shotgun blasts. He tensed, expecting the agony of scatter shot flensing the flesh from his bones or a solid shot punching a giant crater in his chest.

But he felt nothing – then realised the shots had come from Silver's direction.

'Run!' yelled Silver, firing again into the group of Bronzes, forcing them to find cover. She'd bought him time and he mentally chalked it up as one he owed her. He scrambled to his feet and crawled round the flattened milling machine, reaching up to grab the petri dish as he went.

Feeling pretty pleased with himself, he didn't notice the last Jackboy until he almost crawled on top of him.

For a second neither moved until Snowdog launched himself forward, lowering his head and slamming his forehead into the shaven-headed ganger's nose. The Jackboy roared in pain, hands flying to his face.

Snowdog sprang onto the squirming Jackboy and forced the barrel of his gun under his chin. He closed his eyes and pulled the trigger. The Jackboy's head exploded, showering Snowdog with blood and brains, the crack of the gun's discharge lost in a cacophony of shotgun blasts that erupted around him.

Splinters of concrete and glass showered him and he desperately attempted to squeeze himself into as small a target as possible. He could hear Tigerlily and Silver yelling colourful curses and threats at the Bronzes. He tried not to picture the images in his head.

It was clear this situation had gone way too far. Something drastic was required. He checked the clips of each pistol. Each had less than half a mag left. He slowed his breathing, getting ready to go for it. Death or a blaze of glory. Muscles tensed, he was about to move when he caught sight of a dark sheen of metal underneath the Jackboy's bloodstained overalls. He grinned as he reached down and pulled out a leather bandolier with crude, homemade grenades hung along its length.

Some with his name on, he guessed. He was about to unsnap one of the grenades from the bandolier then stopped, smiling to himself.

To hell with it.

He quickly pulled the pins on all the grenades and rose to his feet, swinging the heavy belt round his head. Yelling an obscenity, he lobbed the bandolier towards the sheltering Bronzes.

The boom of a shotgun caused him to duck back behind the crate. But not before he had time to savour the cries of alarm as the Bronzes realised the deadly nature of what he'd thrown them.

The frag grenades simultaneously detonated in the midst of the Arbites troops. Razor-sharp pieces of white hot metal scythed out from the explosion and men died as the shrapnel shredded their bodies. Snowdog covered his ears at the terrific blast as the pressure wave rolled over him, tumbling him from his hiding place. The echoes of the detonation rolled back and forth, mixed with the shrieks of the survivors and the dangerous groaning of tortured metal.

The roof now took on a noticeable downward bulge, water beginning to pour from rapidly developing cracks. With hundreds of tonnes of metal above him, that move with the grenades probably wasn't the best idea he had ever had.

It was time to get greasy and slip away.

He stood and sprinted towards Silver and Tigerlily, sparing a glance at the carnage he'd caused. Three of the Bronzes were dead, a fourth on his knees, clutching his ruined belly, vainly trying to hold in his bloody entrails. The leader he couldn't see. It was too much to hope that Gunderson had been killed; that fragger was way too slippery for that.

Sure enough a black figure rose from behind the wreckage and levelled his shotgun at the running ganger. Silver fired on him, but he didn't flinch. A fragger he may be, but he was a brave one, Snowdog admitted grudgingly. Silver's shot impacted on his armour, but the thick breastplate deflected the shot. Snowdog ducked as Gunderson fired, feeling lashes of hot fire rake across his back as scatter shot scored through his leather waistcoat, shirt and skin.

His ears were ringing with gunfire, but not before he heard the metal ceiling of the factory give out one last hideous metallic scream of protest, chunks of plascrete and metal crashing to the floor. He saw Silver discard the empty shotgun then, following Tigerlily, dart into the corroded sewer entrance they had earlier tagged as their escape route if things went loco. With a wild yell, he lurched and skidded along the floor, following them into the darkness of the sewer entrance.

SNOWDOG BREATHED DEEPLY, then wished he hadn't. The stench of the Erebus Hive sewer network was overpowering, shot through with the reeking odours of six million people's waste.

He stood knee deep in foetid, rank effluent, sludgy with refuse. Man, he was never gonna get this off his boots! The darkness was absolute; a number of turns in the sewer had cut off the little light that filtered down into the waste pipe. Snowdog reached into his pocket, grunting as pain razored up his back from the trails the scatter shot had blazed, and withdrew his lighter. He flicked off the brass cap and struck the flint.

Weak light flickered, revealing the full extent of their refuge. The steel pipe was perhaps one and a half metres in diameter and stagnant with filth. The murky liquid was unmoving, blocked further up the pipe by piles of trash and rubble.

'You okay?' asked Silver genuinely. 'I was sure that Bronze had you tagged for sure.'

'He almost did. He's a stubborn one, that Bronze. He's been lookin' for me for Spirit only knows how long. Didn't get me yet though,' replied Snowdog.

'I think we might be near the bug nests,' said Tigerlily, the fear in her voice unmistakable. 'We're gonna have to step lightly, less we want to end up sliced and diced.'

Snowdog nodded. Ever since the Space Marines had kicked the tyranids off this world, the local boys of the Imperial Guard and Defence Militia had had their hands full hunting the remaining tyranid creatures that had gone to ground in the underhive. Despite their efforts there were still broods of the smaller beasts nesting in the moist darkness of the lower levels of Erebus Hive. When the 'nids had attacked

the hive, Snowdog had fought hand-to-hand in a militia
unit as sickle armed beasts burst through every culvert and
recyc unit, slaughtering hundreds of the lower hive dwellers.
Snowdog had seen enough bugs to last a lifetime and certainly didn't want to see any more.

But the war had been over for three months now and
Snowdog had wasted no time in getting back to the serious
job of dealing in illegal narcotics and guns. The devotional
vids and posters might claim it was every citizen's job to
help in the eradication of the tyranids, but for Snowdog it
was back to business as usual.

'You get the Kalma drops?' asked Tigerlily, a carefully hidden longing beneath her casually asked question.

'Yeah, I got some. But nobody gets none 'till we're homef
ree. Last thing we need is you smacked out if the bugs come
for us,' said Snowdog, stuffing the petri dish into the pocket
of his waistcoat.

He grimaced and pointed down into the rank depths of
the sewer tunnel. It sloped downwards at a shallow angle,
descending into darkness.

Now that he had illumination, he noticed the walls were
covered in a glistening ooze, a sticky residue that he didn't
like the look of at all.

'Looks like we got a long walk ahead of us,' he said. 'Come
on, let's go. I don't wanna be hangin' round here longer'n
we got to.'

GUNDERSON THREW HIMSELF forward as tonnes of metal and
concrete came crashing down. He yelled as a steel beam
smashed into his back, slamming him into the ground and
he rolled as blocks of stone and iron thundered around him,
the noise drowning out his cries of anger and pain. He saw
Enforcer Delano crouching next to him, blood streaming
from his temple. He jerked his thumb in the direction of the
sewer entrance he'd seen Snowdog go down.

The ceiling continued to groan in protest and Gunderson
knew that to stay here was to die. Rubble was sure to keep
falling around them and it would only be a matter of time
until they were crushed flat. Gunderson and Delano slithered

their way towards the tunnel. Snowdog had a head start, but he wouldn't be expecting any pursuit.

Gunderson would make him pay for that lack of vision.

THE INTERIOR OF the sewer tunnel wasn't the worst place Snowdog could remember being in, but it came pretty damn close. The stench was appalling and he didn't want to think what the wriggling movements within the effluent were.

As escape routes went, he'd used better ones.

But any gunfight you walked away from in one piece and with a pocket full of Kalma was a good one, so he guessed he couldn't complain.

At last the tunnel began to brighten slightly before emerging into a high vaulted chamber of dim light and dripping echoes. Tunnels branched off the chamber in all directions and without hesitation Snowdog dropped from the tunnel into the chamber. Picking an opening to his left, he began wading towards it.

They had travelled perhaps ten steps when they found the bodies.

Five Wyldern gangers, their skeletons picked clean of meat. The water around them was still stained with blood, so whatever had done this had reduced them to their bare bones in seconds. The underhive was full of creatures that could kill a man stone dead, but Snowdog didn't know of any that could do this to a person so quickly. At least not ones of this world. The killing of the Wylderns reeked of tyranids and he knew they must be close to a nest. Time to get moving.

The Wyldern nearest to Snowdog still clutched a shotgun in a death grip and he grinned as he quickly bent to pick it up.

'Don't even think about it,' snapped a voice from behind him.

He slid his hand towards his holster until the sharp click of a shotgun slide being racked convinced him that it would be unhealthy to continue. He slowly turned and raised his hands in time to see a pair of blood-streaked Enforcers emerge from the tunnel he and the girls had just come from.

Gunderson dropped into the water-filled chamber while the second Enforcer covered them with his shotgun.

'That weapon is Imperial property,' said Gunderson. 'Touch it and I'll blow you away.'

'You'd like that, huh?'

'More than you know.'

'So why haven't you?' asked Snowdog.

'Oh no,' replied Gunderson. 'You don't get off that easy, punk. I'm taking you in Snowdog. I'm going to chain you up like the animal you are and let the world see me drag you in.'

Snowdog looked over at Silver and Tigerlily, but, like him, they knew that reacting now would just get them all killed. The two Enforcers were on the edge. Their blood was singing and it would only take the slightest hint of resistance to start them blasting. He'd have to play this one ice cool.

'Listen man. You see these skeletons?' said Snowdog, nodding towards the bodies. 'These boys got their asses fragged by the 'nids that went to ground after the war and my gut tells me there's a nest nearby. You start firing that cannon of yours, you're gonna bring a whole bunch of 'em down on us, so what you say we all just keep calm, ok?'

'You killed my men!' shouted Gunderson. 'Don't you dare tell me to be calm! I am calm! Delano, get down here with the cuffs.'

A hoarse gurgling was the only reply to Gunderson's order and he risked a glance behind him to see what the hell Delano was playing at.

Enforcer Delano still crouched in the sewer outlet, but a massive long talon now protruded from his body, just above his hip. A look of almost comic surprise twisted his features and he groaned in pain as blood dribbled from the corner of his mouth.

'What the hell–' managed Gunderson as the talon was wrenched from Delano's body and the Enforcer toppled into the water. Behind him, its claws stained bright red, was a lithe, muscled creature with a ridged body and lethal looking talons. The beast hissed, exposing glistening fangs and its pale eyes burned with alien malevolence.

Its powerful hind legs uncoiled like a powerful spring as the creature leapt from the sewer outlet towards them. It exploded in mid-air as the solid shot from Gunderson's shotgun blew it apart, the echoes of the blast ringing from the concrete walls. Hurriedly he chambered another shell and ran to help the struggling Delano to his feet as the sound of scrabbling claws and alien hissing came from all around them.

It seemed to issue from every outlet. And it was growing in volume.

'Damn,' whispered Snowdog as he tried to pinpoint the source of the noises. 'Look what you gone and done now!'

Another one of the creatures dropped from the roof of the chamber, landing with a splash just behind Snowdog. Its talons lashed out at his neck. He ducked and lowered his head straight into the second beast as it powered from the water, its bony skull smashing into his unprotected face. Blood burst from his nose and he yelled in sudden pain, splashing backwards into the water.

Gunderson's and Delano's shotguns fired again as the outlet pipes erupted with dozens of the horrifying beasts, an alien tide of rippling armour plates, chitinous blades and fangs.

Snowdog hauled himself to his knees as two of the creatures stalked through the foamy water towards him. The creatures were hunched over, the front pair of their limbs ending in long, scythe-like blades.

He recognised them almost immediately as hormagaunts, and he'd fought enough of these beasts during the war to know they were in serious trouble. Their bestial faces were drawn and pale, white, lidless eyes seeming to glow with a killing light.

The lead hormagaunt lifted its head, cocking it to one side, tongue darting in and out of its mouth like a snake's. Snowdog put a bullet between its eyes as the second 'gaunt launched itself at him. He threw himself flat and the creature sailed over him, landing in a thrashing pile of claws. As it picked itself up, Snowdog emptied the last of the clip into the back of its head.

More of the creatures dropped from the roof or rose from the sewage around them. The heavy boom of shotgun blasts echoed deafeningly around the chamber as Gunderson and Delano fell back towards Tigerlily and Silver, firing as they went. Tigerlily drew her daggers and hammered them through a 'gaunt's neck, almost severing its head, as Silver snatched her pistols from her weapons belt. Before she could fire, a pair of 'gaunts leapt from the tunnel behind her and smashed into her back. She cried out and was knocked sprawling, face-first into the water. The beasts' claws tore at her back, their talons raised to strike.

Snowdog slammed a fresh clip into his pistol and fired twice into the soft underbelly of one of the 'gaunts, blasting it from Silver's back. Gunderson slammed the butt of his shotgun into the second creature's head, splitting it apart with a sickening crunch. He kicked the alien away as Tigerlily pulled the spluttering Silver to her feet. Snowdog stood and waded towards the girls. He could see more 'gaunts emerging from the tunnels around them and counted at least a dozen. Suddenly his autopistol seemed scant protection.

Gunderson glared at Snowdog, his rage an almost physical thing. Snowdog grinned, knowing that the Enforcer now realised that he would need Snowdog's help if he was to survive the next few minutes.

Delano propped himself against the concrete wall, his groin and legs awash with blood and his face ashen. A circle of hormagaunts surrounded them, at least twenty now. Snowdog hoped they had enough ammo left to deal with this number of aliens.

He dodged as a hormagaunt leapt at him, its talons slashing. He blasted its chest open and dodged as another pounced. He pulled the trigger and the hammer dropped on an empty chamber. He quickly snatched his knife from his belt.

The bug attacked wildly. Snowdog dodged, spun inside its guard and drove the blade deep into its neck, wrenching it upwards. They splashed into the water, the 'gaunt spasming weakly as its lifeblood pulsed from the ruin of its throat.

Snowdog sprang upright, knife at the ready and slashed out at the 'gaunts next to him. Silver tossed him a fresh clip for his pistol and he slid it home. Gunderson fired into the mass of creatures, each blast blowing a 'gaunt into bloody shreds.

'We got to get out of here!' shouted Snowdog.

'You think?' Gunderson snapped

'Head for the tunnel behind us, it's the only one these things ain't come from!'

Gunderson nodded and began falling back. The 'gaunts surrounded them in a rough semi-circle, fangs bared and talons raised. The noose slowly closed, but the aliens held back, seemingly content just to watch their prey.

'Why aren't they attacking?' whispered Silver.

'Who cares?' said Tigerlily. 'Let's get the hell out of here!'

'Sounds good to me,' agreed Snowdog, backing in the direction of the tunnel. The 'gaunts closed in, moving in time with their beleaguered group. Why weren't they attacking, he wondered? Almost as soon as he formed the thought, his question was answered as a terrifying screech echoed from the tunnel behind the circle of 'gaunts and a monster from the darkest of nightmares pushed its alien bulk into the chamber.

Snowdog had seen some hellish monsters in his time fighting the tyranids and had paid close attention when the commissars had shown them the instructional vids detailing the various identified types of alien creatures and their horrifying abilities.

But he was still shocked by the hideous appearance of this creature.

Standing taller than a man, its spine was curved and ridged, with overlapping plates of chitinous, red armour. Its head was distended and burnt looking, with white orbs for eyes and a vast jaw filled with row upon row of needle-like fangs. Its rear legs were muscled like the 'gaunts' and, like them, its forelimbs ended in gigantic scythe-like talons. The limbs on its thorax bore clawed hands and the muscles there bunched and relaxed, the fingers flexing rhythmically in time with its foetid breath.

The beast's chest was a wetly glistening mass of rippling tissue, pink and raw looking. Barbed hooks clicked on the exposed bone of its exo-skeleton, almost as though they had a life of their own. Perhaps it had once been a 'gaunt like the others and the isolation from the hive fleet had driven its internal evolution into overdrive, producing this terrifying pack leader. However it had happened, Snowdog realised, it was bad news for them.

'Emperor save us...' whispered Gunderson. Silver hurriedly scrambled into the outlet behind them and reached back to pull Tigerlily up.

'Come on!' said Silver, extending her hand towards Snowdog. He gripped her wrist and hauled himself into the sewer tunnel as the monstrous beast took a thundering step into the water. Snowdog looked back as Gunderson and Delano faced the huge beast.

'Well shoot the damn thing!' he yelled.

Delano needed no further prompting and squeezed the trigger of his shotgun. At such close range he couldn't miss and Snowdog watched as a blaze of purple energy flared around the beast simultaneously with the shotgun's blast. As the searing afterimage of the flash dissipated, Snowdog saw that the creature was unharmed and knew that it was protected by a kind of naturally generated energy field. He'd seen some of the larger tyranid beasts protected by something similar during the war.

The creature's chest suddenly spasmed, the pink folds of skin rippling and undulating with a grotesque peristaltic motion. Thick cords of tough muscle fibre whipped out towards Delano. The barbed hooks punched through the Enforcer's carapace armour and snagged his rib cage, digging into the meat of his body. The flesh hooks retracted on powerful muscles and hauled the screaming Delano off his feet. Gunderson made to grab him, but wasn't quick enough to prevent the beast from dragging him into its deadly embrace.

Delano slammed into the creature, his screams cut off abruptly as its upper talons stabbed repeatedly into his body. Soon the Enforcer's body was reduced to a pulped mess of torn and bloody flesh, barely recognisable as human. While the beast destroyed Delano, Gunderson leapt for the sewer outlet as the beast dropped the mangled corpse into the water. Snowdog helped him up and they sprinted deeper into the sewers, the high pitched ululating screeches of the 'gaunts telling them that the tyranid creatures weren't far behind them.

Gunderson led the way as they moved further into the tunnels, a torch on his shotgun providing some illumination. Snowdog brought up the rear of their small group, casting nervous glances behind him as the screeching increased in volume.

'Come on, come on,' he hissed. 'Let's pick up the pace here people!'

His breath came in short gasps, and he could almost feel the creatures' hot breath upon him. He threw a glance over his shoulder as he ran and swore as he saw the outline of the giant beast behind him. Too close, too close by half!

The tunnel turned and widened into a large inspection chamber, one with a corroded iron ladder at its centre leading up into darkness. The others were past the ladder, still running, but he knew that to keep going deeper into the tunnels wasn't an option. The beast was too fast and there were more of the smaller ones than they had bullets left.

'Woah!' he yelled, skidding to a halt. 'Up here!'

Snowdog scrambled up the ladder, fear lending his limbs extra speed. He climbed into a wider concrete tube, finally emerging into another tunnel, larger than the one they had just left, but with a sliver of light casting a weak glow from one end. Silver crawled from the hole and rolled to one side as Gunderson's head emerged behind her. No sooner had he clambered out when Tigerlily hooked her arms around the manhole's edge and began hauling herself free.

She screamed suddenly and Snowdog grabbed her wrists and pulled as powerful alien limbs began dragging her back down. Tigerlily continued to scream horribly as Silver and Gunderson lent their strength to holding her.

A horrifying ripping noise sounded, and at first Snowdog thought her clothes were tearing. Then, a scarlet gout of blood flooded from the girl's mouth and the three fell backwards, still clutching the upper half of Tigerlily's torso. The glimmer of life was still in her eyes and Snowdog watched in horror as the girl's agonised shrieks trailed into a hideous gurgling.

With a deafening cry, the tyranid creature hauled its bulk through the floor of the tunnel and Snowdog howled his rage at the beast. He rolled to his knees and drew his pistol in one motion, aiming towards its head. He squeezed off several shots, but none were able to penetrate the creature's energy field.

It lashed out with a taloned arm and sent him flying, slashed from hip to shoulder. Gunderson fired his last few shells at the creature as Silver snatched up one of Tigerlily's fallen knives.

The beast towered over Snowdog and he knew that this was it, this was how he was going to check out of this world. Not exactly how he'd planned it.

Its powerful clawed hands, the ones it had used to tear Tigerlily in two, reached down and picked him up, raising him to its fanged maw. Snowdog heard Silver scream his name as he fired the last bullets from his pistol at point blank range into the beast's face. It screeched in agony as one bullet somehow managed to defeat its protective field and blow out its left eye. Its grip convulsed, the claws digging further into Snowdog's body, and he screamed in agony, blood streaming down his sides.

He scrabbled for another weapon, almost insensible from the pain as the claws dug further into his flesh. His hand closed over something in his pocket and he rammed it deep into the creature's throat. He kicked backwards, powering free of the creature's grip, its talons scoring bloody grooves in his body. He felt a bone-jarring impact as his face connected with the concrete and tasted blood as his teeth snapped.

He heard another boom of a shotgun discharge followed by the snap of a hammer slamming down empty. The beast lashed out again at Gunderson's chest, its talon smashing through his armour and laying him open to the bone. The Enforcer tumbled back, unconscious, and dropped his shotgun.

It was all over now, Snowdog realised, and he waited for the fatal blow to land. But for long seconds nothing happened. Then he heard a tortured groaning and an alien hiss of incomprehension.

Snowdog felt a crashing thump beside him and closed his eyes. Eventually, he forced them to open and looked around. The tunnel was eerily quiet, only the sound of ragged breathing and the gentle lap of distant water disturbed the silence. Then Silver laughed, a high pitched laugh of terrified relief and released tension. Snowdog pushed himself painfully to a sitting position and leaned back against the tunnel wall and stared, disbelieving, at the sight before him.

Flanks heaving slowly with its laboured breathing, the vast tyranid creature lay unmoving on the tunnel's floor. Its fanged head was close enough for him to touch, thick saliva drooling from its jaws. He closed his eyes and replayed the last few moments in his head: Tigerlily's death, the gunshots and him ramming something down the alien's throat. It obviously hadn't been a grenade as he'd hoped, but what had it been? Then he noticed a few red capsules trailing from between the creature's jaws and suddenly knew exactly what he'd done.

Six hundred Kalma drops in one go!

As he watched, the alien's chest hiked one last time and its heart finally gave out under the sedating effects of the drug. Its long, rattling death cough faded to a low hiss and Snowdog could feel hysterical laughter building inside him. The beast had overdosed on Kalma. Not really surprising, considering it had taken all six hundred doses of the powerful narcotic in one hit. Silver helped him to his feet and together they stared at the beast that had almost killed them all.

'Some day, huh?' remarked Silver.

'Some day,' agreed Snowdog.

Silver nodded towards the unconscious Gunderson and said, 'What you wanna do about him? You want me to finish him off?'

Snowdog shook his head. 'No, I don't think so.'

'Why not? He'd kill you.'

'Probably,' conceded Snowdog. 'But just think how much it's going to eat at him, knowing we could've killed him, but didn't.'

Silver shrugged and said, 'Have it your way.'

Snowdog winced in pain as they limped towards the light at the end of the tunnel, dizzy from blood loss. But any battle with an alien monstrosity you walked away from in one piece was a good one, so he guessed he couldn't complain.

Yeah, thought Snowdog, it was business as usual alright.

DEFIXIO

Ben Counter

'ORKS!' SCREAMED SOMEONE over the radio, and the concussions of the first crude shells rang through the ground into the reeking, cramped interior of the *Defixio*. Samiel shouldered the massive weight of the sponson's heavy bolter and squinted through the vision slit. He could see nothing of the ambush, just wisps of smoke drifting in from the front of the convoy, but he could already hear the confusion of noise building up – broken voices over the comms, dull thuds from up ahead, and the Exterminator crew around him getting to battle posts.

He was bad luck, they said. Samiel was beginning to think they were right.

'Crew, load up!' came Commander Karra-Vrass's voice over the rumble of the tracks and the ringing of explosions. Samiel glanced round to see Graek heaving the autocannon rounds into their chambers, gang tattoos rippling across his back. Above him, the skinny form of Damrid crammed itself into the turret gunner's chair.

'*Defixio* requesting target locations,' barked Karra-Vrass into the comms, but all he got was static shot through with screams. He turned back and shouted over the noise of the *Defixio*'s engines. 'Crew, I want targets, now! Light armour and infantry priority!'

There was a vast, terrible, crunching explosion and Samiel's vision was filled with an orange-white sheet of flame billowing towards him.

He darted back from the sponson as a tongue of fire licked through the vision slit, his gas mask's intake suddenly choked with smoke and fumes. There was a hideous wrenching sound as Dniep gunned the engine and the *Defixio* ploughed through the wreckage of the shattered tank ahead of them.

'What the bloody hell was that?' bawled Karra-Vrass.

'Hellhound!' shouted back Samiel. 'They got Lucullo's Hellhound!'

Burning bodies tumbled across the dark earth outside, and Samiel was thankful he couldn't hear them scream.

'Targets!' The voice was Damrid's, up in the turret, bringing the *Defixio*'s autocannons to bear.

Kallin, on the opposite sponson, opened up and suddenly the *Defixio*'s interior was full of the staccato battering of the heavy bolter's reports, hot shell casings everywhere. 'Come get some, ya groxlickin' sons a' bitches!'

Karra-Vrass swung open the front hatch and put his head out to see what was happening.

When he came back down the side of his face was dark with soot. 'Get the halftrack!'

Samiel didn't hear over the din, but he knew that Damrid would be muttering a word to the Emperor, like he always did, just before the twin thunderclap of the autocannon blanked out the world for a split second.

All of *Defixio*'s firepower was brought to bear on the orks apart from Samiel's sponson. He couldn't see the orks, and now thick smoke was sweeping across the valley from what must be half the convoy burning up ahead. It was choking the interior, too, but the crew barely noticed. Every breath a Chem-Dog took was drawn through a respirator or jerry-built gasmask, and most of them were used to breathing stuff that would kill most people.

Graek yanked the glowing-hot shells out of the breech and slammed another two home, and Kallin continued to fill the air with bursts of heavy bolter fire.

'Samiel, get me targets!' shouted Karra-Vrass. Unlike the rest of the crew his voice was unimpaired by ugly implants or a gas mask – Savlar aristos didn't have such things because back home they breathed clean, imported air.

'Nothing, sir!' replied Samiel, and even as he said it a monstrously crude jet intake sucked the smoke away and he was looking at the underside of the ugliest, squattest aircraft he had ever seen. It flew so low it must have clipped the vox aerial, sounding like a nuclear wind and followed by a score of rickety buggies, half-tracks and bikes crewed by insane greenskins, teeth bared and guns roaring. They barrelled down the side of the valley at astonishing speed and one of them slammed into the *Defixio*'s side, so the tank slewed wildly and Samiel was thrown onto his back. Gunfire rattled along the *Defixio*'s armour and Damrid swung the turret towards the horde.

Then, the roar of the dog-nosed fighter again as it spiralled down for another pass. This time cannon shells lanced down from above, ripped chunks out of the ground, and burst through Samiel's side of the *Defixio* like a hammer through glass. Samiel heard no noise, because the din had built up into a wall of white noise that filled his ears. Through the yawning hole in the tank's side he saw a swarming mass of greenskin maniacs sweeping down into the valley.

Samiel realised he had been blown clear across the tank's interior, and that Kallin's gun was still firing wildly even as the wall of white noise toppled over and everything went blank.

WHEN HE WOKE, all he saw was the grim grey sky of Jaegersweld. There was only one planet Samiel had seen uglier than this one, and that was Savlar itself. The Guard was supposed to be a way of getting off Savlar and the Dead Moons, with their chem-pits and convict-cities. All the Guard had done for him was drag him from planet to misbegotten planet, kill

his friends, make him a jinx. Because he had been a sole survivor, he had used up more than his fair share of luck already
and whoever had to serve with him next would have that little bit less luck to go round. Sole survivors were as unlucky
as it got.

Still, he wasn't dead yet.

He sat up and felt the ache running down his limbs, and
the sharp shots of pain where his skin had been hit by
shrapnel. He took a breath of Jaegersweld's damp,
unhealthy air, and heard the metallic sigh as it was forced
through the implants inside his ribcage. Samiel's implants
were more sophisticated than most, because those willing
and able to work as administrators were worth keeping alive
for longer than the average Chem-Dog. But the Guardsmen
of the Savlar regiment, of course, had little respect for such
skills.

They were towards the top of the valley slope. The *Defixio*
stood nearby. The profile of the Exterminator-class battle
tank was broken by all manner of salvaged and stolen bits
Dniep had bolted on – armour plates, trophies, stowage.
Kallin had tied a string of ork hands around his sponson
mount, the freshest still glinting with moistness, the oldest
shrivelled and rotted. The Savlar regimental marking were
stencilled onto one side of the turret – on the other, splattered on in Dniep's loose hand, were the bold white letters
that read *DEFIXIO*.

The tank had been sprayed in the drab brown-grey cam-
ouflage scheme common to everything on Jaegersweld, but
the various shades of the bits and pieces bolted and tied on
made it something very different from what must have
rolled out of the factory on some far-flung forge world.
Samiel was coming to realise that it was their tank now, their
home and their protection as well as the weapon they were
ordered to use. And because it was theirs, the crew made
sure that in the process of repairing and maintaining it, they
left it looking like it had been through its fair share of battles and firefights – they said almost everything had been
replaced on the hulking vehicle, until it was almost entirely
composed of what they had installed or repaired. The tank

belonged to the crew far more than it belonged to the Imperial Guard, and that was just how the crew wanted it. Dniep himself was kneeling at the *Defixio*'s other side and welding a huge sheet of salvaged metal over the hole in the side armour, which would become one more battle wound carried proudly like a badge of honour.

'Looks like all yer luck's used up after all.' Samiel looked up to see Kallin standing over him. Kallin was a big guy, tall and broad-shouldered, with skin so appallingly pitted and eroded by the constant rain of chemicals he had lived through that Samiel had seen healthier-looking corpses. The unsophisticated respirator implants under his jaw confirmed he had grown up in the chem-mines of the Dead Moons, which was a feat in itself. 'Miracle we made it this far, with a jinx.'

'Save it for the greenskins, Kallin.'

Kallin stooped down and pushed his ravaged face close. The ork bones hanging round his neck jangled like wind chimes. 'You're a jinx, boy. One of them things sent down to plague us, like the greenskins ain't bad enough. Don't you start thinkin' we'll look out for you or miss you when you're dead. Graek's dead and we're on our way out, and it'll all because we went and took in a jinx.'

'Graek's dead?'

Kallin indicated the loader's body, laid out in the shade of a rock, one side of his torso dark red and swollen under the tattoos. 'Dead as they come. Busted all his ribs, turned his guts to groxfood. Like I said, miracle if any of us make it now. Jinx and a Guild boy, Emperor's teeth.' He saw Samiel's confused frown, and smiled with a mouthful of teeth stunted from inhaling acidic air. 'You didn't know about Karra-Vrass? You know that damn stick he carries?'

Samiel nodded. Karra-Vrass always carried a silver swagger stick, but Samiel had assumed it was just a gimmick, like other officers insisted on wearing full dress medals or parade swords.

'It's a badge of office. Made of titanium. He's not just any aristo, he's from the Guild. When he's not playing soldier with a tank full of us plebs, the bastard sits in orbit and sells the filth we churn out of the Dead Moons. People like him worked everyone I know near to death. Most of us aren't even cons, we're second generation or more, but they don't care. Long as they keep the trade going, we're just machines to make them creds. Used up Graek like he used up half the men on the Dead Moons.'

When Karra-Vrass approached with Damrid, Samiel couldn't help noticing the shining swagger-stick the officer still held in his hand. In the other was a salvaged visor-scope, just one of the pieces of 'non-standard' equipment that tended to turn up in any Chem-Dogs vehicle.

'We're not rejoining the convoy,' said Karra-Vrass.

'Why not?' asked Dniep, looking up from his hurried weld job.

'Because it's not there. We lost about three-quarters strength in that ambush, and the tail-end must have retreated. We can't hook up with them because our comms are out and the orks have us cut off.'

'Then what do we do?' said Kallin, quick to anger. 'Wait for a greenskin patrol to skin us alive?'

'The nearest regimental HQ is the Cadian 24th, fifteen hundred kilometres west.'

'Three days across ork-held land?'

'Exactly, Kallin. I wouldn't like to think you were questioning this course of action.'

Kallin muttered something under his breath that Samiel was glad he didn't quite catch.

'Now, crew,' continued Karra-Vrass, 'Since Samiel is back with us I think this is an appropriate time for a reading. Damrid?'

'Sir.' Damrid stepped forward, fishing a small prayer book from his ill-fitting fatigues. He began to speak of hope and duty, of how they were all sinners who wanted only to survive that they might redeem themselves in the Emperor's service. The words were familiar to Samiel, who had heard such things so often before in the chapels of the administrative colony where he had once lived. But he knew they were not meaningless, even if he had trouble believing them – devotion was the only thing keeping many Guardsmen sane. And even he, sometimes, found himself calling to the Emperor for help – especially when he fought his way out of a flaming wreck and felt the flames on his back as he leapt from the white-hot explosion behind him...

He was a sole survivor. Perhaps the Emperor had already heard him once, and wasn't ready to grant a miracle a second time. Maybe that was why he was supposed to be so unlucky.

Samiel and Damrid buried Graek's body quickly – orks were little more than animals, and they could home in on a spoiled corpse like any other beast. Samiel didn't object when Damrid rifled through his dead comrade's fatigues and pocketed the few trinkets and ammo rounds he found – he'd done the same himself, to friend and foe.

'Is it wrong...?' asked Damrid falteringly. 'Is it wrong to lose a fellow man and think we're better off without him?'

'I don't know,' replied Samiel. 'I didn't know him long.'

The last handful of damp earth was thrown over the dead man's face. 'You didn't want to. He was bad. The worst.'

'What did he do?' It wasn't a question that was generally asked of a Chem-Dog, for a man's crime was his own damn business. But Graek was dead, and he wasn't about to complain.

'A slaver. He ran with the... the uncleans. Some Arbites tracked him down, but he found them first, and when he finished with them they say you couldn't tell they had ever been human.

'And he never changed, that was the worst. He never saw the light. He never stopped hurting people. When we evacuated the civilians out of the south, he went missing for days, and after he came back we'd hear stories about families burned in bunkers and children hunted down for sport. They blamed it on the orks, but Graek had some... some things he kept. I think he was the worst sort of person.'

Samiel was grateful for an unhealthy shudder from the *Defixio*'s engines as they kicked protesting into life. 'Dunno if they'll hold together,' Dniep was saying. 'Fuel's not a problem, you can run a Leman Russ on boot leather and bad language. But she took a big hit back there and the track drives are looking shaky.'

'Will it last?' Karra-Vrass's voice was dispassionate – he must have known that his life depended on the *Defixio* not breaking down, but he didn't sound like it.

Dniep stood up, wiping the oil off his hands onto his stained fatigues. 'Three days? Be surprised, sir. But then again, sometimes even I get surprised by how much punishment these things can take.'

'Good.' The officer raised his voice. 'Burial detail, are you finished?'

Damrid raised a hand. He had rolled up the sleeves of his fatigues and for the first time Samiel noticed something – a tattoo, a skull surrounded by barbed wire, with a barcode underneath, at the top of the boy's arm. It was one of the many symbols branded on the fresh convicts brought in to keep up the population of the Dead Moons, which meant that Damrid wasn't second generation like Samiel had assumed. He was a con. What had he done, this boy? You heard tales of kids slung into the chem-mines for stealing loaves of bread or failing to cheer when the planetary governor waved to the crowds. Poor lad. Life could be bad enough without being sentenced to a slow death when you were hardly old enough to know what right and wrong really were.

'And weaponry?'

'Loaded and ready,' came Kallin's voice from within the hull.

'Very well. The orks will have patrols out looking for survivors and we must not give them the chance to find us. We roll immediately.'

They clambered into the *Defixio*, Damrid into the turret to take the first lookout, with Karra-Vrass alongside Dniep at the front. Kallin and Samiel, meanwhile, slumped against the sponson mounts to catch some of the noisy, cramped downtime that passed for sleep on the move.

You can't dream when you're not asleep, but it still felt like a nightmare. It wasn't that long ago it had happened, but he knew it would be burned across his mind's eye until he breathed his last. It was the reason he was on the *Defixio* at all, and the reason they all thought what only Kallin spoke – that Samiel was a jinx who had used up too much of his luck. His previous tank, an Executioner, had found itself surrounded and outnumbered by the light vehicles and bikes the greenskins rode like madmen.

He saw the billowing black-red of the fire and felt the heat across his face. He felt the cold earth against his back heating up as fuel spilled over the ground and rippled towards him, on fire.

He could see, as if they were in front of him right then, the silhouettes of his old crewmates, fire at their backs and orks at their front, blasting away with sidearms at their assailants. When the magazines had gone up from a lucky warbike shot the rear of the tank's hull had been torn off and Samiel had tumbled out while the burning wreck slid to a halt, and there his crewmates had made their stand.

Living on a planet like Savlar meant you valued every scrap of pride you scrounged, and the men who crewed the shattered tank weren't going to let themselves be taken prisoner by anyone or anything. Samiel watched as one was cut down by explosive shellfire, another ground beneath the wheels of a warbike that slewed insanely close.

And then the plasma coils went critical. An expanding globe of white-hot energised plasma, like a new star, incinerated the crewmen and burned a hole in the ork attack.

When the smoke cleared and the bodies were recovered, Samiel was the only one alive. His injuries were minor, and the orks hadn't even noticed him in the confusion. He heard them all say he was the luckiest Guardsmen on the planet.

But they weren't smiling when they said it.

'No use, sir. Goes as far as I can see.' Samiel snapped out of his half-sleep, and once more he was back inside the stale hull of the *Defixio*. He knew something was wrong because the tank was only moving slowly now, and Karra-Vrass was replacing Damrid at the turret hatch.

Damrid dropped down onto the floor.

'What's happening?' asked Kallin, also jolted out of his own half-dreams.

'Minefield,' came the reply, and Samiel realised it was probably the worst possible answer. Orks made no attempt to conceal their minefields, but they laid a hell of a lot and didn't care if they lost a couple of their own to them, meaning the fields were always big with no way through. They also had a habit of packing them with so much explosive they left craters the size of command bunkers – current Guard wisdom was that the orks laid mines more because they liked the noise than for any strategic advantage.

Karra-Vrass came back down and pulled a folded-up map from inside his greatcoat. He laid it out on the floor – it showed the northern part of the continent across which the *Defixio* was trying to travel. Samiel saw just how far they had to go, and how much of the ground they had to cover was covered in the green markers of known ork camps and outposts.

Karra-Vrass stabbed at the map with the end of his swagger stick. 'Dniep, is this our position?'

'Near enough.'

Between the *Defixio* and the Cadian HQ lay a plain bounded by contours – in the world outside, those contours were ragged, torn ranges of loose earth and landslides. No kind of country for a tank.

'The minefield will have no safe channels, and the high ground is not an option. However, the field is not particularly deep. Defusing is possible.'

Everyone looked at Dniep. He had a knack with anything technical – Samiel had heard tell of the miracles he had worked with the stubborn Leman Russ engines, and no doubt he could have taught the Tech-Guard Engineers a thing or two about clearing mines. 'I could do it,' he said, with an uncharacteristic bravery that made Samiel realise just how desperate a situation they were in.

'What about patrols?' said Kallin. 'We'd be waiting here for hours, the bloody greenskins could pick us off for fun.'

'Dniep could stay.' It was Damrid who spoke – by now all the crew were crowded around the map. 'If someone marked the mines first, he'd defuse them in half the time. We'd have a driver in case we got jumped. He'd have to go out and clear a path afterwards, but not for as long. We'd still be targets, but we'd have a better chance.'

'And we'd leave a man behind if we had to run for it,' added Kallin grimly.

Karra-Vrass began folding up the map. 'We're not leaving anyone. But we may find ourselves in a firefight a man short. We're already down a loader.'

'So, who do we need the least?' said Dniep.

And this time, they looked at Samiel.

IT WAS DARK by then. Jaegersweld had two moons, one large and bright, but its light was filtered through many layers of ever-present cloud and a sickly, grey glow fell over the landscape. The minefield was obvious enough – some explosive-packed devices stuck above the ground, more of a challenge than a trap. But while they might have been animals, orks were a very cunning type of animal. They would have some buried so you couldn't see them, and those were the ones Samiel would have to spend a long time marking so Dniep's foray would be as short as possible.

Samiel told himself it could be done – it wasn't far across. And it certainly had to be done, for the loose, muddy hills on either side would be near-impossible for the *Defixio* to clamber across, even with Dniep at the controls.

Hopping down from the front hatch, Samiel was acutely aware of just how exposed he was. Outside the tank, he felt soft and vulnerable.

Inside the tank he was on home ground, a tiny bubble of the Imperium around him. Now he was behind ork lines, and alone. He checked his gear – flare gun, bayonet (another of Dniep's 'finds'), a bag of spent shell casings to mark the mines.

It wasn't slow work, but there were a lot of mines, densely packed to make the huge chain explosions the orks liked so much. He looked up every now and again to check for glints of approaching machinery against the grey-black horizon, and listened for the juddering drone of an ork engine. Once or twice he heard the chatter of gunfire far off, but that might mean anything in a ork warzone – they could be launching a major assault or just taking pot shots at one another for fun.

That they were so difficult to predict was the worst thing, because you couldn't just herd them into killing zones or cripple their economic base or any of the other things that worked with good old-fashioned humans. The only thing that worked was hatred. There was no sympathy, no honour. You had to exterminate them, all of them, because they were seemingly designed to spring up again at the slightest chance. Samiel knew that war against the orks would never end – even if they were wiped of the surface of Jaegersweld, the Guard would just be packed off to the next planet that became infested, and it would begin all over again. For Samiel, it had become a case of getting out alive and hoping that some distant commander would grant him a plot on a conquered planet as reward for a lifetime of fighting, so he could let someone else do all the hating. But if he really had used up all his luck already, as the others suspected, then he didn't fancy his odds.

The sound that alerted him was the squeal of metal on metal as the *Defixio*'s turret turned to face something he couldn't see. Samiel looked around him – he was more than halfway across the minefield by now, a long trail of shell casings marking the hidden mines. The *Defixio* was too far away – if he ran for it now it would probably move before he got there and he'd be left standing full in view of whatever was attacking. He obeyed the first rule of the Imperial Guard, and kept his damn head down.

The autocannon fired and an explosion bloomed some way off. A group of vehicles was illuminated for the briefest moment – bikes, huge clunking things like battering rams on wheels with speeds limited only by the insanity of their riders.

Orks. They had been found, and now the greenskins were moving in for the kill. They were crazy, these bikers, but they were as dangerous as it got for a tank – they carried the crudest of explosives which could crack open a Leman Russ with ease. Samiel had seen it done. And now it was going to be done to the *Defixio*.

The red-hot exhausts and muzzle flashes were visible now as the bikers careered down the valley at tremendous speed, and the *Defixio* was moving. It was heading the only way it could – towards the nearest ridge of surely impassable ground. Karra-Vrass was gambling on the tiny chance that the *Defixio* might make it, because the other chances were the minefield and the approaching orks, and those odds were worse still.

It wouldn't make it. No way. Kallin's sponson chattered away at long range at the bikes, and after a worryingly long wait (Damrid must be having to load it himself, thought Samiel, remembering Graek's shattered ribs) the autocannon fired again. Two bikes tumbled flaming to a standstill, but the others sheared through their wreckage and stayed on course.

The *Defixio* was at the foot of the ridge and began to climb, the loose earth already slipping under its tracks. The tank wouldn't have outrun the bikes at the best of times and now it was slower still, hauling itself painfully up the crumbling slope as the bikes roared around it, sweeping towards its near side. Samiels's sponson fired and the closest bike's front wheel was shredded, flipping the bike over and sending the ork rider somersaulting into the *Defixio*'s side. Samiel realised that Karra-Vrass himself must be manning the gun.

The officer's aim was good but there were only so many rounds he could squeeze off, and the lead biker threw a grenade, fuse sparkling, at the tracks as he slewed past. The explosion was loud even from where Samiel was lying and he saw links of track flying. Three more followed as the bikers passed, Karra-Vrass's gun still firing but blindly through smoke and shrapnel.

Samiel knew they didn't think much of him – in fact, they would probably have preferred one less gunner than a sole survivor and the misfortune he brought. But they were still his comrades, and they were still soldiers of the Imperium up against aliens. He couldn't just let them die.

He stood up, pulling one of the flares out of his bag, and lit it. When his eyes adjusted to the sudden glare he saw the lead biker had spotted the flash in the darkness and was wheeling in Samiel's direction, the others following.

Samiel considered dropping the flare and running – but ork mines were unstable and the weight of a man would set even the tankbusters off. His heart, already racing, quickened further when he realised that the safest thing he could do was stand his ground and face the bikers' charge.

'Come on, you green bastards! Come and get some!' he yelled over the roar of the bikes' engines.

It was probably the bravest thing he had ever done. Probably the last, too. Would anyone survive to tell the story of how he died? Could the crew in the *Defixio* even see what was happening? Samiel couldn't think of an answer because his mind was full of the bikes screaming towards him. He could see the lead bikers' bared teeth in the light from the flare, see the pinpricks of white in its tiny piggy eyes and the blur of the front wheel...

It was some way into the minefield when it careened straight into an anti-vehicle mine so scrappily made it stuck out of the ground half the height of a man. The noise was so vast Samiel was totally deafened, and a column of earth burst out of the ground. An instant later a huge chain explosion erupted with such force Samiel felt himself picked off his feet as the concussion hammered over him. He slammed onto the ground, breath knocked out of him, mind reeling, the whole world a swirling madness of white noise and explosions.

When the noise subsided and he opened his eyes, he saw the air thick with smoke coiling from a rip in the ground longer than the skid from a dropship crash. The wan moonlight made strange shifting shapes in the smoke, and the smell of burnt fuel was dizzying. A bike wheel, licked with flame, rolled slowly along the ground.

By the Emperor, thought Samiel, I'm alive.

I can't believe it. I'm alive.

Through his near-deafness he caught the ragged sound of an engine gunning and the smoke parted to reveal the last biker, blackened and battered with blood-flecked teeth bared, clinging to his bike as it tore towards Samiel through the blast zone. Samiel acted on reflex – he lashed out his gun and fired. It was then that he realised he was armed only with the flare gun.

The sparkling white flare spiralled towards the bike and shattered against the handlebars like a firework, leaving an incandescent comet trail as the bike hurtled forward. Samiel could see the ork's manic grin and the wicked squinting eyes behind its goggles, and knew he was going to die.

There was a massive wash of heat as the bike took off at the last second in a ball of flame, somersaulting over him and cartwheeling across the plain. The rider was thrown off, on fire, further into the minefield – Samiel covered his head just in time to protect himself from the inevitable shower of debris from another detonating mine.

Samiel watched as the flames guttered out. For the second time in half a minute he was quite astonished to be alive. He lay back on the ground, suddenly exhausted, and got his first real sleep for months.

'You ARE ONE lucky bitch, Chem-Dog.' The voice was Dniep's. It was morning, and the sun was flooding the dank valleys of Jaegersweld with drab grey light. Samiel felt he was propped up against the slope. He was aching again, but mostly unhurt.

'Them greenskin bastards cleared us a path,' continued Dniep. 'And that last one, you must've caught his fuel tank. Went up like a flare shell, saw it from here. Even Kallin was impressed.'

Samiel looked across to the minefield – there was indeed a scar running right across it, plenty wide enough for the *Defixio*.

Dniep scratched at the acned skin around his throat implants – he had escaped the worst ravages of the chem-mines because he had been too useful fixing the machines to risk at the workface, but he was still damned ugly. 'So you solved us one problem, Samiel, but now we got us another.' He indicated the hulk of the *Defixio*, smoke still coiling off it. The tracks on the near side had been unpinned and lay limp on the ground. 'We found enough links, but a coupla pins got sheared. Scavved one soon enough, but we can't find another. Not for the life of us. And it'll be our lives, too, 'cause we're stuck out here in the open with a tank that won't move and a bunch of greenskins wondering why their mates haven't come back.'

'You should have woken me, I could have helped–'

'Karra-Vrass said to let you sleep. And didn't none of us argue with him, neither. Besides, we're not going to find it. We need something thin enough to fit but strong enough to take the strain. Miracle we found one.'

But Samiel went out and looked anyway. It wasn't that he dared have any real hope – he just couldn't lie there and wait. The orks would come, he knew, because they had a knack for being everywhere on a planet at once, and many Guardsmen swore greenskins could hunt a man down by scent alone. He kept low and always checked the horizon for approaching orks, once or twice spotting something dark and moving and hitting the ground until he was sure it was gone. And, as he expected, there was nothing that might serve as a track pin half-buried in Jaegersweld's heavy earth, just metal fit only for scrap. There was no hope, but he didn't allow himself be consumed with the knowledge that he would die. Many a time he had heard better Guardsmen than him discover how slight their chances were, then shrug their shoulders and reply that hell, a man's gotta die somehow.

Nevertheless his steps were heavy and his head low as he clambered back over the ridge. And the sound he heard was engines.

He hurried down the loose slope to see the *Defixio* warmed up and ready to roll, smoke pumping from inefficient exhausts, trinkets and grisly trophies shaking with the unhealthy vibrations of the cylinders.

The front hatch went up and Kallin looked out. There were a few more scavenged trinkets around his neck and hanging from his various ammo belts and pouches – a Chem-Dog out foraging always came back with some new toys. 'Samiel, ya grox-lover! Get in!'

Samiel sprinted the last few yards and climbed in – the rest of the crew had been waiting for him. With a nod from

Karra-Vrass, Dniep gingerly backed the Defixo off the slope. Then, it turned and headed across the wide channel across the minefield, towards the other side of the plain and the Cadian HQ beyond.

Samiel didn't ask what had been used as a track pin. Probably the axle off an abandoned ork vehicle, or even a direct replacement from another wrecked Leman Russ tank, of which there must be some lying around.

And then he realised that Karra-Vrass was no longer carrying his titanium swagger stick.

SAMIEL'S TURN AT the lookout came. The last day had been nervous but hopeful – they had hidden under an overhang when a flight of smoking ork flyers swooped overhead, and often lurked behind ridges and rock formations as ork patrols passed close by. Karra-Vrass had told them they were being hunted by orks eager to remove such an impertinent threat as a tank that dared run their gauntlet, and the hunters were closing in. But they had not been spotted, and time was on their side, because they were nearing their destination.

'Maybe you're not as unlucky as you look, Samiel,' Kallin had said, which were probably the most charitable words he had uttered in his life.

And now they had to cross one last hill before the Cadian HQ was in sight. There would be some explaining to do – where had they come from? Why were they alone? Where was the rest of the column? The Cadians would certainly make a point of packing away anything small and valuable whenever the Chem-Dogs approached. But they would be able to eat, maybe sleep, pull a few days light duties before someone figured out how to get them back to the Savlar regiment.

Samiel didn't fancy the *Defixio* to make it, with a half-busted track and a hole in the side, especially since a constant supply of Leman Russ spares was always required. The Cadians would probably break the old Exterminator up and use the bits to patch up their own vehicles in the motor pool. But even Dniep thought it was a better end than a smouldering wreck in the middle of a planet no one really cared about.

And now they were at the crest of the hill, the flats beyond rolling out before Samiel's eyes, the Cadian HQ finally coming into view...

A grinning, lopsided horned skull totem, cut from sheets of metal and bolted together, stood on the roof of the command bunker. Burned-out Leman Russ and Chimeras littered the compound. A Hydra flak cannon stood idle at one corner, pointing down and inwards, barrels still blackened from the fire it had poured into the attackers streaming through the breaches.

Bodies of men and orks lay in piles around the centres of the heaviest fighting – the breach, the gateway, the mess and barracks complex where the men had made their stand. Where the fuel dump had been was a charred crater ringed with corpses. Buildings and bunkers had been turned inside-out by demo charges, their contents – furniture, equipment, occupants – strewn across the ground. Those structures still standing bore scars around windows and doors that had been used as fire points. Bodies in Cadian fatigues were displayed entwined in the razor wire that topped the rings of barricades and fences. Everywhere were bullet scars, discarded weapons, and the dead. Especially the dead.

But the worst was outside. All around the HQ was a teeming city of tents and huts, brimming with greenskins. They fought, argued, divided the spoils and feasted on the supplies they had hauled out of the HQ's stores.

The mad bikers that had so taken to Jaegersweld's landscape were buzzing like flies around the camp, eagerly burning captured fuel in pursuit of the blind speed they lived for. Camp fires smouldered, and the breeze brought the reek of burning and filth.

'Can you see it?' called out Damrid from below.

'Stop,' said Samiel.

The *Defixio* ground to a halt. Damrid was the first out, scrambling over the turret seat and pushing his head out of the hatch.

'Imperator...' he whispered, one hand held to the pocket in which he carried his prayer book. 'Xenos malefica... what about forgiveness? Hasn't it been enough?'

Damrid slithered back into the *Defixio*'s hull. Dniep replaced him, eager to see what had caused such shock in his crewmate.

'Those bastards,' he said when he saw. 'Alien bastards. We shoulda known.'

Samiel didn't know what to say. What can you say, when even what little hope a Guardsman allows himself is torn away?

'So that's what broke the lad,' continued Dniep, more to himself than to Samiel. 'He thought he was forgiven, he really did. That's why he never called you bad luck, like the rest of us. The Emperor was watching, he thought, because he had been forgiven.'

'For what?'

Dniep looked at him incredulously. 'No one told you? Damrid's the worst! I mean, I did fixin' for some pretty rough types, and a few people got hurt, and but I never–' Dniep shook his head. 'The lad was on a frontier world, raising hell since he was born. When they sent a mission to tame the place, Damrid and his boys took exception. You know his prayer book? Used to belong to a Sister there. They say that as Damrid was hacking the poor bitch to pieces all she could say was: "He will forgive you. He will forgive you..." over and over. Threw her to the cudbears when they'd finished with her. He started reading the damn book on the prison ship, and by the time he got to the Dead Moons he got it into his head he was forgiven.'

Damrid? It didn't make any sense... but then, sometimes there was a desperation about the way he believed, as if his faith was his only chance and he had to hold onto it no matter what... 'He doesn't look like he went through the Dead Moons.'

'They kept him safe. A chaplain who believes, that's the rarest thing in the system. Worth keeping alive. And when the Guard said they were raising up another Chem-Dog regiment, he was first in line, ready to fight the Emperor's fight and smite the foes of Humanity.' Dniep shook his head and whistled at the sight of the orks running wild across the Cadian HQ, making belts of skin and necklaces of hands. 'And now this. He should've made it. Really should've. Kid like him, just getting through it all without breaking up, that's like winning the war on your own.'

When they had all looked upon the remains of the Cadian HQ and its slaughtered garrison, they slumped down inside the *Defixio* and were silent.

Suddenly Kallin slammed a fist into the side of the hull. 'For this we fight? We drag this lump of metal across a whole damned bitch of a planet and this is what we get?'

They all looked at him, and Samiel wished he would stay quiet, but like the rest of them Kallin had felt hope building up during the journey's last leg and he couldn't cope with having it torn away from him. His voice was rising to a screech. 'Why now? Why couldn't they take the place a month earlier, or a month later, or any time but now? They can't... what happened? Can't these damn Cadians even look after their own HQ?'

Kallin slumped, suddenly exhausted. Dniep spoke weakly, his voice cracking. 'The Jurn regiment is supposed to be south, past the gulf. If we can get down there, and cross it–'

'No.' Karra-Vrass's voice was strong. That was why he was an officer, thought Samiel grimly. He was as broken as the rest of them, but he could conceal it. 'We would be passing through the ork drop sites. When we are found here we will be executed quickly, for we are on the frontier and prisoners would use up too many supplies. If we break for the south we will be imprisoned, enslaved, probably used as playthings, and then we will die anyway. And the gulf cannot be crossed, there have been enough prisoners that have tried.'

'So what then?' Kallin's voice was like a child's. Samiel was almost sure he was weeping. 'We die?'

Karra-Vrass looked at him. 'We die.'

'But then, everybody dies.' Samiel realised that he was the one speaking.

'The truest of things,' replied Karra-Vrass. 'All lives end.'

'So it is willed,' said Damrid. His face was pale as a dead man's and he had a faraway expression. It was said a man could gain a place at the Emperor's side by his conduct when all seemed lost, for even in the moments of the most terrible desperation, He was watching, He was judging.

This was Damrid's last chance. If he died well, maybe that would mean he'd be forgiven, after all.

'But how many know when their time comes?' continued Karra-Vrass. 'How many can see the end coming, and be prepared? Not many. Of all those of our brothers-in-arms who died, only we can ready ourselves. It is in death, more than anything, that a man can be measured. Isn't that right, Damrid?'

'So it is willed,' said the boy again.

'Their patrols will catch up with us within the hour. Their camp sentries will be onto us long before that. We don't have much time, but it will be enough. We have been given the greatest gift that any man could ask, for now we have a purpose. We will spend the rest of our lives battling the alien foe, not because we are ordered or because we must, but because we choose to do so, to make our deaths mean something. It could be otherwise – we could die in flight, or cowering, or under the slaver's whip. But we will not.'

Samiel looked up. It shouldn't mean anything, for still they were all dead men. But somehow, it did. They could butcher his friends, strip away his hopes, wage a war that forced him to spend his life in exhaustion or fear cooped up in a tank on a planet he hated. They could turn him into no better than a bad seed. But by the Emperor himself, those greenksin bastards couldn't make him die for nothing.

He was on his feet, shivering with excitement and pride. Karra-Vrass stood, too, and smoothed out the creases in his greatcoat.

'Crew, load up,' he said.

EVERY SAVLAR VEHICLE was equipped with hermetic seals around the hatches and doors – these they sealed, so that even breathing the same air as the Chem-Dog crew would be a privilege the orks would have to fight for. Karra-Vrass took off his officer's greatcoat, rolled up the black sleeves of his uniform, and slammed two autocannon shells home into the breech. Damrid calmly recited those hymns that meant the most to him – the ones about never despairing, because every good man has his place in His plan, even if that man in his humility knows it not.

Karra-Vrass checked his sidearm, a duelling pistol that somehow he had managed to keep hold of even though its ivory handle and fine workmanship would have caught the eye of the most honest Chem-Dog. The others did the same with weapons they had as trophies or charms – Kallin's ugly snub-nosed gun looted from a dead ork, a shotgun Dniep hid under the driver's seat, a rusted sergeant's sword Damrid had kept. A rummage through the *Defixio*'s gear produced an old but working laspistol, which Samiel took.

This is the last gift I will ever receive, he thought. It felt like the first.

They did not have long to wait. As darkness approached once again, a greenskin foot patrol approached from the camp. Perhaps fifty strong, they stalked low in the gathering gloom, led by one a head or two taller than the rest, one arm hacked off and replaced with a brutal three-fingered claw that spat sparks from a power field. They had axes, guns, clubs.

Kallin whispered sharply to Karra-Vrass – from his vision slit, he could see one of the bike patrols that had been hunting them approaching fast from the opposite direction. They were trapped.

Good, thought Samiel. If you've got to go, then this is the way to do it.

Karra-Vrass glanced up at Damrid. The lad nodded back.

'Fire,' said Karra-Vrass.

The twin explosions burst in the midst of the orks, blasting two or three to flailing limbs. Some tried to scatter but the leader grabbed a couple by the scruffs of their necks, flung them forward, pointed with his monstrous claw and bellowed a command that could only be the charge.

They ran forward brandishing their weapons. Samiel heard Karra-Vrass roll the smoking casings out of the breech and haul another two shells in, as strongly and smoothly as Graek had done.

'Range?' called the officer, voice strained with the effort of forcing the breech cover home.

'Close!' shouted back Damrid.

'Fire!'

The two blasts merged into one as a hole was torn out of the advancing patrol. Some were thrown forward to collide with their fellows in the front, and two of them were thrown into the air in bits. Samiel took the opportunity – slowed down and in disarray, the leader cracking two heads together to stop his troops from fleeing, the patrol was a fine target. He opened up with his heavy bolter, seeing orks stitched through with explosive shells, illuminated in the muzzle flare. Two or three more went down, and the charge was halted. Now Dniep crunched the gears and the *Defixio* turned towards the orks.

Samiel kept firing, keeping ork heads down, and he could hear the wet crunch of greenskins going under the *Defixio*'s tracks.

Kallin was already firing on his side, meaning the bikers were almost upon them. The foot patrol blazed away with every chance they were given, and shells were impacting fiercely on the *Defixio*'s hull. The noise was appalling, for the orks liked their weapons loud – but Samiel didn't care. They could make all the noise they wanted, they weren't taking down these Dead Moon scummers without the hardest fight of their lives. His heavy bolter roared with the defiance he felt boiling inside him, and another ork was run through on a lance of hot steel.

There was a sound like a thundercrack as a crude ork grenade went off, buckling the metal patching the hull at Samiel's side. Shells ricocheted off the edge of Samiel's vision slit, but he didn't flinch. His ammo belt was running out and Karra-Vrass rammed another one into the heavy bolter's breech. Samiel glanced at him in gratitude, saw the officer understood, and went back to firing. He could barely see the targets now, his vision was full of a heaving press of green flesh as the orks tried to swamp the *Defixio*.

Another grenade went off and Kallin swore, his heavy bolter torn off its mounting by the explosion. Without pausing he grabbed his ork gun and opened fire at the talons clawing at the breached hull. Samiel could hear the bikes now, even above the rest of the din, as the riders dismounted and added their weight to the assault.

There was shriek of metal and suddenly the *Defixio* was open to the sky – the lead ork was standing over them, power claw holding the turret he had just ripped clean off the tank. Damrid tumbled back down into the hull, grabbed the sword and began to hack at the green arms and heads that appeared over the edge of ragged metal. Kallin's side gave way seconds later and he was fighting back the encroaching greenskins with his bare hands, ammo expended.

One of the greenskins got Dniep, an axe swinging down and burying itself in his back. Karra-Vrass opened fire with his duelling pistol, each shot hitting home, and Samiel followed suit, laspistol bolts burning into green skin. He heard Kallin yelling obscenities as he was dragged through the hole in the hull by a dozen clawed hands, and Samiel felt sure Kallin would have wanted to go out swearing.

The massive ork reached down and grabbed Damrid in its claw, hoisting him clean out of the tank, shearing through the boy's skinny body, tossing him aside, roaring its rage and showing its huge fangs. Karra-Vrass grabbed an autocannon shell and rammed it into the monster's mouth with the strength of a man who knows he has run out of time. The ork swiped at him with the power claw, batting him aside, and shots from the swarming orks tore into the officer's torso.

Samiel snatched up Dniep's discarded shotgun. He could feel the greenskins all around him, teeth biting into his legs, claws sinking into his shoulders. But there was no pain, not at the end, not while he still had his mark to make.

He fired a single round from the shotgun, aimed right into the face of the immense ork leader. With a roar like the end of the world the autocannon shell lodged in its jaw detonated, blowing the beast's head clean off, tearing a huge chunk out of its monstrous body. It swayed, as if it hadn't realised it was dead – then it fell.

Knowing that he had died giving as good as he had got, his heart pumping sheer glory through his veins, Samiel fell under the heaving mass of greenskins and felt no more.

'YOU'RE A LUCKY swine,' said the voice. It wasn't Savlar – the accent was different. 'Well enough to talk?'

'Just.' Samiel was surprised to hear his own voice replying. He opened his eyes – Jaegersweld's sunlight was never very bright, but he still squinted after so long...

Asleep? Unconscious? Dead?

The shadow in front of him became the shape of a man. A lined face and grey hair, dressed in Cadian fatigues. A colonel, Samiel saw from the chevrons on his shoulder.

'You mind telling me what happened here, son?'

'Ran into some orks, sir.' Samiel could hardly believe he was speaking. He had thought he must be dead before, twice... but this time he had been certain. He had been there waiting for it, and when it came he faced it and refused to let it take him without a fight.

He struggled into a sitting position. Behind the colonel was the smoking shell of the *Defixio*. He wouldn't have recognised it as a tank at all had he not spent the last, greatest moments of its life inside it. Skeletons surrounded it, just as charred.

The massive jawbones and beetling craniums of orks were everywhere, with a couple of human skulls that once belonged to his comrades.

'Took a lot of them with you. Must've thought you were dead, eh?'

'I was sort of counting on it, sir.'

'Like I said, one lucky swine. Fuel tanks went up and threw you clear. Week or two with the Sisters in the field hospital and you'll be back in action.' The colonel looked over Samiel's tattered fatigues, and the gas mask that hung round his neck. 'You from Savlar?'

'Yes, sir.'

'Steal anything and we'll hang you.'

'Yes, sir.'

Samiel could sit up but he couldn't walk – one leg was busted so bad he couldn't feel it. As he was loaded onto a stretcher he could see the rest of the Cadians clearing up the debris of the ork camp they had overrun in recapturing their HQ. The ork totem was being taken down from the roof of the command bunker, and the bodies lined up in mass graves.

Nothing Karra-Vrass had said was true. His friends (they were his friends in those final hours, without a doubt) had died no better deaths than the hundreds of Cadians days earlier, or the poor souls killed when the convoy was hit. They hadn't achieved anything, not really – the war on Jaegersweld would carry on without them. The Imperium was exactly the same as it would have been had none of them ever lived.

But that wasn't the point. They felt they were achieving something in death. Even Karra-Vrass believed his own words, of that Samiel was sure. They believed they were dying for a cause, they had been allowed to confront their deaths head-on and not have it finding them without warning as they cowered alone. How many Guardsmen on Jaergersweld could say that?

It was a terrible place, this galaxy, that ate up the lives of men. But sometimes, there was hope. Sometimes, there was something you could salvage from it, some dignity and pride, even if it was right at the end. It was more than most men got in the Guard, or on the Dead Moons, or anywhere else. Samiel couldn't properly understand it himself. But the crew of the *Defixio* had won a fine and noble victory of their own.

Now, of course, Samiel was a sole survivor twice over, and it would be a miracle if anyone would ever so much as look at him without muttering something dark under their breaths about how that man had used up enough luck for a hundred men. But there were worse things. In fact, he had something to be proud of – he had died a total of three times now, and two of those were pretty good send-offs. That wasn't a bad strike rate.

The Cadians began to carry him back to the HQ compound, through the wreckage of the ork camp. One of the stretcher-bearers glanced round at him, and must have wondered why, when he had a shattered leg and every one of his friends was dead, all this crazy Savlar kid could do was smile to himself.

INFERNO! is the indispensable guide to the worlds of Warhammer and Warhammer 40,000 and the corner-stone of the Black Library. Every issue is crammed full of action packed stories, comic strips and artwork from a growing network of awesome writers and artists including:

- William King
- Brian Craig
- Gav Thorpe

- Dan Abnett
- Barrington J. Bayley
- Gordon Rennie

and many more

Presented every two months, Inferno!
magazine brings the Warhammer worlds to life
in ways you never thought possible.

For subscription details ring:
US: 1-800-394-GAME   UK: (0115) 91 40000

For more information see our website:
http://www.blacklibrary.co.uk/inferno